## Praise for HUGH HOLTON

"When I ventured into Hugh Holton's *Windy City* there was no exit for me until I finished **the final fiery pages**. Authentic police procedures entwined with the shocking antics of a deliciously evil villainess and a perspicacious top cop's braintrust of mystery writers combine to produce one of the **most suspenseful and enjoyable crime novels I have read in recent years**."

—Robin Moore, author of *The French Connection*

"Holton writes with the stark, gut-wrenching realism of a cop who knows the slime pit cops work in."

—William J. Caunitz, *The New York Times* best-selling author of *One Police Plaza*

"Where in the world did Hugh Holton come from? He is a true, immensely talented writer."

—Dorothy Uhnak, *The New York Times* best-selling author of *False Witness*

**"Chicago now has a police officer–writer to join the ranks of William Caunitz and Joseph Wambaugh."**

—*Fraternal Order of Police Newsletter*

"I've spent my life working the street. Hugh Holton's writing is as gritty and real as it gets!"

—Michael Levine, author of *The New York Times* best-seller *Deep Cover*

"It's the rare reader who'll put this one down as it hurtles—one chilling event after the next—to its finale. A bravura performance."

—*Kirkus Reviews*

**Forge Books by Hugh Holton**

*Presumed Dead*
*Windy City*

## Hugh Holton

A TOM DOHERTY ASSOCIATES BOOK
NEW YORK

NOTE: If you purchased this book without a cover you should be aware that this book is stolen property. It was reported as "unsold and destroyed" to the publisher and neither the author nor the publisher has received payment for this "stripped book."

This is a work of fiction. All the characters and events portrayed in this book are either products of the author's imagination or are used fictitiously.

WINDY CITY



A Forge Book
Published by Tom Doherty Associates, Inc.
175 Fifth Avenue
New York, N.Y. 10010

Forge® is a registered trademark of Tom Doherty Associates, Inc.

ISBN: 0-812-56714-5
Library of Congress Card Catalog Number: 95-14708

First edition: August 1995
First mass market edition: April 1996

Printed in the United States of America

0 9 8 7 6 5 4 3 2 1

I would like to dedicate this book to my daughter Elizabeth Frances Holton, whom I've loved and been proud of since the day she was born.

## ACKNOWLEDGMENTS

Although the Brain Trust in *Windy City* is fictional, I have depended on a real Brain Trust in Chicago to help me as writing teachers, resource persons and very good friends. They are authors Barbara D'Amato, D.C. (Debbie) Brod, Mark Zubro, Doug Cummings, Michael Allen Dymmoch and Bill Love. Then there are the cops: Assistant Deputy Superintendent Raymond Risley, Chief of Detectives (retired) John T. Stibich, Commander John Richardson, Police Officers Edna White, Elmer Atkinson, Lawrence Terry, Eddie (Chaser) Garrett, Ron Beach, Jocelyn (Jo Jo) Gregoire-Watkins and all the hardworking men and women of the Second and Third Districts of the Chicago Police Department.

Hugh Holton
*November 1994*

# Cast of Characters

## The Chicago Police Department

| | |
|---|---|
| Larry Cole, Sr. | Deputy chief of administration for the Detective Division |
| Cosimo "Blackie" Silvestri | A lieutenant assigned to Cole's staff |
| Manfred Wolfgang "Manny" Sherlock | A sergeant assigned to Cole's staff |
| Judy Daniels, a.k.a. the Mistress of Disguise/High Priestess of Mayhem | A detective assigned to Cole's staff |
| Jack Govich | Chief of Detectives |
| Terrence Jonathan "Terry" Kennedy | First deputy superintendent |
| Frank Dwyer | Deputy chief of detectives—Field Group A |

**The DeWitt Corporation**

| | |
|---|---|
| **Margo and Neil DeWitt** | **Sole owners of the DeWitt Corporation** |
| **Wayne Tolley** | **Attorney and former Illinois governor** |
| **Seymour Winbush** | **DeWitt Corporation vice-president** |

**Significant Others**

**Paige Albritton**

**Lisa Cole**

**Larry "Butch" Cole, Jr.**

# 1

**"What about the child in Lincoln Park?"**

**—Margo DeWitt**

# CHAPTER 1

**June 4, 1996**
**10:47 a.m.**

Registration for the summer semester at the downtown campus of Roosevelt University was in progress. It was a hot, muggy day. The air-conditioning unit in the second-floor lounge—a high-ceilinged room of old marble and varnished wood, where the registration was taking place—was operating at maximum.

The Roosevelt Alumni Association had provided the funds for complimentary popcorn and lemonade stands. So far the lemonade stand was much busier than its popcorn neighbor. Twice, the two harried volunteers manning the lemonade stand had run out of ice. They were getting low on the crushed crystals again and dreading another trip to the cafeteria located on the other side of the building.

A man approached the lemonade stand and took a cup of the tepid liquid. He turned and walked over to the other stand and picked up a bag of popcorn. He crossed the lounge to the entrance to one of the vacant study rooms. There he stopped and turned around.

He wore a broken-down denim sailor cap covering his head to the ears and a pair of tinted glasses with bright silver frames. His features were sharp, and he had one of those carefully crafted, health-spa tans sometimes referred to as "golden." He wore a white silk shirt, a heavy gold watch on his left wrist and denim slacks.

From the study-room entrance he surveyed the registration area, pausing to observe a teenager in jeans, a well-preserved gray-haired woman in a jogging outfit and a dark-haired woman in a green dress. His eyes remained on the woman in the green dress longer than on any of the others. Then the man entered the study room.

# CHAPTER 2

**JUNE 4, 1996**
**10:52 P.M.**

Paige Albritton was registering for the first three hours toward a bachelor's degree in General Studies. She was thirty-four years old and had been out of school for fifteen years. Mack had convinced her to go back.

She received her class assignment sheet at Station Three. "Advanced Pro-Seminar—General Studies—Sat.—9:00 A.M. to Noon—Dumas, A."

She came to Station Four. A young black girl with a ponytail looked up at her from the registration table. "Does your employer provide tuition assistance or are you applying for financial aid?"

Something inside Paige snapped and she unfocused. She went back to when she was a teenager in Oklahoma.

"You have some lovely children, Mrs. Albritton," the male social worker from the Department of Public Aid said. He looked at the then thirteen-year-old Paige seated beside her mother. "Are you sure," he asked, "the public assistance will be sufficient to meet their needs?"

It hadn't been. Later, in an Oklahoma whorehouse, a madam had told her to save her tips.

"You won't have your looks forever," the madam had said.

* * *

"Excuse me," the black girl in the here and now said. "Are you all right?"

She blinked her eyes. "Sure, I'm fine."

Paige went on to the next station. As she moved through the registration process, she was conscious of many stares directed at her. Most were from men, but a few were from women. All her life, or at least as far back as she could recall, men had stared at her.

She was tall, five feet nine in her stocking feet, and well proportioned with prominent breasts, a narrow waist and hips that she thought were beginning to flare too much.

But Mack had called her "the sexiest woman on Earth."

Her hair was back to its natural dark brown color now. For many years she had dyed it blond. She had good features. Not necessarily beautiful, but good. Her eyes were green, but she didn't have much naturally in the way of eyebrows and lashes, so she had to resort to makeup to achieve the exotic look so popular in her former profession. Her skin was pearl white. She was capable of tanning, but she had to do so carefully. She had been a big hit among those who preferred blond hookers in the call operations she worked in Oklahoma City, Las Vegas, and finally Chicago. She had even gotten marriage proposals.

She finally made it to the last step of the registration process. Here she had to pay for her class. Even though this was the end, she had dreaded this step most of all. Mack had given her a signed blank check. All she had to do was fill in the name of the "payee" and the amount. A year ago, a man giving her a check like this would have been in real trouble. Now she felt uncomfortable using Mack's money. Using his money to further her neglected education.

She stepped up to the cashier's window. The cashier reminded Paige of a jail warden.

"That will be one thousand, two hundred seventy-one dollars, if you're going to pay it all," the cashier snapped.

"If not, you'll have to go through that door and make arrangements for installment payments with the bursar."

Paige felt a chill descend on her. She leaned toward the grating over the cashier's window. The dried-up cashier recoiled.

"Look, I'm paying it all, which means I'm the customer and you're the employee. You got that?"

"Yes, ma'am," the cashier said politely. She took the check, stamped it paid and returned a receipt in the name of Paige Albritton.

Paige crossed the registration area and entered one of the study rooms. The place was deserted except for a man wearing a denim hat. He was seated on a couch by the far wall reading a book.

She walked over to a couch near the door and sat down. She scanned her book list. She was considering a trip to the bookstore when the man sat down on the opposite end of her couch.

Startled, she turned to look at him. His head was in his book and he did not look up at her. She examined the book jacket. *Killing Streets* by Jamal Garth. Paige had read this book, but hadn't liked it. Too much violence.

She looked at the man again. He still did not look back. Stuffing her school registration papers and book list into her handbag, she stood up and left the room. She glanced back as she crossed the registration area. He was not following. For his sake she was glad.

# CHAPTER 3

**JUNE 4, 1996**
**11:35 A.M**

He gave her a head start. Enough time for her to cross the registration area to the staircase. Another few seconds and she would be down the first flight of stairs leading to the main lobby.

Casually, he closed the book and stood up. By the time he reached the banister and looked down the main staircase, she had reached the first floor. She did not look up.

With his book tucked under his arm, he followed.

# CHAPTER 4

**JUNE 4, 1996**
**12:15 P.M.**

Larry Cole struggled under the three-hundred-pound bench press. Clarence "Mack" McKinnis was his training partner.

"C'mon, Larry!" Mack screamed encouragement. "Push that sucker up! Push it off you, man! This bastard'll go, do you hear me?"

The weight inched upward. Cole's face was constricted

with exertion. The tendons and muscles of his neck and upper body stood out.

The right side of the barbell was coming up faster than the left. Mack didn't want the weight to shift and pull Cole off the bench. He reached down and gently touched the left underside of the bar. The imbalance corrected, it continued to rise.

With a final grunt, Cole locked his elbows and Mack helped him place the bar back on the rack.

Cole sat up. Sweat was streaming off him. There was a glint of satisfaction in his eyes.

"You did it, man," Mack said, slapping him on the shoulder. "You've got to be the strongest command officer in the department."

"I told you to leave that 'command officer' crap in the locker room."

"Sorry, I forgot. Let's stretch and get a shower."

Larry Cole and Mack McKinnis were cops. They were about the same age and black. Cole was a wiry, muscular man with a medium brown complexion and curly black hair showing a few telltale streaks of gray. Mack was a dark-skinned, heavily muscled man with short, jet black hair.

They had met in high school, where they had played defense on one of the best teams ever to come out of Chicago's Mount Carmel High School. Cole had been a defensive back, Mack a linebacker. Cole made All-City, Mack All-State. Cole had gotten an athletic scholarship to the University of Iowa, Mack to Notre Dame. Complications in his early college career had forced Cole to return to Chicago, where he joined the police force. At Notre Dame, Mack had become an All-American; he was drafted in the second round by the NFL's New England Patriots.

Cole's career with the Chicago Police Department had been spectacular. Blessed by St. Michael, the patron saint of cops, whom the police chaplain was fond of invoking, Larry Cole had stumbled accidentally into more big-time, headline cases than most cops even hear about in a thirty-five-year career. His rise had been meteoric. Before his fortieth birthday, Cole had made deputy chief under Chief Jack Govich.

Mack's career as a professional football player did not live up to his college press clippings. He started a few games for the Patriots and looked promising. He had size, speed and strength. What he lacked, in the words of a Patriot defensive coach, was "the killer instinct." The drive not just to tackle an opponent, but to end his career.

Mack was simply too nice a guy to do anything like that. After four seasons with the Patriots, he was traded to the New Orleans Saints, where he was used sparingly for a franchise that won only seven games over two seasons. After being cut by the Saints, he bounced through Dallas for a season with the Cowboys before heading home to Chicago.

At Notre Dame, Mack had earned a degree in Political Science, but what was he going to do with it now? He was about to go looking for a construction job when he ran into Larry Cole. Cole had convinced Mack to take the police exam. That was eleven years ago.

Cole and Mack sat in the sauna. Cole noticed how quiet Mack had become.

"A week from Sunday you'll be a married man," Cole said.

"Yeah," Mack responded listlessly.

Cole felt the heat settle over him. "You're not having second thoughts, are you?"

Mack shrugged. "I guess I am, but it's not because I don't want to marry Paige."

"Then what?"

He took a deep breath and released a long, slow gush of air. "I guess it's this interracial thing. It bothers me."

"I thought we talked that out a long time ago?"

"It's not me I'm concerned about, Larry. It's Paige. How's she going to adjust to being married to a black man? I mean, she's from the South. She's been treated like a queen in places where they'd have my black ass shot if I even looked wrong at her. Now she's going to be forced to live on the other side of the tracks. The preacher says, 'I now pronounce you man and wife' and 'Shazzam!' she becomes an instant nigger!"

Cole was surprised at the bitterness in Mack's voice. "I think you've been over all this with her before."

"Yeah, but then we were just talking about what it was going to be like. Now it's going to be the real deal."

"I don't think she's going to have a problem with it, Mack. She's a strong lady. Doesn't see the world through rose-colored glasses."

"That's for damn sure."

"She also knows what she wants, and that's sitting right beside me on this bench."

Mack turned to look at Cole. He extended his palm. Cole slapped it with his open hand.

# CHAPTER 5

**JUNE 4, 1996**
**1:15 P.M.**

Paige purchased the four books for her class from the book store on Wabash. She then walked to the State Street subway and caught a northbound train. The platform downstairs was crowded, so she didn't notice the man in the denim hat and white shirt follow her onto the northbound train. He watched her through the window of the adjoining car. At one point, she felt a strange uneasiness. She looked around the car. No one was paying her any attention. She glanced at the window of the adjoining car. It was empty.

At Morse Avenue she got off. On a whim she hailed a

passing cab. Once inside she felt safe again. The man in the blue hat managed to flag a taxi as well.

Jumping inside, he dropped a twenty-dollar bill on the front seat. "There's another one of those plus the fare if you follow that cab, and I don't want to be noticed." He spoke in a voice that was a duplicate of actor Jack Nicholson's.

"You got it, pal," the unshaven, cigar-smoking driver said. "Your girlfriend or your wife?"

"Something like that."

Paige and Mack had moved in together six months after he busted the call operation she worked for. He had passed himself off as a john. She had gone to his Loop hotel thinking he was an out-of-town businessman visiting Chicago for the electronics convention at McCormick Place.

"I've seen you someplace, haven't I?" she said as he uncorked a bottle of champagne. "Have you ever been on television?"

"Once a week on Sundays during the fall."

"You're a football player! You played for the Cowboys!"

"Briefly."

"It's a real pleasure meeting you." She extended her hand, which got lost in one of his. "I'm from Oklahoma City originally. Been a Cowboy fan all my life. When it comes to college ball, of course, I'm a Sooner fan. Where'd you go to college?"

"Notre Dame."

"Boo! But then once a Cowboy, always a Cowboy."

"Does that rate me a discount?"

"Sorry. I wish I could, especially for you, but it's a thousand straight and anything more costs extra."

"I'm sorry too," he said. "But you're under arrest."

She smiled. "Well, this is a surprise. Were you really a Cowboy?"

"Cross my heart."

"That's too bad, because I meant what I said about being sorry for not being able to give you a discount."

Their apartment was in a new multi-unit complex in Rogers Park, where the apartments were arranged around a courtyard decorated with trees and ivy surrounding a large swimming pool. Mack and Paige lived in a one-bedroom second-floor apartment overlooking the pool. She was hot and tired by the time she stepped inside.

The air-conditioning blew cool air through the vents. Kicking off her shoes, she crossed the living room and hit the Replay button on the answering machine.

"*Hi, baby,*" Mack's voice came over the speaker. "*I'm going to the police gym for a workout with Deputy Chief Cole. I should be home at three. You know what I want for dinner.*"

She knew exactly what he wanted, but then she'd also have to fix him something to eat.

She went to the refrigerator and checked the freezer. It would take too long to thaw anything if he was going to be home at three. That meant she'd have to go to the store.

She washed her face, applied a dab of makeup, and headed for the street.

The man in the blue hat watched her leave. He had seen her enter Apartment 27 and matched the apartment number against the tenant directory at the courtway entrance. The names there were in white plastic letters on a black cloth background: ALBRITTON—MCKINNIS. A roommate? The idea of two of them excited him. But then perhaps he should wait. No! He wanted her now!

But Margo had told him to be more cautious.

He entered the courtyard and crossed to the staircase leading up to Apartment 27. A janitor emerged from the back of the complex lugging pool-cleaning equipment and a large bucket with a skull and crossbones on its side. He paid the man no attention.

The man in the denim hat kept walking as if he belonged there. He traversed the second-floor balcony, while keeping an eye on the janitor. Then he examined the lock to Apartment 27. It was sturdy, but his lockpicks were exquisitely precise. It took him less than twenty seconds to get inside.

# CHAPTER 6

**JUNE 4, 1996**
**2:45 P.M.**

"I really appreciate you giving me a lift, Deputy," Mack said as Cole drove his unmarked Chevy police car north on Lake Shore Drive.

"We back into titles again?"

"When we're in the gym that's one thing, boss. Out here in the world is something else."

"But we're alone."

"That really doesn't matter. I'm real proud of what you've made of yourself. Every place I go people talk about Deputy Chief Larry Cole. About you and some of the cases you've broken. That guy Zalkin a few years back. And then bagging Tuxedo Tony DeLisa, not to mention the changes you put the dear, departed Rabbit Arcadio through. Some people say you're gonna be the next black superintendent of police, but I don't agree with that."

"Oh?" Cole said, somewhat surprised.

"Yeah. I think you're going to be the *next* superintendent of police."

"Give it a rest," Cole said.

"I'm real proud to have you stand up with me and Paige. I mean a lot of regular, dog-ass street cops wouldn't be caught dead anywhere near City Hall the day we get hitched, not to mention some bosses, who've been acting like I got leprosy complicated by AIDS."

Cole nodded but said nothing.

A short time later Cole pulled up in front of Mack's apartment building.

"You want to come up for a beer?" Mack offered.

"No, but thanks anyway. I promised Lisa I'd be home early."

Mack glanced at his watch as he opened the car door. "I told Paige I wouldn't be home until three. Again, thanks for the ride and I'll see you tomorrow."

Cole drove away. Mack started for the entrance to the courtyard. He noticed the janitor working around the pool as he passed.

# CHAPTER 7

**JUNE 4, 1996**
**2:47 P.M.**

The man was going through the dresser drawers. The top one held skimpy woman's lingerie in various colors. Everything was scented. He figured she knew how to turn a guy on. He felt under the stack of underwear. There was a thick plastic tube hidden there. He began breathing harder when he pulled it out. It was a vaginal lubricant.

He noticed that a padlock and hasp secured the bottom drawer. Intrigued, he knelt on the floor and pulled out his lockpicks. The lock opened easily. He pulled the drawer out and stiffened when he saw its contents. Then the front door opened. He froze.

"Paige!" The deep voice echoed through the apartment. "You home?!"

The man looked back into the open drawer.

Mack dropped his gym bag on the living-room floor. He stood still and listened to the silence of the apartment. When he had opened the door he'd sworn he heard something. When Paige didn't answer he figured she was out shopping.

He walked into the kitchen, removed a bottle of beer from the refrigerator and pried off the cap with his thumb.

Sipping the beer, he walked toward the back of the apartment. He was debating whether to watch the White Sox game on TV or to read the new Debbie Bass police procedural Paige had picked up at a local bookstore.

He had decided on the book by the time he turned into the bedroom. There facing him was a man in a blue denim cap, sunglasses and a white shirt. The man held Mack's Model 686, six-inch barrel, .357 magnum revolver. It was pointed right at Mack's chest.

Mack looked down at the padlocked drawer where he kept his guns secured. It was open. Anger flared as he looked back at the man. Mack took a step toward him just as he pulled the trigger.

The janitor was a fifty-four-year-old alcoholic, who had managed to hold on to his job despite being almost continuously drunk. Once a week he was supposed to clean the pool. He was already two days late and the snotty building manager was getting nasty.

But he figured he deserved a couple of hits from the half-pint bottle of gin in his back pocket before he started. He particularly needed the booze because he didn't like working with muriatic acid. That stuff could melt the flesh right off his bones.

As he was heading back for the basement he heard a muffled popping noise. He shrugged and went off to drink his gin.

When he got back twenty minutes later his bucket of muriatic acid was gone.

# CHAPTER 8

**JUNE 4, 1996**
**4:17 P.M.**

Sergeant Manfred Wolfgang Sherlock turned onto the street where Paige Albritton and Sergeant Clarence McKinnis had lived. A knot of marked and unmarked police cars narrowed traffic to one lane. Manny pulled in behind a marked unit. Before he turned off the engine, his passenger, Lieutenant Blackie Silvestri, was out of the car and headed for the courtyard entrance.

With Manny right behind him, Blackie reached the entrance to Apartment 27. He flashed his badge at the officer outside the door and brushed past him.

Commander Richard Shelby of Area Three Detectives was standing in the middle of the living room. When he saw Blackie his eyes narrowed. Shelby knew that Blackie worked for Deputy Chief Cole. This didn't cut any ice with Shelby. It was still his case.

Shelby waited for the lieutenant to come to him. He knew the scowling, heavyset cop wouldn't like this, but then he didn't give a rat's ass about that either.

"How you doin', Commander?" Blackie said.

"Good, Silvestri. I thought we'd have more brass from downtown on a cop killing?"

"They're coming. I'm kind of an advanced guard."

"Wouldn't it make it easier if I waited until everyone got here so I won't have to go over this a bunch of times?" There was no warmth in Shelby's tone.

"Whatever you say, boss, but maybe you could get one

of your guys to give me an idea of what went down so I can let Chief Govich know if he calls."

"Why can't Govich talk to me?"

Blackie shrugged. "He could do that too, boss. Again, whatever you say."

Shelby gritted his teeth. Silvestri was on Govich's staff. It was likely that the chief would talk to the commander-in-charge at some time during this investigation, but then he would also ask Silvestri for input. If the lieutenant was kept in the dark, then Govich might not look at Shelby too favorably. That's the way Govich was. Shelby didn't need any new problems right now.

"Let's go outside," the commander said.

Leaving Sherlock behind, they stepped out onto the balcony and walked to the end away from the ears of any curious cops or civilians. The residents of the complex had turned out to watch the spectacle, and each of the four balconies, as well as the courtyard below, was filled.

"This Sergeant McKinnis," Shelby said in a hushed voice, "is shacked up with an ex-hooker. They get into some kind of beef. She gets one of his guns and pops him. But she's not through, vicious bitch she is. We've got a drunken janitor lugs a ten-gallon barrel of muriatic acid out to clean the pool. He slips off to take a couple of hits from a half pint of gin. When he gets back our lady fair has put the dead sergeant in the bathtub and doused him with the stuff. Ate the flesh right off his bones."

With an impassive expression, Blackie asked, "She confess to all this?"

Shelby laughed. "You kidding? She tried the hysterical act on us. Shouted, screamed, cried, the whole bit."

"Where is she now?"

"They took her over to St. Anne's Hospital. The doctor says she's close to going into shock, but I think she's faking. If it was up to me she'd be on her way to the shithouse right now."

Blackie nodded. "Can I see the body?"

"Sure. We're all one big, happy police department, aren't we, Silvestri?"

Blackie ignored the sarcasm and went back inside. He crossed the living room and walked down a corridor leading to the rear of the apartment. The Crime Lab technicians were finished with the scene, but he could still see areas circled with chalk, such as the bloodstains on the floor outside the bedroom.

The acrid smell of acid stopped him at the bathroom door. An acrid smell mixed with the unmistakable odor of burned flesh.

Despite the smell filling the room, Mack appeared to have simply fallen asleep in the tub. When Blackie stepped closer, the sight of the nude body startled him. The acid had scalded everything it touched: the enamel sides of the tub, the metal fixtures and even the tiles where a few drops had spilled onto the floor. But the most damage had been done to the flesh of the dead policeman. It had melted off the bone to form simmering gobs of a smoldering goo-like substance at the bottom of the tub. The bones of Mack's lower body, from his rib cage all the way to his toes, were exposed. They had been bleached white by the acid, making them stand out in startling definition to what was left of his ebony skin.

Blackie backed out of the bathroom. He could see through the apartment to where Shelby stood by the front door talking to a couple of detectives. Blackie wondered what had happened to the container the acid had come in. Probably it had been inventoried, but it would have been damned heavy. He wondered if Shelby had considered this when making Paige his one and only suspect?

Blackie headed for the front of the apartment. Before he could get there, Shelby dashed outside. Blackie followed.

Out on the balcony Blackie could see Shelby hightailing it toward the courtyard entrance, where the superintendent and first deputy were just getting out of chauffeur-driven cars. Chief of Detectives Govich was in the car with the first deputy.

Blackie went to the bottom of the stairs, but moved quickly out of the way when the superintendent's entourage swept by. Shelby was talking a blue streak. Blackie had a pretty good idea what he was talking about.

Manny Sherlock stepped up beside Blackie. The sergeant was six foot four, but not as lean as he had once been. His years in the Detective Division had given him not only bulk but greater confidence. In Blackie's estimation he was destined to do great things on the Chicago Police Department.

"How's it look?" Manny asked.

"It don't, kid. This whole thing is getting real screwed up. Shelby thinks he's got it all locked up and he's about to put Paige Albritton's neck in a noose."

"What can we do to stop him?"

"C'mon. We've got to catch the boss before he gets here."

# CHAPTER 9

**JUNE 4, 1996**
**4:35 P.M.**

Larry Cole stepped off the elevator onto the fourth floor of St. Anne's Hospital and saw the uniformed police officer sitting on a folding chair outside a room down the corridor. When Cole approached, the officer stood up and assumed a parade-rest stance. Cole flashed his gold badge at her, which she studied closely before stepping back and saluting.

"At ease, Officer . . ." He read her name tag. ". . . Fletcher."

"Probationary Officer Fletcher, sir!"

Cole smiled. A recruit. Very official. Uniform spotless. He wondered how she'd react if she met Judy Daniels, the infamous Mistress of Disguise/High Priestess of Mayhem, who was a detective on his staff. It would undoubtedly change Probationary Officer Fletcher's entire concept of police work.

He knocked lightly on the hospital room door before entering. Fletcher whispered from behind him, "She's been sedated, sir, but I believe she's conscious."

Cole thanked her and closed the door behind him.

Paige was lying on her back, her dark hair splayed on the pillow. Cole crossed to the bed and stood over her. Her eyes fluttered open.

Cole watched her face twist in anguish as she said, "Why?"

He took her hand. "I don't know, Paige. But I'm sure as hell going to find out."

Carefully, he began questioning her. It was difficult, because of the drugs they'd given her, but finally he had a place to start.

# CHAPTER 10

**JUNE 4, 1996**
**5:10 P.M.**

They were conducting a "round table" in Shelby's office in the Area Three Police Center at Western and Belmont. Detective Commander Shelby; the commander of the 24th Police District Henry McNamara; and the assistant Cook County state's attorney for the Felony Division, Anne Johnson, were present. They were preparing to file first-degree murder charges against Paige Albritton for killing Clarence McKinnis.

So far, Shelby and Johnson had done most of the talking. When McNamara tried to get in a point, they either ignored or dismissed him. As the senior district commander on the force, McNamara didn't like this, but he was eight months shy of retirement and didn't need the hassle.

Anne Johnson and Richard Shelby had known each other for fifteen years, during which she'd climbed the ladder from the Felony Review Unit to being chief prosecutor of the Felony Division in the State's Attorney's Office while he had gone from being a mediocre homicide detective to commander of a Detective Area.

A more unlikely pair for a professional partnership could not be found. Black, short and stocky, Anne was abrupt with people to the point of rudeness and dressed in odds and ends that looked as if she had picked them up at a Salvation Army garage sale. She never wore makeup. Her work was her life, and many in the legal profession, both opponent and ally, thought she was just a bit overzealous when going after certain types of defendants.

Shelby looked like a 1950s version of a nerd. One of a vanishing breed who still rubbed liquid Vaseline into their hair before slicking the short tresses back in a severe, greasy, off-the-forehead style, he wore brown horn-rimmed glasses and suit coats with trousers that rarely matched and looked to have come from the same garage sale where Anne purchased her clothing.

No one had ever accused Dick Shelby of being a good detective. Many barely saw him as adequate. He lacked instinct and was totally inept at conducting investigations. Some detectives were born with instinct and most acquired it after years of fieldwork; every detective had to work on the ability to conduct thorough investigations. Shelby lacked both, yet he managed to survive and even prosper in a highly competitive field.

The reason? Dick Shelby was a ruthless bastard. Once he

got on to a suspect, guilty or innocent, he would go to any lengths to secure an indictment and conviction. Even if such lengths took him beyond the realm of legality.

Now, as the white-haired Commander McNamara looked on, the team of Johnson and Shelby were constructing the cross they intended to crucify Paige Albritton on.

"Who rented the apartment?" she asked.

Shelby flipped through the volume of photocopied pages he had assembled. "They both signed the lease, but the rental agent, a Mrs. Carter, said the Albritton woman came alone to look at the apartment."

"Okay," Johnson said smugly. "She constructs her little love nest first and the stupid cop flies in figuring he'll get a little free trim. But she has marriage on her mind. Do we have anyone who can corroborate our victim having second thoughts about this broad's matrimony scam?"

"Don't worry, Counselor," Shelby said. "I'm sure we'll come up with someone who can testify that the dead sergeant was going to be an unwilling bridegroom."

"What about her prior police record?"

"No convictions, but we're getting copies of every piece of paper ever made out on her from Oklahoma, Texas and Nevada. They should be here by tomorrow."

"You know what we really need to make this thing stick? If she has a history of violence with her tricks. Maybe a stabbing or shooting."

"What about tossing acid?"

"That would be great, Dick! I can see the jury now when I drop that one on them. We might get a woman executed in Illinois yet."

The phone on Shelby's desk rang. He answered it. "Yes?"

He listened for a moment, frowned and snapped, "Okay," before hanging up.

"What's the matter?" Johnson asked.

"That was the Nineteenth District desk downstairs. Deputy Chief Cole is on his way up. He wants to sit in on the round table."

"Well, tell him he can't! This is your show, not his!"

"I can't, Anne. He outranks me. If he wants in, he's in."

McNamara took this as his cue. "That means you won't be needing the likes of a poor patrol type like me any longer. This is a Detective Division show now. You folks have a nice day."

With that, McNamara was out the door. Before it could swing shut, Larry Cole walked in.

Cole smiled. "I hope I'm not too late. We have so much to talk about."

# CHAPTER 11

**JUNE 4, 1996**
**5:15 P.M.**

Mrs. Margo DeWitt was hosting a reception at the Chicago Cultural Center honoring Chicago's Greatest Writers of the Twentieth Century. Standing alone, without her husband, Neil, she greeted each guest with a forced smile. She was worried about Neil. He should have been here by now. The only excuse for his absence she would accept would be his death, and she'd only accept that because she would be unable to kill him.

Margo DeWitt was not an attractive woman, but rather one who wore her money well. Rich all her life, she had married into the DeWitt real-estate fortune of Chicago, whose only surviving member was her missing husband.

Many members of the North Shore society crowd, of which Margo and Neil were members, secretly wondered why a man with Neil's money and good looks would fall for a stuck-up, pretentious woman like Margo. No one had yet been able to come up with the simple answer. The two of them had a great deal more in common than any of their friends could ever imagine.

Margo managed a personal greeting for each guest by reading the names written on the tags pinned to their left breasts. The tags were made up at the table outside by Cultural Center employees.

A name tag loomed in front of her that made her forget her absent husband. She looked from the piece of plastic-encased cardboard up into the ruddy, smiling face of Terrence "Terry" Kennedy—the first deputy superintendent of the Chicago Police Department. She recognized him from his appearances on television. Margo brightened. In a way, cops were her thing.

"Mr. Kennedy, how nice of you to come. I'm Margo DeWitt."

"Not my idea," Kennedy said bluntly, cocking his head at the woman standing beside him. Margo read the name tag: SANDY KENNEDY.

*God*, Margo thought, *I once owned a dog named Sandy.*

Sandy smiled at Margo. "I'm the intellectual in the family, Mrs. DeWitt. If it doesn't have the DC Comics label on it, Terry won't go near a book."

"C'mon, now," Kennedy said. "I'm not that bad. Give me a good mystery or a bloody suspense thriller by some of our local authors like B.S. Zorin, Jamal Garth or Martin Wiemler and I'll eat it up at one sitting. This longhair stuff puts me to sleep."

Margo reached up to touch an imaginary stray hair, which could not possibly have escaped from her Vidal Sassoon Salon–done coiffure, and managed to smile. "Of course. Welcome to our little affair anyway. I'm sure you'll both find something to stimulate you as the evening progresses."

The Kennedys walked past her into the columned hall. They were heading for the bar when Margo called, "Oh, Terry, perhaps later we can have a little chat about crime. It's kind of a hobby of mine."

Kennedy's normally good-natured front crumbled into an

"oh no not another one" look, and he said, "I'll be looking forward to it, Mrs. DeWitt."

She was aware he said something to his wife when he turned around. She lip read the first part and guessed the second. First Deputy Superintendent Terrence Jonathan Kennedy had called his hostess a "stuck-up bitch."

Margo smiled at the thought. Yes, she was, wasn't she?

The greetings over, Margo found a phone in one of the offices. She punched out the penthouse number and waited. Five, six, seven rings and still no answer. She opened her purse, extracted a pack of Virginia Slims and lit one with a sterling-silver lighter.

Fourteen rings, fifteen rings, sixteen rings.

She snubbed out the cigarette. "Answer the frigging telephone, Neil, or Mama's going to burn your pubic hair off." To emphasize her words, she ignited her lighter and let the flame dance in the air.

On the twenty-first ring, Neil picked up the phone, *"Hello?"*

"Neil, you're supposed to be in your tux and down at the Cultural Center right now, or have you forgotten?"

*"I . . . I . . . I can't, Margo. Some . . . some . . . some . . . "*

"Say it slowly, Neil. Concentrate. You can do it."

*"Some-thing hap-pened. There . . . was . . . this . . . this . . ."*

"Take your time, Neil," she ordered, "and tell Margo all about what a bad boy you've been."

It took a while, but he did.

# CHAPTER 12

**JUNE 4, 1996**
**5:30 P.M.**

They gave an award to a writer whose book had sold less than five hundred copies but had been critically acclaimed for its sharp literary style and depth of content. The author, a bearded man with long hair and granny glasses, accepted the award and mumbled some inanities about art, literature and life.

"Looks like a hippie to me," Kennedy whispered to his wife.

"Probably is. Why don't you spray him with your Mace and if he screams 'Oh, wow!' or 'Off the pigs!' we'll know he's for real."

"We don't carry Mace anymore."

A young woman in a smartly tailored business suit appeared at his side. "Excuse me. Are you First Deputy Superintendent Kennedy?"

"Yes, I am."

"Mrs. DeWitt wondered if you and your wife could join her in the salon?"

The salon was located one level above. The young woman ushered them across an ornate hall into a smaller side room. The room itself had been perfectly restored to the state of the private reading room it had once been, when the library was new, at the turn of the century.

"Would you look at this?" Sandy Kennedy said in awe.

The Kennedys studied the tapestries, carpets and hand-carved bookcases filled with leather-jacketed first editions. All the furniture in the room was of genuine leather.

"They say that this desk once belonged to Teddy Roosevelt," Margo DeWitt said from her seat on one of the couches. "Teddy was supposed to have used it when he was vice-president. That was before the assassination of William McKinley."

The Kennedys exchanged questioning glances.

Margo stood up. "Won't you join me? Things must have gotten terribly boring for you downstairs." Turning to their escort, Margo said, "That will be all, dear. I can handle things now."

Margo proved to be an extraordinary, if somewhat strange, hostess. She had plundered the cash bar downstairs for ice, a gallon of white wine and a tubful of beer packed in ice. They sat down on a couch across from her.

Their hostess lit a cigarette with her sterling-silver lighter, took a sip of white wine and said, "I, like you, Mrs. Kennedy . . ."

"Please call me Sandy."

"Of course," Margo said with a tolerant smile.

"And I'm just Terry," Kennedy said.

"Oh, this is so delicious!" Margo gushed. "You're easy to talk to. It is so seldom that I find people I can really be comfortable with. May I speak frankly?"

"Of course," Sandy replied.

"Literature has been an abiding passion of mine most of my life. My husband, Neil, who is unable to be with us tonight, feels the same way. However, too many people would call the type of writing which I really enjoy not even worthy of the coinage 'literature' at all."

"What type of writing do you mean?" Sandy asked.

Margo pointed at Terry. "The type he likes. The raw, gritty stuff. Crime fiction. What life is really all about. Life, that is, and death."

Kennedy smiled and reached for a beer. Sandy responded. "I would say crime and mystery fiction have come a long way toward legitimacy in literature during the past few years. In fact, there are some who believe that crime fiction has always had a niche in legitimate literature dating back to the works of Wilkie Collins and Edgar Allan Poe."

"My, Sandy," Margo gushed. "You are well read on the subject."

"English teacher," Kennedy interrupted.

"But earlier you talked about those mystery authors you enjoyed so much, Terry. Would they ever be considered for awards like the one we gave tonight to our eggheaded friend downstairs?"

He shrugged. "I don't know. They write contemporary stuff, but good contemporary stuff, if you ask me. But maybe I'm not the one to ask?" He looked at his wife.

She came to the rescue. "I don't know if there's any way to tell. A hundred years from now will they still be reading Hemingway or F. Scott Fitzgerald, or will they be reading . . . ? Who were those authors you mentioned, honey?"

"Zorin and Garth were a couple."

"But what makes them good to you, Terry?" Margo asked.

"I guess what they write about is very real to me. After all, I am a cop."

Margo set her glass down on the cocktail table. "I have a difficult time giving any credence to the abstract in literature when there is so much good work being done in the areas where life is portrayed in its most basic terms. Where we see the real horror of our existence most blatantly displayed. Most blatantly displayed by violent death!" She unfocused for a moment. Then she looked at Kennedy. "Tell me, Terry, I heard on the news today that a police officer was killed in a rather horrible fashion. Wasn't there something mentioned about acid being used?"

Kennedy frowned, but didn't answer.

"And what about that little boy in Lincoln Park?" Margo added.

Kennedy put his empty beer can down on the cocktail table. It made a dull clunk that carried through the old, stately room.

# CHAPTER 13

**JUNE 4, 1996**
**7:15 P.M.**

As they pulled from the Grant Park underground garage, Kennedy growled, "We've got another fucking leak in the Department."

"A leak? I don't understand," Sandy said.

He gripped the steering wheel and hunched over it, glaring through the windshield at the traffic on Columbus Drive.

"Somebody's talking out of school, and on a cop killing, to boot."

"That stuff Margo DeWitt mentioned? About the acid and the child in Lincoln Park?"

"What child in Lincoln Park?"

"Terrence Jonathan Kennedy Don't go getting your hackles up at me. It's Mrs. Moneybags you're mad at, not me."

He calmed down a degree or two, but took out his frustration by banging his fist against the steering wheel. "Okay, we've got a dead cop. Guy named McKinnis. A sergeant in the Organized Crime Division. Shacked up, now get this, with a former high-priced call girl."

"Oh, Terry, did she do it?"

"We don't know. The dicks are handling it. Too many unanswered questions, but Larry Cole's on it and this case might end up having more wrinkles than ten pounds of chitterlings."

"What are chitterlings?"

"I'll tell you later. But the one thing we kept out of the press about McKinnis's murder was that after he was shot somebody poured a ten-gallon bucket of acid over his body.

"Now I go to a reception a few hours after the murder and everybody knows about it. The security in the Department stinks." Again he banged his fist against the steering wheel.

"Everybody there didn't know about it, Terry."

"What'd you say?"

"The only person that mentioned acid was Margo DeWitt."

"And where do you think she found out about it? She wasn't there?"

"I guess not, but you still haven't answered my question."

"What question?"

"What about the child in Lincoln Park?"

# CHAPTER 14

**JUNE 5, 1996**
**DAWN**

They were dragging the Lincoln Park lagoon for the body of ten-year-old Bobby Easton, who had been reported missing from the Cabrini Green Day Camp during an outing to the nearby zoo the day before. An all-night search by Area Three Youth Officers had failed to find him.

Then a witness was discovered.

Thelma Chisholm was a homeless person, a bag lady. A gnarled, wrinkled woman of indeterminate age, she carried all her possessions in two plastic trash bags.

At three in the morning she was awakened on a park bench by a uniformed police officer.

"Okay, I'm going. I'm going," she grumbled. "How'd you like someone to wake you up by shining a flashlight in your face!"

He laughed. "My sergeant does it all the time, mother."

"I'm not your mother. And you keep a civil tongue in your head when you're talking to a citizen."

"Yes, mother."

She forgot the smart-mouth cop and headed for the park exit at North Avenue. As she did she noticed a lot of cops prowling around the zoo and the park. They were looking for someone. She loitered around the periphery of a group of cops. She caught bits and pieces of what they were saying. A ten-year-old boy wearing a White Sox T-shirt was missing.

Thelma remembered. Yesterday, at about noon, she had seen a woman with a little boy in a White Sox T-shirt. The woman had been wearing some kind of blue sailor hat and dark glasses. She'd been feeding the little boy hot dogs, popcorn and cotton candy like it was his last meal. Thelma figured the woman would have turned up her nose and told her to get lost if she'd simply asked for some spare change. Thelma had even considered approaching them, but thought better of it. The last time she saw them they were walking hand-in-hand toward the stone bridge over the lagoon.

Thelma waited until she could approach one of the lady cops, who were always easier to talk to than the men. The lady cop said a far from cordial, "And what can I do for you, mother?"

But Thelma was their only lead and a request was made to the Fire Department for a search of the lagoon.

As the sun came up on a day when the temperature would soar well into the nineties, the masked head of a diver broke the surface of the lagoon beneath the stone bridge. He gave a thumbs-up sign and in a matter of minutes the ashen gray body of the drowned boy was pulled from the water.

The cops and firemen were wrapping things up when First Deputy Superintendent Terrence Jonathan Kennedy's black police car pulled into the parking lot beside the lagoon. They were all surprised. A woman was in the car with Kennedy, although she didn't get out. The first deputy conferred briefly with the sergeant-in-charge at the scene before returning to his car.

Sandy Kennedy sat in the front seat of the police car. She was smoking a cigarette. Although she was trying to give up smoking, when she got tense or upset, she reverted to her old habit. "Do you think that Margo DeWitt had something to do with the little boy's death?"

"I don't know what the hell to think. This is crazy. How in the hell did she know about the acid used in the McKinnis killing and up until a few minutes ago that dead kid was only a routine missing person. That wouldn't have made the news."

"So what are you going to do?"

"I don't know, but this isn't simply a case of some cop in the know shooting off his mouth. I wish it was. There's more to it than that."

# CHAPTER 15

**JUNE 5, 1996**
**9:05 A.M.**

The meeting was in Chief Jack Govich's office on the fifth floor of police headquarters. Present were Deputy Chief Frank Dwyer of Field Group A of the Detective Division, Commander Richard Shelby, Assistant State's Attorney Anne Johnson and Deputy Chief Larry Cole.

Govich had called the meeting. The subject under discussion was what they were going to do with Paige Albritton.

Frank Dwyer was Shelby's immediate superior.

Govich was attempting to head off a major incident between the Department and the Cook County State's Attorney's Office. It would be his final decision as to how the criminal-justice system in Chicago would proceed against Paige. Larry Cole waited for Anne Johnson and Dick Shelby to have their say. He was in no hurry to show the chief of detectives what a complete mess the state's attorney and Shelby had made of the McKinnis murder investigation.

So far Shelby had made a comment or two, but, for the most part, the state's attorney did most of the talking.

"So, Chief Govich, we have to ask ourselves why a high-ranking member of the Chicago Police Department would want to get involved in an investigation outside his area of responsibility. It is no secret that Deputy Chief Cole is a personal friend of Paige Albritton. However, it is impossible for me to say how deep that friendship goes. At least at this stage of the investigation.

"But for whatever reason," she continued, "Cole shows up at the hospital, where our prospective defendant is being held under guard, and conducts an unauthorized interrogation of her without the consent of Commander Shelby, who is the officer in charge of this case, or with the consent of my office. Then he proceeds to mount an equally unauthorized, totally obstructionist investigation of his own. An investigation that I must charge has totally jeopardized the state's case against murderess Paige Albritton."

"Are you prepared to put these allegations against Deputy Chief Cole in writing?" Govich said.

"I most assuredly am, sir," she said. "I have never . . . !"

Govich held up his hand, silencing the state's attorney, and turned to Cole. "Maybe it's about time we heard from the accused."

"Yes, sir. There are a few things I'd like to say."

Cole had worked for Jack Govich for the past five years. It was on Govich's recommendation to the new superintendent of police that Cole was promoted from commander of Area One Detectives to become deputy chief of Detective Division administration. In Cole's opinion Govich was one of the smartest, toughest cops around.

Cole leaned forward and folded his hands in front of him on the table. "I must disagree with Ms. Johnson as to my engaging in what she called an 'unauthorized, obstructionist investigation.' My duties as deputy chief of administration in this division charge me with the specific responsibility for insuring that thorough investigations are conducted of all crimes reported in Chicago."

"A thorough investigation was being conducted," Anne Johnson exploded.

Govich slapped his open palm down on the table. "Order in the court, Counselor! Deputy Chief Cole gave you your say; please give him his."

Cole continued, "After I discovered what Commander Shelby's investigation had uncovered, I did go to the hospital to see Paige Albritton. I knew her through the deceased Sergeant McKinnis. Before questioning her I advised her of her constitutional rights. She agreed to talk to me without a lawyer being present. I recorded her responses to my questions on a supplementary report, which was made available to Commander Shelby this morning."

Govich looked at Dwyer and Shelby. "Did you get the report?"

"Yes, sir," they answered together.

The chief turned to the state's attorney. "That's basic procedure in the Department, Counselor." Then he nodded for Cole to go on with his story.

"Ms. Albritton wasn't able to tell me a great deal. We went over everything she'd done that day from the time she got out of bed yesterday morning until she found Sergeant McKinnis's body."

He quickly ran through the account of Paige Albritton's day. School registration, the bookstore visit, the El ride and her taxi ride to the apartment were covered.

"The only things she told me which were out of the ordinary were a man behaving strangely at the school registration and a general uneasy feeling she had on the way home. The description Paige gave of the man at the university was that of a white male of medium height with a slender build wearing a blue denim hat, white shirt and sunglasses. She couldn't remember anything else about him except that he was carrying a book. The title was *Killing Streets* by an author named Jamal Garth."

"I know Garth," Dwyer said. "Not a bad writer, but has a tendency to be a little gory."

Govich looked at the other deputy chief with surprise. "You *know* him?"

Dwyer shrugged. "I'm a mystery fan, Chief. I know a lot of local mystery and suspense authors. I'm an associate member of Mystery Writers of America's Midwest Chapter."

"We've got to talk about that sometime," Govich said. "Sounds interesting."

Cole continued. "There was a student passing out popcorn at registration. A Pakistani named Syed Shafiq, an engineering major. He remembers Paige and the man in the denim hat and white shirt. Shafiq added to Paige's description. Along with the denim hat and white shirt he was wearing tailor-made denim slacks and a Princeton class ring with a red stone. The year on the ring was sixty-nine."

Shelby glanced nervously at Anne Johnson. She refused to look back.

"The student recalled Paige leaving registration," Cole said. "He saw the man in the blue hat leave a few minutes later. Shafiq said the man followed her from the university."

The office was very quiet now.

"After leaving the bookstore on Wabash, Paige boarded a Howard Line subway train at Jackson and rode to the Morse Avenue stop. When she got off, she took a taxi to the apartment. There are about six independent cab companies operating on the North Side and in the northern suburbs; that is, along with the larger Checker and Yellow Cab companies. We took a shot at the independents first. We didn't come up with anything until we talked to the afternoon dispatcher at the last company.

"The Nicholas Brothers Cab Company is a ten-taxi operation run out of a garage at Devon and Western. We talked to the radio dispatcher and found out that all their drivers have to maintain a log of the locations where they pick up fares and their intended destinations. One driver, guy named Sidney Vukhovich, picked up a fare at the Morse El at about the time Paige caught a Checker taxi at the same location. But on Vukhovich's trip sheet no destination was entered. The dispatcher called him on it, and Vukhovich told her he'd forgotten to write in the destination because he hadn't been given one.

"Seems the fare, a guy in a blue hat and sunglasses carrying a book, told Vukhovich to follow a Checker taxi which had just picked up a good-looking woman in a green dress in front of the El station. Paige was wearing a green dress yesterday. The fare tells the driver of the Nicholas Brothers cab that the woman was either his wife or his girlfriend, but the driver couldn't remember which it was. Both cabs let their fares out at about the same time in the 2300 block of West Lunt. Paige lives at 2316 West Lunt. There's one other thing. Vukhovich said the fare talked just like Jack Nicholson. Said he even gave the guy a hard look in the rearview mirror in case it was Nicholson and he could ask for his autograph."

Govich looked away from Cole to Dick Shelby. The Area Three commander kept his eyes down. If Shelby had looked up, he would not have liked what he saw.

"We have one final witness who saw our man in the denim hat," Cole said. "She's a Mrs. Frances Adams. She's the Police Beat Representative on Beat 2423. She lives at 2255 West Lunt. Very active in the Neighborhood Relations Program. She's forty-five years old and her husband's a doctor with a suburban practice. Her hobby is crime prevention. Yesterday afternoon"—Cole consulted a sheet of paper in his folder—"she observed a white male, age thirty-five to forty-five, approximately five feet eight to five feet ten inches tall, medium build, deep tan complexion, wearing a blue broken-down sailor cap, expensive sunglasses, a short-sleeve white silk shirt, blue denim slacks and white shoes. He was walking up and down the 2300 block of West Lunt after he exited a taxi. Mrs. Adams didn't get the name or the license number of the taxi, but she did recall that it was brown and white. Nicholas Brothers taxis are painted with a brown-and-white color combination. Our suspect was carrying a book with a red cover and appeared to be watching the building at 2316 West Lunt.

"According to Mrs. Adams, he was on the street between five and ten minutes before a tall, dark-haired, white female exited the 2316 building and walked west on Lunt. At that point the man stopped his aimless pacing and walked in a decisive manner to the courtway entrance and entered. Mrs. Adams lost sight of him. She did not see him leave the courtway."

Govich looked at Anne Johnson. "Any thoughts, Counselor?"

"Deputy Chief Cole has done a very thorough job," she said. "The one thing we don't have is a motive for the murder of Sergeant McKinnis."

"I drove Mack home yesterday," Cole said. "Our man in the denim cap could have already been in the apartment and Mack walked in on him."

"So he's a burglar with a homicidal quirk?" Shelby interjected.

"That's possible," Cole said. "But there could also be another possibility."

"Such as?" the state's attorney asked.

"He followed Paige. He was after her. Killing Mack could have been in self-defense from the offender's perspective, but the part with the acid is something else. Exactly what I don't know, but my staff's working on it."

"Until you find your mystery man, Paige Albritton will remain the state's number-one suspect," she said.

"You said 'suspect,'" Govich said. "Does that mean you're not going to charge her now?"

Grudgingly, Anne Johnson took her time saying, "In the light of the current circumstances, no. But that doesn't mean I won't later."

"Okay," Govich said. "You know what to do now, Larry."

Cole nodded and stood up to leave. "I'll find this guy, Chief. Don't worry about that."

Dick Shelby and Anne Johnson watched him walk out. The looks they gave him were far from friendly.

# CHAPTER 16

**JUNE 5, 1996**
**11:02 A.M.**

Probationary Police Officer Elizabeth Fletcher sat outside Paige Albritton's hospital room. A tall, attractive black woman stepped off the elevator and stopped briefly at the nurse's station before heading toward the guarded room. The police officer stood up as she approached.

"Hello," the woman said. "I'm Lisa Cole. Deputy Chief Larry Cole's my husband. He was supposed to call about my coming to pick up Ms. Albritton."

"Yes, ma'am. I know all about it. The deputy wanted me to wait until you got here before I returned to my regular assignment. If you want, I can wait and escort you out of the hospital."

"No, that won't be necessary. I can handle everything. Thanks for asking."

"You're welcome, ma'am," Fletcher said as she turned to leave.

Neil DeWitt sat in his silver Mercedes in the hospital parking lot. He had read in the papers this morning that a suspect in the murder of Sergeant Clarence McKinnis was being held by the police.

Margo had still been asleep when he slipped out of the penthouse. She'd been angry with him because of the problem with the dead cop. If she knew where he was going this morning she would have been furious. He was dressed in a blue business suit with a gray porkpie hat. He also carried an attaché case. He had on his horn-rimmed glasses, and his silver hair was perfectly combed. He figured he would make the right impression appearance-wise.

He had gone to the apartment building. A police car had been parked in front of the courtway entrance. He left the Mercedes a half-block away and returned on foot. A lone cop in the car was sound asleep.

Neil knocked softly on the passenger-side window. The policeman abruptly awakened and looked out the window. His apprehension was evident.

B.S. Zorin's private detective Emil Zielinski had run a scam on a cop in *A Good Day to Die*, the third book in the Zielinski series. Neil decided to run the same scam.

Although Private Detective Emil Zielinski never appeared in the movies or on television, Neil always pictured the fictional detective as looking a great deal like the TV Mike Hammer. Not the one played by Stacy Keach, but instead Darren McGavin in the 1950s. With the ease of a man slipping on a pair of very old familiar shoes, Neil molted into his impression of the gravelly-voiced actor with the slightly bowlegged gait.

"I'm Zielinski, investigator for Amalgamated Insurance."

"Yeah."

"I guess this is what you call protecting the crime scene?"

The cop's eyes widened. "I'm supposed, uh, to be watchin'. . . ."

"What's your supervisor's name, buddy?"

"Sergeant . . . uh, Sergeant Best, sir."

"Well, what do you think he'd say if he knew I caught you asleep at the switch?"

The cop had gone pale. "Uh, who did you say you was?"

"The guy whose company insures the tenants in this building, pal. We've got a multi-million-dollar damage suit staring us in the face. Now I come along and find you sleeping and all you want to do is dish me out a ration of shit."

"I'm sorry, sir," the cop said.

"Okay, forget it. We're all in the same game. Right?"

The cop nodded.

"Look, I need some information."

"What kind of information?"

"That suspect you people arrested yesterday. What hospital did they take him to?"

"You mean the broad?"

Neil couldn't help it. He smiled, but continued to play fictional private eye Emil Zielinksi to the hilt. "Yeah, the chick. What was her name?"

"Paige Albritton. I understand she's in St. Anne's under guard, but . . ."

"Thanks, pal." Neil walked away from the police car. "I owe you."

At the hospital, Neil had parked his car and gone inside. He found a public telephone and looked up the hospital's number. Once connected, he requested Patient Information. He looked around in time to see a clerk seated behind a desk across the lobby pick up the ringing telephone.

"*St. Anne's Hospital, Mr. Josephson.*"

"This is Lieutenant Catizone, Homicide," Neil said, imitating classic, tough-talking gangster actor George Raft. B.S. Zorin had written that Catizone, a foil for Private Eye Zielinski, sounded a lot like Raft. "You got a patient there name of Albritton being held under police guard?"

"*Yes, sir, we do.*"

"I wanna talk to one of the cops guardin' her."

"*Hold on, please.*"

There was a brief pause and then, "*Nurse's station.*"

Neil repeated his request in the Raft voice.

"*I'm sorry, Lieutenant, but the police officer just left.*"

"What?" He lost the Raft imitation.

"*Ms. Albritton's in the process of being released. Didn't you know?*" There was suspicion in the nurse's voice.

He had hung up. He left the hospital and hurried back to his car, where he turned on the ignition and switched the air-conditioner on high. As cool air blew through the car he had stared at the hospital entrance. He wasn't sure what he was going to do next.

Then they came out. The excitement that charged through him at the sight of the two women—one white, the other black—was as intense as an electrical charge. He recognized the white one as the woman he followed yesterday. She still had on the green dress, but now she looked tired and worn-out. Paige Albritton. Interesting.

He was turning his attention to her companion when a car pulled into the driveway and stopped in front of them. A heavyset man got out and opened the back door for them. The women got in. As the man started to get back under the wheel he stopped and removed his sports jacket. His shirt had perspiration circles under the arms. Neil also noticed the large gun he carried in a belt holster.

The nurse had said the Albritton woman had been released and her police guard pulled. But a cop was driving the car she was in and maybe the black woman was a cop, too. He wondered where they were taking her. He was just about to follow them when his car phone rang. It was Margo.

# CHAPTER 17

**JUNE 5, 1996**
**11:15 A.M.**

"Get me the reports on the Sergeant Clarence McKinnis slaying," First Deputy Superintendent Kennedy said to his secretary. "I also want anything that comes in on a kid's body pulled from the Lincoln Park lagoon. And see if Larry Cole is in. I'd like to talk to him."

But Cole wasn't in, and before Kennedy could have him

beeped Alderman Sherman Ellison Edwards called. Edwards was the chairman of the City Council Police and Fire Committee and a chronic pain in the ass for the Department.

The secretary announced him on the intercom. *"Boss, Alderman Foghorn Leghorn's on line one."*

It was an inside joke in the department. Edwards spoke and postured exactly like the blustering rooster cartoon character Foghorn Leghorn with an Alabama drawl so exaggerated it sounded like a put-on. Even the superintendent, a woman not rumored to be gifted with a great sense of humor, found it hard to keep a straight face when Edwards started talking, and he talked a lot.

Steeling himself, the first deputy picked up the telephone. "Kennedy."

*"First Deputy, suh, ah protest most ve-he-ment-ly yo department's unbristled inference in affairs in mah ward."*

After a fifteen-minute, wordy prelude detailing the shortcomings of the Chicago Police Department, as Alderman Sherman Ellison Edwards saw them, he got to the real reason for his call. One of his ward committeemen had been given a ticket for parking in front of a fire hydrant. Edwards wanted the ticket "nonsuited," which was a polite way of saying "fixed." Kennedy told him to send the committeeman to court. In a huff, the alderman hung up, promising the first deputy that he had not heard the end of this.

Kennedy buzzed his secretary. "Try Larry Cole for me again."

*"Deputy Chief Cole is here, sir."*

# CHAPTER 18

**JUNE 5, 1996**
**11:35 A.M.**

Blackie Silvestri stomped into Detective Division headquarters and headed for his cubicle. Manny Sherlock saw him and figured he'd better cool him off before some unsuspecting detective got in his way.

Sherlock slipped quietly into the enclosed area. Blackie sat slumped behind his desk. His shirt was plastered to his flesh with perspiration. He glared at Sherlock.

"The air-conditioner on my squad car's out again. How many times have those assholes in the motor pool claimed they've fixed it?"

"Four since the beginning of May."

"This will make five. About once a fucking week. I've had it with them."

As he snatched up the phone Manny said, "The boss wants to see you. I think it's important."

Blackie paused with the receiver halfway to his ear.

"I've got an idea," Manny said. "Why don't I take your car to the shop and you take mine for the rest of the day? I don't use the air-conditioner that much anyway."

"What do you do? Sweat?"

"I roll the windows down. Fresh air is good for you."

Blackie shook his head. "Health nuts."

Cole's office air-conditioner was in perfect working order, and Blackie could feel his disposition improving as fast as his sweat dried.

"Did you get Lisa and Paige to my place?" Cole asked.

"No problems except my damn air-conditioner went out."

"Again?"

"Yeah. Manny's going to take it to the shop for me. He's probably afraid I'll kill one of those pricks calling themselves mechanics if I do it."

Cole changed the subject. "I've got something of a mystery the first deputy handed me a little while ago."

Blackie waited.

"Seems Kennedy went to the Cultural Center for an awards presentation last night and some socialite there was talking about Mack being doused with acid after he was shot."

Blackie's eyebrows arched. "If there's a leak it didn't come from this office, boss. I'd point the finger at Shelby's Area Three people. With an idiot like him for a commander you got to figure them for a bunch of goofs anyway, give or take a few."

"Ordinarily I'd agree with you, but there's more to it than just the information about Mack. Seems this rich socialite, who was throwing the affair, knew about the kid pulled out of the Lincoln Park lagoon this morning. The problem with that is she was talking to Kennedy at seven o'clock last night. The body wasn't discovered until about twelve hours later."

Blackie's frown deepened. "But how in the hell . . . ?"

"I asked Kennedy the same question and it comes down to only two ways it can be: she either talked to the killer or killers of Mack and the kid or she killed one or both of them herself."

"Who is this broad?"

"Name's Margo DeWitt." Cole noticed Blackie sit up a little straighter. "You know her?"

"Her and her old man Neil are out of my league, Boss, but I've heard of them. Neil DeWitt is the heir to a pretty healthy real-estate fortune. Besides being worth about a quarter of a billion dollars, he owns half the land in the

Loop and a good portion of North Lake Shore Drive. His family has been buying and leasing property in and around Chicago for over a hundred years. In fact, the land this building sits on is owned by Neil DeWitt."

Cole stared blankly at the lieutenant. "You're kidding."

"It's gospel. The city leases it from him. Margo's got a pile of dough of her own from some family enterprises out in Colorado, but she amounts to peanuts compared to her husband. He's right up among the top five richest Chicagoans and I'd say he's in the top one hundred in America."

"How did you come to know so much about the DeWitts?"

"Bobby," Blackie said, referring to his only son, an investment banker on LaSalle Street. "He's in to all that wealth and prestige crap. Last Easter he was joking about changing his name from Silvestri to Silver. His mother threw such a conniption he's been apologizing ever since."

"How do you feel about him changing his name?"

"I really don't give a shit. I'm proud of the kid. He's gonna make his first million before he's thirty. Silvestri or Silver, he'll still be my son. He comes around, we sit in the basement, crash a few beers and talk about money, which means we talk about people like Margo and Neil DeWitt."

"What else do you know about them other than the size of their bank accounts?"

"They give away a lot of money to charity, throw a lot of big parties, and, if I'm not mistaken, Bobby was saying something about them being mystery buffs."

It was Blackie's turn to notice Cole react. The deputy chief was obviously surprised.

"I say something wrong?" Blackie said.

"Every place I turn in this thing mysteries keep popping up. The guy following Paige was carrying a mystery novel, and before Margo DeWitt started blabbing to Kennedy about Mack and the drowned boy she was talking about mystery fiction. On top of that, Frank Dwyer's a member of some kind of mystery writers' organization here in Chicago. Coincidence?" Cole queried with a raised eyebrow.

"But that's fiction. How Margo DeWitt found out that stuff she told the first deputy is not. How do you want to handle it?"

"The old-fashioned way," Cole said. "We're going to pay an unannounced call on Mrs. DeWitt. Let's go."

# CHAPTER 19

**JUNE 5, 1996**
**11:55 A.M.**

Located on Michigan Avenue not far from the Hancock Building, DeWitt Plaza was a dual-purpose, fifty-story skyscraper, with the bottom twenty-five floors devoted to business and the top twenty-five to residential living. Its sole owners were Margo and Neil DeWitt, who lived in the three-story penthouse with a helicopter landing pad on the roof.

The Michigan Avenue high-rise was not the only DeWitt residence. They had an estate in suburban North Lake; a Michigan summer home on 150 acres of the Upper Peninsula; a private residence converted from a ski resort in the mountains near Aspen, Colorado; an eight-room apartment on Park Avenue in New York City; an apartment in Paris; and a chalet outside Zurich, Switzerland.

Life had been very good to Margo and Neil, but what they had was not enough. They wanted more. A great deal more.

Neil rode the elevator up from the parking garage. He stepped off the elevator into the southern branch of the U-shaped hall running completely around the first level of the penthouse. His heels clicked on the polished wood floor as he headed for the library where Margo usually was this time of day. He was halfway there when he caught the aroma of Governor Wayne Tolley's cigar. Neil stopped.

"This is really quite an extraordinary find, Margo," Tolley was saying. "Must be worth a fortune."

"Actually," Neil heard his wife reply, "it's priceless. But you know how Neil and I feel about you, so we wanted it to be kind of an early Christmas present."

"Christmas is nearly six months away." Neil noticed the same disapproving edge in Tolley's voice that he'd had when he was the Cook County state's attorney, prosecuting racketeers.

"Well, you certainly can't call it a bribe," Margo said. "After all, you haven't held elected office in over four years."

*Good for you, sweetheart!* Neil could imagine the starch going out of the old bastard's spine when she hit him with that one. The good Governor Tolley had not only been forced to resign from office, but had come very close to trading in the Governor's Mansion in Springfield for a cell in the federal penitentiary in Lexington, Kentucky.

Tired of the eavesdropping, Neil stepped inside. "I hope I'm not intruding?"

"The man of the house!" Tolley said. He still held the jewel-handled scimitar Margo had given him. "How are you, Neil?"

Neil held up his hands in mock surrender. "As long as you have no intention of using that wicked instrument on me, I'm fine."

"Oh, this," Tolley said, carefully fingering the sharp blade. "Your wife just gave it to me as an early Christmas present. I must admit that I have some problems about accepting it."

Neil moved across the room to Margo's side. He put his arm around her and kissed her cheek. "You could have waited a bit longer to give it to him, dear. Say until the end of July."

"Oh, Neil, we did buy it for him when we were in Egypt. Why can't he just take it now and we'll give him something else for Christmas? Convince him."

Neil looked at the former governor. "The lady has a point, Wayne. What do you say?"

Tolley looked down at the blade. He was an addict for ancient artifacts.

Neil and Margo exchanged glances. They knew he was about to give in.

"I'll tell you what, Wayne," Neil said. "Margo and I are going to pop over to my office while you make up your mind. There are some papers she must sign that will only take a moment. We'll have some refreshments brought in for you. What would you prefer, soft or hard?"

"I could stand a small vodka martini."

"Shaken not stirred, of course," Margo said, as she preceded Neil to the door.

"Is there any other way?" Tolley said.

They crossed the hall to Neil's corner office with the view of Michigan Avenue below. When they were inside with the doors closed, Neil spun toward his wife. "What's that idiot doing here?"

Margo walked across to Neil's desk. Picking up the telephone, she dialed an in-house number connecting her with the servants' floor. "Yes, Mrs. Gaynor. Governor Tolley's in the library. Please have someone deliver a properly chilled pitcher of martinis to him with a single glass. A snack tray would be fine. Of course, caviar!"

When she hung up, she glared at her husband. "Tolley's here, my darling husband, because the way you've been blundering around following women on public transportation, breaking into apartments and killing cops, I'm sure we'll be needing legal representation very soon. You do remember that our former crooked governor is a senior partner at Leahy, Leach, Strong and Kinch, don't you?"

Neil blanched. "You think the police are looking for me?"

Margo opened a silver box on the desk. Extracting a cigarette, she held it in her hand, waiting for him to pick up the matching desk lighter and do the honors for her. "If the police aren't looking for you then I'll be surprised. You've left such an obvious trail of clues even Edward Parchman could find you."

Edward Parchman was a blind detective created by author Debbie Bass.

Neil picked up the lighter. "I've been very careful, Margo. Nobody could be on to me."

She inhaled smoke. "Sit down, Neil, and let me explain a few things to you about being careful. If you had the brains God gave a cockroach I wouldn't have to do this, but then one must take pity on less fortunate creatures, musn't one?"

Obediently, sulking over the insult, he walked behind the desk and sat down. He was too afraid of having made a critical error to risk countering the barb.

She began pacing the floor in front of the desk. With each pass, she blew smoke into the air.

"We've been doing pursuits how long, Neil?"

He shrugged. "You were doing them before me."

"I mean together. I know I was doing them before you."

"Seven years."

"When you go out pursuing what is the first rule?"

"Become someone or something else. Don't get recognized."

"Very good."

He brightened.

"So before you went pursuing yesterday you took off your class ring and the Lucien Piccard watch I bought you for your birthday?"

His face fell.

"But then you don't have to worry too much, darling," she said, stopping at the center of the desk and looking down at him.

He perked up again.

"How many men in the nineteen sixty-nine graduating class at Princeton wear class rings with ruby stones, custom-made Lucien Picard watches, fit your general description and live in Chicago?"

"But who would have noticed my watch and ring? I didn't go around advertising myself yesterday."

Margo shook her head from side to side as she chuckled softly and resumed pacing. "Neil, Neil, Neil. What am I going to do with you? All this money and you're as dumb as a box of rocks. Are you sure your parents weren't related? It only takes one witness to make a positive ID and send you on the road to a rendezvous with a lethal injection."

Something changed in his face. The fright was replaced with a cruelty very close to that which his wife displayed. "Like the witness who saw you with Sylvia Garrett the night before her body was found on Christmas Eve nineteen eighty-nine?"

Margo stopped. "You were that witness, Neil. Are you planning to turn me in?"

"No. I . . . uh . . ."

"You what?"

The phone rang.

"Answer it" she snapped.

He obeyed instantly. After listening a moment, he said, "Hold on," and looked up at Margo. "There are two policemen downstairs to see us. One of them is a deputy chief."

She smiled. "Very good. It's just what I expected. Now do you see why I have Tolley here?"

"But what shall I tell security?"

"Tell them to escort the officers up, Neil. We'll receive them in the library with our attorney, Governor Tolley."

"Of course."

The security officer who escorted Cole and Blackie to the DeWitt penthouse looked more like a young executive than a cop. Dressed in a blue blazer, with a DeWitt crest on the breast pocket, and gray slacks, he was clean-shaven, alert and unflappably polite.

When the elevator doors opened, the security officer said, "Mr. and Mrs. DeWitt are waiting in the library. You will find it halfway down this corridor on the left. Have a nice day, gentlemen."

"Welcome to heaven," Blackie said, looking around.

"The guy downstairs said they occupy every inch of space on the top three floors of the building," Cole added. "Just the two of them."

"I'd get lost in this joint. Give me a southside bungalow anytime."

Cole led the way to the library and knocked. A man's voice called from inside, "Come in."

There were three people in the room. The policemen recognized Tolley. A slender man with a deep tan and silver hair crossed to the library entrance with his hand extended. "Gentlemen, I'm Neil DeWitt."

Cole took the offered hand.

"I'm Deputy Chief Cole. This is Lieutenant Silvestri."

"Please come in."

"This is my wife, Margo, and of course you know who this gentleman is," he said, indicating Tolley.

"Mrs. DeWitt, Governor Tolley," Cole said. Blackie nodded in their direction.

"So what can we do for you?" Neil asked.

"Actually, we came to talk to Mrs. DeWitt," Cole said.

This surprised Margo. "I don't understand. Why me?"

"Just a minute, Margo," Tolley interrupted. "Is this in connection with an official investigation, Officer Cole?"

"I really can't say at this point, Governor, because we really don't know."

"You don't know?"

"That's right. We don't know. We would just like to find out how Mrs. DeWitt came into possession of certain information she disclosed to First Deputy Superintendent Kennedy yesterday evening."

"Has this . . . ?" Tolley began, but Neil cut him off.

"What kind of information?"

"Neil, I don't think . . ." Tolley tried.

Margo jumped in. "Did I say something to Terry and Sandy that I shouldn't have?"

Cole smiled. Tolley was trying to get them to shut up but Neil and Margo were actually eager to talk. He figured it was time to exploit this gap in attitudes. "I'm quite sure Mrs. DeWitt hasn't done anything wrong and we're probably wasting our time, as well as yours, by coming here. But then that is our job."

"Of course," Neil said. "We're always happy to help the police."

"We understand perfectly," Margo echoed. "It's our duty to give you whatever assistance we can."

Tolley was seething. "I must advise both of you that it would be imprudent to make any admissions. In fact, I'd strongly caution against you saying anything until we find out what this is all about."

"The governor's got a point," Blackie said. "Maybe we should advise Mr. and Mrs. DeWitt of their constitutional rights, boss."

"Oh, would you really." Margo said excitedly.

"I think you'd better tell us what this is all about," Tolley demanded.

Cole smiled at the governor. "Oh, I plan to do just that, but first I think Lieutenant Silvestri should advise them both of their rights."

Margo and Neil stood up and raised their right hands.

"I don't think that will be necessary," Blackie said.

# CHAPTER 20

**JUNE 5, 1996**
**4:45 P.M.**

Paige was dreaming. She and Mack were at a society ball in Dallas with women in expensive gowns from Neiman-Marcus and men in Stetsons, Western-cut suits and gleaming cowboy boots. Everyone was white. She and Mack were the center of attention. She was terrified.

"They love us, baby," Mack said with a broad grin.

She turned to look into his face. His head was sitting on a skeleton's body. She screamed.

The scream shocked her awake, ringing in her ears as she jerked into a sitting position on the bed. Drenched with sweat despite the window air-conditioner going full blast, she didn't know where she was. She looked around. This was a child's room. A little boy's. There were stuffed Muppet animals and toy cars shoved into a corner out of the way. A full-length poster of Batman looked down at her from the back of the bedroom door, which swung open suddenly.

Lisa Cole rushed in. "Are you okay?"

Paige managed to smile. "I had a bad dream. Probably a reaction to all that dope they poured into me at the hospital. I'm okay now."

Lisa studied her for a moment. "When's the last time you ate?"

"I really can't remember. Sometime yesterday."

"Why don't I fix you something and bring it up on a tray?"

"I think I've spent enough time in bed, Lisa. I'd like to

take a shower and come downstairs to eat, if it's okay with you."

"I'd like that. The bathroom is across the hall. I'll lay out a fresh towel for you."

In the bathroom Paige turned on the water and stepped under the shower. As she closed her eyes and let the stinging spray hit her in the face, the image of Mack lying dead in the tub doused with acid jolted her. She nearly lost her balance. She sat down on the floor of the tub and curled her knees up under her. Then she cried for a long time.

Lisa was broiling hamburgers and Italian sausage links on the patio grill when Paige came down.

Paige stepped outside. It was still hot, but she felt good being outdoors.

Lisa flipped a couple of patties and turned to her guest. "You look hungry."

"I am. I didn't really think about it until I smelled the food."

"Why don't you sit down out here while I make some lemonade?"

"C'mon, I'm not an invalid. I'll make the lemonade for you."

"Okay, if you feel up to it. Everything you need is in the cabinet over the sink."

"Be right back."

Half an hour later they were seated at the patio picnic table. Paige had consumed two hamburgers with all the fixings, an Italian sausage sandwich with sweet peppers, and three glasses of lemonade. Lisa was trying to get her to eat more.

"No, I couldn't," Paige said laughing. "If I keep stuffing myself I'll be as big as a house."

"You've got a ways to go before you get there," Lisa said as she began to clear the table. Paige helped. In the kitchen Paige also demanded to wash the dishes. With no other options, Lisa sat down.

"What's it like?" Paige asked. "I mean being a cop's wife."

"It can be rough," Lisa began. "A few years ago I actually walked out on Larry because I couldn't take it. The hours can be horrible and then there's always tension. You know that the people he's after are not only bad, but in a lot of cases crazy or doped up. You try to be understanding, but then you care so much.

"The day I got back with Larry that time he got trapped by this maniac who was stalking a Catholic nun. The guy drugged Larry and then nailed his hand to the floor of a chapel."

Paige spun around, horror on her face. Horror and a great deal of anger.

Lisa saw this. "He's dead. The nun killed him that same night."

"Good for her," Paige said, turning back to the dishes.

"Larry loves his job. Sometimes I get jealous of it. But when he comes home after making a good arrest or cracking a complicated case, then you can actually feel the satisfaction radiating off of him. Sometimes he gets together with Blackie. . . ."

A horn sounding in front of the house interrupted her. Getting up, Lisa said, "That's Butch. He's in day camp."

"How's he going to feel about me taking his room?"

"He won't mind," Lisa called over her shoulder. "I think he likes sleeping with us."

A few minutes later Lisa came back into the kitchen. She had a boy of about eight in tow.

Paige instantly saw the resemblance. The child had Lisa's facial features and bone structure, but his father's eyes and curly black hair. He stared back at Paige with a shy curiosity, but no fear.

"Larry Cole, Jr., this is Ms. Albritton," Lisa said. "She's a friend of your daddy's and mine. She's going to be staying with us for a while. Paige, this is Larry, Jr., but we usually call him Butch."

"Hello, Miz Albritton," he said.

It had been a long time since she'd been around children, but she did remember a few things she'd learned growing up in a house with four brothers and six sisters. She crossed to the kitchen and knelt down. Her eyes were level with his. "It's nice to meet you, Butch." She extended her hand.

He looked at the hand for a moment before reaching out and clutching her fingers. He smiled.

She smiled back. "Ms. Albritton is such a big name for a little boy to say, Butch. If your mommy doesn't mind, I want you to call me Paige."

He looked up at his mother. Lisa nodded her approval.

"Paige?" he said. "That's a funny name."

"Yes, it is," she said, laughing. "It is a funny name."

She had found a new friend.

# CHAPTER 21

**June 5, 1996**
**6:15 P.M.**

Dick Shelby was still in his office in the Area Three Police Center at Belmont and Western. He was brooding over the events of that morning. The private line on his phone console rang.

"Shelby."

"*What are you doing*?" It was Anne Johnson.

"Sitting here counting my fingers and toes. Where've you been?"

"*Here and there. You sound depressed.*"

"Shouldn't I be? Cole made me look like a rookie in front of Govich and Dwyer."

"*It's not over yet, Dick. In fact, it might only be just*

*beginning. Deputy Chief Cole might have bitten off more than he can chew.*"

"I don't understand."

"*Do you know where the Barrister's Club is in the Loop?*"

"On Plymouth Court near the Federal Building. It's members only."

"*We've got an invitation from a member for dinner.*"

"Who?"

"*It's a surprise. Just meet me in the lobby at seven.*"

With that she hung up.

Shelby said into the emptiness of his office, "Why not?"

# CHAPTER 22

**JUNE 5, 1996**
**7:10 P.M.**

Former Governor Wayne Tolley got out of the chauffeur-driven limo. The top-hatted doorman in front of the Barrister's Club said a cheerful "Good evening, Governor."

Tolley managed one of his old campaign smiles as he crossed the sidewalk to the double doors marked with the letter "B." Another doorman was waiting there, "Good evening, Governor."

Inside the lobby, at least five people gave him warm greetings; however, an equal number, including a few who had been former colleagues, ignored him.

A heavyset black woman and seedy-looking white man crossed the lobby toward him. He turned his back on them, wondering how these two gate-crashers had gotten into the lobby of his private club. Then he heard the woman call, "Governor! Governor Tolley! It's Anne Johnson."

He stopped and turned around. He couldn't believe it.

This woman was the assistant state's attorney in charge of the Felony Division. He glanced at the man. If this was Johnson, then the guy with her, who looked like a pickpocket, had to be the police commander. Hell, he didn't even look Irish. The former governor wondered what the world was coming to, as he smiled his politician's smile and said an expansive "Ms. Johnson and Commander Shelby. How good of you to join me. I've reserved a private dining room for our meal."

He could tell they were impressed. They were supposed to be. Neil and Margo were not only picking up the tab, but would also be paying his five-hundred-dollar-an-hour fee. The clock had started running two hours ago.

Two waiters and a wine steward attended them in the private, third-floor dining room. When brandy was served, Tolley dismissed the help. He could summon them by pushing a button beneath the arm of his chair.

"I want to begin by again thanking you for coming this evening and also give you my assurances that nothing said in this room goes beyond these walls."

He watched the cop shoot the state's attorney a questioning look. She gave him a reassuring nod.

"Let me start off by saying that I represent a very important family in this city. A family whom I believe is on the verge of being severely and unnecessarily harassed by a high-ranking member of the Chicago Police Department. Now, it is my understanding that there was an investigation conducted into the death of an off-duty police sergeant yesterday. An investigation which targeted the common-law wife of this sergeant as a suspect. An investigation which uncovered enough evidence to justify the arrest and incarceration of this suspect. An investigation that also disclosed that this suspect is of somewhat questionable character."

Shelby's eyes darted to Johnson and then back to Tolley. The former governor looked at the female attorney. She was cool, possibly just a bit anxious, but not scared. She could be someone who would make an admirable adversary.

"My sources, whom I don't need to disclose at this time, have also informed me that this high-ranking member of the Department's Detective Division, who was also a friend of the deceased officer and the suspect, intruded in the conduct of the investigation. That he conducted an independent investigation of his own which diverted attention from the suspect in custody. Diverted that attention in another direction. That direction is the reason I asked for this meeting. I represent the party, or shall we say parties, at whom this scrutiny is aimed."

"You mind telling us who your client or clients are, Governor?" Anne said.

"I don't think I need go into that at this time."

Johnson shook her head. "I think you do. Guarantees of confidentiality to the contrary, what we're doing here right now could be considered at some later date a conspiracy to obstruct justice. If we're going to enter into some type of pact, understanding or whatever, I think we all need to be honest with each other. Don't you think so, Dick?"

"Y-yes, of course. We need to be honest with each other."

Tolley could see who was running the show.

"My clients are Neil and Margo DeWitt."

This stunned even the calculating state's attorney. "Cole suspects the DeWitts of murder?"

"I don't know what he suspects, but he's already questioned them once," Tolley said.

Johnson and Shelby exchanged amazed looks. When they turned back to Tolley, she said, "Go on, Governor. This is very interesting."

# CHAPTER 23

**JUNE 5, 1996**
**9:35 P.M.**

The DeWitts listened to Tolley's report over the speakerphone in Neil's office.

*"So apparently Cole has formed a link between this phantom in the blue cap and white shirt following the Albritton woman, and the sergeant's death. To my way of thinking that does no more than show that another guy was interested in her. She would still be at the top of my hit list for a murder indictment."*

Margo had been making notes on a legal pad. During Tolley's narration of the information he had obtained from Anne Johnson and Dick Shelby, she had asked him to spell the names of each of the witnesses. There were three: the Pakistani student, Syed Shafiq; the cabdriver, Sidney Vukhovich; and the concerned citizen, Frances Adams. Margo drew exaggerated exclamation marks behind each name.

"Wayne," she said, "is Cole trying to say that Neil is the man who followed the Albritton woman?"

*"He hasn't disclosed anything like that, at least as far as my contacts have been able to discover."*

"Then why did he come to see us today?"

*"It could be just as he told us, Margo. You said something last night to that other cop Kennedy, which made him suspicious, and Cole came to check it out."*

"That's ridiculous. What could I know? I was a bit smashed when I talked to Kennedy and his horrid wife. Maybe I made something up. Narrated a scene from some book I recently read. That isn't enough to send police officers around banging on people's doors."

Neil stared at his wife. She didn't look back at him. He could tell she was nervous, something few people were capable of detecting. So, she had disclosed something last night. Either about what he had done, or what she'd told him she had done to the little boy in the park. What was that she'd said earlier about parents being related?

Tolley was speaking again. *"He could have used your meeting with Kennedy as a smoke screen. I heard Cole's a smart cop. But he's sniffing around looking for something. I've got my ear to the ground and my sources are reliable. I'll be in touch if I come up with anything more."*

After Tolley hung up, Neil asked. "What in the hell did you say to Kennedy anyway?"

"Don't use that tone of voice to me, Neil. Not after all your screwups!"

"Okay, but you never caught me getting a snootful and singing an operetta to no cop."

She glared at him. "And who did you borrow that from?"

"Borrow what from?"

" 'Singing an operetta to no cop.' Those aren't my Neil's words."

He lowered his eyes. "A bad guy named Fishbait said them to Kirk Slade in *Killing Streets*. But that's got nothing to do with the whole point of this thing. It was you and not me that brought the flatfoots down. . . ."

"Oh, Neil, please." She howled. "You keep this up and you're going to give me a hernia. 'Flatfoots'?"

He tried to suppress the grin, but couldn't. The urge to continue the argument was oozing out of him. She could always do this to him.

As quickly as her laughter began it halted. "We've got to stay a jump ahead of Cole. We can't let him get any closer to us than he already is."

"How are we going to do that?"

She fingered the edges of the legal pad on which she'd

written the witnesses' names. She made an addition to the list and handed it to Neil.

"So what about them?"

She shook her head in that disapproving way she reserved just for him. "If something happens to Cole's witnesses, he has no case, my darling husband."

He started to ask what was going to happen to them, but caught himself in time. "When do we start?"

"In the morning, at the top, with Mr. Shafiq."

He looked back at the paper. There were four names on it. The last was Paige Albritton.

# CHAPTER 24

**JUNE 6, 1996**
**7:30 A.M.**

Neil and Margo were up early. They had breakfast served to them in the library, where they spent the morning browsing through mystery novels. As they read, Margo chewed listlessly on a dry English muffin, while Neil devoured spinach quiche and fresh fruit.

With an orange marker she underlined passages in a number of books before passing them to Neil. He would glance at the passage between bites and nod or grunt approval. Finally, these responses got to her.

"Don't you have anything at all to add? Can't you at least disagree on one of them?"

With a mouthful of food he stared at her. Dabbing his lips with a napkin and chasing the quiche with a swallow of sweetened grapefruit juice, he picked up the last book she had given him. He looked at the cover. *A Minute to Die* by Martin Wiemler. He read what she had highlighted. When he finished, he tossed the book on the floor.

"Okay. It stinks. Find something else." He went back to his breakfast.

She walked over and picked up the book. "Serves you right for asking, stupid," she mumbled.

Mrs. Schiller, the work-study program director at Roosevelt University, took the call shortly after she arrived in her office that morning. The caller had a British accent, which reminded her of the actor Terry Thomas because of the pronounced lisp.

"You're looking for an engineering student of Pakistani origin," Mrs. Schiller said. "What type of business did you say you were in, Mr., uh . . . ?"

*"That's Colonel Farquart-Smyth, dear lady. Colonel Hugh Montague Farquart-Smyth of the Farquart-Smyths of Kent. We're into the design and manufacture of farm implements for Third World nations. After all, one must do what one can for the less fortunate. Don't you agree, dear lady?"*

Mrs. Schiller flipped through an index card file on her desk. The only Pakistani engineering student in residence for the summer was Syed Shafiq.

*"Splendid!"* Colonel Farquart-Smyth said. *"I'd like to make arrangements to collect the dear Mr. Shafiq at his earliest convenience."*

Shafiq sat on a pillar in front of the Michigan Avenue entrance to the university. He was excited over the prospect of getting a job that would earn him a decent wage. He was eager to get into the American workforce, to obtain some experience as a capitalist.

The dark blue Buick pulled to the curb and honked. Shafiq stared at the shiny car. Since coming to America he had been in no vehicles other than a friend's twenty-year-old Volkswagen and CTA buses. Again the horn blew.

The power window on the passenger side rolled down. A woman with long red hair sat behind the wheel of the car.

"Are you Shafiq?"

He stood up tentatively and took a step toward the car.

"C'mon, Shafiq, move your ass. This is a bus stop I'm parked in!"

He quickened his pace. As he opened the door, the automatic window went up. He slid onto the leather seat and buckled his seat belt.

"Hope you move faster'n that when you're working," she said around a wad of chewing gum. Then she slammed the car in gear and peeled rubber pulling away from the curb.

"I'm sorry," he said. "But I did not know whom to expect."

" 'Whom to expect.' Ha! Where'd you learn that lingo? Baghdad?"

This rankled Shafiq. He had been complimented on his excellent English many times at the university. "Baghdad is in Iraq. I am from Pakistan."

"Well, excuse the hell out of me, honey. I didn't mean no offense."

He glanced sideways at this brash, loud American woman. The red hair was obviously a wig. He had seen them worn at the school. She had on enormous sunglasses that covered her skinny, pinched face as effectively as a mask. And her voice! She sounded like one of those crazy American actresses who hurled insults in screeching tones that could raise goose bumps.

"So, when do you graduate?"

"June of nineteen ninety-seven."

"By that time you should be pretty well off if ya' go to work for the colonel."

"Who is this colonel?"

"Colonel Hugh Montague Farquart-Smyth, retired."

Shafiq frowned. "The same as the one in the book?"

The woman stiffened. "Just don't let him hear you say that. He started to sue that writer. I mean a name like Jones or Johnson is one thing, but Hugh Montague Farquart-Smyth! Can you believe it?"

"You cannot copyright a name," Shafiq said. "The colonel would have been wasting his money if he had tried to sue Mr. Wiemler."

"For an engineering student you seem to know an awful lot about American fiction."

"Foreign students at the university are required to take English familiarization courses. One of them is a Contemporary American Literature seminar. Mr. Martin Wiemler was a guest speaker last semester. I own the autographed copy of his book."

"*A Minute to Die*?" she asked.

"That is it. The one whose hero is Colonel Hugh Montague Farquart-Smyth, retired, of the British commandos. It was very interesting how he solved that series of poison murders. No one suspected . . ."

She skidded into a parking lot west of Navy Pier. As the Buick raced down the rows of tightly parked cars, Shafiq noticed the conspicuously posted signs stating, PRIVATE PROPERTY—VIOLATOR'S CARS WILL BE TOWED AT OWNER'S EXPENSE. The logo over the sign bore the name THE DEWITT CORPORATION.

She pulled the Buick into a spot at the far end of the lot and got out. Slowly, Shafiq unharnessed his seat belt and followed.

She crossed the grass parkway surrounding the lot and walked rapidly toward the street. He was forced to run to catch up with her.

"Where are we going?" he asked.

"Lunch," she said without breaking stride.

He stopped. She continued walking into a small tree-lined park and proceeded to a picnic table and placed the large shoulder bag she carried down on it. Then she turned and crooked a finger beckoning him to join her.

Something about this was wrong, but he couldn't figure out what. He resorted to his excuse for everything new he encountered in the foreign land where he was being educated: "This is America, not Pakistan."

He looked around the park. There was no one in sight except a man operating a portable hot-dog stand. Shafiq noticed that the man wore a white chef's cap and white apron.

"Sit down," she ordered. "I don't know how you do things in your country, but if you're going to work for the colonel you'll have to learn to move a great deal faster than what you've been doing with me so far."

She slapped a white, lined pad on the table. "Do you have a pen?"

He reached for the disposable ballpoint in his shirt pocket.

"I want you to write out your name, age, address and educational background *neatly.* When I come back I'll tell you what I want you to do next."

"Where are you going?"

"To get our lunch. What do you want on your hot dog?"

"I'm not hungry." He began printing his name on the pad.

She dropped a thick envelope on the table. It bounced onto the pad and struck his hand skewing the *h* in his name.

"That's your advance. Ten thousand in cash. The colonel's already checked you out with the school. You're in. Now all I need is the particulars."

With trembling fingers Shafiq reached out and grasped the envelope. Fumbling with the flap he peered inside. The stack of hundreds he found there nearly stopped his heart.

"I'll ask you again, Shafiq," she said in that acid-toned voice that now sounded like music to his ears. "What do you want on your hot dog?"

"Everything," he said, still eyeing the money.

Neil DeWitt stood under the umbrella of the hot-dog stand and watched Margo and Shafiq. He had to admire her. She was good.

Margo headed for the stand. She had that look as she approached. She had him! Neil could have kissed her.

"Okay, my darling husband," she said adjusting her wig. "Two dogs, one plain, the other a special with the works."

He looked blankly at her. "So what should I do?"

She ground her teeth. "Fix me two hot dogs, Neil. One plain for me; the other with everything in the special bun."

He looked dumbly at the hot-dog boiler and bun warmer.

"Oh, for crying out loud. Can't you do anything right?"

"You didn't say I'd have to make the hot dogs."

"Okay. I can handle this. Look over my shoulder. See what our dear Mr. Shafiq is doing."

"He's still staring at the money."

"Keep watching him. Let me know if he looks this way. Where did you put the special buns?"

"They're in the container on top."

"Good. This will be one hot dog our Pakistani snitch will never forget."

# CHAPTER 25

**JUNE 6, 1996**
**12:30 P.M.**

They waked Sergeant Clarence McKinnis at the A.A. Rayner Funeral Home on East Seventy-first Street. The funeral was held the next day in the Catholic church across the street. The mass began at 11:00 A.M. The celebrant was the police chaplain Father Michael Ivers; the concelebrant was Father Ken Smith from Our Lady of Peace parish, where Mack had gone to grammar school.

Paige Albritton, accompanied by Lisa and Larry Cole, attended both wake and funeral. Cole, wearing his dress uniform, was worried initially over how well Paige would bear up under the scrutiny of thousands of people, including

Mack's surviving family and the majority of the 12,500-strong Chicago Police Department, who would be attending the services.

At the cemetery, when taps had concluded and the last volley of the twenty-one-gun salute had been fired, they slowly made their way back to the cars. Lisa, whimpering softly, clutched her husband's arm. Cole's face was set in stone.

Paige accompanied Mack's mother back to the limousine, but that's as far as she went. There she embraced her almost mother-in-law, said polite goodbyes to the other family members and rejoined Cole and Lisa.

Before they could escape the knot of cars clogging the narrow cemetery lane, Terry Kennedy intercepted them. The first deputy was on foot and leaned down to look in Cole's open window.

"Lisa, Miss Albritton," he said, tipping his hat. "How's it going, Larry?"

"Good, sir. With you?"

"Operational Services is a nightmare as usual, but so was my last tax audit. How'd you come out on that thing you were looking into for me?"

"I want my witnesses to take a look at the husband. He and his wife are a strange pair, but I figure that he could be our guy. The kid's death is still up in the air until I get more from the M.E., but it looks like he sustained a broken neck before he went into the water. I've got to play this one close to the vest. They've got some heavy legal representation."

"Who?"

"Wayne Tolley."

Kennedy sneered. "He was never more than an overpriced mouthpiece with political connections and an out-of-season tan. You make a good enough case, all he'll be able to do is plea-bargain for a commuted sentence of life imprisonment. Look, maybe tomorrow you can stop by my office and we can kick this around."

"Sure thing, boss."

"Have a good day," he said again, tipping his hat to the ladies. He started to walk away from the car and stopped. He looked back at Paige. "I really haven't had the opportunity to personally convey my condolences to you. Mack was a good man. He'll be missed by all of us."

Surprised, Paige said a shocked "Thank you, sir."

She cried all the way back to the house.

# CHAPTER 26

**JUNE 6, 1996**
**5:45 P.M.**

Syed Shafiq was in his dorm at the university making plans to spend his money. He would send some home to help his brothers and sisters. He needed new clothes and . . . the idea had seemed so outlandish just a short time ago: he would buy himself a car! He was trying to make up his mind on the color when the first pain hit him.

He had felt hot and uncomfortable for the past half hour. The window fan was blowing cool air into the cramped area. He had never felt this way before. He was also having difficulty breathing.

Too much excitement. Plus, he hadn't eaten since . . . He remembered the hot dog and soft drink he'd had with that horrible woman, who had become his guardian angel. A woman whose name he couldn't remember. Then he realized that she'd never told him her name. Just the colonel's. Colonel Hugh Montague . . .

The sharp pain tore through him like a sledgehammer blow to the gut. He doubled over and slid off his desk chair onto his knees. He clutched his stomach, hoping this pressure would keep him from exploding from within. Bright pinpoints of light danced across the insides of his closed eyelids. He felt sweat pouring off him, yet suddenly he was as cold as he had been on that winter day he had arrived in Chicago.

God, what was happening to him? Then in one brilliant flash of insight he knew. He had been poisoned. Poisoned by the loud woman wearing the red wig.

The room started to spin. *But why had she done this?* He remembered the man in the chef's hat at the hot-dog stand. He had been too far away for Shafiq to see him, but he had to have helped her.

*Colonel Hugh Montague Farquart-Smyth!*

It was becoming increasingly difficult for Shafiq to breathe. He didn't think it possible, but the pain inside him had intensified. Fighting it, Shafiq pulled himself upright. Using the desk as a brace, he remained standing. He searched the titles in his bookcase. This was difficult, because he was going blind. Finally he found the book, which he succeeded in clutching to his chest the instant he toppled backward to the floor.

Thirty seconds later Syed Shafiq was dead.

# CHAPTER 27

**JUNE 6, 1996**
**6:45 P.M.**

*"Base to Sidney. Base to Sidney. Hey, Sidney, you out there?"*

Sidney Vukhovich rolled his eyes at the roof of his cab. Marian never could master proper radio procedure. Snatching up his microphone he depressed the transmit key.

"This is Cab Twelve to base. I read you. Come back."

*"Is that you, Sidney?"*

"This is Cab Twelve, base. Come back."

*"Stop playin' cop, Sidney, and go pick up a fare in front of Loyola University on Sheridan Road. Lady with a dog. Asked just for you. Going downtown to the Mag Mile."*

"You're supposed to use proper radio code when transmitting, Marian."

*"Aw, stuff it and go pick up your fare. You've been loafing all day."*

He tossed the mike on the car seat. "What's the use?"

In front of Loyola he pulled to the curb. The woman had white hair, probably a wig, wore dark glasses despite the approach of twilight and had a white toy poodle on a leash that looked big enough for a Great Dane. Dragging the little dog, who was reluctant to go with her, she crossed the sidewalk and got into the cab. Sidney smelled the odor of alcohol right away, but he didn't mind. He enjoyed a drink from time to time himself.

"Where to, ma'am?"

"You are Sidney, aren't you?" Her speech was slow and thick.

"Sidney Vukhovich. Just like on the license."

"My friend Janine told me to ask specifically for you. She said—that's my friend Janine—that you're very good. Are you very good, Sidney?"

He looked in the rearview mirror at his passenger. Not a bad-looking broad. Maybe a little skinny for his tastes, but then she looked like she had dough. He'd been propositioned before by women fares. In fact, more than once. And he had taken a couple of them up on the offer, too. But then his job was cabdriver, not stud for rent on the meter. On top of that, he could pork some drunk who, when she sobers up in the morning, starts screaming rape. Then he would be in the shit. It wasn't worth it.

"Yes, ma'am, I'm good. Best cabbie in Chicago. Get you where you want to go safe and fast as the law'll allow."

"Good! I want to be taken . . ." The little dog began

barking. She did something that made it yelp in pain. "Sssh, Fifi. Mama's talking."

Sidney didn't like this. He didn't like people who hurt defenseless animals. If it wasn't that he hadn't had a fare in a couple of hours, he would have ordered this drunk bitch out of his cab.

"So where'll it be?"

"You sound angry, Sidney," she pouted. "Are you mad at me?"

"Just tell me where you want to go, lady."

"Downtown. North Michigan Avenue. Anywhere near DeWitt Plaza."

"I'm not going to get out until you have one drink with me, Sidney."

There must have been a thousand people walking up and down the block on North Michigan Avenue where he had stopped. To Sidney it seemed like they were all looking right at his cab.

"Look, lady, I told you I'm on duty. I drive for a living. I can't drink with you."

She had produced the silver flask right after he pulled away from the spot where he picked her up. Although he never actually saw her drink from it, she handled it enough to indicate she wasn't holding it in order to occupy her hands. Now she wanted him to have some.

"I'll double your tip," she said, flashing a hundred-dollar bill and dropping it on the front seat.

The toy poodle started getting nervous. It was pawing around the backseat looking for a way out. Sidney only hoped the little dog didn't have a weak bladder or worse.

"Stop it, Fifi, or Mama will hurt you. Now what about it, Sidney?"

"Tell you what, you keep the tip and I'll just . . ." The poodle let out such a howl of pain the hairs on the back of Sidney's neck bristled.

"What're you doing?" He spun around to face her over the backseat.

Her face was split in a teeth-bared snarl. He couldn't see what she was doing with her right hand, but whatever it was froze the dog rigid with pain.

"Let it go!" He reached for her.

Her snarl was turned on him. "You touch me and I'll have your ass jailed for battery!"

The dog's howl had turned to pitiful whimpering. Sidney felt hot tears sting his eyes.

"Please. Don't hurt it anymore."

The glasses she wore were dark, but he was able to see her eyes widen in surprise behind the lenses. "I won't hurt it anymore if you drink." She held out the flask to him.

It tasted awful. He didn't even think it was booze at all until it burned its way down into his gut. The taste it left made him gag.

"What in the hell was that?" he gasped.

Carrying the dog, she was getting out of the cab. She stopped with her feet on the sidewalk. "Aged cognac, with a little something to give it an extra kick. See you around, Sidney."

She slammed the door and walked off down the street.

He started to yell after her that she'd forgotten the change for the hundred-dollar bill, but he could no longer see her. Chalking it up to another weird experience as a hack driver in the Windy City, he headed back for the North Side. He only hoped she wouldn't hurt the dog anymore.

Three hours later, Sidney Vukhovich collapsed in a diner on Lincoln Avenue. He died in the ambulance taking him to the hospital. Forty-five minutes after he was pronounced dead, the Dead Animal Removal Unit of the Police Department was called to DeWitt Plaza. A poodle had been found in the lobby. The little dog's neck was broken.

# CHAPTER 28

**June 7, 1996**
**6:30 a.m.**

The alarm clock snatched Cole from a sound sleep. He stared at the bedroom ceiling. He had been off yesterday for Mack's funeral, and today he would have to mount an all-out investigation to build a case against his friend's killer—a killer he strongly suspected was Neil DeWitt.

He headed for the shower. When he came downstairs, Lisa was in the kitchen fixing breakfast. After kissing her, he sat down at the table and opened the *Times-Herald*. The second page was devoted to Mack's death and funeral. There was a picture of Paige in the black dress she had worn yesterday. Under the photo was the caption "Murderess or victim?"

"Has she seen this?"

"No," Lisa said, placing a cup of coffee in front of him. "But I don't think we should try to hide it from her. She can handle it."

"Where is she?"

"Still asleep. I looked in on her when I got up. She's out like a light."

"Where's Butch?"

"In bed with her. He fell asleep while she was reading him a comic book. I tried to take him about eleven, but she was holding him and he had his arms wrapped around her so I left him there. They hadn't moved when I looked in this morning."

"He doesn't usually take to strangers so easily."

Lisa smiled. "I don't think she does either."

* * *

Detective Judy Daniels had just returned from a two-month detail to the Organized Crime Division. While there, she had adopted a number of her patented disguises to go undercover against a group of Outfit types vying to occupy the throne of top Chicago Mob boss—a throne vacated two years before by Antonio "Tuxedo Tony" DeLisa, a man Judy had tried to beat to death one chilly spring night after he had kidnapped her.

Her regular job was on Deputy Chief Cole's staff. Whatever the deputy chief needed, Blackie Silvestri, Manny Sherlock or she would be dispatched to obtain. They also had the luxury of operating out of the Chief of Detectives' Office. This enabled them to call on just about any cop in the city for help. That was how the three of them had uncovered the information Cole had used to temporarily clear Paige Albritton.

On this hot summer morning, Judy was going through the twenty-four-hour incident report and noticed the names Syed Shafiq and Sidney Vukhovich. They had witnessed the man following Paige on the day Sergeant McKinnis was murdered. Both witnesses had died within hours of each other. The cause of death in both cases was listed as "Undetermined."

She took this information to Blackie. When Cole walked in at eight-thirty, they were waiting for him.

# CHAPTER 29

**JUNE 7, 1996**
**10:15 A.M.**

Bill McGuire worked in the Cook County Medical Examiner's Office. He had been there for eight years and gotten a lot of mileage out of being a dead ringer for the actor Christopher Reeve. Since he'd been with the M.E. he'd been nicknamed "Soupy," which was short for the character Superman, whom Reeve had portrayed in movies. However, today he wasn't feeling very super. Seated across from him in his small office above the morgue were Larry Cole, Blackie Silvestri and Judy Daniels.

"You've got to autopsy those bodies again, Soupy," Cole said. "Those two guys were murdered. I'll bet my pension on it."

"Larry, we did a standard post on them when they were brought in. There was nothing to indicate foul play."

"But there *was* foul play," Blackie said. "Like we told you, they were witnesses in the McKinnis murder investigation."

"Okay, hold it a minute," Soupy argued. "I worked on McKinnis myself. A gunshot killed him. The acid wiped out most of his vital organs, but we did find the bullet. Now, these two"—Soupy tapped the autopsy reports lying on his desk—"fit the pattern of any number of natural-cause deaths they bring in here every day. Not a mark on them."

"But your reports list their causes of death as 'Undetermined,'" Cole said.

"Well, one thing's for sure," Soupy said, "they weren't shot and burned with acid. These guys were as clean inside and out as they would be if they'd died in a hospital bed."

"Did you check their livers?" Blackie asked.

"We always check the liver, Blackie. It's standard procedure in a post."

"Were you checking for poison?" Cole said.

"We check the blood and stomach for your standard poisons routinely."

"Suppose someone's using something unusual or exotic?" Blackie asked.

Soupy was being bounced back and forth between them like a Ping-Pong ball, and he didn't like it. Thousands of bodies went through the morgue in this town every year. In at least a few hundred cases, a grieving relative or cop with an itch wanted to create a murder where none had been committed. Soupy had handled situations like this before. He knew exactly what to do.

"Okay, you guys want the whole thing done over. You win. I'll have both Shafiq and Vukhovich reworked."

"That isn't all we want," Cole said. "We want you to examine the liver, the lungs, the heart and whatever else you guys look at to see if you can find traces of not only poison, but maybe difficult-to-detect violence."

*Difficult-to-detect violence!* Soupy wondered who Cole thought he was. Quincy?

"I'll go over them from head to toe personally," Soupy said. "But you're gonna have to give me a couple of days. I'll have to do it on my own time."

"You come up with anything, we owe you a steak dinner," Cole said.

"What about pizza?" Blackie countered.

"Let's see if I find anything before we start ordering dinner."

Judy didn't say anything until they were in the squad car.

"He's not going to do anything, Boss."

Cole turned around to look at her. "What do you mean? You know Soupy McGuire?"

"No, but I know the type. As an undercover you learn to spot straight talkers and bullshitters. That guy's a bullshitter."

"I tend to agree with Judy," Blackie said. "How will we know if he does what he said he was going to do or just sits on the reports for a few days and tells us he didn't find anything else? All we can do is take his word for it."

"Then I'll go straight to the M.E." Cole said angrily. "This is a murder case he's screwing around with."

"I don't think that's going to do any good either, Deputy," Judy said quietly. "The commander I worked for in Narcotics went to the M.E. over one of our snitches a dealer gave a 'hot shot' to. Another of those 'undetermined'-cause deaths. Not only did they not reautopsy the snitch, the M.E. wrote a letter of complaint to the superintendent about the commander's interference."

"I've got to chance that," Cole said. "The DeWitts somehow killed both Shafiq and Vukhovich and I'm pretty sure they did Mack, too. Without knowing what they used on the witnesses we won't be able to find out how they did it."

"With an 'undetermined' cause of death we won't be able to charge them even if we can make a case," Blackie said glumly.

"Mack wasn't an 'undetermined' cause," Cole said.

After a few moments Judy said, "I don't know what the M.E.'s going to do, but maybe there's a way we can find out the 'how' of all the murders."

This time they both turned to look at her.

She smiled. "You're not going to like it."

# CHAPTER 30

**JUNE 7, 1996**
**11:00 A.M.**

Anne Johnson was in a bad mood when she exited the courtroom on the third floor of the Criminal Courts Building at Twenty-sixth and California. She had just blown an extortion case she thought she had a lock on.

Stomping through the corridors, she kept a frown on her face. Dick Shelby was waiting outside her office. Her frown deepened when she saw that bloodless, "I'm scared shitless" look on his face.

Her secretary tried to give her a handful of urgent messages, but she waved the woman off. From the looks of Shelby, most of them were probably from him anyway. He followed her into her private office, which resembled a waste-paper storeroom.

Anne took the only available chair behind the desk. Because papers, files and books covered everything else, Shelby was forced to stand.

"Okay, let's have it," she said.

"Let's have what?"

"You're so pale it looks like Dracula's had his fangs in your neck all night. On top of that, your hands are shaking like you've got D.T.'s."

"Have you talked to Tolley lately?"

"Not since the other night at dinner. Why?"

"Two of Cole's witnesses are dead."

This got her attention. "What are you talking about?"

He pulled two crumpled sheets of paper from his inside

pocket. When he handed them to her, the dampness from his perspiration made them collapse.

"Those are from the twenty-four-hour incident report. As you can see . . ."

She had already found them. "It says that the cause of death in both cases is 'Undetermined.' "

"Aw, c'mon, Anne!" His angry shout surprised her. "One of them I'll buy, but not two within hours of each other!"

"Relax, Dick. Sit down. Pull yourself together."

He looked around the cluttered office for a chair.

"Throw the stuff off that chair onto the floor. Not that chair!" But it was too late. She watched the files on the case she had going to a jury trial at three land in an untidy heap at Shelby's feet. He sat down.

"Okay," she said, massaging her temples. "What do you think happened?"

"I don't know, but I'll bet Tolley does. Two witnesses don't drop dead so close together wihout a reason."

She studied the incident-report excerpts again. "They really weren't close together as far as geographical proximity, and the times are actually hours apart."

"We still need to talk to Tolley about this."

"Do you think he killed them?"

"I don't know what to think, but those guys are dead. It might be coincidence. One thing's damn sure: Cole's not going to buy coincidental deaths without an investigation."

Picking up the phone, she said, "Let's see what the good governor's got to say, but I really don't think we have anything to worry about."

"Yeah, and I don't know how 'good' he is either," Shelby mumbled.

# CHAPTER 31

**June 7, 1996**
**12:30 p.m.**

"That's horrible, Wayne," Margo said. They were in Neil's study, but Margo was not using the speakerphone, so Neil stood anxiously by.

"Well, I don't know how anyone could implicate Neil or myself, Wayne. You did say they died of natural causes, didn't you? Oh, 'undetermined.' What does that mean? But if they can't tell, how do they suspect foul play?" She winked at her husband. "If Officer Cole wants to come back and talk to us, he's welcome anytime, but I can assure you, Neil and I have never met those men whose names you mentioned."

A few moments later she hung up.

"They're so stupid," she said. "All they've got is two stiffs. They don't even know how they died."

"But could they find out?" Neil asked.

"Of course they could find out if they had time, the expertise and didn't have from ten to fifteen fresh murder victims every day. I used a little extract of castor-bean oil on Shafiq and a dose of nicotine sulfate mixed with something to slow down the reaction flavored with cognac for my friend Sidney. Very slow deaths."

"So what about the other two?"

"I think we'll wait a few days before we move on them. Let Shafiq and Vukhovich cool a bit. Maybe get buried. They might even send our little Pakistani student home for burial. That would make exhumation damned hard."

"You said 'we.' "

"What are you talking about now?"

"You said 'we' will have to wait a few days before we move on the other two. You promised they would be mine."

"Yes, I did, Neil," she said without enthusiasm. "I did promise."

# CHAPTER 32

**JUNE 7, 1996**
**2:16 P.M.**

"The last time Syed Shafiq was seen," Manny said, "he was on his way to meet a man who identified himself to the college work-study program director as a Colonel Hugh Montague Farquart-Smyth."

"You're kidding?" Blackie said, deadpan.

"No, sir, I'm not. The name's the same as the main character in a book by an author named Martin Wiemler. The book's title is *One Minute to Die*. When Shafiq was found he was clutching that book to his chest. Rigor had set in and they had to wait for it to recede before they could pry it away."

They were in Cole's office, going over everything they had on the deaths of Shafiq and Vukhovich.

"Do we know where this Wiemler was yesterday?" Cole asked.

"In New York at a meeting with his agent and publisher," Judy said. "The NYPD checked it out for us."

Manny continued. "Shafiq was on a scholarship and did odd jobs around the college to make spending money, about fifty bucks in a good week. Well, he had ten thousand dollars in new one-hundred-dollar bills in his room."

Blackie let out a low whistle. "Maybe the kid was good at saving money."

No one commented.

"The cabdriver had a slow day, according to his dispatcher. The only thing out of the ordinary was a call for him to pick up a fare in front of Loyola University on North Sheridan Road. The fare asked for Vukhovich by name, but according to the dispatcher this wasn't unusual because he was very popular on the North Side."

"Was that the last time he was heard from?" Cole asked.

"No, Deputy," Manny responded. "He dropped that one and took two others before he went out of service at the Lincoln Avenue Diner. But he dropped the fare he picked up from Loyola a half-block from DeWitt Plaza. Among Vukhovich's effects was a one-hundred dollar bill. It was also new and as crisp as the ones we found in Shafiq's room."

Silence followed. The seconds ticked by rapidly. Glances were exchanged, although no one looked at Cole.

"Okay," Cole finally said. "It's a go. Does everyone know what they're supposed to do?"

As one they nodded.

# CHAPTER 33

**JUNE 7, 1996**
**4:45 P.M.**

The tall, auburn-haired woman walked into DeWitt Plaza. She crossed to the information desk. The security officer smiled. "May I help you?"

"I'm interested in purchasing a condominium in the

Tower," she said in a husky voice. "Is there someone I could talk to?"

"Certainly." He picked up the telephone. "Trident Realty has an office here. I'm sure someone is available to help you."

A gushing agent with a blue rinse in her hair was sent to collect the woman. The security officer studied the sway of her hips as she walked to the elevators.

A few minutes later a tall man, with long hair tied back in a ponytail and tinted glasses, approached the desk.

"Hey, man."

The security officer studied the newcomer with a disapproving frown. "Can I help you?"

"Where's Sounds, Inc., man?"

Before the security officer could answer him, the telephone rang. It was an outside call.

"Good afternoon, DeWitt Plaza."

The voice was deep and gravelly. "*There's a bomb planted there.*"

"What did you say?"

"*There's a bomb in that building set to go off in the next five minutes.*"

"Who is this?"

The caller hung up.

"Hey, man," Ponytail asked again. "You wanna tell me where Sounds, Inc., is?"

"Level Four," the security officer managed to mumble, as he tried to remember the proper procedure to follow for a bomb threat.

"Thanks, man," the ponytail said, turning away from the desk. Then he stopped. "Somebody left a package here on the floor, man."

The security officer's eyes became wide as saucers. He leaned over the counter. A shoebox-sized parcel wrapped in brown paper and tied with twine was lying on the floor beside the desk.

"You want me to hand it to you, bro?" The ponytail bent to pick it up.

"No!" The security officer's scream rocked the lobby. "Don't touch it!"

Margo and Neil DeWitt were on the elevator en route to the garage. The ceiling speaker crackled on. The security chief's voice echoed through the car. *"All residents, shoppers and employees of DeWitt Plaza are asked to proceed immediately to the nearest exit. You are requested to avoid the elevators and instead utilize the staircase to proceed to the main floor. There is no cause for alarm. Please do not run. Anyone who is unable to use the stairs please dial seven-four-zero on the house phone and a security officer will be dispatched to your location."*

"What in the hell's going on?" Neil asked.

"They're evacuating the building." Margo's usual confidence had deserted her.

Anxiously, they watched the elevator floor-indicator numbers as the car descended. They exhaled a sigh of relief when the doors opened in the basement parking garage. A security officer waited by their limousine.

Before either of them could speak, the security officer explained, "We've had a bomb scare. The information desk received a call and . . ."

"You evacuated the building because of a telephone call?" Margo snapped.

"There's more to it than that, Mrs. DeWitt. Suspicious packages have been discovered in the lobby and on Level Four outside Sounds, Inc. We've also got unexplained smoke on the condo model floor."

The DeWitts exchanged anxious looks.

"Well, we have an engagement," Neil said hurriedly, ushering his wife to the car. The chauffeur held the door.

"Yes, we'll call later to see how things turn out," Margo said, ducking into the car.

"Let's get out of here," Neil snapped at the chauffeur.

Moments later they were blocks away from DeWitt Plaza. They would not return until an all-clear was given some hours later.

# CHAPTER 34

**JUNE 7, 1996**
**5:01 P.M.**

The Chicago Police Department's Bomb and Arson Squad responded to DeWitt Plaza. Michigan Avenue was cordoned off in front of the building by district cops, and the street was clogged with police cars, fire trucks and hundreds of curious spectators. The area was backlit by minicam spotlights, giving the scene the appearance of a theatrical set. In fact, what was happening was staged. The director of the production, wearing a visored helmet and explosive-resistant suit, exited the blue and white van along with five other similarly clad cops. They crossed the sidewalk and were escorted into the lobby by a uniformed lieutenant.

With no insignias of rank visible on the bomb technicians' suits, the lieutenant addressed the lead officer, who also happened to be the tallest of the sextet.

"As far as we can tell, everyone is out. We've isolated the package over there"—he hooked a thumb at the lobby floor by the information desk—"and the one on Level Four. The smoke on twenty-six set off the detectors, but there wasn't enough heat to trip the sprinklers. Despite the call, it looks like a prank to me."

The tall bomb technician reached out and patted the lieutenant on the shoulder. Then he turned and pointed to the Michigan Avenue door. The lieutenant took the hint and left.

The six bomb technicians began moving as soon as they

were alone. Two went to the box in the lobby. Two more proceeded to Level Four, where the wrapped shoebox's twin had been left next to a trash container. The remaining two, which included the tall one and a shorter, stockier man, headed for the elevators.

Outside on Michigan Avenue the man with the ponytail approached the auburn-haired woman who had requested the condo tour.

"How's it goin', mama?"

She shot him a disapproving look. "The key to any successful disguise, Manny, is knowing when to take it off."

"C'mon, Judy," he said. "Live a little."

She turned to look back across the street. A squad of uniformed cops, under the command of the intense lieutenant, stood guard over the entrance to DeWitt Plaza. "I'll start living again when the boss and Blackie come out of there."

The smoke on the twenty-sixth floor was caused by a small pyrotechnic device, which produced an ever-expanding, nontoxic fog, but harmed nothing. Judy had set it while she was being given the overpriced condo tour by the talkative agent with the blue rinse. Now Blackie, still wearing his bomb helmet, picked it up with an asbestos-gloved hand and carried it into the marble-lined bathroom.

He doused it in the tub, causing the smoke to increase briefly before stopping. What was left of the low-grade incendiary he placed in a sack slung over his shoulder; then he headed back for the elevator. The twenty-sixth floor remained enveloped in a light fog. The air-conditioner would clear it completely in fifteen minutes.

The elevator was being manually operated by Cole. He turned the key to close the doors, shutting off the fog floor, and pushed the button for forty-eight.

"So far so good, Boss," Blackie said.

"That's the same thing the guy said who fell off the Sears

Tower," Cole said. "At each floor he called out 'So far so good.' "

They stepped into the deserted hall on the first level of the penthouse.

"We'd better check it out," Cole said.

Blackie nodded.

They split up. It took ten minutes to check the first level. They were alone.

"What about up there?" Blackie said pointing to the upper floors, which could be reached by a winding staircase.

Cole checked his watch. "We're running out of time. If we get a chance we'll take a look later, but we can't stay in here forever. C'mon."

They went to the library. At the door Cole turned on the lights.

"Why here?" Blackie asked.

"Mystery novels," Cole said, crossing to one of the floor-to-ceiling bookcases. "This has something to do with mystery novels."

Blackie wandered around the room as Cole began checking the titles in the bookcase. There was a stack of six books on an end table beside one of the couches. Blackie read the title of the top book and froze. "Larry!"

Cole rushed over. He read the book jacket over Blackie's shoulder. *A Minute to Die*! With a gloved hand Cole picked it up. Flipping through the pages, he stopped at the orange-highlighted passages. He began reading out loud:

*"Helen Kelly beckoned the Oriental doctor to the table. 'Do you like American food?' she asked. He nodded, but said, 'I'm not hungry.'*

*" 'Oh, I forgot, Colonel Farquart-Smyth told me to give you this.'*

*"Chang looked at the jade statue in awe. He had spent half his life searching for it. He reached for it. She jerked it away. Picking up the tray of canapés from the table, she offered them to Chang.*

*" 'What is this?' He was suspicious.*

*" 'Chopped liver. You'll like it.'*

*"Keeping his eyes on the jade figurine, he took a canapé and bit into it. She looked at her watch. Chang had a minute to die."*

Cole turned to Blackie. "Poison. They used some type of poison."

Blackie picked up another book and opened it to a page that had been dog-eared. "Look at this."

Cole glanced at the title. *Killing Streets* by Jamal Garth.

"Halfway down on page one-eighty-one," Blackie said.

Cole's eyes scanned the print. He began to read. Blackie watched him go rigid. When he looked up, Cole said tightly, "It's the same thing that was done to Mack. The exact same thing."

Blackie nodded.

# 2

**"Just like a corpse."**

**—Margo DeWitt**

# Chapter 35

**June 9, 1996**
**10:30 a.m.**

Barbara Schurla Zorin was the president of the Midwest Chapter of Mystery Writers of America, headquartered in Chicago. At the age of forty-seven and writing under the names B. S. Zorin, Malcolm Blackburn and Jill Fontaine, she'd written thirty-two books, most of which were mystery novels set in Chicago. She had created four series characters: private detective Emil Zielinski; amateur sleuths Mavis Adams and Esmeralda West; and Chicago Police homicide detective Joe Clancy. Although as an author Barbara Zorin possessed a wealth of knowledge on police procedure gleaned from the research for her books, she had never actually met a real cop. That's why she was shocked when she received a call from Frank Dwyer that morning.

Dwyer had only recently joined MWA. As a nonpublished associate member, he had been attending monthly meetings since February. There wasn't a great deal Barbara could remember about him other than that he was a tall, scholarly-looking man, who was well read and knew a great deal about the local mystery scene. She actually had never really considered what he did for a living.

"You're joking?" she said after he told her he was a cop.

He cleared his throat. "No. I'm not, Barbara."

"Why didn't you tell us, Frank?"

"I wasn't trying to fool anyone. It's just that at times people react negatively to police officers. I figured it would be best if everyone just got to know me as a regular guy first."

"So you were kind of working undercover?"

"No. I would never spy on you. I just wanted you to treat me just like any other associate member."

"But this is great, Frank. We do think of you as just another member and it'll show everyone that policemen are just like anyone else. Of course, you're going to get a million questions."

"I was afraid of that," he said glumly.

"Tell me," she asked. "What do you do on the force?"

"I'm the deputy chief of Field Group A of the Detective Division."

She gasped. "That means you're Joe Clancy's boss."

"I guess I would be," Dwyer said. "If Detective Clancy were real."

"That settles it. You're going to be in my next book."

"That brings me to the real reason I called. There may be another cop you'd be more interested in writing about. Guy's a real legend on the job and he's very interested in attending an MWA meeting."

"What's his name?"

"Larry Cole."

"The one who bagged Steven Zalkin and Tuxedo Tony DeLisa?"

"The same." There was a purr in Frank Dwyer's voice.

Midwest Chapter meetings of MWA were held in the lower level dining room of Binyon's Restaurant on Plymouth Court in the Chicago Loop. As a rule, monthly meetings were suspended for the summer, from May to September; however, this was an emergency meeing called by President Barbara Schurla Zorin at the request of associate member Frank Dwyer. Dwyer had expected ten or fifteen members to respond. Instead seventy-five showed up, the largest turnout in the chapter's history.

Dwyer noticed the heavy traffic in front of the restaurant when they turned onto Plymouth Court off of Jackson Boulevard. Blackie Silvestri was driving Cole's squad car with

Cole up front beside him. Judy Daniels was in the back with Dwyer.

"I don't believe it," Judy heard him murmur.

"Don't believe what, Deputy?"

"Nothing," he said, shaking his head. "Must be a private party in one of the other rooms."

He was wrong.

They were seated at a table at the far end of the oblong dining room. The membership had been jammed into the remaining space. Only cold cuts were available from the kitchen and beer and soft drinks from the bar, but there were no complaints. Everyone paid the twenty-five-dollar meeting fee.

"I thought you said they wouldn't be able to get many members on such short notice," Cole whispered to Dwyer.

All he could do was shake his head. "I didn't know you'd be this popular."

"What do you mean, I'd be popular?"

"It was part of the deal I made with the president to get her to call the meeting."

"What kind of deal?"

Dwyer smiled. "They want you to give them a short talk. Say twenty or thirty minutes' worth."

"What am I supposed to talk about?"

"Police work. They'll love your war stories. I think you'll get a lot of mileage out of the Zalkin and the DeLisa cases."

"Hey, boss." Blackie was seated on the other side of Dwyer. "You can talk about the Salter Project. That'll really get them stirred up."

"I never heard of that one," Dwyer said.

Cole turned to look at the sea of curious faces staring back at him. "It didn't get a lot of notoriety. Are you writing a book too, Frank?"

"Sure am."

"What's it called?" Judy asked.

"*Dragnet*."

Cole, Blackie and Judy went silent. Cole was about to

suggest a title change when Barbara Zorin stood to introduce him.

Cole told "war stories" for an hour and fifteen minutes. Not one member moved. At the end, when his voice started to fail, Barbara came to the rescue, and they gave him a standing ovation.

They broke into small groups. Each of the cops—Cole, Dwyer, Blackie and Judy Daniels—was the center of attention in each respective gathering. There were a lot of questions asked.

Cole was asked, "If I attach a silencer to a three-fifty-seven magnum revolver, will the noise be completely suppressed or will the gun make one of those coughing noises like they do in the movies?"

Cole studied the questioner. She was about thirty, with short brown hair and a very soft voice. She had been introduced to him as Debbie Bass. He had thumbed through a couple of her books. He had expected someone who resembled Mickey Spillane. Instead she looked more like the actress Madelaine Stowe.

"A revolver can't be silenced," Cole explained. "The cylinder of a revolver is open, which allows the gases to escape when the weapon is fired. The exploding gas creates the sound. Silencers can only be used with automatics, which have a closed construction."

A murmur of awed revelation rumbled through the group.

Dwyer was asked, "What would you say goes into making a good detective?"

"The two most important attributes a detective should have are diligence and patience. One can't work without the other."

"But what about Joe Clancy and Mike Hammer? They shoot first and ask questions later."

"Any cop who shoots first and asks questions later will

end up either in jail or with their badge sued off. There's a little thing we've got in this country called civil rights."

The group around Blackie Silvestri didn't need to ask questions. He was into war stories and was a great deal more graphic than Cole had been. He also had the largest group.

"February nineteen seventy-six. Me and Deputy Cole were working tact out of the old one-nine on the North Side. So we scam up on this hit's supposed to go down. The old Arcadio Mob wants to cancel the ticket on Rabbit Arcadio's bookkeeper, Felix 'Big Numbers' Albanese. So the Rabbit sends his nephew Frankie Arcadio and a wheelman named Tony Lima to do the job. Me and Larry slip up on Lima, who is one mean little . . . uh . . . guy."

Barbara Zorin was in Blackie's group. "Leave the language in, Blackie. It reads better."

He shrugged. "If you say so. Like I was saying, Tony Lima's a mean little motherfucker. So me and Larry . . ."

Judy Daniels had a smaller audience consisting solely of crime-fiction author Dan Cassidy, who was certain he was falling in love. They had distanced themselves from the others in a corner of the dining room by the bar, where they spoke in low tones over glasses of Coke.

"People sometimes say my books are too highbrow," Cassidy, a balding man wearing horn-rimmed glasses, said. "I have a master's in psychology from the U. of C., so my detective is a psychologist. He actually solves crimes by getting inside the criminal's head."

"That's fascinating," she said. "How does he do that?"

"Oh, any number of ways. My character, Dr. Max Burns, is a consultant for the New York Police Department. Once in a while he'll take on a case for the F.B.I. or the C.I.A."

"I'd like to read one of your books sometime."

Cassidy smiled. "I'd like you to read them all. I could bring you some autographed copies and we could go out to dinner one day next week. That is if you're free."

"Friday?" Judy asked.

"You're on."

Jamal Garth, the author of *Killing Streets*, was one of the members Barbara Zorin had particularly wanted present at the special meeting, because Frank Dwyer had given her Garth's name along with Martin Wiemler's as writers they wanted to talk to. She had been forced to plead with Garth, however, before he would agree to attend. He hadn't shown up until after the formal program had concluded.

As the cops conducted their individual question-and-answer sessions at various locations around the dining room, Garth, a well-dressed black man of about sixty with a full head of curly silver hair, skirted the fringes of each group. He never asked any questions, but merely observed. He thought he had found exactly what he had expected. Then he began having doubts.

He watched Frank Dwyer. Barbara had explained to him that Dwyer had not wanted to reveal what he did for a living because people were often uncomfortable around cops. Well, Jamal Garth would say a hearty "Amen" to that.

At his group, Blackie Silvestri had launched into another cop tale that held Barbara Zorin and ten published mystery authors enthralled.

"It's cold, the abandoned Loop hotel is as dark as Lucifer's heart and I got a flashlight with batteries just about ready to give up the ghost. But we want this asshole. We want him bad.

"Larry's got a scalp wound, but I couldn't have kept him out of that place with the entire Eighty-second Airborne. Larry's got one of those multicell Kelites that can throw a beam with the same intensity as a squad-car spotlight. So, in we go after this guy. And we had problems."

Barbara interrupted him. "Wasn't that the Loop hotel that had the serious rat problem?"

"The same. I mean those were brown Norway rats, some

weighing up to three, four pounds. Them, along with the bats, made the search for our fugitive very interesting."

"Bats?" The strangled voice of a muscular male writer who had just signed a six-book contract escaped from the audience.

"Yeah," Blackie said. "Little critters about this long with wings extended." He spread the thumb and forefinger of his right hand. "Won't hurt you, though, but I'm here to tell you they can make you hurt yourself. Especially when a herd of about a thousand of them drop down around your ears."

The gasp from the group was in unison. Garth walked away as Blackie continued the story.

"How you doin', Jamal?"

Garth turned. Dan Cassidy had called to him from the end of the bar. He was with a young woman. Garth could tell she wasn't another of Cassidy's usual airhead dates, who exhibited much too much cleavage, yawned during meeting presentations and told authors that instead of reading their books they'd wait for the movie versions. The one tonight was different; he hoped that Cassidy would have enough sense to hang on to this one.

As he walked to the group surrounding the last cop, Garth studied Cole: tall, athletic-looking, articulate, intelligent and obviously successful, just as Garth had always wanted to be. But it simply hadn't worked out that way. He turned away from Cole's group and walked to the bar.

Cole, who had been explaining some of the finer points of a crime-scene search, watched him go. The policeman knew Garth's story. He knew it well.

The busboys had cleared the tables, and the waiters and the rest of the members were gone.

Seated around the table at the center of the room were Larry Cole, Frank Dwyer, Blackie Silvestri and Judy Daniels representing the Chicago Police Department, and mystery and suspense authors Barbara Zorin, Debbie Bass, Martin Wiemler and Jamal Garth. The previous night in the DeWitt library, Cole and Blackie had discovered orange-highlighted passages detailing the commission of violent crimes in books written by each of the authors present.

Cole paused a moment before standing to address the authors. Zorin and Bass looked intelligent, but both women hardly seemed the types to produce the hard-core crime fiction detailed in their books. Then he glanced at the men: Wiemler, a former traveling salesman, fiftyish and overweight, and Jamal Garth. They didn't seem like the hard-core types either.

Cole didn't know what he wanted of them. How much could he tell them about what had already happened? How much would they be able to tell him? What did he really hope to find out? As there was no time like the present, he stood up.

"We're working on a somewhat complicated series of homicides," he began. "We believe that our killer, or possibly killers, has used your books to come up with the methods used to commit these crimes."

Shocked looks passed among the authors. Martin Wiemler said, "Now, that's taking being a fan a bit too far."

This was followed by halfhearted laughter.

"But how do you know this killer is using our work, Chief Cole?" Barbara Zorin asked. "I mean, we do come up with some unique methods of dispatching characters in books, but I don't think there's anything under the sun that hasn't been tried somewhere at some time in the past."

Cole glanced at Blackie and Judy Daniels, the only two present aware of the bomb-scare ploy they had used to get into DeWitt Plaza the previous night. "Let's just say for the time being that we have a fair certainty that some of the things you've written have been used to commit crimes."

"Some of the things all of us have written?" The question came from Garth.

"Yes," Cole responded.

"How?"

"Could we just let that one ride for the time being? In that way we could . . ."

Garth stood up. "Do we look like fools to you, Cole? You come in here with this . . . this story about a series of murders, which means you're looking for a serial killer in all likelihood. Am I right?"

"That's possible," Cole said evenly.

"Then you say this serial killer has used our books to commit his, her or their crimes?"

"We didn't say we had a serial killer on our hands, Mr. Garth. You did."

"Don't play games with me, Cole. You're not in my league."

Wiemler interrupted. "Why don't we hear the man out first, Jamal?"

Garth glared at Wiemler. "Why don't you let me have my say, Marty, then you can do whatever the hell you want? And I don't understand what in God's name has gotten into the rest of you. You let these people just waltz in here, take over your organization and then start questioning you about what you write, and you're willing to start running off at the mouth without really knowing what they're talking about."

Barbara Zorin stood up and faced Garth. "I know what they're talking about, Jamal, and I made the decision to let them come here tonight. I do have that authority as the duly-elected chapter president."

"I know you mean well, but there are too many questions that need to be answered and he's already started out by being evasive." He pointed a finger at Cole.

"What do you want to know, Mr. Garth?" Cole asked. "I'll answer any questions I have that I feel won't compromise the Department's investigation. I hope you can respect that."

"I don't know you well enough to respect anything about you, Cole, but we can cut through the crap if you answer one question for me."

Cole waited.

"Will any of us ever be considered suspects in your investigation?"

"I don't think that's likely."

"Suppose you find that one of us is working in collusion with your serial killers? What then?"

"You already know the answer to that one, Mr. Garth."

"So we could very well be suspects and all you're looking to do is tie the noose tighter around our necks?"

"I didn't come here to accuse anyone of anything. I came to ask for your help. Someone is using your books as instruction manuals to commit murder. I don't think that any of you has ever written anything intended to do more than simply entertain your reading public. I was hoping to get some ideas from you that might give me some insight into the type of criminal mind we're dealing with, as well as maybe give us some clue as to what to expect next. Any cooperation you give will not only be totally voluntary, but kept in the strictest confidence."

Garth flashed Cole a chilly smile. "Isn't that the same as saying, 'You have the right to remain silent'?"

"Maybe if you turn it upside down and inside out, you could come up with something like that, Mr. Garth."

"Then I'm exercising my rights. Good night."

He stormed from the room.

# CHAPTER 36

**JUNE 10, 1996**
**11:30 A.M.**

Butch was excited. He was going on an outing to the Chicago Historical Society. It would be just like a lot of trips he had gone on with the day camp. Only this one would be better because Paige was taking him.

They were going because of Abraham Lincoln. Butch had

seen Daddy reading a book one night. A book that had lots of old black-and-white photographs.

"What's that, Daddy?"

"This is a history book about the Civil War. Do you know what that was, Butch?"

Butch didn't know anything about the Civil War, but then that was okay because he climbed up beside his father and together they looked at pictures until Butch fell asleep. Before he nodded off they came across a picture of a very tall man with a beard.

"Who is he?" Butch asked.

"Abraham Lincoln. He was the president of the United States during the war. He came from Illinois. They call this state the Land of Lincoln."

"Is he dead?"

"Very," Cole said. "Has been for more than a hundred and thirty years."

Butch looked back at the picture. "Will they remember us that long, Daddy?"

"They might, son. They just might."

They talked about things that belonged to Lincoln. His carriage, which Daddy explained was like a stagecoach, and replicas of the cabin where he was born and the room in which he died were in a place called the Chicago Historical Society.

"Can we go there someday?"

"Definitely, Butch."

But his father was busy and Paige offered to take him. His mother hesitated before saying yes.

"I've been there before, Lisa," Paige said with that funny way she had of talking. "Mack took me a couple of months before he died."

Butch noticed that whenever Paige talked about Mr. McKinnis she looked kind of strange, like she was going to cry or something.

"You're not supposed to go anywhere without a policeman

with you," Lisa said. "Larry thinks there could be some danger after what happened to those two men."

"Lisa, I can't stay cooped up here forever. Hell, I'll go nuts. Let the officer come along. Do him a world of good seeing a Reb like me getting educated about Old Abe."

So Butch's mother had relented.

The day of the outing a girl in pigtails showed up at the door. Butch knew who it was, but Mommy didn't.

Lisa Cole studied the teenager through the peephole before opening the door. "May I help you?"

The girl was chewing gum with her mouth open. She emitted a loud popping smack after every other bite. "You Mrs. Cole?"

"That's right." Lisa frowned. The girl did seem familiar, but . . .

"Heard around school you was looking for a baby-sitter for a bad little boy named Butch."

Lisa's eyes flared before revelation dawned. "You got me again, Judy. I should have known."

Standing behind the door, Butch laughed. Of all the people Judy Daniels was able to fool with her disguises, she had never been able to deceive Deputy Chief Cole's son. She had never been able to figure out why.

In the kitchen, Lisa introduced Judy to Paige.

"You're a police officer?" Paige said skeptically.

"At your service," Judy said, extending her hand.

In addition to the pigtails, Judy wore blue jeans, running shoes and a size-too-large Chicago Bears sweatshirt. Her hair flaming red, and there was a smattering of freckles across her nose. She looked no older than sixteen.

Paige looked to Lisa for reassurance.

"Remember the story I told you about Antonio DeLisa?" Lisa said.

Paige's eyes went wide. "You beat up Tuxedo Tony?"

Butch was playing demolition derby with a couple of toy cars on the living-room floor.

"I was actually trying to kill the bastard," Judy said. "He slapped me."

"Well, honey, you're my girl," Paige said. "I hope you like museums."

"I'm crazy about them," Judy said as they went to collect Butch. "Especially when I get paid for going to one."

# CHAPTER 37

**JUNE 10, 1996**
**12:15 P.M.**

Margo DeWitt was being driven back from a meeting of the Friends of the Library Association, which was held monthly at the Orrington Hotel in downtown Evanston. On the way back she told the chauffeur to take Sheridan Road instead of Lake Shore Drive. This would give her time to think.

Margo DeWitt had a genius IQ and could accomplish just about any task she put her mind to. She was puzzled over Cole's reaction to the deaths of Shafiq and Vukhovich. He had done the unpredictable: nothing.

As the limousine wound its way south past Addison and then Belmont, Margo studied the streets with passive interest. So what was Cole doing now? Tolley had been unable to find out anything more. His snitches, the state's attorney and the police commander, were spooked. Even Tolley himself had seemed a bit tense when she talked to him this morning. She didn't regret Shafiq and Vukhovich. It was indeed bold, but she was a bold woman: She had not only thrown down the gauntlet, she had flung it right in Cole's face.

The stretch limo crossed Diversey and swung into Lincoln

Park, where the trees were lush with summer greenery and the sky was a clear, bright blue. To the east the waters of Lake Michigan sparkled, reflecting sunbeams off its surface.

They had not heard from the police in two days. This would be the third day. Everything had gone along in a maddeningly normal fashion since the nosy Pakistani student and the talkative cabdriver had been dispatched into eternity—everything, that is, except the bomb threat the other night. Margo jerked forward in her seat. The bomb threat. A phony. Building evacuated. Chicago Police bomb technicians searched the place. Searched everywhere including the penthouse.

She was staring out the window with her thoughts racing through the possibilities when she saw them. They didn't register in her mind right away. In fact, she'd never seen any of them before. At least not in the flesh. But she had seen photographs in the newspaper of one of them. The tall, well-built woman with the dark hair. It was Paige Albritton! Paige Albritton with a little boy and a teenaged girl. Margo's eyes glistened with anticipation at the sight of the child. She remembered the other one a few days ago over by the zoo. Perhaps she needed to throw down another gauntlet for Cole? Give him another dead little black boy in Lincoln Park. But then the main prize was the Albritton woman. Maybe she could eliminate both of them? The teenager would be just for fun.

"Pull over!"

The chauffeur was used to unexpected commands from the DeWitts. He maneuvered the car to the curb.

"Wait here," she said, bounding out and trotting up LaSalle Street toward the Chicago Historical Society.

# CHAPTER 38

**JUNE 10, 1996**
**12:32 P.M.**

Larry Cole pulled into the parking lot beside Houston's Restaurant about a mile south of the Historical Society. Entering the restaurant, he walked through the bar to the maître d's desk. A young woman in a Scotch-plaid vest smiled at him. "May I help you, sir?"

"I'm meeting Mrs. Barbara Zorin for lunch."

"Yes, sir. Mrs. Zorin's already here."

She led him back through the restaurant to a rear booth. As Cole approached, he saw the mystery author seated there. Someone else was with her. Cole was stunned when he found it was Jamal Garth.

He hesitated a moment before sitting down, eyeing Garth warily.

"Please join us, Larry," Barbara said.

Garth stood up and extended his hand. "I'd like to apologize for last night. I said some things I really didn't mean. I'd be honored to give you any help I can."

Cole shook hands with him and sat down. "Well, this is a surprise."

"I talked it over with the others," Barbara said, "and they've all agreed to help as well. But we really don't know what you want us to do."

Last night, before Garth's abrupt exit terminated the meeting, Cole had not known how much he could tell them, but Garth had made a point. He had to let them know a lot more than he had originally intended.

"Okay," Cole said. "Let me start at the beginning."

And he did, with the death of Mack and the case he had made to clear Paige. He mentioned the comments made to Kennedy at the Cultural Center and the mysterious undetermined-cause deaths of Shafiq and Vukhovich. The only information he failed to disclose concerned the staged bomb threat at DeWitt Plaza and the names of the DeWitts.

"If these people did everything you said they did, Larry," Barbara said, "then they are two very fascinating characters."

"Fascinating?" Cole said with a raised eyebrow.

"I mean that from a purely literary standpoint. The villain is as important to the success of a book as the hero or heroine. You've got a pair of really classic villains here. Ruthless, bold and even literate. Not your usual combination. Wouldn't you agree, Jamal?"

Garth was listening, but with the vacant expression of someone whose mind was elsewhere. "Yes, but you did say they had highlighted the murder passages in our books?"

"That's right," Cole said. "They used the gunshot victim whose body was burned with acid on my friend Mack. The entire two and a half pages of that scene in *Killing Streets* were highlighted."

"And you saw this?" Garth questioned.

"I did. Please don't ask me how."

"So what do we do now?" Barbara asked. "Thousands of people read our books, but there's no way we can provide a clue as to which readers would actually kill anyone. What the heck, we seldom get a chance to meet fans except at conferences and book signings."

"Would it make a difference if these people were fairly prominent?" Cole asked.

"You might be climbing the right tree, Larry, but I think you're out on the wrong limb," Garth said.

"What do you mean?"

"I haven't got it completely myself at this point, but let's look at it from a different perspective. Someone got the idea to shoot your friend and douse his body with acid from one of my books. Now, where did I get the idea?"

Barbara and Cole stared back at him. "Okay," Barbara said. "I'll bite. Where did you get the idea?"

"About five or six years ago I read a story in the *Times-Herald* about a Colorado state trooper who had the same thing done to him. He was shot to death with his own gun and dumped into a bathtub in one of the rooms of this ski resort, then doused with a gallon of sulfuric acid. I keep a file on ususual murders, so I held on to the clipping.

"A year or so later I happened to be out West researching a book on a series of child murders in the Denver area. To make expense money I was doing a magazine piece paralleling the Denver cases with the Atlanta child murders."

"I remember that," Barbara said. "You published the article in *Chicago* magazine. All of the victims in both cases were young black male children under the age of twelve."

"At least in Denver they were," Garth said. "Anyway, while I was doing this research I discovered that the trooper found in that tub had also been investigating the Denver child murders and had told one of his superiors the morning of his death that he was on to something."

"Did they ever make any arrests or come up with any suspects?" Cole asked.

"They brought in a lot of people, mostly those with records for child molestation and the like, but the dead trooper was apparently proceeding in a different direction. He had recorded the name of a Margo Rapier in his notebook three times and had supposedly questioned her twice before he died. However, his notes were indecipherable."

"Who was she?" Barbara asked.

"A local socialite. Had lots of money, went to all the big affairs, got her name in the papers a lot and came from a family that supposedly fought Indians from the Canadian border to Mexico before the Spanish-American War."

Cole had become very still. He leaned across the table toward Garth. "What happened to this Margo Rapier?"

Garth shrugged. "Nothing. It made quite a splash in the papers at the time, but she had some very powerful friends, as well as high-priced legal assistance. She got married a short time later. The guy was from Chicago. Rich to boot. Name's . . ."

Cole's fist slamming onto the table punctuated his screamed "Neil DeWitt!"

Besides scaring the writers into bloodless shock, this turned every head in the restaurant in their direction.

# CHAPTER 39

**JUNE 10, 1996**
**12:42 P.M.**

Lincoln's black carriage was one of the most beautiful things Butch had ever seen. Although he couldn't touch it, he could see the beauty of its lines and even imagine it rolling down the street pulled by four white horses. He didn't want to ride in the coach; instead he wanted to sit up top holding the reins, driving down the street while everyone looked. He would let Mommy and Daddy ride in the carriage. Paige and Judy, too.

"Would you look at this?" Paige said, reading a paper mounted on a pedestal. "Old Abe paid for this thing on the installment plan."

Judy stepped in to take a closer look.

Butch didn't care how Lincoln paid for it. If he was dead as long as Daddy said he had been, then it really didn't belong to him anymore anyway. Butch began dreaming of driving the carriage across the old Western frontier like they showed in the movies. The horses now pulling the carriage in his imagination were black stallions with white hooves.

"C'mon, Butch," Paige said. "Let's go see the log cabin."

Reluctantly, holding Paige's hand, Butch allowed himself to be pulled away. He kept staring back at the coach.

Margo DeWitt watched them. She stood in the shadows of an eighteenth-century Illinois exhibit at the other end of the gallery, studying the little boy. There was something very familiar about him. She wondered . . . That would really be too much. Casually, she began moving toward them.

"Looks like the house where I grew up," Paige said.

They were standing in front of a replica of the log cabin in which Lincoln had been born.

"Aw, c'mon, Paige," Judy said. "Nobody lives in places like this anymore."

"We did. Maybe it was a bit bigger and there weren't any logs like that. But there were boards the wind used to blow through. In the winter it'd get damned cold."

Butch asked, "Can we go back and look at the carriage some more?"

"Haven't you got tired of that thing yet?" Paige said.

"No. I liked it."

"C'mon, Butch," Judy said. "We need to see some more of this stuff. You'll find something else you like just as much."

Margo waited at the exhibit of the boardinghouse room where Lincoln had died. She stared into the space filled with the narrow bed and overstuffed furniture; however, she saw none of it.

They stepped up to the railing beside her. Margo turned. Her eyes briefly met those of Paige. Paige smiled. Margo walked by her as if she were invisible.

Butch and Judy paid the woman no attention.

"He was too tall for them to lay him straight on that bed," Judy said. "After Booth shot him at Ford's Theater, they carried him to this room. He died there the next day."

Paige was looking at the spartan furnishings. The chest of drawers, the pitcher and washbasin. Even in the shack she had grown up in down in Oklahoma there had been indoor plumbing.

Butch slowly slid his hand out of Paige's. He half-listened to Judy's narrative of the events that had taken place on Good Friday of the year 1865. His eyes drifted back down the gallery to the carriage exhibit. An exhibit to which the thin woman, who had been standing where they now stood, was heading.

Pausing at the log cabin, Margo let her eyes drift over the contents of the exhibit before swinging them back down the gallery. Only the child was looking this way.

She realized now that there was no way she could do anything with all three of them present, not in a public place where at any second another museum visitor or employee could come wandering into the area. But she had wanted the Albritton woman. Maybe she could wait a moment or two longer. She made another slow inspection. What she saw made her heart leap. The little boy was coming down the gallery toward her. He was alone.

"John Wilkes Booth was a very successful actor," Judy was saying. "He came from an acting family and had even been invited to Lincoln's second inauguration in March of that year. It was there that he got the idea to kill the president, because it was so easy. Back then, after the Civil War ended, they didn't think Lincoln was in danger anymore. Assassination was thought to be something strictly European or Asian. They didn't think an American, either from the North or the South, capable of it."

Paige lowered her head. Tears stung her eyes. "Sometimes I think murder is something we enjoy in this country whether it be a president or a policeman."

Judy stepped toward her. It was then that she noticed that Butch was missing. She spun away from the display and stared frantically up and down the gallery. It was empty.

"Butch," Judy called. "Butch!"

* * *

Butch was again at the carriage, his fantasies soaring as he stared at the black sides and the large spiked wheels. He did not hear the lady step up behind him. He was unaware of her until she placed her hands on his shoulders. Then he heard Judy calling him. He turned around and looked up at the lady. She stared down at him. What he saw in her eyes frightened him.

Judy and Paige raced down the gallery toward the carriage exhibit. When they arrived, there was no sign of Butch.

"Where could he have gone?" Paige was near hysterics.

"He's got to be here somewhere." Judy said, fighting a rising panic of her own. "He was standing between us only seconds ago."

"We've got to do something, Judy! I'll never be able to live with myself if anything happened to him!"

"Calm down," Judy ordered.

"What's the matter?" Butch said.

They both jumped at the sound of his voice. He was standing beside them, looking up. He had come from the other side of the exhibit.

With a choked scream, Paige collapsed to the floor.

An attendant on the first floor provided smelling salts and a cup of cold water. Paige came around, but looked like hell.

They were seated on a bench in the lobby. Judy held Paige in her arms. The tall woman's head rested on Judy's shoulder. Butch sat on the other side, rubbing her hand. Visitors entering the museum stared curiously at the trio.

"Do you think you're strong enough to walk out of here?" Judy asked. "I could always call an ambulance."

"No," Paige said with a hoarse voice. "I can walk. I've been pampered too much as it is. But, boy, Butch," she managed with a weak smile. "You scared ten years off my life."

"I'm sorry, Paige," he said, lowering his head. A tear ran down his cheek. Paige reached out and pulled him to her.

"It's okay, baby," she said. "I just love you so much I couldn't stand to have anything happen to you."

His tears stopped quickly.

However, Judy was not so compassionate. "Why did you leave us, Butch? Something could have happened to you."

"I wanted to see the carriage again. And the lady was there."

"What lady?" Judy asked.

"The one who asked me my name."

Judy frowned. "Did you tell her?"

Butch nodded.

"You told her your name was Butch?"

Again a nod.

"Is that all she asked you?"

"No. She asked if that was my real name. I told her no. That my real name was Larry Cole, Jr. Then she laughed and walked away. That's when you and Paige came."

Paige and Judy exchanged questioning glances. Then they looked back at the child.

# CHAPTER 40

**JUNE 10, 1996**
**3:27 P.M.**

Larry Cole, Barbara Zorin and Jamal Garth stepped out of the air-conditioned restaurant. The temperature hovered at ninety.

"I've got an appointment at Border's on Wabash at four," Barbara said. She looked around for a taxi.

"It's on my way," Cole said. "I'll drop you. What about you, Mr. Garth? You need a ride?"

The invitation startled the writer. Barbara stepped forward and grabbed his arm. "Jamal, you live in Presidential Towers, which is almost in sight of police headquarters. At least that's what you always tell me."

On the ride downtown most of the conversation was between Barbara and Cole. Garth sat in the back maintaining a stony silence.

After they dropped Barbara at Kroch at Border's bookstore, Garth climbed into the front seat. They rode to the Presidential Towers apartment complex in silence. When they pulled up in front of the entrance, a doorman jumped forward to open the car door. The writer was about to get out when he turned to Cole. "You got a minute?"

"Sure."

"Can he park the police car for you?" Garth nodded toward the doorman.

"As long as he's got a license and doesn't go joyriding with the siren on," Cole said, following Garth into the building.

Garth lived on the twelfth floor of the North Tower of the Presidential Towers apartment complex. His condominium consisted of six rooms with two baths and an east wall of glass facing the Chicago Loop. The author opened the door and led Cole across a hardwood foyer to a spacious living room with a panoramic view. Soft jazz drifted through the apartment from undetectable speakers. As they stepped into the living room a woman wearing a black leisure outfit stood up to greet them. She had been seated on a U-shaped couch, which occupied most of the space in the immense room. She had ebony skin, a short Afro and a sensuous way of moving.

"Good afternoon, Jamal. You are early." She spoke with a pronounced foreign accent. Her dark eyes swung to Cole. "Good day to you, sir."

"Hello," Cole replied.

"Angela, this is Deputy Chief Larry Cole of the Chicago Police Department."

The woman's eyes shifted nervously from Cole back to Garth. The writer laughed. "I'm not in any trouble, dear. In fact, I'm giving Cole a hand with one of his cases."

She managed a forced laugh, but it was apparent she was not comfortable with Cole's presence.

"May I offer you some refreshments, sir? A cocktail or perhaps some iced tea?"

"The iced tea will be fine."

"I'll have the same, Angela," Garth said. "We'll be in my office."

She bowed as Garth led Cole back through the apartment.

The writer's office contained a black leather couch, a plain metal desk and a matching chair on rollers. A stack of yellow legal pads, a plastic cup full of inexpensive ballpoint pens and a compact word processor were on top of the desk. The only other items in the room were two gold-framed photographs hanging on the wall opposite the desk. Cole glanced at them. One was of a pretty black woman with a small girl. The other was of a woman in her twenties, which closer examination revealed was the little girl in the first photo, grown up.

"My wife and daughter," Garth said, taking the seat behind the desk and motioning Cole to the couch. "My wife's been dead since nineteen sixty-four. My daughter Francesca lives in France. She refuses to return to this country. Do you know why?"

"I've heard stories," Cole said.

"How long have you been a cop in Chicago?"

"Twenty-four years."

There was a knock at the door. Angela came in carrying a tray with two glasses of iced tea on it. She handed one to Cole and the other to Garth. She hesitated a moment while casting a concerned look at Garth. The author ignored her. Slowly, she turned and left the room.

"Your wife?" Cole asked.

Garth shook his head. "I'll never marry again. Angela's my companion. We've been together for twelve years. I could never love any other woman as much as I did Pat."

Cole waited.

"You know, don't you?"

"You got quite a lot of press when you returned to the States and were acquitted of all charges."

"I was accused of the murder of my wife and a police officer. One of your cop organizations demonstrated outside the Criminal Courts Building. They threatened to lead a campaign to oust the judge and state's attorney from office if I was acquitted."

Cole's eyes never left Garth's. "I don't belong to that organization, and both the judge and state's attorney were reelected."

Garth turned away from the policeman. He stared out the window at the west side of the city sweltering under an ozone haze. But he wasn't looking at the buildings out there. Instead his mind was back in the year 1964.

"I was born Thomas Walter Holman in Greenville, Mississippi, in nineteen thirty-four. My family moved to Chicago after World War Two. We lived in an apartment in the Ida B. Wells projects. My father, who'd been a sharecropper most of his life, went to work at the Main Post Office. Me and my older brother James attended Wendell Phillips High School.

"Dad could barely read or write, but he was big on education for us. I listened. Jimmy didn't. He quit school, joined the army and got killed in Korea.

"Even back in high school I wanted to be a writer. Not a newspaper reporter or a journalist, but a novel writer. And I wanted to write best-sellers not for the money, but so my words could be read by millions and millions of people.

"I would always carry a little notebook around with me. I'd jot down descriptions of things, places and people, overheard conversations, stories, jokes, just about anything that would strike me as being future grist for my writer's mill; was branded an oddball in school, but I didn't care."

The story continued. The aspiring writer from the ghetto received a scholarship to study English literature at the University of Chicago. While there he published a few stories in literary magazines and compiled an anthology of early frontier tales for a paperback publisher.

"It wasn't until after Pat and I were married that I even discovered there were such things as black cowboys in the Old West, and even then I wasn't patient enough to do the research to uncover this information. I used the excuse that Negro cowboys were part of history. I was interested only in literature."

Thomas W. Holman completed the undergraduate and master's programs in English literature with honors. He was offered a teaching position on the university staff, and his anthology was published, earning him a slight honorarium. A short time later his daughter was born. In the summer of 1964, Professor Holman took his wife Patricia and two-year-old daughter Francesca for a walk in Grant Park on a hot, humid night.

"We were strolling past the old band shell. There was no concert that night, but there were couples and even entire families sitting on blankets in the grass. It was so peaceful you could almost feel as if you were one with nature. In fact, I made a comment to this effect to Pat only seconds before the police car showed up.

"Everything happened so fast. The policeman was alone. He pulled the car up onto the sidewalk behind us. We didn't know he was there until he hit his Mars light and bright headlamps. Francesca started crying. Pat tried to comfort her as the cop jumped out and came at us with his gun drawn.

"His name was William Hickman," Garth said solemnly. "He grabbed me and shoved me toward the police car. He was screaming that there was a 'colored boy' who looked like me running around the park raping white women. I tried to tell him I was a professor at the University of Chicago. I even groveled, calling him 'sir' and 'officer.' I tried to tell him that this was my wife and child with me, that I was no rapist, but he wouldn't listen. In fact, I think he was laughing at me all the time.

"But Pat wasn't afraid. She stepped forward and grabbed Hickman's arm. She shouted something at him. Something about him being a racist. He turned toward her. I remember when the gun went off it didn't sound like they do on television. This one made more of a loud pop, like the cork coming out of a champagne bottle. I didn't know what had happened until Pat fell to the sidewalk.

"It stunned both of us. Francesca was screaming and there were some people a short distance away sitting on a blanket in the grass."

"The Lowensteins?" Cole asked.

With a tired, sad expression Garth nodded. "My one-armed man."

"I beg your pardon?"

"My one-armed man," Garth repeated. "In the story of *The Fugitive*, Dr. Richard Kimball chased this one-armed man he saw running from the house where his wife was beaten to death. Kimball figured if he could find the one-armed man he could prove he was innocent of the murder. I felt the same way about the Lowensteins, but I didn't find out their names for nearly twenty-five years. They were going to keep silent and let me go to jail for a crime I didn't commit."

"But you did kill the policeman?"

Garth's eyes flared a terrible hatred. "Yes, I killed Officer Hickman! I would kill him again today if he'd done what he did to me that night. You would too, Cole. I can see it in your face. You would too."

"Because he accidentally killed your wife?"

"No. Because he turned the gun on me."

"He was going to kill you?"

Garth had turned to stone. "He'd already made one mistake. He figured to cover it up with another body. For all I know, he planned to throw Francesca in for good measure. But I never gave him the chance."

Cole waited.

"I ran," he finally said in a hoarse voice barely above a whisper. "I took my daughter and I ran. I had someone at the university. A colleague of sorts. She'd approached me more than once about joining the Communist Party. A few years after I escaped to Europe, she was tried and convicted of spying for the Soviet Union. She wanted me to defect to Russia, to tell my story of an oppressive life here in the United States. I was confused. Francesca was still a baby. I was alone, so I went along."

He turned away from Cole. "I considered turning myself in. Facing the . . . what do you call it . . . 'music'?"

"There are different ways of saying it, Mr. Garth, but I understand what you mean."

"Instead, I ran. I ran into a nightmare of underground transportation, false papers and intrigue. My daughter"—his eyes misted—"knew no other life for years.

"We traveled through Canada, Cuba, South America, Europe, the Middle East. It was an adventure and a nightmare all at once."

Cole had been waiting for a chance to ask the question. "They, that is the Russians, tried to use you?"

Garth didn't look at the cop. "I became a pawn. We . . . me . . . us, as so many people who have no other choice, do. I knew that. I tried to resist, but my lone venture into violence had turned me off it for life.

"I became invaluable to them. They stopped trying to get us, Francesca and me, to do propaganda movies, and instead used my brain. I understood America. At least the literature of America. I also came to a revelation, Cole. A revelation about people. There's really no difference in us. We're all the same. Black, white—Russian, Afghan—American, Vietcong—we're all the same. There are good and there are bad."

"Is that where Thomas Holman ended?" Cole asked.
"No. That's where Jamal Garth began."

# CHAPTER 41

**JUNE 10, 1996**
**7:45 P.M.**

Neil DeWitt had grown tired of waiting. Since he'd killed the cop, Margo had forbidden him to do anything. She had handled both the student and the cabdriver, but then they had been men. Neil's thing was women. Especially attractive types like Paige Albritton.

He and Margo had sex occasionally, but afterward Margo either complained or became sullen. He rarely enjoyed making love to her and, in fact, avoided it. With the others it was always new and unique—a one-time encounter, since his partners never survived.

On the day he had stalked Paige Albritton he had been setting her up to be one of his paramours. Neil would never consider using the term "victim." Breaking into her apartment had been the prelude. A form of foreplay. This was the way he got to know them intimately. He went through their things, which told him of their likes, dislikes, hobbies and pastimes. If he was lucky this also revealed their darkest, deepest secrets. Paige Albritton would have been the third woman whose apartment he had invaded in the week prior to Sergeant McKinnis's death. It would have been the first one he'd had a problem with in over a year.

Now he sat in a North Michigan Avenue bar nursing a beer. The after-work crowd from the downtown office buildings was beginning to fill the place. He watched them come, studying the faces of each of the women.

Sheila McNulty came in with her usual crowd. She was a little brunette with a decent figure. Neil had seen her twice before with her little crowd of file clerks and copyboys. Most of them drank beer or white wine. Sheila drank Scotch and drank it fast.

That first night Neil hadn't approached her, but instead had followed her home. She lived in a New Town apartment off Broadway. For a brief instant he had considered a direct approach, because she staggered slightly due to the six Scotch-and-sodas she had downed in the bar. But there were too many people around and he didn't have the lay of the land, as Margo called it.

A few days later, while Sheila was at work, he returned to the building. She lived in an overpriced efficiency flat overlooking an air shaft. Using his lockpicks, he slipped inside without being seen.

The place was a mess. Clothes, dirty dishes and empty fast-food containers were strewn everywhere. But he was able to discover a great deal about her during his visit. She owned a new Sony television and VCR. She read romance novels and movie magazines. She was also on birth-control pills. The most interesting thing he found out about Sheila McNulty came from the black-and-white 8½-by-11 photograph he found hanging on the living-room wall. A wilted rose was stuck behind the frame. The inscription scribbled in black ink in the lower right-hand corner of the picture read, "To my little Sheila, all my love, Uncle Sean—Belfast—May, '83." The man in the photo looked to Neil like your average Mick. Pug features, a shock of unruly hair sticking out from under a knit cap, and a lopsided grin.

There was little else in the small flat to tell him more about Sheila. The only papers were unpaid bills, and he didn't even find any letters from this Uncle Sean or any other relative. He later found he wouldn't need anything else.

That night Neil returned to the bar. There he discovered the piece of the puzzle that pulled all the rest together. On her fourth Scotch and beginning to feel it, Sheila began preaching about the Irish Republican Army cause and how her uncle Sean McNulty had been gunned down by the British Army on the bloody streets of Belfast. At this point Neil figured the rest would be easy. But Sergeant McKinnis had forced a postponement of his plans for the little Mick drunk. Now he was back and literally ready for the kill.

Every night, after her third drink at the Michigan Avenue bar, Sheila McNulty became depressed. She would begin mourning her dead relatives "across the pond" on the "old sod" where the "Troubles" had made many a widow and the blood ran freely in the streets of Belfast. Patrons in the bar avoided her. On this summer evening she was alone. The bartender only approached her to pour a fresh drink. A man wearing an expensive red wig slid onto the stool beside her.

"Would you be cryin' for a relative who's died in the Troubles of a faraway land?"

Sheila's eyes went wide as saucers. She stared at him in shock before tears streamed down her face and she let out a wail that alerted the bartender and the bar's "security specialist."

The man in the wig was stunned.

"So what'd you do to the lady, pal?" the security specialist said, resting a heavy, thick-knuckled hand on the man's shoulder.

The bartender gave the bouncer a "be cool" look. Then he asked Sheila, "What's the matter, honey?"

"He . . . he . . . he sounds just like my Uncle Sean used to."

The bouncer removed his hand and the bartender poured the sobbing woman another drink. The man in the wig motioned that this drink was to go on his tab.

When he and Sheila were alone, the man lowered his voice. "Don't go screamin' that way again, girl. There's people lookin' for me on this side of the pond."

Sheila blew her nose with a cocktail napkin. Her eyes

darted around the bar. "Why would somebody be looking for you?"

"Why were they after Sean McNulty?"

"You knew Uncle Sean?"

"Keep your voice down, girl."

"You knew Uncle Sean?" she whispered.

"Is the South of Ireland Protestant?"

"No," she said with a frown. "It's Catholic. The North is Protestant."

He didn't say anything for a moment. "Let's have another drink."

"But you said the South was Protestant." There was suspicion in her voice.

"A code, darlin'," he said smoothly. "We in the movement have got to be damn careful."

"Oh, I see," she said. Actually, she didn't and never would.

Sheila was very, very drunk. She didn't remember how many Scotches she'd consumed, but it had been far above her limit of six, or was it seven? She didn't know at what point she staggered to the ladies room and puked up her guts. But after that she'd washed her face, rinsed out her mouth, and gone back to have another round with "Himself." She'd asked his name, but he had told her he didn't want to say it in a pub. The walls had ears. She guessed that made sense. So she had taken to thinking of him as "Himself." She'd always wanted to refer to someone by that title. It sounded just grand.

"I didn't get to go along with the boyos when they took out that British pig," he'd told her.

"Wha' Brish prig?" She picked up her drink. Some of it sloshed over her hand.

"Mountbatten. Lord Mountbatten."

The next thing she knew the bartender was standing in front of them.

"No more for her, friend. She's drunker'n the law allows. Just get her out of here."

Then she found herself sitting on the floor, but she couldn't remember how she got there. Arms were pulling her up and someone was carrying her.

There was the motion of a car moving and she thought she was going to be sick. There was music playing. Stevie Wonder was singing in French. Sheila tried to sing along. "My cherry armour!"

She came to in her apartment. She was lying on the bed. It was dark. She had a splitting headache and her mouth tasted like the floor of a saloon. And her arms hurt.

She tried to rub them, but found that she couldn't move her hands. Fear raced through her when she realized she was bound spread-eagled. She was nude.

Then "Himself" stepped out of the shadows. But he looked different than she remembered he had back in the bar. It was his hair. The wig was gone. He had a full head of silver hair and was much better looking than she'd originally thought. The light in the bar hadn't been that good anyway. He was also naked.

"Okay," she managed. "We can do this if you want, but I don't like it kinky. An Irish gentleman would never . . ."

He was across the room so fast her brain barely had time to register that he had moved at all. He shoved a cloth into her mouth. It gagged her. She recognized it as the rancid, greasy dishcloth from her sink. Sheila couldn't remember the last time she used it.

She attempted to close her throat, but she could feel the terrible residue dripping down across her palate. When it mingled with the booze she had consumed she expected to be very sick.

His face was there very close to hers. His tone was pleasant, almost soothing. His words were not. "Listen, you drunken slut." The accent was gone. "We're going to have a good time, you and me. You're going to please me any way I like and as often as I like."

He tied something around her neck. It was soft, but had a hard object inside. Slowly, he began tightening it. Terror and the obstructing rag cutting off her air made her eyes bulge, as her face reddened.

He snatched the rag from her mouth. She gulped in a deep, gasping breath. She planned to scream her lungs out. But he tightened the thing around her neck. The hard object dug into her windpipe. Her scream came out a weak croak.

"No, no, no, my little cunt. No screaming tonight. Not tonight, nor tomorrow night, or ever."

He held the thing around her neck until her eyes began to roll back in her head. Then he released it.

"Now, let's start at the beginning." His face was an inch from hers. "You're in for the night of your life."

# CHAPTER 42

**JUNE 11, 1996**
**6:32 A.M.**

Margo DeWitt had been up all night reading. The book was a ten-year-old Jamal Garth novel, *Day of the Terrorist*, written while the author was still a fugitive. She had started the 428-page book at about midnight. Now, as the morning sun spread its rays across Chicago, Margo paused before beginning the final chapter.

She glanced at the grandfather clock in the corner of the library, then back at the open library doors. She expected her husband at any minute. He never stayed out too far past dawn. Possibly, like the fictional vampire, Neil figured that if he did, the sun would scorch the flesh right off his bones. Yes, Margo thought, Neil was just that stupid.

She returned to *Day of the Terrorist*, but only half her mind was focused on the author's words.

As she scanned the final pages of the novel that had

occupied the top spot on the *New York Times* best-seller list for thirty-two weeks in 1986, she considered the future of her marriage.

Margo was tired of Neil. She never really knew what she had seen in him to begin with. A thought occurred to her, which made her smile in spite of herself. She remembered when they had met, out in Colorado. She had thought him to be nothing more than a simpering nitwit with too much money. The first time he asked her out she had actually laughed in his face. The next time she heard from him was on the telephone. On that occasion he had imitated the voice of movie star Keven Costner to perfection. It was at that point she knew Neil was someone different from the rest of the dreary men she came in contact with. It didn't take her long to find out how much different. And he was wealthy to boot.

Now she was entitled to half that wealth. Actually, all of it could be hers if something were to happen to her dear, dear husband. There were a smattering of DeWitt distant relatives around the planet, but she was the wife. If anyone tried to tie her up in probate, Margo would deal directly with them by a simple act of murder. If necessary, several acts of murder. However, there weren't that many DeWitts left. In fact, she was the last of her kind as well. She didn't use her family name of Rapier, because she wasn't talking about families.

The first Rapier had set foot on the soil of the New World long before the Revolutionary War. There had been talk down through the years that this first ancestor had fled France after committing a number of capital offenses against the French Crown. Murder had never been mentioned because the respectable Rapiers over the centuries had preferred treason, a more palatable crime, against a long-extinct monarchy. But somehow Margo had known it had been murder. Perhaps a number of them.

For countless succeeding generations the Rapiers had been adventurers, explorers wandering across the lonely frontiers fighting Indians and soldiers alike while giving true allegiance to no man. Progeny had been produced in a haphazard fashion. There was a great deal of mating with the Indian tribes of the Midwest territories. A few of Margo's ancestors found their way as far south as Haiti; a good number settled in Louisiana, and there was mention that the Rapier line had some strains of black blood in it. Perhaps, Margo considered, that was why she had such a particular hatred for the little black boys she stalked before either strangling them or breaking their necks.

She closed the book and studied her hands. The fingers were exceptionally long, with digits just a bit too thick to be called graceful. Since birth she had been gifted with abnormal hand and forearm strength. Margo had learned from studying her family tree that such strength could be developed by wielding sharp knives to skin the hides from buffalo and other game. Even the occasional scalp, Indian or Caucasian. The thought made her smile.

She flexed her right hand into a fist. She could employ enough force on Neil's hand during a simple handshake to make him cry out. When she was two years old, a doddering aunt had given her a small kitten. The first day, Margo had "broken" the little animal. To this day she could recall her mother's shrieks of horror. The dear woman never again looked at her daughter without fear. This fact never bothered the girl, who had grown into a psychopathic woman. She had found it rather convenient when she needed to get her way.

Every other generation or so there had been a scandal in the Rapier family. A Rapier scout employed in the service of General Andrew Jackson's Army during the War of 1812 had been rather efficient at assassinating British officers. "Old Hickory" had the scout hanged when he discovered the same assassination tactics were being employed by Rapier against American officers.

In post–Civil War New Orleans, a Rapier reportedly engaged in a bizarre series of "Jack the Ripper"–type slayings. However, there was a difference. Both women and men had been the killer's victims. That particular ancestor fled the Louisiana parish where the slayings occurred only moments before a platoon of soldiers came for him. All of the victims were former slaves.

Margo felt a particular kinship with this ancestor. His name had been Jean Claude Rapier, and she had a very old photograph of him. He looked like John Wilkes Booth. Margo's mind flashed briefly back to the little boy at the Chicago Historical Society. He had first told her his name was Butch. Yes, just as Margo had once been called "Margie" by a hated teacher. A teacher who had drowned mysteriously while swimming alone in the school swimming pool. No one had ever called her Margie again. But the little boy had also told her his real name: Larry Cole, Jr.

With her hands at his throat it could all have been over in seconds. But then, the Albritton woman and the teenager had been close by. Possibly not close enough to see her commit the act, but close enough to raise an alarm. Unlike her overdue husband, Margo did not take unnecessary chances. Then, what purpose would the random death of Cole's son serve? The nosy policeman deserved much more than that, and Margo intended to give it to him. It was part of her plan. Hers and Magda's.

In the novel she was reading Garth's fictional hero was pursuing a terrorist who had planted an atomic bomb in downtown Philadelphia. Margo's mind drifted easily from the words on the page to another of her ancestors, the one responsible for building the bulk of the Rapier fortune in post–World War I Denver. David (pronounced "Daveed") Paul Rapier built up a lucrative retail furniture business from nothing. He was another handsome, slender man with the soulful eyes of the poet and the good looks of the thespian.

Between Christmas 1919 and the summer of 1925, fifty-seven men, women and children in the Denver area simply vanished. No bodies, remains or other traces of them were ever found. A nosy Irish detective in the Denver Police

Department named O'Hara had somehow begun suspecting David Rapier, because two of the last four missing persons had been seen with the furniture magnate. Perhaps it was because three of the young women, two of the men and a messenger boy all worked for the Rapier Furniture Company.

Detective O'Hara came after David with the tenacity of a bull terrier. O'Hara was kind of David's Larry Cole, she thought, with a smile. O'Hara took a rather close interest in some of the furniture coming out of the Rapier factory, particularly certain fabrics, lampshades and slipcovers. On the same day in 1925 that the Denver Crime Laboratory discovered that the suspect furnishings were made from chemically treated human flesh, Detective O'Hara vanished.

A rather sensational criminal trial followed. A jury returned a verdict of Not Guilty, because no bodies were ever found and there were no witnesses to the suspected crimes.

Acquitted, but publicly disgraced, David quietly moved his family back to New Orleans, where they resided in inconspicuous opulence for a generation. Then Margo's grandfather, Clement David Rapier, moved the family back to Denver, in 1950. By then the Rapier Furniture Company murders had been forgotten by all except a very few crime-history buffs. It had been simply bad luck for Margo that one such crime-history buff was a certain Colorado state trooper investigating a series of child murders in the late eighties. Bad luck for her, but particularly bad luck for him.

Her attention was diverted from her book and thoughts of her family by the front door of the penthouse being unlocked. This would be Neil. Dear, dear tiring, bumbling Neil.

Margo listened to his steps as he approached the library door.

When he walked into the library, there was a supreme look of triumph on his face.

"Guess what I've been doing?" he purred.

She stared across the room at him. He was so full of

himself. He reminded her of a dog bringing a dead bird back to its master; like the dog, he would expect an approving pat on the head. She could simply ignore him and watch the starch drain out of him. But then, she had just decided on a plan that would get rid of him while leaving her with the entire DeWitt fortune. She would even let the meddling, inquisitive Larry Cole do the job for her. Then, she would return the favor for the cop and, yes, his little son Butch, too.

Margo flashed Neil a chilly smile. "Why don't you come over here and tell Mama what a bad boy my Neil's been?"

As he came, like the dog with the bird in its mouth, her eyes never left him.

# CHAPTER 43

**JUNE 11, 1996**
**11:45 A.M.**

Manny and Lauren Sherlock were preparing to go to the annual St. Jude picnic when the telephone rang in their North Side apartment. Lauren was in the kitchen preparing what she called "an old-fashioned picnic-basket lunch," and was within arm's reach of the wall extension.

"Hello?"

*"Hey, babe."*

Lauren, a hazel-eyed woman with pretty features, frowned. "Hello, Virgil."

*"The sarge in?"*

"Just a minute." She put the phone down on the counter, as if something distasteful were on it, and went in search of her husband.

Manny was half-in and half-out of the storage closet at

the rear of the apartment. He was attempting to pull a lawn chair from behind the boxed artificial Christmas tree, the humidifier and the old VCR.

"Manny!" She had to shout to be heard over the racket he was making.

"Yeah!"

"Your friend Detective Virgil Davis is on the phone."

Reluctantly, Manny gave up the struggle with the stubborn chair. He started for the phone, but she stopped him.

"What does God's gift to the human race want now?"

"ESP's down today, honey. I'll have to talk to him to find out."

She let him pass. Then she stepped into the closet, collapsed the offending chair and easily pulled it out into the hall.

Probably in every class that has ever been convened, in which twenty-five or more human beings participate, there is a misfit. Generally classified as the "class clown" or "class cutup," this individual can generally be counted on to screw up on a fairly regular basis. In Manny Sherlock's 1990 Chicago Police Detective School class, Virgil Davis had assumed this role, which he had been playing all his life.

Manny picked up the kitchen phone. "How's it going, Virg?"

*"You ready to turn in your sergeant stripes and come back out in the street where we work for a living?"*

"I'll put in my papers the first thing Monday morning. So what's up?"

*"We got a body in the Twenty-third District. White female. Name was Sheila McNulty. Found tied up and mutilated in a ritualistic manner. A witness saw a guy come home with her last night. Could be your perp."*

Manny's hand gripped the receiver tightly. Deputy Cole had wanted them to keep an eye on any unusual murders in the city. He had told the staff not to go through the normal channels to do this, but to use their own individual "old boy" networks. Each of them—Manny, Judy and Blackie—had contacts throughout the Department.

Cole had also told them he wanted to keep a particular eye on things in Commander Shelby's area. The only one on the staff who knew any of the detectives assigned to Area Three was Manny. However, Virgil Davis had a reputation for being supremely unreliable.

"How sure are you about the ID, Virg?"

*"We got a building superintendent and a nosy next-door neighbor. In fact, the neighbor says the guy's been in the apartment before. Even gave us a date—June third. She, that's the neighbor, said that at the time she thought he was a repairman or something, because he had a key. The building super says there haven't been any repairmen around for a month. On top of that he doesn't give out passkeys. He goes with any workmen and stays with them. So you gotta figure this guy's casing her. There's something else."*

"What?"

*"I heard it on the jungle grapevine that your boss made my boss, who I think is a grade-A asshole, look bad on that Sergeant McKinnis thing. I also heard your guy turned up a suspect who was supposedly following the sergeant's lady. A guy wearing expensive shades and a denim sailor cap."*

Manny waited.

*"Okay, Sergeant Manfred Wolfgang Sherlock,"* Virgil said with a flourish, *"the nosy neighbor gives this description of the guy who went in the dead girl's apartment on the third, and I quote: 'White, male, thirty-five to forty, medium height, medium build, wearing a broken-down denim sailor cap, dark glasses and a light-colored shirt.' Says she thinks it was the same guy came back with the dead girl last night, only this time he had on a red wig."*

"Where are you?"

*"In a restaurant on Broadway near Diversey. A coupla blocks from the scene."*

"I think I'll stop in and take a look on my way to the picnic."

*"Be sure to bring your old lady with you,"* Virgil laughed. *"I'm sure what's left of this McNulty broad'll do wonders for her appetite at the St. Jude bash."*

# CHAPTER 44

**JUNE 11, 1996**
**2:15 P.M.**

The St. Jude Police League annual picnic was being held in Jackson Park. The day was overcast and warm, with a hint of rain in the air. Off-duty police officers, their families and friends packed the grassy area just off Sixty-third Street a block east of Stony Island. Picnic tables were set up, and there were two open-sided pink-and-white-striped tents. One was where free beer, soft drinks and hot dogs were distributed to the picnickers; the other was the VIP tent. The superintendent of police presided at the head table beneath this tent.

Although a bit apprehensive, the superintendent put on a good show of enjoying herself. On her right, descending by order of rank, were First Deputy Superintendent Kennedy and his wife, Sandy; the deputy superintendents and their spouses; on down to the chiefs, deputy chiefs and assistant deputy superintendents; and finally the commanders.

The superintendent's father and grandfather had been cops, and at an early age it was quite clearly conveyed to her that she was expected to marry a cop, or at least a fireman. She had other plans.

She was the first female superintendent and the second-youngest in history at the age of forty-five. She hadn't necessarily designed it this way, but when it happened she accepted it and set out to do the best job possible.

She looked down the table at her subordinates. Two present were females with their husbands. Only one out of the entire group was younger than she was, and most of them conveyed that they were uncomfortable in her presence. She found that a little fear could reap positive results in an organization that demanded strict obedience in order to function. She also realized that too much fear could strangle productivity. It was her job to strike an adequate balance.

Father Michael Ivers, the police chaplain, sat on her immediate left. He was on loan from the archdiocese and so far thrived on the duties that had him rushing out in the middle of the night to hospitals where his job was to comfort the loved ones of wounded or dying policemen, providing spiritual support for those in need, and in some cases had him celebrating requiem masses for deceased officers like Sergeant Clarence McKinnis.

"Have you turned up anything on the McKinnis investigation, Superintendent?" Father Mike asked.

She turned to look at him. A green stovepipe hat, a beard and a shillelagh added would have made him a good candidate for a leprechaun impersonator. However, he possessed no accent, save a bit of New England. He'd received a master's in theology from Boston College.

"I've been so busy lately, Father," she said, looking at her first deputy, "I haven't had a chance to keep up with it."

Kennedy took the hint. "Deputy Chief Cole has been working on it. Got some interesting theories, but no arrests yet. I'm sure he'll come up with something soon. I think I saw him a little while ago," he said, glancing around the VIP tent.

The first deputy spied Chief Govich. "Jack, where's Larry Cole?"

"At the big game, boss. He plays first base on the Detective Division team. You want me to go get him?"

"No," the superintendent said. "I'll go. I need the exercise."

Kennedy and Father Mike stood up with her. She motioned them back to their seats. "I can do this alone, boys. Give me a chance to check out the festivities firsthand."

She stepped out onto the grass. The sky had a slate gray, midsummer overcast that could spew rain at any minute.

The superintendent strolled slowly away from the VIP tent toward the refreshment area. She could feel the eyes of those she passed following her. What had one of her aides said they called her? "The Iron Maiden"? Maybe not so much iron beneath the pink blouse and denim skirt she wore, but definitely not cotton.

Out in the center of the grassy area of the park, a softball game was in progress. She could see a tall black man in a red Chicago Police cap playing first base. She had noticed Cole, minus his wife and son, wearing a red cap when he arrived earlier.

She started toward the makeshift diamond. As she walked along, feeling the grass squiggle through the openings of her sandals, a sense of well-being descended on her. She took in a deep breath; the air was fresh and warm, with just a hint of moisture mixed with the faint aroma of freshly cut grass. For a moment she forgot that she was the chief executive officer of the second-largest police department in the country.

A short distance from the players, she stopped. She was unobserved, because everyone nearby was focused on the game. She noticed that the red caps were all members of the Detective Division, who were also wearing matching red shirts with the logo CPD DICKS across the back. The team name made her frown briefly. Then she mumbled to herself, "Why the hell not?"

The other team was dressed in blue caps with matching shirts as well. Across their backs the team name in white lettering read CPD DOG ASSES, which was the slang name for beat cops. Folding her arms across her chest, the superintendent shook her head. Cops would never change, she thought.

The game was apparently coming to a close. She was able to pick up from the shouting that the Dicks were behind by a run and it was the bottom of the final inning. The first batter, a red-faced, beer-bellied detective commander named Tim Shroeder, stepped to the plate. A grizzled old cop in a blue cap, who was the Dog Asses' manager, began shouting changes in the defensive positions of his team on the field. He then made a series of hand and arm motions to his pitcher.

Shroeder was tossed four underhanded pitches by the gangly young man with the bushy mustache on the mound. He swung at each of them. He only tipped one. On the final strike Shroeder spun around so violently that the superintendent was certain he was going to corkscrew himself right into the ground.

As Shroeder skulked away, his head hung in shame, the man she had come in search of stepped to the plate. The superintendent was surprised at Cole's size. With a business suit on he didn't look this big. In fact, she had always thought he was kind of thin. Now, with him wearing a short-sleeved Dicks shirt, his upper body muscles were quite evident. She recalled the report she'd read on McKinnis's death. Before Cole had driven him home the two of them had been lifting weights at the police gym. It was obvious that Cole's time there wasn't wasted.

The manager of the Dog Asses and the bushy-mustached pitcher went through a few more of their coded gymnastics. The pitcher wound up and flipped the sixteen-inch softball toward home plate. Cole seemed to coil into himself before springing to smack his bat into the ball. The impact made a loud whack, as the leather-and-twine sphere rocketed into the outfield. The Dog Asses' center fielder was forced to play the ball on a hard hop. The Dicks' hitter had a very loud, long single.

The next batter was closer in appearance to Shroeder than to Cole. Hatless, he had a receding hairline, a thick middle, and heavy arms covered with black hair. He wore a scowl arranged around a cigar stub stuck in the corner of his mouth and carried a bat over his shoulder that resembled a caveman's war club. As he approached the plate, the Dicks' bench shouted: "Get 'em, Blackie," "Bring the boss home, Blackie" and "Let's kick some dogs' asses, Blackie!"

The superintendent had never set eyes on Lieutenant Blackie Silvestri before, but she definitely knew of him. If he was anywhere near as tough as he looked, then most of the stories were probably true.

Blackie stepped to the plate and glared at the pitcher. The kid grinned back, but somehow it appeared phony. It was as if in that brief exchange between them Silvestri had won something, or rather taken something away from the gangly Dog Ass.

The gnarled manager was shouting encouragement and gesticulating like a windup toy. He, too, seemed to be a bit more frantic than had been the case with Shroeder and Cole. Interesting, the superintendent thought. This Silvestri had a presence and he had made that presence felt.

The first pitch was a ball. Standing with his club-sized bat slung casually over his shoulder, Silvestri watched it go past with an expression verging on boredom.

The pitcher looked from the umpire to his manager. The beginnings of panic flickered on his face. The manager gave him some arm music. The pitcher shot a glance at Cole on first base. The deputy chief gave him a mocking smile. Wiping sweat from under his cap, the pitcher turned back to the plate.

There was something happening here. The superintendent could feel it. There were forces at work not openly evident, but powerful nonetheless. An intensity had enveloped the makeshift softball diamond in Jackson Park. The superintendent wished she could transfer this intensity from the playing field into the squadrooms and patrol cars all over the city. If she could indeed accomplish this feat, the crime rate would be cut in half within a year.

The pitcher threw the second ball and then a third. Silvestri did not move.

The old manager called time and trotted out to the mound. The superintendent was at least forty-five yards from where they stood, but she could tell what was being said. The manager was giving the kid a pep talk, which didn't appear to be working. When the manager turned to run back to the Dog Asses' bench, he looked worried. On the mound the pitcher fidgeted nervously.

Silvestri continued glaring. For his part, the pitcher tried to tough it out. He squared his shoulders and returned Silvestri's gaze. The kid went into his arm-swinging windup and delivered a ball headed straight for the heart of the plate. It never made it.

Unlike Cole, Silvestri did not coil before swinging. He swung from the heels with everything he had.

The superintendent, Cole, the members of both benches, the spectators and all the Dog Ass outfielders watched it go on, and on, and on. As the two Dicks, Cole and Silvestri, circled the bases, the rains came.

The superintendent turned from the site of the now concluded game and head back for the VIP tent. She would let Kennedy find out how far Cole had progressed on the McKinnis investigation. She had a department to run. As she walked alone through the summer downpour there was a smile on her face.

# CHAPTER 45

**JUNE 11, 1996**
**6:37 P.M.**

I'm sorry I missed the game, Blackie," Manny said. "But I figured the boss would want to get the skinny on this McNulty murder."

Blackie took a long pull from a sixteen-ounce can of Miller and stuffed his cigar back in his mouth before saying, "Sherlock, you're all cop. I'm proud of ya, but you missed a game-winning home run of truly epic proportions."

They were in Cole's den. The rain had fallen steadily since the end of the game in Jackson Park. The forecast was for no letup for the next twenty-four hours. Manny and Lauren didn't get to the park until everyone was heading home. Lauren was not happy about this development.

"I'd love to have seen the expressions on the faces of the Dog Asses," Manny said. "We haven't won a game from them in four years."

"Next year," Cole said. He was sprawled on the couch. "Blackie's still our secret weapon. What did you find out at the homicide scene?"

He shrugged. "Nothing, boss. I shouldn't have listened to that crazy Virgil Davis. That guy couldn't find his ass with a road map."

"So the ID Davis told you about was no good?" Cole said.

"It all hinged on the next-door neighbor's identification of the suspect," Manny said. "But with her eyes, even with glasses, she didn't look to me like she could see more than five feet in front of her. On top of that, the hallway was dark even during daylight hours. An electrical problem keeps burning all the ceiling lights out. The janitor said an electrician was supposed to be out to fix it, but he hasn't shown up yet."

"Could the neighbor have seen well enough to give us a description of the guy's clothing?" Blackie asked.

"I guess so, but what good's that gonna do in court? The last time she saw him, before last night, was over a week ago."

"The day Mack was killed?" Cole asked.

"Day before, boss," Sherlock said. "Then the perp was supposedly wearing a denim cap and shades, but there have got to be a hundred guys walking around in New Town with those same type caps on."

Cole swung his feet to the floor and sat on the edge of the couch.

"What is it, Larry?" Blackie said.

"So we figure Neil DeWitt, wearing a denim hat, followed Paige from the Loop to the North Side. He enters the apartment after she leaves to go shopping and Mack surprises him. Now we got a guy, in the same kind of cap, doing the same thing to this dead girl the day before Mack is iced. He cases the place, maybe makes contact with her somewhere, and comes back later to kill her. I bet that's his MO."

"But how are you going to tie the McNulty murder to Neil DeWitt?" Blackie asked. "From what Manny's said, the eyewitness is something less than reliable."

"How did they handle the scene, Manny?" Cole said.

"Pretty good. Janitor found her and called nine-one-one right away. Twenty-three thirty-four got the call. When they found the girl was dead, the beat cops sealed it real good. Crime Lab went over it and even my friend Virg looked like he knew what he was doing for a change. They probably collected a ton of physical evidence out of the place."

"What about the girl?" Cole questioned.

Manny's face fell. "He hacked her up real good and enjoyed doing it. Had a half-dollar twisted inside a nylon stocking tied around her throat. He can ease or tighten the stocking easily enough. That way he controls her breathing with the coin wedged against her windpipe. The lab guys say they think the cause of death was probably strangulation and not necessarily from the wounds. And there were a lot of wounds."

"*Killing Streets*!" Cole said, jumping up and going to a plastic bag on his desk.

They watched him rummaging around inside it. He pulled out a handful of paperback books, stacked them on the desktop, picked one up and showed them the cover. It was the novel *Killing Streets* by Jamal Garth.

Cole returned to the couch and began thumbing through the book,

"Ain't that the guy took a walk on you the other night from the mystery-writers meeting, boss?" Blackie said.

"Yeah, but he had his reasons."

"Like what? If you ask me, he acted like a total asshole."

"The name Thomas W. Holman ring a bell for you, Blackie?" Cole did not look up.

Blackie became very still. Manny noticed and asked his lieutenant, "What's wrong?"

Blackie didn't respond, but his eyes never left Cole.

"Here it is!" Cole said, pointing to a passage in the book. "The nylon stocking was used by one of Garth's murderers, only he used a silver dollar inside of it."

"Larry," Blackie said in a voice that was barely audible.

Cole looked up. "Yeah?"

"Thomas Holman's a cop killer."

"I know," Cole said, going back to the book.

# CHAPTER 46

**JUNE 11, 1996**
**7:01 P.M.**

Neil DeWitt lay asleep on an immense circular bed beneath black silk sheets on the second level of the penthouse. Heavy drapes and soundproofing kept his slumber from being disturbed by the flashing lightning and ear-shattering thunder accompanying the sheets of rain falling on the city

In the repose of sleep the multimillionaire looked at extreme peace with himself. A slight smile played at the corners of his mouth and his hands were folded across his chest.

A figure stepped from the shadows and ascended the two stairs to the carpeted platform on which Neil's bed rested. A voice spoke into the darkness. "Almost like a corpse."

The words, although spoken in a whisper, disturbed the solitude of his sleep. His eyes popped open. For a moment he was disoriented. He realized where he was at the same time he became aware of the spectral figure standing beside his bed. He lurched into a sitting position. His heart raced.

"Get up," Margo said. "I have something for you to do."

"What?" he asked, but she was already half way to the door, and did not turn around.

He checked the luminous dial of his wristwatch. He had slept the entire day. Of course, he'd had quite a night. With a grin he remembered the last moments of Sheila McNulty's life.

It took him nearly an hour to shower, shave and dress.

Margo was in the library waiting for him. She had a new book open.

"What's that?"

She closed the book and showed him the cover.

"*Excessive Force* by Clancy Blackburn," he read out loud. "Cop thriller?"

She took a plastic bookmark from the end table to note her place before closing the novel. "Your basic police thriller. Lots of cops running around acting a lot smarter than they are in real life."

"You said you had something for me to do?"

She smiled. "It's time we disposed of one of our remaining two witnesses."

"Paige Albritton?"

Margo took a cigarette from a gold filigree box on the cocktail table. She lit it with her silver lighter. Blowing smoke into the air, she said, "Isn't one in twenty-four hours enough for you?"

"It wouldn't have to be involved. I could just eliminate her."

Margo gave him a cold look. "Why don't you go and just eliminate the woman who saw you from her apartment window? This Frances Adams. Then we'll see about Paige Albritton."

He shrugged. "Okay. How do you want me to do it?"

There was a pitcher of orange juice with glasses and a tray of sandwiches on the end table beside the couch. She reached out and poured a glass and, offering it to him, said, "I spent the day looking through some of B.S. Zorin's books. She wrote one a few years ago which I feel contains the perfect method for you to use."

Neil looked from the glass back to his wife. There was a wariness bordering on outright suspicion on his face.

Seemingly oblivious to his look, she poured a second glass. After taking a healthy swallow, she said, "Delicious."

He also drank. The fruit juice was so good that he drained off the entire glass. He was also hungry and grabbed a sandwich from the tray. It was chicken salad, one of his favorites.

"So, what's the perfect method you found in the Zorin book?" he said with his mouth full.

Margo flashed him the warmest smile she had bestowed on anyone in many years. "Chloroform," she said.

"Chloroform?"

"Chloroform," she repeated.

# CHAPTER 47

**JUNE 11, 1996**
**8:32 P.M.**

Probationary Police Officer Elizabeth Fletcher was assigned to guard duty outside the home of Frances Adams. She was in a squad car with a faulty air-conditioner on a hot, humid night. The rain had fallen steadily since she left the station after roll call. Expected to spend her entire tour here, she would be relieved for a half-hour lunch at nine, and a sergeant would spell her for brief personals, which she was to request on her walkie-talkie. If she didn't ask for more than two, the sergeant wouldn't get too cross. The rest of the time she was on her own.

According to the limited information she had been provided, the order to guard Mrs. Adams had come from Detective Division headquarters. She recalled that the other guard-duty assignment she'd had was ordered by the Detective Division. It was like everything else Fletcher had encountered so far in life. Shit rolled downhill.

A car pulled up directly behind the squad car. She looked up in the rearview mirror, but the glare off the fogged-up back window was blinding.

She put on her cap and grabbed her Kelite from the front seat. She thought about the raincoat in the back, but it would take too long to put it on and whoever was back there had extinguished their headlights. She got out of the car.

She didn't know much about vehicle makes, but she could tell the one parked behind her was expensive. A Lincoln maybe. The driver was already out and walking toward the sidewalk.

"Excuse me, sir!"

He stopped. He wore a dark fedora with the brim broken down to shield his face in shadow. The trench coat also looked expensive, but she didn't pay as much attention to the style as she did to the fact that his hands were in the pockets. This froze her at the rear bumper of the police car.

"I'm Detective Moran from Deputy Chief Cole's office. Gotta talk to the Adams woman."

He sounded like someone she'd heard before, probably a cop. The sneer in his voice from talking out of the side of his mouth, the gravelly quality in the tone from too many unfiltered cigarettes and too much straight whiskey, and the obvious toughness were all there. As if he could—what was the saying she'd heard an old cop use?—"chew nails and spit tacks."

He also seemed a bit unsteady, as if he had been drinking.

"Nobody told me," she said in an unsure voice. When it rolls downhill the one at the bottom is always the last to know.

"Can't help that, sweetheart," he said, turning toward the house.

Maybe he was just being funny, but something didn't feel right. The last words he'd spoken, especially the slurred "sweetheart," enabled her to place the voice. He was doing a perfect imitation of Humphrey Bogart. So he was playing games with her! Well, to hell with him and this Deputy Chief Cole.

"Just a minute, sir!" This time she let her anger come

through. "I'll have to call this in and get an okay from my supervisor!"

He was at the bottom of the stairs leading up to the front porch. She stepped around the rear bumper of the police car. Suddenly, he spun toward her. She saw the muzzle flashes from the automatic weapon just as he opened fire.

# CHAPTER 48

**JUNE 11, 1996**
**9:15 P.M.**

The rain had turned to a fine mist, and the heat-baked streets looked like sheets of glass. The unmarked squad car sped north on Lake Shore Drive, its flashing headlights spearing warning beams at the cars ahead. The siren's wail wrapped the occupants of the car in a cocoon of tension.

Cole held the wheel of the car so tightly his knuckles bulged noticeably through the skin. Still wearing his red Dicks cap, he had lost the cheer and satisfaction of victory and was now grim. Beside him sat Blackie, looking equally cheerless. Manny was in the back. He looked simply numb.

From two blocks away, they could see the blue lights of the police cars in front of the Adams house. An officer in a nylon raincoat directed them to a parking place behind the first deputy's car. They noticed Shelby's car in front of it.

Kennedy was standing at the bottom of the steps conferring with Shelby and State's Attorney Anne Johnson. Cole, flanked by Blackie and Manny, approached. Cole questioned silently why Johnson was there.

Kennedy was still dressed in the same sports outfit he'd worn to the picnic. The falling rain was being absorbed by his shirt like a sponge.

"You didn't have to come out on this one, Larry," Kennedy said. "I could have briefed you on the phone."

"The duty officer at Operations Command said that what happened here tonight closed my case for me," Cole said. "He also said a cop was shot. I guess the combination was too much to resist."

"Oh, no, Larry. There was no cop shot here, although the son of a bitch tried. Had an Uzi. Come over here."

They walked to the side of the front porch where a canvas-draped figure was laid out half on the lawn and half on the sidewalk. Kennedy snatched back the covering. Blackie and Manny had followed their boss. The three of them looked down into the face of Neil DeWitt.

The killer's eyes were open and there was a very neat bullet hole right in the center of his forehead.

"Damndest thing I ever saw in thirty-two years on this job," Kennedy said. "This prick fires twenty rounds at this Probationary Officer Fletcher. She lets one go from a four-inch Smith and Wesson thirty-eight. Hits him right in the fucking head. Dead before he hits the ground."

"Crime Lab checked him out yet?" Cole asked.

Shelby answered. "Besides the Uzi, he had a bottle of chloroform and some gauze pads on him."

"What was he planning to do with them?" Anne Johnson asked. "Put someone to sleep?"

"Chloroform can kill," Cole said. "If it's applied long enough. Most people don't know that. Our boy here could have."

Kennedy shivered in the rain. "Well, Counselor, I guess Mr. DeWitt here clears Miss Albritton completely."

Anne Johnson snorted. "I guess so." Then she abruptly turned and stomped away.

Shelby took a parting look at the body before following her.

"Where's the probationary officer?" Cole asked Kennedy.

"Inside. Mrs. Adams fixed her a cup of hot tea. The kid's

taking it pretty good though. Employee Assistance is sending out a counselor."

"I'd like to talk to her."

Kennedy stifled a sneeze. "C'mon, I'll go with you. I could use some of that tea myself."

At that instant a lightning bolt split the sky, followed by deafening thunder. All of them jumped. The four policemen retreated into the Adams house, leaving the dead body of Neil DeWitt alone.

# CHAPTER 49

**JUNE 12, 1996**
**MIDNIGHT**

On the terrace on DeWitt Plaza, Margo, clothed in a black full-length cape, stood in the rain. As lightning spread across the city, sending bolts spearing into the Loop, she raised her hands and let the cape fall off. She was naked beneath it.

The first few drops of cold rain made her gasp, but she quickly got used to it. Keeping her hands raised, she moved forward. Dangerously close to the edge fifty floors above Michigan Avenue, she stopped.

Lightning snaked out from the heavens to lick close to the nude woman, but she did not flinch. Instead she stood her ground with legs splayed apart as if defying God Himself. The accompanying thunder made her ears ring, but she still didn't move.

Slowly, the storm retreated out over the lake. It was as if it had tested her with its power and been found wanting. She had stared down one of the mightiest forces of nature and survived.

She could now feel her own power, the same power her idol in literature, Magda, possessed. Margo had emulated Magda right down to the killing of children. But up until now, Margo had merely copied Magda's crimes. Now she felt that she was indeed becoming Magda!

A howl of insane laughter escaped her throat to rise above the still blowing wind and rain. A howl that no human ear could hear. To the demon in human form that was Margo DeWitt, it was a howl of triumph. To the entities of the heavens it was a challenge.

**“You’re all in this together.”**
**—Margo DeWitt**

# CHAPTER 50

**JUNE 15, 1996**
**12:35 P.M.**

Larry Cole was riding a Schwinn Airdyne stationary bicycle at the police gym. When he worked out, Cole's brain went into a form of cruise control. His problems, particularly the police-related ones, would be put on hold; however, he had developed the ability to let them rattle around in his head on their own. More than once, he had come up with a solution while his brain was so engaged. Some people slept on their problems; Cole exercised his.

Later, after a shower, as he was driving past the new White Sox park, his conscious mind picked up the thread of the problems he had put aside when he hefted the first barbell.

He pulled into the parking lot at Eleventh and State streets south of the police headquarters building. Less than a minute later he was in his office.

There was a videocassette on his desk. A stick-on note with the heading "Police officers never miss a beat" was attached to the case. Cole knew the note was from Manny. Lauren had apparently bought him a year's supply of them. The note read: "Deputy Cole, this is the tape you wanted. I made it myself."

Cole inserted the cassette into his department-issue video recorder and sat back to watch.

The tape began with a segment from the local NBC affiliate's news program of the previous night. A stunning Hispanic woman was talking.

"Earlier today, real-estate tycoon Neil DeWitt was cremated following a brief family service at the Baird and Livermoore Funeral Home."

As she talked, a prerecorded picture of the exterior of a red brick building with white columns appeared on the screen. A row of black limousines was parked in the funeral home's driveway.

The picture switched again. Margo DeWitt, dressed totally in black with a veil over her face, emerged from the funeral home. As Cole watched, former Governor Wayne Tolley, walking beside her, reached for her arm. Suddenly, he jerked his hand back. Cole figured she'd either done or said something to make him recoil like that.

"Mrs. Margo Dewitt is the lone surviving relative of Neil DeWitt," the commentator said. "He was shot to death by Police Officer Elizabeth Fletcher this past Saturday night after he attempted to kill the officer. Officer Fletcher was guarding a witness in a murder investigation. Two other witnesses in that same investigation, Syed Shafiq and Sidney Vukhovich, died last week under what authorities are calling suspicious circumstances.

"Mrs. Adams, police believe, would have eventually implicated Neil DeWitt in the brutal slaying of off-duty Chicago Police sergeant Clarence McKinnis."

The scene switched. Chief Govich's face appeared on the screen. He was standing outside police headquarters. His name and title were stenciled on the screen. He was talking to an off-camera reporter. "We think we're on solid ground with this now, Doug. Neil DeWitt was a suspect while he was alive and his actions last weekend indicate he had some involvement in Sergeant McKinnis's murder."

"Were there any other suspects in the sergeant's death, Chief?"

"None of any relevance."

"Do you think you could have gotten a conviction had you prosecuted Neil DeWitt?"

"You know speculating on convictions is iffy. Maybe we would have had enough to put Mr. DeWitt away for Mc-

Kinnis. Maybe we wouldn't. But I know we would have definitely nailed him for the murder of Sheila McNulty."

"Because of the physical evidence?"

"That's right. We were able to ascertain with a scientific certainty that Mr. DeWitt was in the McNulty apartment and had sexual relations with the deceased possibly only moments before she died."

"Was Mr. DeWitt a serial killer, Chief?"

"Hard to say. A sociopath, perhaps. A homicidal maniac? Serial killers usually stick with the same types of victims. Of course, we've got some new theories on that, too."

"Such as?"

"We're still working on them. You'll be the first to know if anything breaks."

"Thanks, Chief."

The tape switched back to the newscaster in the studio. "Although Mrs. Margo DeWitt would not discuss her husband with reporters, former Illinois governor Wayne Tolley served as spokesman for the DeWitt family and said that no legal action would be undertaken against the Chicago Police Department for the death of Mr. DeWitt. Governor Tolley also said the DeWitt family is completely satisfied with the circumstances surrounding his death."

A head shot of Tolley followed. He was standing outside the funeral home. A half-dozen microphones had been thrust under his chin. He looked completely at ease.

"Had Mr. DeWitt ever been treated for a psychological disorder, Governor?" A reporter yelled.

"No. Neil never sought psychiatric treatment of any kind. In all the years I've known him he always behaved as a sensitive, responsible individual. His death came as quite a shock to me."

"But the family's not pursuing it!" another reporter shouted.

"That's correct. There will be no action taken by anyone, either from the DeWitt family or the DeWitt Corporation, as a result of Neil's death."

"But you're not satisfied?" A third reporter entered the fray.

"Gentlemen and—" He turned his head slightly to the left and looked down before saying, "Ladies. I am the attorney for Mrs. Margo DeWitt. It is my job . . . No, correct that. It is my duty to follow the wishes of my client to the letter."

Cole's intercom buzzed. Blackie's voice came over the speaker. *"Boss, Soupy McGuire called from the M.E.'s office. Said he needs to talk to both of us as soon as possible."*

Cole frowned. "About what?"

*"He said the autopsies we requested, but I don't think that's all."*

Cole thought for a moment. "Who's out there?"

*"Just me."*

"Then I guess it's gonna be just you and me. Kind of like old times."

Blackie laughed.

Cole was about to turn off the set when a story, telecast on the news after the DeWitt piece, began. Manny had apparently taped it by mistake.

The studio commentator was again talking. ". . . makes the sixth child accidentally killed in the past three weeks. All the victims have been black males between the ages of four and twelve. The black community is up in arms over this situation."

Alderman Sherman Ellison Edwards appeared on the screen. Standing at the podium in a meeting hall, he was sweating profusely. "And I ain't gonna let that lady po-lice superintendent just sweep our complaints under the rug. No, Lord, you can bet I'm not!"

The camera swung to take in the audience. About twenty people, mostly senior citizens, occupied chairs. At the alderman's words they clapped and shouted "Amen!"

The epidemic of young black male deaths did have the department alarmed. They had discussed it at a meeting in

Govich's office that very morning. The problem was that all of the deaths appeared to have been accidental.

Cole made a note on his desk pad to have the files pulled when he got back. Then he went to get Blackie.

# CHAPTER 51

**JUNE 15, 1996**
**1:40 P.M.**

The two cars pulled up in front of the apartment building in Rogers Park. The lead car, a black Mustang convertible with the top down, was driven by Paige. Seated beside her, strapped securely in the front bucket seat and having the time of his life, was Butch Cole. The little boy had never been in a convertible before. In the dark gray Toyota behind the Mustang were Lisa Cole and Judy Daniels. None of the three women, either the driver of the Mustang or the two in the Toyota, were looking forward to why they were here.

They got out of the cars and met on the sidewalk. Butch ran to the wrought-iron fence surrounding the courtyard and stared in through the bars at the swimming pool.

"Wow, Mommy, look! They got a pool!"

Lisa walked over to her son. "They sure do, but it looks kind of deep for you to swim in."

"Paige'll take me in!" he squealed. "Won't you, Paige?"

She was looking up at the door to the apartment where she had lived briefly with Mack. She had not heard what the little boy said.

"I'm sure she will, honey," Lisa said. "But I don't want you going near it by yourself. Promise?"

Butch said a grudging, "I promise."

They entered the courtyard and ascended the stairs. The

door to the apartment was smeared with fingerprint powder and the remnants of a barrier tape hung from the frame. With her shoulders squared, Paige unlocked the door.

The interior of the apartment was more upset than in disarray. The furniture looked out of place and the dust from the fingerprint powder was on just about every surface.

Paige took a couple of steps toward the back of the apartment and stopped. Lisa and Judy detected a slight tremble in her movements. Butch was confused.

"Tell you what, Paige," Lisa said. "Why don't you take Butch out to the pool while Judy and I straighten up in here? I'm sure it won't take long."

"No." Paige said in a voice barely above a whisper. "This is my place. I got to clean it myself."

Lisa and Judy noticed that her accent had deepened. This only happened when she was under stress.

Paige took another step toward the back, hesitated, and then walked purposefully forward. They followed.

At the bathroom door she stopped. The acid scoring was everywhere.

"I don't know how I'm gonna get them stains out. You got any ideas, Lisa?"

"No, but I'm sure we'll find something. Maybe Judy can take Butch to the store and look for a detergent."

Judy took the hint. "C'mon, Butchie. I'll buy you an ice-cream cone when we get there."

Paige and Lisa entered the bedroom. Paige went to the closet. The first sliding door she opened revealed a rack of men's clothing. With a casual gesture, Paige pushed them over to one side. There were women's clothes there, too. She had shared this closet with Mack, shared it the same as she had shared the bed, this apartment, and had planned to share the rest of her life.

She took down a dress with a wild floral pattern. Tossing it on the bed, she began stripping off the blouse and slacks she had borrowed from Lisa. Everything in the apartment had been impounded pending the outcome of the police investigation, including her clothes.

"I'll wash those things and return them to you," Paige said, pulling on the dress.

It appeared too small, and for a moment Lisa couldn't figure out why she would put on such a thing. When Paige began pinning back her hair, Lisa understood. The dress was a work outfit she would wear to clean up.

"I was gonna start in the bathroom," Paige said, "but won't be much I can do until Judy gets back with some cleaning stuff. Probably the easiest place to do would be the kitchen, then the living room. If you all stay I'll fix you the best fried-chicken dinner you ever ate."

Paige slipped a pair of open-heeled sandals on her feet. She was heading for the living room when Lisa stopped her.

"Are you sure you're up to this?"

There was a sadness in Paige's eyes, but there was also something else. A strength, or possibly more than that: a determination to go on regardless of the obstacles. It was something life had never required Lisa to possess. At least not yet. But it was something she could recognize and understand.

Paige's answer was simple. "I can handle it, Lisa."

Then she was on her way to the living room.

# CHAPTER 52

**JUNE 15, 1996**
**2:10 P.M.**

The lawyers, accountants and executives of the DeWitt Corporation were assembled in the penthouse office atop DeWitt Plaza. Chairs had been brought in to accommodate the coterie of assistants accompanying the three executives in the gleaming shoes and tailored suits. They sat in the deeply upholstered leather chairs in front of the desk. Everyone present looked properly contrite over the death of a man half of them had never seen and only a select few had ever met.

Seated behind Neil's desk was Margo DeWitt, casually smoking a cigarette. Seated to her right was Wayne Tolley.

The chief accountant for the DeWitt Corporation, a totally bald man wearing horn-rim glasses and a perpetually petulant expression, had just concluded his report on the financial status of the corporation. Margo was satisfied that her holdings were in excellent shape.

"Excuse me, Margo," Tolley leaned forward to whisper. "They're waiting for an answer."

She realized at that instant that the ex-governor was beginning to irritate her.

"I didn't hear the question." She noticed a smirk pass between two junior-level executives standing one row back in the pecking order from the big boys up front. She stared until they both reddened and dropped their eyes.

"They want to know if you plan to name a transition team?"

"Why would I want to name a transition team? They've been doing a competent job. I'm satisfied with the profit index. I do plan to take a closer look at the day-to-day running of the corporation; however, for now things may go on as they've been."

"If there's nothing else, maybe we should let the boys get back to work?"

Margo studied the faces in front of her carefully. Almost exclusively white males. Mostly Anglo-Saxons. The one there in the third row at the far end near the topographical globe could have been Hispanic, but the more she studied him the more she doubted this. The closest his ancestry had come to having Hispanic blood would have been via Spain at the time of Cortez.

There was an Oriental. In fact two, but the second had some Caucasian blood in him. They were both junior-level executives. Probably accountants. No blacks or women. She didn't think they allowed things like this to happen anymore. It was supposed to be un-American.

"Yes, Wayne," Margo said with the acid tone she reserved for her supreme displeasure. "We'd better let the *boys* get back to work so they can keep making all those dollars to keep me happy and ignorant up here in this jaded tower!"

*That puckered an anus or two!* Even Tolley looked distressed. Before the former governor could jump in with something else stupid, Margo snapped, "Do we have an affirmative-action plan for the company?"

Surprised, Tolley looked over at the company's executive vice-president. Margo knew the distinguished gentleman was named Seymour Winbush. He looked like a silver-haired Ronald Reagan, minus the wrinkles. He had attended her and Neil's wedding. Thirty-five years with the company. Harvard graduate. He and Neil always bet on Harvard-Princeton football games.

Winbush shook his head in the negative.

Margo kept her eyes on the DeWitt Corporation vice-president as she asked, "Do we have a minority apprenticeship program? A woman's issue committee? A minority executive development program?"

To each of these questions Winbush's leonine head of immaculately combed and barbered hair rotated from side to side in a negative.

Margo understood. Seymour Winbush was paid over a million dollars a year and had extensive stock holdings in the DeWitt Corporation. She could fire him, but then he probably had a contract that would cost her a pretty penny to buy him out of. Winbush didn't realize that Margo was very innovative when it came to breaking contracts, whether they were with a spouse or an employee.

She spoke directly to the executive vice-president. "Then I suggest that someone look into initiating each of the programs I've just mentioned and have a feasibility study on this desk"—she tapped the area next to her ashtray—"no later than noon tomorrow!"

Winbush, along with the rest of his front-row colleagues, looked to the ex-governor for help. Hurriedly, Tolley began whispering intercessions on their behalf. He managed to gain them a week to complete the feasibility study.

Margo had taken over the reins of the DeWitt Corporation with a flourish. Now, for the remainder of the day, she had a more interesting task to occupy her time.

# CHAPTER 53

**JUNE 15, 1996**
**2:20 P.M.**

Cole and Blackie found Soupy McGuire in the morgue. At the door to the lab the two policemen stopped. A red sign on a white background above the door flashed: AUTOPSY IN PROGRESS—ENTRY FORBIDDEN.

Through the glass in the upper door they could see a masked and gowned Soupy performing an autopsy on the body of a young black male. Cole estimated the age as between eight and twelve. The M.E. was being assisted by a young female. Both pathologists were so intent on their work that they were unaware of the two policemen outside.

The boy on the table looked simply asleep to Cole. He had seen his son sleep in exactly this same position many times. Cole resolved to make more time for Butch. To do things with him. Before . . . *Before what*? Cole refused to dwell on the thought.

Inside, Soupy was handed a scapel. Using it, he made an incision under the rib cage and began a precise cut from the boy's solar plexus to the navel. Blackie coughed and turned away. Cole hesitated a moment longer before joining him. They stood over against the far wall where they couldn't see what was going on inside the autopsy room. Ten minutes later Soupy came out.

He was pulling off his cap and mask when he saw them. His gloves were stained with blood. There was more blood on his gown and apron, along with lumps of a milky, viscous substance.

"You guys got here pretty quick," Soupy said. "I thought it would be at least a day before I heard from you. Let's go upstairs. I've got something very interesting to tell you."

In his office Soupy dumped his stained work outfit in a laundry bag and went into the washroom to wash his hands. Cole and Blackie took seats on the other side of his desk.

"You asked me to reautopsy those two cases we got in last week, Shafiq and Vukhovich," Soupy said, sitting down behind the desk. "Well, I did and I came up with zilch. A big zero. Exactly nothing."

Blackie frowned. "Is that why you had us come all the way over here, Soup? Just to tell us you came up empty?"

"Keep your shirt on, Blackie," the M.E. said. "I wouldn't get you guys away from doing important police-type stuff without a good reason. I got something for you."

He got up and went to a refrigerator in the corner. "Can I offer you a soda or maybe some ice cream?"

"What kind of soda?" Cole asked.

"Strawberry."

The stains on Soupy's apron sprang back into their minds.

"No thanks," they said in tandem.

"Suit yourself." He removed an individual-serving ice-cream container and a plastic spoon from the refrigerator and returned to his seat.

They noticed that the ice cream's flavor was Raspberry Surprise.

"Okay, so you guys got me to thinking about—what was that you called it, Larry, 'undetectable poisons'?"

Cole nodded watching McGuire spooning red and white ice cream into his mouth.

"But there are no such things as 'undetectable poisons.' If it's foreign to the human body then we should be able to find it."

"But you said you didn't find anything in Shafiq or Vukhovich."

A dab of Raspberry Surprise had gotten on the corner of Soupy's mouth. Both cops found it hard to take their eyes away from it.

"So what are you saying?" Cole said tightly. He wished Soupy would wipe the damn ice cream off his mouth.

On cue the M.E. ran the back of his hand across his mouth. The ice-cream stain vanished.

"When I heard that this millionaire Neil DeWitt could have possibly been involved in the case you were investigating, I took a real close look at him when he was brought in."

Soupy handed Cole a folder that bore the typed label "Neil DeWitt—Deceased—Gunshot." As Cole opened it, Soupy continued.

"The cause of death was indeed by gunshot. A nice neat hole right here." Soupy touched an index finger to his forehead.

"We saw him," Blackie said.

"But he was full," Soupy said, "and I do mean full, of a little barbiturate called Dalmane."

"Dalmane?" Cole said.

"It's a powerful depressant. Relieves anxiety, insomnia, strictly prescription stuff."

"Can it kill and was there enough in him to kill him?" Blackie asked.

"That's hard to tell, but for once I decided to play Quincy. How many guys do you know go out with an Uzi and a bottle of chloroform to take on a cop and possibly kill a witness, and beforehand take enough barbiturates to sedate, or maybe even kill, a horse? Sounds to me like somebody slipped this guy a mickey before he started. The reaction was delayed because it was taken with food. Maybe whoever gave it to him didn't want him coming back."

Cole and Blackie glanced at each other and then at Soupy McGuire. "You know," Cole said, "if you ever get tired of slicing and dicing over here I can guarantee you a job as a detective."

Soupy grinned and went back to his ice cream.

# CHAPTER 54

**JUNE 15, 1996**
**4:52 P.M.**

The *Lady Margo* was a seventy-five-foot cabin cruiser berthed at its own wharf a short distance from the DeWitt Corporation administration building on the Chicago lakefront. It could go to sea with a crew of six, including a chef, or be taken out by one experienced seaman. During the summer months Margo had been known to take it out at least once a week.

Margo drove her Jaguar XJ-9 toward the security gate, but was waved through without stopping by the guard. She parked next to the wharf and bounded aboard before the crew was aware of her presence.

A blond young man with a deep tan met Margo in the companionway as she was going down to her stateroom.

"Good afternoon, Mrs. DeWitt," he said, flashing a toothpaste-ad smile. "We didn't know you were coming aboard today. We're all sorry about . . ."

She brushed past. At the bottom she said, "How many others are on board?"

"The usual crew minus Jack. Mr. Winbush gave him the day off."

"Get everyone else off. I'm taking her out alone."

"Are you sure that's what you wanna do, ma'am," he said carefully. "I mean it's a nice day and all, but the wind's making the water kinda choppy."

Margo glared at him. He got the message.

Three minutes later she was powering up the *Lady Margo*'s engines and heading out onto the lake. She loved the water. As the Ken-doll crewman had said, it was quite choppy for such a clear, cloudless day. But she wasn't in a dinghy either.

She traveled south along the Chicago lakefront, skirting the smaller craft lying closer to the shoreline. A few waved or blew foghorns as she went by, but she returned no seaman's greeting.

The farther south she traveled, the fewer boats she encountered. She powered back and studied the packed beaches. The heat had brought the poor ghetto dwellers out in droves. Most of the beaches on the South Side were occupied almost exclusively by black people. This was what she expected.

She motored on slowly. South of the Sixty-third Street Beach, she saw what she had been looking for. Snatching a pair of binoculars from a footlocker, she studied the rocks lining the shore. Four boys, ages ten to fourteen, although the tall one could be big for his age. And he was the one she wanted.

Margo dashed belowdecks to the equipment locker. She stripped naked before donning an oxygen tank, mask and flippers. A sharp combat knife with a serrated edge went into a sheaf strapped around her right ankle; a skindiver's watch went on her left wrist. Back on deck she again checked the position of the swimming boys.

One of them, a smaller boy, was looking out at the *Lady Margo*. She swung her glasses to the tall one again. He was skinny and so very, very black. She could feel her breathing quicken, as her nipples hardened until they ached.

Moistening her lips, she tested her mouthpiece and lowered the mask. On the side of the boat away from shore, she dropped into the water.

The cold shocked her, but she soon got used to it. Using the *Lady Margo* as a reference point, she swam underwater toward the rocks.

The water was amazingly clear, and she could almost see the bottom some twenty feet below. She maintained a depth of about ten feet. She watched the bottom sloping upward, indicating that she was approaching shore. She studied the water ahead of her. For a long minute she could see nothing. Then there was movement off to her right. She studied it. Yes, it was them. They dived off the rocks into the water, stayed under briefly and swam back to shore. She paddled toward them.

Forty feet from the divers' spot she stopped and watched until she knew each of them individually. The tall one was wearing aqua-green trunks that were a size too big for him. Every time he hit the water he had to yank at the elastic waistband to keep them on. She watched him do this twice.

The boy, who went in right before the tall one, actually jumped with his knees tucked to his chest and his arms wrapped around his legs. He was lighter-skinned than the tall one and heavier, too. He was out of the water almost as fast as he got in. The one that followed the tall one was the smallest and also looked to be the youngest. His dives were shallow and he splashed around noisily, as if he had yet to overcome his fear of the water. Neither of them would be able to see her. Even if they did, what would they describe?

She tensed in anticipation of the tall one's next dive. When he hit the water, she sprang toward him.

# CHAPTER 55

**June 15, 1996**
**5:15 p.m.**

Larry Cole and Blackie Silvestri were seated in Chief Govich's office. Govich listened patiently to their story, concealing his skepticism.

"So to put it in a few words, Chief," Cole concluded, "everything points to Margo DeWitt."

Govich nodded. "I agree, Larry. At least theoretically. But what proof do you have?"

"Neil DeWitt didn't intentionally fill himself full of this barbiturate Dalmane before going out to kill a cop and kidnap or kill a witness, boss," Cole argued. "It wouldn't make sense."

Govich spread his palms on the desk. "Okay, let me play devil's advocate on this for you. Kind of like Anne Johnson versus Perry Mason."

"I'd love to see that, Chief," Blackie said.

"They say you like car wrecks too, Silvestri. So, here we go. Larry, how do you know DeWitt didn't overdose himself with Dalmane? Suppose he was scared, needed something to calm his nerves, and popped a couple of capsules?"

"Soupy McGuire said DeWitt had approximately six to eight capsules' worth inside him," Cole countered. "That's a lot of nervousness."

"But we get junkies overdosing in this town everyday," Govich pressed. "DeWitt wasn't wrapped right anyway. People like him are more likely to do something stupid."

Blackie cleared his throat. "Begging the chief's pardon, but wouldn't a guy going out to raise hell with an Uzi maybe snort a little coke or pop a few amphetamines instead of taking a depressant?"

"That's a good point, Blackie," Govich said, "but there's no way to prove it in a court of law."

"Then we've got Shafiq and Vukhovich," Cole said.

Govich shook his head. "Undetermined-cause deaths, and even if we could prove murder all the fingers would be pointing at your boy Neil DeWitt."

"Somehow I don't see him being in it alone," Cole said stubbornly. "Just didn't strike me as brainy enough."

"But he did Mack and Sheila McNulty," Govich said.

"Yeah," Cole admitted.

"And he did them alone."

"From all indications, he did them alone," Cole said.

"C'mon, Larry!" Govich's voice rose in more amusement than anger. "Do you think he took his wife with him while he went around casing broads to rape and murder?"

"But Margo DeWitt's bent too, Chief," Cole said.

Govich's face tightened. "That's the story you got from Garth about her being a suspect out in Colorado."

"Yes, sir. He's got some documentation on it he's putting together for me. It should tell us more."

Govich looked at Blackie. "Excuse us, Lieutenant. I want to talk to my deputy alone."

Blackie nodded and left the office quietly.

"What's with you and this Garth, Larry?" There was an edge in the chief's voice.

"He's part of the mystery writers' organization I mentioned. He and Barbara Zorin have the widest reading audience of anyone in the group. We've got it on good information that the DeWitts took an interest in a number of local MWA authors' books."

"You find that out when you pulled that phony bomb scare at DeWitt Plaza?"

"Sir?" Cole said innocently.

"Innovative to the point of genius, Larry. And clean. Wished I had thought of it myself."

Cole still wasn't about to confess.

"But you do know that Garth, Holman or whatever the hell his name is now, killed a cop a few years back?"

"He was acquitted of that, boss. There might have been some extenuating circumstances in his favor."

"Don't let anybody hear you say that, Cole!" Govich flared. "Too many good officers have died in the line of duty, while juries have dismissed their killers because of extenuating circumstances! Circumstances like it was too dark in the warehouse for the burglars to see the cop they shot, or the guy with the butcher knife was too drunk to recognize the cop he stabbed in the chest, or the gang of thugs didn't hear the detective shout 'cop' before they beat him unrecognizable with baseball bats. So don't tell me about any goddamned extenuating circumstances."

Cole remained stock still. He had no retort for Govich. He didn't know if one existed.

"I'll limit Mr. Garth's involvement in my investigation, Chief," Cole said quietly. "Now, if there's nothing else . . ."

Govich's anger ebbed away. "What are you going to do next?"

"I don't really know, boss. Maybe have another meeting with the mystery writers. They're pretty inventive people. I might get a few ideas from them."

"I thought we were the ones supposed to be giving them ideas?"

"What is that old saying? 'Turnabout is fair play'?"

"Then you're still going after Margo DeWitt?"

Cole nodded.

"It was all over the financial pages this morning, Larry. She's taking over the DeWitt Corporation. That makes her a billionaire."

"Steven Zalkin was rich too."

"Compared to Margo DeWitt, Zalkin was on welfare."

Govich's intercom buzzed. He picked it up.

"Yes, Superintendent," he said. Govich grabbed a pen and memo pad. He began scribbling information rapidly on it.

"Right away, Superintendent. Yes, ma'am. We're on the way. We'll meet you there."

When he hung up, Govich looked across at Cole. "We got another dead black kid. Apparently drowned on the South Side while swimming in a restricted area. But this one's going to be a problem."

Cole waited.

"There were three kids swimming with the drowned boy. They're saying a shark got him. A big shark."

"Sharks don't swim in fresh water," Cole said. "At least not the kind with gills."

# CHAPTER 56

**JUNE 15, 1996**
**5:45 P.M.**

Las Vegas was just too fast a town for me, Judy," Paige said. "I wanted to go back to Dallas, but the people I worked for decided on Chicago."

"Suppose you had just said no and gone back to Dallas on your own?"

"I was in Tuxedo Tony DeLisa's organization. I even saw him once at a Vegas party for some high rollers. I thought he was an undertaker, the way he dressed in all that black. It was even kind of funny, but nobody laughed at him. And you could say there were some really tough hombres down there. They ran things real tight, but with a smile. If I'd have gotten on the wrong side of them I'd have ended up in a grave out in the desert."

They were in Paige's living room. The television set was on, but turned low, providing background noise that none of them was paying any attention to. Lisa, with Butch asleep with his head in her lap, and Judy were seated on the sectional sofa. Paige was on the floor with her legs tucked beneath her.

"Larry told me DeLisa's organization pretty much fell apart after his death," Lisa said. "No one mobster seems to have enough muscle to pull it all together."

"There are still a lot of Mob-controlled rackets in this town, but a lot of stuff goes on without the Outfit having anything to do with it at all," Paige said.

"Could I ask you a question?" Judy asked, after casting a glance at Butch to make sure he was still asleep. "Did they ever hassle you about just walking out on them?"

"Sure they did. In fact, Mack had to do some serious talking to me before I would even consider it. Even then, I was so scared I just stopped going to work. It was about the time we rented this place. It took me a while, but I managed to stop looking over my shoulder."

"No one ever bothered you?" Lisa said.

"Not really. There were a couple of telephone calls, but Mack was working Organized Crime and knew a lot of the people I worked for. I guess he kind of went to them and made them see it would be best to just leave me alone." Paige hesitated a moment. Her memories made her shiver.

Lisa looked at her watch. "We'd better get on the road, Judy. I'm going to have a hungry husband home soon and I haven't a clue what I'm going to fix him for dinner."

Lisa sat her son upright on the couch. He moaned sleepily, "You gonna come back home with us, Paige?"

"Not tonight, honey," she said, reaching over and kissing him on the forehead. "But you've got to come back and visit me real soon. Okay?"

"Yeah, I will." He rubbed his eyes.

"Let me take him to the washroom before we hit the road," Lisa said, pulling the little boy behind her down the hall.

"I'm sorry I couldn't get anything to remove those stains

in the bathroom," Judy said. "You might want to consider retiling."

"Good idea," Paige said. "You got a minute?"

As Judy nodded, Paige sprang to her feet and headed for the rear of the apartment. Judy followed.

In the bedroom Paige fingered the open padlock on the drawer where Mack's guns had been secured. She pulled the drawer out. It was empty except for a sheaf of green foolscap pages.

"What in the hell did they do with them? Mack had an arsenal in here."

Judy reached down and removed the green sheets. "They inventoried the guns, Paige. It's standard procedure in cases . . . like . . . this." Her voice trailed off.

"When can I get them back?"

Lisa came out of the bathroom with Butch. "What's wrong?"

Judy explained.

"I'm sure Larry can help you get them back," Lisa said.

"After a bunch of red tape," Paige said.

"We can always get someone to stay with you tonight or at least until . . ." Lisa began.

"No, thanks. I've been a burden long enough. I'll be okay. I just thought they would have left the ones that weren't used."

Lisa and Judy exchanged glances. They could see that Paige was terrified.

At the car Judy stopped. "Mrs. Cole, you got to clear this with the boss for me later."

"Clear what?"

"Leaving my piece with Paige. I got another at home."

"Don't worry," Lisa said. "He'll give it to you in writing if you need it."

Back upstairs Paige opened the door. Judy shoved a 9mm Beretta at her, butt first. "Eighteen rounds in the clip, one in the chamber. It's equipped with night sights. Flip the safety off and you're ready to rock and roll."

"Mack had one just like it," Paige said. "But I couldn't . . ."

Judy was already on her way back down the stairs. "Have a nice night, Paige, and remember, keep the safety on unless you plan to shoot someone."

"Yes, ma'am," Paige said, waving. "I certainly will."

# CHAPTER 57

**JUNE 15, 1996**
**DUSK**

Raoul "Rocket" Ramirez and Jaime "Scarface" Blanco were members of the Latin Lords street gang. Rocket, eighteen, and Scarface, sixteen, both had lengthy police records as gangbangers on the west side of the city. Rocket had been shot twice and stabbed or slashed five times. Scarface's name was derived from the razor cut running from his forehead to his chin inflicted by a member of a rival street gang when he was fourteen.

On this summer evening, Rocket and Scarface had wandered far from their usual stomping grounds, because the Gang Crimes Unit of the Police Department was rounding up all the Lords in connection with a gang execution. Rocket and Scarface had been responsible. Now, having shed their gang colors, they were down on the lakefront.

So far the day had been uneventful for them. They hadn't even been hassled by a cop. Scarface had recommended sleeping on the beach. Rocket was considering doing just that as dusk descended. As they had no money, this was the only option available. Going back to the neighborhood was too risky.

Then they spied the old DeWitt Corporation security guard.

"Jaime!" Rocket said, stopping his friend across the street from the shack where the guard's post was located. "Look what we got here, bro."

The guard's head was propped up against the glass wall of the telephone-booth-sized security shack. He was sound asleep.

"What the fuck's he guardin'?" Scarface questioned.

"Just that old dock. Don't make no sense."

"But he's got a piece. Maybe a three-fifty-seven!"

"Split!" Rocket gave the order and the two boys separated as if they'd rehearsed it.

They circled toward the booth in the rapidly falling darkness. The shack stood outside the twelve-foot-high fence protecting the private DeWitt wharf from the street. They reached it at the same time.

The guard came awake with a start, but it was too late. He screamed, but there was no one to hear him. Rocket wielded a six-inch-blade folding knife honed to razor sharpness; Scarface used his fists and feet. The guard would have died from the stabbing and beating if his heart had not given out first.

"He's dead, bro!" Rocket said, pulling Scarface from the narrow shack. "You keep stomping him you gonna hurt yourself."

Scarface was indeed in a frenzy. His eyes were wild, and his entire body trembled violently. Outside the booth he had to take long, deep breaths to bring himself under control.

As his nickname signified, Rocket was back inside the booth so fast he seemed propelled. He removed the gun from the guard's holster. He frowned. It was a standard Police Positive .38. It was also rusty and empty.

"This motherfucker ain't got no bullets on him, Jaime! Who the fuck is he anyway? Barney Fife?"

Scarface was still caught in the grip of his mania and incapable of seeing the humor in his companion's statement.

Rocket went through the guard's pockets. The wallet, covered with blood, contained a twenty, a five and three singles. With his back to Scarface, Rocket balled the twenty up in his palm.

"All he's got on him is eight lousy bucks, man!" Rocket raised the remaining money for Scarface to see.

The killer outside the booth frowned. He had seen Rocket hide something in his hand. He was about to challenge him on it when the lights of a large boat coming in from the lake illuminated the wharf.

They turned.

"Let's split, man!" Scarface hissed.

"Wait a minute!" Rocket pulled his accomplice into the shadows of the narrow security shack. It was crowded with the dead guard in there with them, but they made it.

"What are we gonna do?"

"There's a fancy ride parked down there," Rocket said. "Only one car. Maybe it's some dude out on the lake with a broad. Just the two of them. Be a cinch for us to take them. What do you think a guy like that'll have on him?"

"A bunch of worthless credit cards," Scarface said.

"Maybe. But he could also have a Rolex or some gold rings and chains. Then there's the woman."

"Yeah!" There was excitement in Scarface's voice.

"Think you can make it over to that car without being seen?"

"Easy, bro. Where you gonna be?"

"Right behind you."

Margo was dazed with pleasure. It had been wonderful. She had grabbed the black boy and pulled him down with her. He fought mightily, but she held on. She was stronger than him, and fear, along with his frantic fight for life, weakened him quickly.

She had looked into his face, right into his eyes, and experienced that one great tremendous moment when the light of life went out inside him. The excitement that coursed through her at that instant doubled her up with its intensity. Some twenty feet below the water she screamed into her mouthpiece. The orgasm lasted but a second. It was never long. But then the intensity of the emotion made up for the brevity.

She managed to weakly swim away. She hardly made it back aboard the *Lady Margo*. She put her slacks and blouse back on and came up on deck. She towel-dried her hair, as she watched the frantic activity on shore.

A crowd was gathering. They were all running around and looking down into the water. A muscular man finally dived in. It was at this point that Margo started the engines and headed back north.

She took a long, slow cruise, savoring the wind and spray off the lake surface. As darkness approached she headed back north.

She was still dwelling on the ecstasy of the death she had caused as she pulled into the wharf. It was then that she saw the dark figure dart behind her Jaguar.

Curious more than frightened, she studied the spot out of the corner of her eye. Yes, there was someone there. In fact, she was certain there were two of them. Oh, this just couldn't be!

She felt a giddiness go through her that made her insides quake and her knees tremble.

The *Lady Margo* bumped the wharf. She was supposed to tie her down, but that could wait. She left the bridge and descended to her cabin. She wondered whether they were bold enough to come aboard after her.

She considered waiting to see, but she had no patience. Opening the equipment locker, she removed a Glock automatic pistol and checked to make sure it was fully loaded. Taking off her canvas shoes, she slipped into a pair of high heels. They made her feel more regal.

Then she headed for the deck.

"The bitch alone, man!" Rocket whispered in the dark. "We gonna have a ball with her!"

Scarface's breathing was so excited it had an asthmatic wheeze. "Here she comes!"

"Wait now, *hermano*, just wait," Rocket urged, but it was too late.

Margo's feet had barely touched the wooden planks of the wharf when Scarface leaped from behind the car to confront her. He expected to see stark fear in her eyes. What he saw confused him before terror set in. He turned to look at his *compadre* in crime for support, but it was too late. Raising the automatic, Margo shot Scarface through the neck. At such close range the bullet's force nearly decapitated him.

Shocked by the sound and splattered with Scarface's blood, Rocket screamed. He dropped the empty pistol and ran for the gate. He could hear the staccato clicking of the woman's heels on the asphalt surface of the parking lot as she followed him.

Rocket almost made it to the gate when Margo shot him. He pitched forward headfirst into the fence. There was a massive hole in his back. He was fading fast when she stepped up and knelt down beside him.

He stared at the thin-faced woman until the shroud of death dropped over him. The last thing Raoul "Rocket" Ramirez experienced in life was the woman kissing him on the mouth.

# CHAPTER 58

**JUNE 17, 1996**
**6:36 P.M.**

Butch was packing his Chicago Bears gym bag in preparation for spending the night with Paige at her apartment. In it he placed his replica of an F-15 fighter jet, toy police car with flashing lights and siren and his Superman, Batman and Flash toy figures. As an afterthought he packed his G.I. Joe machine pistol. He barely had room for the junk mom laid out for him. He managed to get in the clean pair of jeans, the shirt and underwear, but it didn't look like the pajamas, toothbrush and comb were going to make it. Leaving the discarded items on the bed, he managed to get the bag closed. Now he was ready.

"How do I look?" Lisa Cole said.

Turning from tying his tie in the bedroom mirror, Cole studied his wife.

She was wearing a beige and black dress and beige high-heel pumps. As usual, he thought her makeup and hair were flawless. "You look great, honey."

"But do I look literary enough? Writers and artists can be real bohemians at times."

"Bohemians?"

"You know, like hippies. Long hair, jeans, granny glasses. Maybe smoke a little pot."

"Not in front of me they won't!"

"You know what I mean," she said, checking the hem of her dress in the full-length mirror behind the door. "They'll be intellectually deep, talking in abstractions and expounding various theories concerning the origins of the universe and the true meaning of life."

Stepping up behind his wife, Cole placed his arms around her waist. "I think you have my mystery writers all wrong, Lisa. They're just as normal as you, me, Blackie or anybody else we know."

She frowned. "I never considered Blackie or Manny really normal. In fact, I think their boss is kind of strange too."

"Barbara Zorin, Martin Wiemler and Debbie Bass are just regular, down-to-earth people."

"What about Jamal Garth?"

Cole didn't answer.

"Larry?"

"Garth has had his problems. I only hope he doesn't end up causing me any."

There was a knock at the bedroom door followed by Butch pushing it open. He dragged his gym bag in behind him because it was too heavy to carry.

"What have you got in there?" Lisa asked.

"My stuff," Butch said innocently.

"All of it?" Cole said with a raised eyebrow.

They were driving Butch to Paige's apartment. Judy, who would also be spending the night, would meet them there.

"Do you think the writers have come up with anything you can use, Larry?" Lisa asked.

Cole managed a weak smile. "I don't know, but even if they could, what am I going to do with it now?"

"You still suspect her, don't you?"

Cole nodded. "I've handled a lot of crazy cases in my time, but this one takes the cake. I mean it's not really complicated or difficult to figure, it's just crazy.

"She did her old man with the barbiturates. She set him up to the point he would have been killed or caught no matter what he did. Fletcher just got to him before he could do any damage. Maybe with a little time and a couple of leads I could prove it, but then she goes out and blows away two of the worst gangbangers this city's ever seen. Gun's registered out of state and legal. We could charge her with some minor weapons-ordinance violation, but the press would crucify us. On top of that, the superintendent's going to present her with the Distinguished Award of Merit and the mayor's talking about making her Woman of the Year."

"So maybe it's time for you to throw in the towel on this one," Lisa said. "You'll still have the best track record in the department."

"I thought of that, honey. It would be easy. Govich wants it, the superintendent wants it, and maybe somewhere deep down inside I want it too. We got her old man and I guess that evens things for Mack. What else is there?"

"That's my line," she said.

"What do you mean?"

" 'What else is there?' Something's still bothering you about Margo DeWitt. What is it?"

Cole twisted around to look at his son. Butch's head was in a comic book.

"You know that thing Alderman Edwards has been making all the noise about?"

Lisa also checked their son before answering. "The little boys?" She kept her voice at whisper level.

Cole nodded. "The alderman's such an idiot it's hard to take anything he says seriously, but for once he might be on to something."

"The accidents?"

"There's nothing to indicate they were anything else but accidents. At least medically speaking, and we've got Soupy McGuire and his people going through every one of them as thoroughly as is humanly possible. But then there are other things."

"Such as."

"Kids falling down stairs or off high places and breaking their necks with no accompanying injuries, sometimes not even bruises. A couple ran into hanging clotheslines and ended up choking to death. But by rights even if they did panic, they should have been able to extricate themselves before they died. Another fell out of a tree, got caught in a lower branch, again by the neck, and hanged himself. No bruises, not even a scratch. And then there was the last one."

Lisa checked Butch again. He had dozed off with the comic book open on his lap.

"The one supposedly attacked by a shark?" she said.

"Yeah, but there are no sharks in Lake Michigan. I'm surprised with all the pollution that we even have any fish left.

"From all indications he dived in the water, maybe caught a bad cramp, couldn't make it back to the surface and drowned."

"But you don't buy that?"

"I talked to one of the kids who was there. Little tyke only seven years old named Petey. Lives over in the Robert Taylor Homes with his mother, six brothers and four sisters. Father long gone. But little Petey's not your average ghetto kid, Lisa. He's sharp. Very observant."

"Was he the one who gave you the story about the shark?"

"No. He didn't see any more of the drowned boy after he dived in the water and didn't come up. He did see a big, white boat that stopped about two hundred yards from where they were swimming right before the kid drowned. He also saw, now get this, a woman studying them through binoculars before it happened. He didn't remember seeing the boat leave because of all the excitement."

"I don't get it," Lisa said.

"When Margo DeWitt played vigilante on those two punks she claims attacked her she had just come in from the lake. Her boat is a seventy-five-foot cabin cruiser named the *Lady Margo*. She was out on it alone."

"But why would she do such a thing, Larry?" Lisa asked revealing the horror she felt.

"I don't know, but unless I get a break soon this case is going to be closed along with all the other strange deaths.

Then Margo DeWitt can sit comfortably in her penthouse and thumb her nose at the world."

Lisa turned to look at their son asleep in the backseat. When she turned back to her husband she said, "You can't let that happen, Larry."

"One thing's for sure," Cole said. "I'm going to give it my best shot."

The elderly woman stood in front of the apartment building where Paige lived. She walked with a cane and had a back bowed by age into a curl. Her hair was completely gray, the flesh of her face slack and her hands liver-spotted. She watched the Coles' car pull to the curb.

"I'll take him in, honey," Cole said, getting out of the car.

"Isn't Judy supposed to be here to meet us?"

"She might already be upstairs," Cole said, opening the back door and gently shaking Butch.

His eyes opened and he looked around with a squint of confusion. Finally, he realized where he was. He came around much faster.

"Excuse me, sir," the old woman on the curb said. "Could you help me?"

"Yes, ma'am," Cole said turning to face her.

"I called a taxi an hour ago. They were supposed to pick me up right here, but they haven't showed. I'm late for tea with my cousin Emma Mae and my bad hip's paining me something furious. And I'm so tired."

The woman sniffled noisily before beginning to cry. She removed a dainty lace kerchief from her pocket and dabbed at her eyes.

The usually unflappable deputy chief of detectives looked uncomfortable. He turned to Lisa for help. She looked as distressed as he was. Butch got out of the car, stepped around his father and walked over to the old lady. He studied her for a moment. She ignored him.

He turned to his father. "It's okay, Dad. Judy doesn't have a cousin named Emma Mae."

"Darn!" the old woman said in a much younger voice. "You got me again!"

"I don't believe it," Cole said with genuine awe.

Lisa was speechless.

"It took me hours to put this makeup on. I've been practicing the voice and gestures for weeks," Judy moaned. "How do you do it, Butch? What's your secret? Somehow I must be tipping you off."

"I don't know," Butch said, shrugging. "I just knew it was you. I always do."

"Someday, Butchie," Judy said before turning back to her boss. "At least I can still fool some people."

Cole cleared his throat. "We'll call to see how things are going when we get home, Judy. Uh, you all have a nice time with Paige. Be good, Butch." With that he trotted around to the driver's side of the car and got in.

Butch and Judy waved as the car pulled away.

A block away, a Chevy Blazer was parked in the shadow of a huge tree. In the front seat a woman had watched the entire scene in front of the apartment building. Now she lowered her binoculars and pressed the dash lighter. As she inhaled to get the cigarette going her features were illuminated.

Exhaling smoke, Margo DeWitt marveled at the strange transformation the old woman had made. "Now that was interesting," she said to herself. "Very interesting."

# CHAPTER 59

**June 17, 1996**
**7:16 P.M.**

Barbara Zorin lived in a tenth-floor condominium overlooking Lake Michigan. Her building was approximately half a mile from DeWitt Plaza, where she often shopped and had once even had a book signing at Benedict's Book Emporium on the seventh level.

Present when the Coles arrived were Jamal Garth, Debbie Bass, Martin Wiemler and their hostess. To Lisa's surprise, the table the writer set consisted of carry-out pizza, a relish tray, beer and lemonade. For dessert they had fudge-nut brownies. Lisa had expected unprocessed yogurt and raw vegetables.

Martin Wiemler was the biggest eater. Of the three extra-large pizzas brought from the kitchen by Barbara, he consumed most of one by himself. Larry and Garth did substantial damage to most of a second, while Lisa, Debbie and Barbara managed to eat enough of what remained to leave very few leftovers.

Dinner-table talk was not about either the meaning of life or the origins of the universe, as Lisa had expected. Debbie and Marty, which Lisa found Wiemler was called for short, were Chicago Cubs fans. Their views on the chances of the North Side club winning the National League East pennant were met with good-natured opposition by Garth and Cole, who were diehard White Sox fans.

"You know I've never been able to understand how people can get so emotional about a simple game like baseball," Barbara said to Lisa.

"Yes," Lisa replied, feeling that she had discovered a writer who would take her to the heights of esoterica she'd been anticipating. "I agree with you. There are so many more important things in life."

"I know you were different the moment we met," Barbara said with a smile. "So what do you think of the Bears going back to the Superbowl this season? I think they'd better do something about their offense."

"Definitely" was all Lisa managed to say before catching her husband's eye.

He was smiling broadly. He gave her a wink, which she ignored.

After they cleared the table, Barbara led her guests into the living room. They got down to cases.

"We've had some lengthy discussions about what the DeWitts have been doing with our work, Larry," Barbara began. "And the one thing all of us agree on is that it makes us very angry."

Marty struggled forward to sit on the edge of the couch. His angry posture belied the pizza-filled gut hanging down in front of him. "I spent fifteen years on the road as a salesman. I learned to write taking home-study courses and reading every mystery and suspense novel I could get my hands on. Started to quit a million times, but somehow I stuck with it. Now fortune has shined on me, but everything I wrote was original. Every word and idea came out of my own head. To have someone use it like this is criminal."

Debbie Bass broke in. "It's more than just criminal. It's a sin. Maybe we're not Hemingways, Faulkners or Dreisers, but what we write is our own. It's between us and our readers. Not for someone to copy for their own evil intentions."

Finally, Jamal Garth spoke. "Perhaps the worst part of it all is that they've used our writings to actually commit crimes. That defiles not only the work, but each of us who spent the time to produce it."

Cole listened patiently. When Garth finished, he said, "I

think that what has happened was terrible. But it is also over. Neil DeWitt's dead. I don't think you'll be bothered by this type of thing again."

Barbara and Garth exchanged looks. "I'm afraid you've got that wrong, Larry," she said.

"Yes," Garth added. "From what I've been hearing on the news you've got a bigger problem now than you did before."

"I don't understand what you mean," Cole said. "There've been no more copycat killings taken from your books."

"Not from ours," Barbara said. "But from Harry McGhee's."

"Harry McGhee?" Cole said.

"He's probably the most famous mystery and horror writer the Chicago area has ever produced," Lisa said. "I remember reading his books when I was in high school."

Garth took over. "Harry McGhee did write both horror and suspense fiction, Lisa. On occasion he would even mix the genres, which some critics claim is a no-no."

Debbie snorted. "Not to play too heavily on words, what do they know?" One of her detectives was a practicing witch who occasionally used her craft to extricate herself from dangerous situations in books.

"Anyway," Garth continued. "In a nineteen-seventy-two book called *Bless the Children*, old Harry had a villain who was a shape-shifter."

"Is that like a werewolf?" Cole asked.

"It can be," Barbara explained. "But Harry didn't give it a label like werewolf or vampire. It was just something evil that fed off the killing of children."

"I remember it now," Lisa said. "It needed the fear generated by the violent death of its victims to live. It possessed a female personality; I think they called her Magda. It preyed on young female victims aged seven to twelve. The story was set back in the East."

"Turn-of-the-century Boston," Garth said. "Magda would also kill anyone who got in her way. She could become invisible, fly through the air or swim great distances underwater. The only thing she feared was fire. That's how they finally disposed of her."

"Tell him the rest of it, Jamal," Wiemler said from where he had collapsed back on the couch with a sleepy expression on his face.

"Harry McGhee shrouded Magda's origins in myth, but she was supposedly the incarnation of an evil Indian goddess uncovered by a group of hunters. After killing a bunch of them in their Rocky Mountain camp, she was captured and brought east by a wealthy Bostonian. He fell in love with her and they were married. Eventually she killed him."

Garth unsnapped a briefcase sitting on the floor beside his chair. From it he removed a thick, well-thumbed paperback book and a folder. The title of the paperback was *Bless the Children*; the folder contained recent newspaper clippings.

Garth held the folder and book on his lap and continued. "You will find very close parallels between the deaths caused by Harry McGhee's creature and the newspaper accounts of the so-called accidents suffered by children here in Chicago. Fatal falls, accidental strangulations, hangings under odd circumstances and mysterious drownings. These"—Garth patted the folder—"follow the same sequence as the book."

Cole and Lisa were listening very closely now.

"Tell him all of it," Barbara said quietly.

Garth hesitated a moment before charging ahead. "We know for a fact that Margo DeWitt, when she was Margo Rapier, owned an autographed copy of Harry McGhee's book."

"You can prove that?" Cole asked.

Garth handed him the paperback. Cole opened it to the title page. The ink was still quite visible on the yellowing paper: "To Miss Margo Rapier, a real horror fan, Harry McGhee—Denver—January 28, 1973."

"Where did you get this?" Cole said.

"In a used-book store in Denver. Came across it quite by accident. I've been out in Colorado researching Mrs. De-

Witt's past for the last few days," Garth said. "I found out quite a bit about her and her family. I also discovered a few interesting facts about her dead husband."

"You didn't have to do that," Cole said.

"I know."

"Tell him the rest," Barbara insisted.

Garth was obviously uncomfortable now. "Harry's creature was finally destroyed in the book, but before she died she had one final victim."

They all waited.

"The detective who was pursuing Magda had a son. The evil entity dismembered the little boy."

"Oh, my God, no!" Lisa screamed.

# CHAPTER 60

**JUNE 17, 1996**
**8:45 P.M.**

Butch, Paige and Judy were watching a videotape of the 1994 movie production of *Frankenstein*. Although billed by the promoters as a "beauty and the beast" love story, this movie had a number of horrible scenes in it. More than once Paige and Judy found their eyes bulging as the monster performed one terrible deed after another. Butch laughed at such scenes. After a particularly terrifying shot Butch had giggled, Paige hit the Pause button.

"Butch, how can you laugh at something like that?"

"Because it's so phony," the little boy explained. "The roadrunner does worse things to the coyote in the cartoons and everybody laughs."

"But this is supposed to be real," Judy said. "Not a cartoon."

Butch looked curiously at Judy. "It's not real. Dad told me so. That policeman's just an actor. The monster's a man wearing a lot of makeup. There's no such thing as Frankenstein or people being brought back to life by lightning."

Paige and Judy exchanged looks. He had them.

"What about some more popcorn?" Paige said, getting to her feet and picking up the empty bowl.

"Okay," Butch said. "And could I have another soda?"

"Sure you can."

As Paige headed for the kitchen, Judy got up, too. "If you don't mind, I'll go with Paige. I've had enough of this crazy movie."

"No problem," he said, without taking his eyes from the screen. "It's almost over, anyway."

"You've seen it before?" Judy asked.

"Dad rented it a couple of weeks ago. That's when he told me about the actors."

"Figures," Judy said. "We'll be back in a minute."

When they were securely out of earshot in the kitchen, Judy said, "He's something else, isn't he?"

"The smartest little boy I've ever seen," Paige said, taking a jar of popcorn down from a shelf. "But unlike a lot of smart kids, he's not a smart-ass or snotty."

Judy laughed. "He wouldn't have survived this long if he was. You don't know the Coles."

The phone rang. Paige answered it.

"Hi, Lisa," she said. "You all must have got home early."

She listened for a moment. "Sure. He's right here. Hold on. Butch!"

The little boy came into the kitchen. "It's your momma. She wants to talk to you."

He took the phone. "Hello, Mom. Yes, I'm okay. Judy's right here. Watchin' *Frankenstein*. But I like it! I love you too. Hold on a minute."

He held the phone for Judy. "She wants to talk to you."

"Yes, ma'am," Judy said. "No. I'll be here. Definitely. My gun's like my American Express Card, I never leave home without it. Paige has still got my Beretta, so we're armed to the teeth. No, we weren't going anywhere. Paige rented enough videos to last a week. Okay, if you want, but I'm sure we'll be okay. Talk to you later."

Judy hung up the phone and looked at Paige. "Now, what was all that about?"

"I don't know," Paige said. "But she sounded worried."

"Could I go back and finish the movie?" Butch asked.

"Sure, honey," Paige said. "We'll be in as soon as we finish the popcorn."

After he left, Judy said, "They're still at the lady mystery writer's place. Lisa said she would call us again when she got home."

A tight expression spread across Paige's face. "You don't think she's having second thoughts about leaving him here with me?"

"Of course not!" Judy said. "Hell, she let him sleep in the same bed with you. She's not worried about you."

"Then what was wrong with her?" Paige said, turning back to the popcorn. "She sounded scared and upset."

"I noticed that too. But she wasn't that way when they left here. Something must have happened at the mystery writers' meeting."

"Like what?"

Judy shrugged. "Maybe one of them told her a scary story. You know writers can be strange at times."

Relief was just beginning to show on Paige's face when something struck the outside of her back door. The dull thump had enough force to shake the frame. Judy and Paige froze.

# CHAPTER 61

**JUNE 17, 1996**
**8:55 P.M.**

Lisa hung up the telephone in Barbara Zorin's study. She felt very silly. Of course Butch was okay. Judy and Paige wouldn't let anything happen to him. But she intended to call again when she got home anyway.

Back in the living room she found that everyone was silent. All of the writers were looking at her husband. Lisa detected an air of anticipation about them.

She sat down beside Larry. He turned to look at her with a lopsided grin on his face, a grin she knew well.

Her husband was not an indecisive man. In fact, she'd never met anyone capable of making decisions, and correct ones, as fast as he did. But occasionally even he found it hard to decide on an immediate course of action. Lisa was glad of this. It made him more human. Without this shortcoming he might have been just a bit too perfect for her or anyone else.

"What is it?" she asked.

The grin remained in place. "Our friends have just come up with a way to trap Margo DeWitt. It's based on Harry McGhee's book."

Lisa remembered. "Wasn't there a group of college professors or some such who got onto McGhee's Magda character in the book?"

"Historians," Garth said. "Three from Harvard; one from Oxford in England. Two males; two females." Garth looked around the circle of writers: Barbara Zorin, Debbie Bass, Marty Wiemler and himself. The same number.

Lisa caught on all too quickly. "They used themselves as bait for Magda. She came after them. She killed them all. Oh, no, Larry, you can't let them do this."

"I haven't said I was going to, Lisa."

"But you are thinking about it?" Barbara said eagerly.

"Seriously thinking?" Wiemler added.

"It'll make one helluva book if we can carry it off," Debbie Bass said. "Nonfiction, of course."

Garth said nothing.

Cole's smiled broadened. Lisa could see that they were winning him over. "Okay, tell me how you'd do this once more."

"Next weekend," Garth said, "we're having our annual Of Dark and Stormy Nights mystery-writing seminar at Northwestern University. We plan to extend a special invitation to Margo DeWitt to attend."

"You think she'll accept?" Cole said.

"She'll accept," Barbara Zorin said. "After she receives the invitation we send her there'll be no way she can refuse."

Lisa was confused. "Okay, suppose she does come to your seminar. What are you going to do then?"

"That's when the fun begins," Debbie said.

# CHAPTER 62

**JUNE 17, 1996**
**9:05 P.M.**

Probationary Police Officer Elizabeth Fletcher was patrolling the north end of the 24th District when the dispatcher's voice crackled over her walkie-talkie: "*Twenty-Four Twenty-Two*."

She acknowledged her call numbers.

"*Stand by for a simulcast, Twenty-Two.*"

She gripped the steering wheel tightly. Another in-progress call! On top of that it was going to be her job! "C'mon, let's go!" she said.

On cue the dispatcher announced: "*Twenty-Four Twenty-Two and units on the citywide, we have a police officer calling for assistance at Two-three-one-six West Lunt in Apartment Two-seven. The caller identified herself as Detective Judy Daniels of Detective Division Administration. That's your paper, Twenty-Two.*"

"Ten ninety-nine," Fletcher acknowledged as she flipped on her Mars lights and siren. She was seven blocks from the Lunt address. She went all the way with emergency equipment going. She skidded to a stop in front of the apartment building and bounded out while the squad car was still rocking to a stop. Flashlight in one hand and service revolver in the other, she ran for the courtyard. Two more units, which she didn't stop to identify, stopped behind her car.

She flanked the door to Apartment 27 and waited for one of her backups, a heavyset cop named Stepaniak. When he was in place she knocked heavily on the door. "Police! Open up!"

Judy Daniels's voice came from inside. "I'm the detective who called! Get somebody around to the back! There was a prowler out there a minute ago!"

Liz looked at Stepaniak. He nodded, slipped away from the door and used his walkie-talkie to order responding units to the rear of the building. Before he could return the door opened.

Judy had her detective star with the black enamel border out for Fletcher and Stepaniak to see. She ushered them into the living room. All the lights were on. Paige Albritton and Butch Cole were huddled together on the couch. They both looked terrified.

"There was a loud noise at the back door a few minutes

ago," Judy explained. "We could hear someone out there, but I wasn't going to open up until I got some help here."

"Isn't she . . . ?" Stepaniak began, looking at Paige.

Fletcher cut him off. "I understand, Detective Daniels. That was the smart move. If you're ready to take a look, we'll go with you."

"Stay with them," Judy said to Stepaniak.

Judy and Fletcher approached the double-locked, bolted door. The detective had the inside key. Using it, she flipped the bolt off. Both women, Judy with a 9mm automatic and Fletcher with her .38, trained guns on the door.

Judy flung it open.

They both saw the dead cat lying outside on the porch. Its neck had obviously been broken before its head had been smashed into a bloody pulp. Blood was everywhere, even smeared on the door against which the animal's corpse had been thrown.

"A prank?" Fletcher asked tightly.

"Probably. But it's not funny. Not funny at all," Judy said.

# CHAPTER 63

**JUNE 19, 1996**
**6:45 A.M.**

Margo was in the library when her breakfast tray was delivered.

"Come," she said from her seat on the couch where she was reading a Debbie Bass hardcover.

The waiter rolled the food cart in. He was a middle-aged man dressed in a white shirt, black vest and red bow tie. He kept his eyes lowered and face expressionless as he unwrapped silverware and poured coffee and orange juice.

He left the lids on the serving trays. When he was finished, he asked, "Will that be all, Mrs. DeWitt?"

She didn't look up at him. "Yes. Thank you." There was never a tip.

He turned to leave.

"Just a minute."

The waiter stopped and turned around quickly. "Yes, ma'am."

"Why are there two place settings?"

"That's what they gave me to deliver, Mrs. DeWitt."

She leaped to her feet. Her white dressing gown streamed behind her as she stomped over to the cart. Snatching the lid off a tray, she studied the plate of lox, onions and scrambled eggs. She never ate such garbage; only her dead husband had.

She slammed the lid down with such force the metal against china impact echoed like a bell through the library.

Margo spied the menu she had made out the night before. She grabbed it preparatory to reading the correct order to the stupid waiter. She stopped suddenly. There it was, like always, in her own hastily scrawled script. Half a grapefruit, dry wheat toast, orange juice and coffee for her. The other meal was for Neil. She checked the date. It was correct. She had made this out yesterday.

"Will there be anything else, ma'am?" the waiter asked.

"No. You may go now."

As the waiter exited, she walked back to the couch still clutching the menu card. Finally, the reason behind this error dawned on her; simple force of habit. She had been making these menus out for the two of them, what . . . ? Six or seven years? So she'd written out the order for Neil subconsciously. No big deal. *Or was it?*

She refused to dwell on it further. She had more important things to do today.

Shortly after ten o'clock she called Wayne Tolley's law office.

*"Good morning, Margo. And how's my favorite client this morning?"*

She ignored the greeting. "Suppose I told you there was a strong possibility that Neil's death was part of a police conspiracy?"

*"Do you have proof of this?"*

"That's what I pay you for, Counselor." The mail had been delivered by the waiter when he retrieved the breakfast tray. There were condolence cards still coming in. A contemptuous smile crossed her features when she fingered the embossed envelope with the 1600 Pennsylvania Avenue, Washington, D.C., address on it.

*"But you said you were satisfied with the police investigation into the shooting."*

"Let's say something has happened to change my mind."

*"What?"*

"I'm not at liberty to say right now, but I think we should take a closer look at Deputy Chief Cole and his operation."

*"Do you want me to make a formal complaint against him to the Office of Professional Standards? I understand he was at the scene of the shooting."*

"No." There was a bloodred envelope with black writing in the mail. Her brows curled when she saw the return address was a post-office box listed to Mystery Writers of America—Midwest Chapter.

*"Margo, are you there?"*

"Yes. No, I don't want you to go to OPS. That would be playing right into Cole's hands. We need to approach this from a different angle." She used a jewel-handled letter opener to slit the envelope. There was a single sheet of matching red notepaper inside. "Have you maintained a relationship with that state's attorney, Anne Johnson, and her friend the cop?"

*"Oh, c'mon now, Margo! I'll be lucky if those people ever speak to me again."*

Margo extracted the paper from the envelope and spread it out on the surface of the desk.

"You sell yourself too cheaply, Wayne. I'm sure you can clear up any . . ."

Everything ceased to exist for Margo DeWitt except the words written on the red stationery.

*"Margo?"*

*His voice brought her back to reality. "Yes! What I was saying is that I'm sure you should be able to cultivate them again. If not, find someone else."*

*She reread the words with more fascination than shock.*

*A sigh of frustration escaped from Tolley's end of the line. "Maybe if you told me what you've got I could have some idea of where to start."*

"You want a place to start? Start with a detective who works on Cole's staff named Judy Daniels. I want to know everything you can find out about her."

*"Then what?"*

"Then, I'll tell you what I want you to do next. Goodbye, Wayne."

Shutting off the speakerphone, she read the words on the red page once more.

MYSTERY WRITERS OF AMERICA
MIDWEST CHAPTER
P. O. BOX 258
WINNETKA, ILLINOIS 62133

Mrs. Margo DeWitt June 17, 1996
One DeWitt Plaza
Chicago, Illinois 60611

Dear Mrs. DeWitt,

You are cordially invited to be our guest at a panel discussion concerning the work of Chicago author Harry McGhee. We will be taking a particularly close look at the 1972 mystery-horror novel *Bless the Children.* We will be attempting to compare Mr. McGhee's fiction with recent actual crimes occurring in the Chicago area.

Panelists will include well-known Midwest Region authors Debbie Bass, Jamal Garth, Martin Wiemler and Barbara Zorin. The panel will convene at 3:00 P.M. on Saturday, June 20th, 1996, in the Alpine Room of Norris Center on the campus of Northwestern University in Evanston, Illinois. This will be the closing activity of MWA's Midwest Chapter Of Dark And Stormy Nights annual mystery writing conference. If you wish to attend all activities that day registration will be at 8:00 A.M. There will be lectures, seminars and manuscript critiques throughout the day, which you may of course feel free to participate in as our guest. However, we are sure you won't want to miss the three o'clock panel discussion.

A cocktail party will follow the panel discussion in the Michigan Room of Norris Center. Hope to see you there.

Sincerelv Yours.

B. S. Zorin

Barbara Schurla Zorin
President

Margo stormed from the study. She stomped to the spiral staircase, climbed to the second level and went to the door to her private quarters, which she opened with a key.

The first room was a bedroom, an exact duplicate of Neil's across the hall.

A hallway led from the bedroom. A spacious, marble-lined bathroom with a sunken bathtub and gold fixtures was behind the first door. The next door also required a key to enter. She removed the key from her dressing-gown pocket. She never went anywhere without it in her possession. The door that the key unlocked revealed a storeroom. Books, papers, clothing and files were strewn around the place in a haphazard fashion.

Margo went to the item she had come in search of. It was a hand-bound book with gold-edged pages. Its binding was of thick, hand-crafted leather, and it came in its own protective sleeve. Margo handled this book like a precious, very exquisite object. Some people handled the passed-down-through-the-generations family Bible in this manner. In a way this was Margo's Bible.

She slid the book out of its covering. The gold lettering on the engraved cover gleamed up at her: *Bless the Children* by Harry McGhee.

The pages were marked in a number of places with smooth plastic strips. Each designated the conclusion of a murder scene. None had been disturbed since Margo last opened the book three days ago. That was when she had plotted the death of a child by drowning in the exact same way that Magda, Harry McGhee's fictional shape-shifter, had carried out the drowning death of a child in the book. Magda had not needed an oxygen tank to breathe underwater, but Margo DeWitt had known her limitations.

Satisfied that the book had not been disturbed, she was about to return it to its place among the debris when she remembered that she had owned another copy of *Bless the Children.* In fact, Harry McGhee himself had autographed it for her. But she had left it in Colorado.

# CHAPTER 64

**JUNE 18, 1996**
**12:15 P.M.**

Anne Johnson didn't eat lunch in restaurants. During the winter, and during periods of inclement weather, she would purchase a cellophane-wrapped sandwich from the automated cafeteria in the Criminal Courts Building. When the weather was mild, as it was on this mid-June day, she usually bought a sandwich from Vito's hot-dog stand, which parked in front of the building from noon until two. She would then walk over to the California Avenue parkway and consume the sandwich on a park bench or while seated in the grass. Wayne Tolley had enough connections left to glean this bit of intelligence about her.

Tolley was in the chauffeur-driven Cadillac limo placed at his disposal when he worked for Margo DeWitt. The limousine was parked a quarter-block from the building entrance. Clad in a charcoal gray pinstripe suit and black homburg hat, Tolley waited patiently in the rear of the air-conditioned car until he saw the state's attorney approach the rather unsanitary-looking sandwich wagon. A dark-complexioned, multi-tattooed man, who had "Vito" written all over him, piled a Polish sausage and condiments into a bun. Anne Johnson paid for the sandwich and a can of soda before heading for the park.

"I'll be back shortly," the former governor said to the chauffeur. Tolley donned a pair of sunglasses as he walked toward her.

The state's attorney sat down on a park bench and began

unwrapping her sandwich. She didn't see him until he was standing over her.

"Madam State's Attorney, what a coincidence."

Johnson had bitten off a mouthful of Polish sausage. When she saw him, she looked as if she was going to spit it out. Somehow she managed to chew and swallow.

"I've got nothing to say to you, Governor!"

"Why do you hold me in such disfavor? I didn't do anything wrong."

She looked ready to explode but managed to keep herself in check. "You know if that student and cabdriver had been reclassified from undetermined-cause deaths to homicides I would have gone after a murder-conspiracy indictment against you."

"Ms. Johnson, I assure you by all that is holy that I have no idea what happened to those two men or why."

"I'll tell you what happened to them, Tolley! Your client killed them! Killed them both! And I gave you the information that helped him do it!"

"That would make you an accessory, wouldn't it, Anne?"

"That's not funny!"

"I agree. So why don't we stop tossing accusations and indictment threats around and talk like two intelligent members of the Illinois Bar?" He sat down on the bench, but maintained a respectable distance from her.

She picked up her sandwich and began eating. "What do you want now?" she said between bites.

"To see justice done."

"Ha! Give me a break, will you? The only justice you serve comes with dollar signs attached."

"You've got me all wrong, Anne. If you give me a chance I'll prove it to you."

"I'm trying to eat my lunch here," she said. "You keep talking like that, I'm going to be sick."

"Two minutes is all I ask. You don't have to say a word."

She kept eating.

"We have three dead men," Tolley began. "All meeting

their demise under strange circumstances and all involved in the same murder investigation. At least that's what Deputy Chief Lawrence Cole would have us believe.

"Now, the case is conveniently closed and my client is dead. But there are also some unanswered questions surrounding his death. My understanding is that he was shot in the head by a rookie police officer."

She was almost through with her sandwich. She would not even look in his direction. It was obvious that when she finished eating, he would be talking to an empty bench.

"Have you seen the autopsy reports on Neil DeWitt?"

She didn't respond.

"If you get a chance, take a look at them. You'll find that he had been administered a massive dose of a barbituate called Dalmane. Deputy Chief Cole was also quite conveniently at the scene of his demise. Now I ask you, Counselor, who would serve to benefit most directly from the death of the student, the cabdriver and Neil DeWitt? If I were a betting man, which experience has taught me not to be, I would say your initial suspect, Paige Albritton, would be the most outstanding beneficiary. The smoke screen Cole began laying down the night of that Sergeant McKinnis's death has now turned into a wall of dead bodies. Everything is now tied into a nice, neat package. Perhaps too neat for my tastes."

Anne Johnson balled the sandwich paper up in her fist and stood. "Good day, Governor," she said, walking away.

"You will take a look at those autopsy reports, won't you, Anne?" he called after her. "I'd like to know what you think. Give me a call. I'm still at the same number."

She didn't respond.

Remaining on the park bench, Tolley watched her go back inside the Criminal Courts Building. "Now I've baited the hook, let's see if I catch anything."

# CHAPTER 65

**JUNE 19, 1996**
**2:13 P.M.**

Jack Govich, Frank Dwyer and Larry Cole were returning from a recruit graduation at the Police Academy. For the occasion, they were in their uniforms, which was unusual for Detective Division brass. When they walked into their headquarters office, they found Barbara Zorin in the visitors' waiting area.

"Barbara!" Dwyer said. "What brings you here?"

"Research," she said, standing up. The three cops dwarfed her. "And I wanted to talk to Deputy Cole."

"Mrs. Zorin," Cole said. "I'd like to introduce you to our chief of detectives. Jack Govich, Barbara Zorin, the famous mystery writer."

"I've read all your books," Govich said. "You created the Joe Clancy series, didn't you?"

"One of my less laudatory accomplishments."

"I think the books are pretty good. Maybe sometime we can talk over a couple of procedural problems I've come across in them."

"Oh, I'd love that! Any time at all, Chief."

"Well, I've got work to do," Govich said, heading for his office. "Nice meeting you, Mrs. Zorin."

"Call me Barbara."

"Ready for tomorrow?" Dwyer asked, referring to the Of Dark and Stormy Nights mystery-writing seminar.

"Loaded for bear," she said, with a smile.

"I don't understand what you mean."

"I think she means they're ready for anything, Frank," Cole volunteered.

Dwyer looked from the writer to his fellow deputy chief. "Why do I get the feeling you two are up to something?"

They didn't comment.

"Okay," Dwyer said. "I'm going back to work and hope that we all make it through tomorrow's conference with all our fingers and toes."

"You don't have to worry about us, Frank," Barbara said. "Might not be able to say that about some of our guests, though."

Dwyer didn't like the sound of that. He vanished inside the safety of his office before he could hear more. Cole led Barbara to his.

"Frank's a nice man," she said once they were seated inside. "But he's too cautious for my tastes."

"He's a survivor," Cole said. "Cops like him have a tendency to spend a lot of years in command positions. You'll find they seldom take chances and never make waves."

"You don't strike me as being that kind of cop, Larry. I mean you're a chance taker and you're probably the first to jump in when you perceive a problem."

Cole smiled. "I think I have to plead guilty on both counts. If I wasn't a bit reckless I wouldn't be involved in what we're planning for tomorrow."

"That's why I'm here," she said, removing a folder from her briefcase.

Cole noticed that it was the same one Garth had shown him a few days ago. He also noticed that it was now twice as thick as before.

"I wanted to share some of the things we've found out about Neil and Margo DeWitt before we kick off tomorrow."

"It looks like you've spent a lot of time on this."

"Most of it was done by Jamal, and he wanted me to tell you that everything here was obtained legally. That he didn't spy on anyone to get it."

"I would never accuse him of doing anything like that."

"From what has been discovered so far, Neil and Margo are as opposite in personality, likes, dislikes and hobbies as any two people can be. He was the last surviving heir of the DeWitt line, which has a history that began back in the days of Fort Dearborn before there really was a Chicago. The DeWitts have always been exploitative businessmen, who have engaged in any type of scheme, both criminal and noncriminal, to increase their fortunes. A Nathan DeWitt was implicated in a phony railroad-bond scam back in the eighteen-eighties and was briefly imprisoned. After his release, he was supposed to pay restitution to those he defrauded, but he never gave up a penny. Carter DeWitt, Neil's grandfather, leased warehouse space to the Capone Gang to store illegal booze during Prohibition. Every generation contributed substantially to the DeWitt fortune. That is, until Neil came along.

"He was a poor student, who was tutored at just about every level of his education. He managed to barely get diplomas from a prestigious East Coast military academy and a well-known Midwestern college prep school. His family money must have accounted for something, but then without it he'd probably have been thrown out on his ear. However, things changed when he got to Princeton. That's when he discovered his true talent.

"He was a liberal-arts major and his grades only improved marginally from what they had been before. But he definitely displayed an aptitude for drama."

She removed three photostats from the file and placed them on the desk in front of Cole. They were reviews of the college productions of three plays: two written by Shakespeare, and the other by Tennessee Williams. The opinions of the reviewers were mixed as far as the overall productions were concerned, but the comments about the performance of Neil DeWitt in the leading roles of each play were stellar.

One review referred to DeWitt as "the second coming of Olivier"; the others included the comments "DeWitt possesses the skill of a young James Earl Jones" and "the '50's produced Brando; the '60's have given us DeWitt."

"His family pay to have this stuff written?" Cole asked.

"No. They're legit. He caused quite a stir in the Ivy League college theater scene back then. I have comments here from some of the people who knew him."

She handed more pages to Cole. These contained the typed transcripts of interviews. "Where did you get this information?"

"Jamal called and talked to each of them. He started with the professor in charge of the Princeton English Department, which dramatic studies is part of. Jamal told the professor he was doing research on DeWitt for a project he was working on. The professor was more than happy to cooperate. He even gave Jamal the names of other people who had known DeWitt. They were very open about our deceased billionaire."

Cole scanned the interviews. Each discussed a man who had seemed a great deal different from the one Cole had met at DeWitt Plaza and whose dead body he had viewed on a North Side street a week ago. The adjectives "brilliant," "mercurial" and "fabulous" were used over and over again to describe him.

"Besides having a tremendous acting talent," Barbara said, "DeWitt was also a born mimic. He could imitate anyone and could even copy accents to the point he could speak a gibberish which sounded amazingly like real French, German, Russian or even Chinese. He knew none of these languages."

"Why didn't he stick with drama?" Cole asked.

"Rumor has it his father wouldn't let him. This supposedly drove DeWitt into a shell. Despite what Mr. Tolley said on television, Neil did receive psychiatric treatment for a lingering depression some years back after he left Princeton."

"This part about the accents," Cole said. "Syed Shafiq was lured from the college by someone using the name

Colonel Hugh Montague Farquart-Smyth, who had a very British accent."

"Marty's character," Barbara said, nodding.

"Officer Fletcher said DeWitt did a Humphrey Bogart imitation before he opened fire on her."

"An authentic genius, but he was unable to escape from beneath his father's heel. Even with the psychiatric treatment, he continued to have problems. Then there were the girls."

"The girls?"

"Yes," Barbara said. "Three young women ages twenty to twenty-six. All raped and mutilated. Neil DeWitt was the prime suspect in each murder."

# CHAPTER 66

**JUNE 19, 1996**
**3:00 P.M.**

Special Agent in Charge Dave Franklin of the F.B.I.'s Chicago office was reviewing reports when his secretary knocked on his door.

"Come."

The secretary stepped inside and closed the door behind her. "We've got a problem on Gold B, sir. Agents Carson and Broy called it in."

"They're on a surveillance, aren't they?"

"Yes, sir."

"What kind of problem are they having?" Franklin asked, turning to the two-way radio set on the cabinet behind his desk and switching it on.

"It's some type of interference. A beeping noise. They said it sounds like a homing-device signal."

"On one of our restricted frequencies!"

"Yes, sir."

There was no voice traffic on the Gold B frequency, only, as the secretary had reported, a faint beeping sound.

"Now, what in the hell can that be?"

"It does sound like a homing device. But we're not using anything like that now, are we?"

"No," Franklin said, with a frown. "But I want it found. Get some people out with direction-finding equipment to locate that transmitter. They can use the base station and two mobile units to triangulate the signal. Then I not only want the plug pulled, but also charges filed with the FCC against whoever's responsible."

"Yes, sir," she said.

# CHAPTER 67

**JUNE 19, 1996**
**3:05 P.M.**

The transmitter broadcasting the beeping noise on the F.B.I. restricted frequency was located under the rear passenger-side wheelwell of Judy Daniels's Toyota Tercel. At the moment Special Agent in Charge Franklin was listening to the unauthorized signal, the car was parked in front of Our Lady of Peace Catholic Church on Washington Park Boulevard.

As Franklin ordered the triangulation search, Judy exited the Our Lady convent carrying a nun's habit encased in a plastic garment bag. Sister Mary Louise Stallings, the lone resident of the convent, walked with the policewoman.

"I'd love to see you in the habit, Judy," the nun said. "In

fact, you kind of look like my novitiate class when I entered the convent."

"Your class?"

"Yes. At one time or another I've seen you in disguises that resemble every one of them."

It took a second for the words to sink in. Then they both laughed.

"This is for a very special disguise, Sister," Judy explained. "For me this will be the same as da Vinci's *Mona Lisa* or Michelangelo's Sistine Chapel."

"Sounds serious. You must be going after someone really dangerous."

They reached Judy's car. The policewoman unlocked the trunk and placed the garment bag inside. She turned to Sister Mary Louise. There was a mischievous smile on her face. "He's not dangerous yet, Sister, but someday he will be."

"Pardon?"

"I'll explain it to you sometime," Judy said getting in the car. "I'll return the habit to you in about a week. Have a nice day."

Judy pulled away heading for Lake Shore Drive. Sister Mary Louise Stallings walked back to the convent. Three blocks away, a black Chevy Blazer with tinted windows was parked on a side street. The Blazer was equipped with an audiovisual receiver that picked up the transmitter's signal and displayed it on an overlay of a Chicago street map designed on the beat configuration of the Chicago Police Department. Utilizing this device, the receiver provided the exact location of Judy's car. The device was accurate up to a distance of five miles.

Now Margo DeWitt watched the indicator light on the map signal that the Toyota had just turned north on Lake Shore Drive. Putting the Blazer in gear, Margo followed.

# CHAPTER 68

**JUNE 19, 1996**
**4:45 P.M.**

Wayne Tolley answered the telephone, "Hello."

*"So, I've seen the autopsy reports,"* Anne Johnson said. *"What have they got to do with Cole?"*

"Let me give you a hypothetical situation," Tolley said. "Neil DeWitt is lured away from DeWitt Plaza and drugged by Deputy Chief Cole or one of his minions. Then, with the obvious cooperation of this Officer Fletcher, Neil is shot under circumstances that make him look like a potential murderer when, in fact, he is an innocent man."

*"What about Sheila McNulty?"*

"Another frame!" Tolley said expansively. "I'm sure a check with your friend Commander Shelby will confirm the possibilities of such a thing occurring."

*"It seems to be a rather complicated way to get someone out from under a murder rap."* There was skepticism in her voice.

"Cole's a headline hunter, Counselor! What more would someone like that crave than a gaudy, media-event case with ramifications that will last for months? Such a man would do anything for his own self-aggrandizement."

Her ensuing silence encouraged him.

Finally, she spoke. *"What do you want from me?"*

"I need to confirm one or two things about the night Neil died," Tolley said carefully, "and perhaps you could obtain some information for me about one of Cole's people."

*"Which one?"*

"I think her name is Judy Daniels."

# CHAPTER 69

**JUNE 20, 1996**
**7:01 A.M.**

They met in the Burger King in downtown Evanston. The cops—Cole, Blackie, Manny and Judy—looked a bit bleary-eyed at this early hour on a Saturday morning. The writers—Barbara Zorin, Martin Wiemler, Debbie Bass and Jamal Garth—were, by contrast, alert, energetic and eager. They assembled at tables in the rear of the restaurant. No other customers were near them.

"Each of you," Cole said, "will be wired. Detective Daniels will take care of that in the security office of Norris Center before registration begins."

"Are you going to use body transmitters?" Wiemler asked. "I get hot at times and have a tendency to sweat a bit. That might interfere with the transmissions."

"No, sir," Judy said. "The transmitters will go on your outer garments. They're less than a centimeter in diameter and should be virtually unnoticeable."

"What do they look like?" Barbara asked.

"Show them," Cole said.

Judy had assumed another identity for this assignment. It succeeded in preventing any of the mystery writers from recognizing her as the same woman who had met them at the meeting a few days ago. In fact, when the writers first walked into the restaurant, they had thought she was an MWA local member named Zoe McAllister, who wrote mystery books for children. The curly blond hair, the granny spectacles and the sallow complexion, coupled with the faded jeans and the worn sweater, made her appear very much the offbeat scholar.

Judy removed an oblong jewelry box from the attaché case she carried and opened it on the table in front of them. There were eight collar pins inside: American flags, miniature silver dollars, a mezuzah, a crucifix and a continent of Africa were arranged on a velvet surface.

"You can select the one you want to wear," Judy explained. She picked up a silver-dollar replica. Each of the writers noticed that the clasp holding the shield in place was noticeably thicker than what would be the case in a normal lapel pin of this type.

Cole noticed that the writers were staring at Judy.

"You've met Detective Daniels before," Cole explained. "She will be present at the conference with you."

"You are very good," Barbara said. "Although I knew I'd met you someplace before. I really couldn't place you. That's a disguise you're wearing."

Judy smiled in character. "I can fool most people at least once, but I have had my problems recently."

Cole continued, "Each of you will be monitored from our surveillance van, which will be parked a short distance from Norris Center. We don't know what's going to happen, but I want to give you some ground rules. Although you will be wired, anything she says to you directly will later be admissable in court. You don't have to worry about eavesdropping on her."

"What about what we say?" Debbie Bass asked.

Blackie leaned forward, placed his elbows on the table, and said, "I spent some time reading *Bless the Children*, so I understand that what you're doing is making yourselves bait. The lady we're dealing with is not the squeamish sort and she ain't stupid either. So if you get too obvious with your play you'll tip her. Then all of this will be wasted."

Manny Sherlock had been silent since they sat down. Now he cleared his throat and said, "I didn't read *Bless the Children*, but instead listened to it on audiocassette. If she's imitating Magda, then Margo DeWitt is a very dangerous person. Playing with her is like toying with dynamite. I suggest that all of you exercise extreme caution."

"Well said, Manny." Cole turned back to his brain trust. "There is danger here. So understand it and be guided by it."

"Questions?" Cole asked.

There were none.

# CHAPTER 70

**JUNE 20, 1996**
**7:55 A.M.**

The surveillance van was parked on Sheridan Road an eighth of a mile from Norris Center. Inside, Cole, Blackie and Manny took turns listening over the headphones to each of the writers. Judy was registered as a seminar participant. She was scheduled to attend various mystery-writing classes throughout the day. Garth, Barbara and Debbie were each giving a class. Garth's was titled "Characterization in Novels"; Barbara's "The Amateur Sleuth vs. the Police Detective," which got a raised eyebrow from Cole; and Debbie's "How to Get Published."

There was only one scheduling problem. Garth's and Zorin's were both at 10:30 A.M. at different locations in Norris Center. Judy would be attending "The Amateur Sleuth vs. the Police Detective." Garth would be monitored closely from the van with Debbie and Marty sitting in on his class.

Cole's plan was for the cops to stay out of sight unless something happened. The deputy chief's fingers were crossed hoping that nothing would. That is, nothing he and his miniforce wouldn't be able to handle.

Frank Dwyer would be there also. He wasn't scheduled

for any of the brain-trust members' classes. Cole had agonized over not letting Dwyer in on what they were doing. If an emergency arose, he would have to. But in such an eventuality Dwyer wouldn't be the only cop Cole would be calling on.

As a courtesy Cole had notified the Evanston Police and the Northwestern University campus police that the Chicago cops would be on campus. He had kept information about what they were doing at a bare minimum. The Evanston day-watch commander was mildly curious, and the sergeant in charge of the campus police contingent was even a bit surly at being kept in the dark. Cole's rank forced both officers to limit their natural inquisitiveness, although grudgingly. Then again, if something went wrong, all the weight would be on Cole's shoulders. He had been in this situation before.

At 8:00 A.M. registration commenced. A hundred and fifty mystery writers and fans streamed into Norris Center. Audio traffic over the CPD surveillance frequencies increased first to a babble and then to a drone of almost indecipherable noise, as the members of the brain trust mixed with other conference participants.

The surveillance van was disguised as a North Shore Juice Company truck. It was big enough for the policemen inside to stand up and even walk around in. There were chairs for each of them, and reading material—mostly books supplied by the writers—and even a television. They had sandwiches and soft drinks in a cooler and coffee in a Thermos jug. It was going to be a long and possibly very hot day. The weatherman had forecast temperatures in the low nineties. The panel discussion at three o'clock loomed seven hours away.

"Shit!" Blackie swore. "I can't understand a word they're saying. A riot could be going on in there and I wouldn't be able to tell."

"Let me have a listen," Cole said, taking the headset and

studying the console controls. Each writer had an individual frequency. "Who are you on?"

"Barbara," Blackie said.

Slipping on the headset, Cole listened. It was indeed hectic inside, but he was able to understand snatches of what was being said.

*"I sent my registration in months ago, Barbara,"* a nasal-sounding woman said. *"I don't understand why you don't have it."*

*"Don't worry, Jennie. I'm sure we can work something out."*

Cole adjusted the volume control. It helped reception marginally. "Where is she?"

"According to the schedule," Manny answered from the other side of the van, "Mrs. Zorin's in the second-floor lobby. That's where the registration and book tables are located."

Cole flipped to Debbie's frequency.

*". . . met him once."* Her voice came across with crystal clarity. *"He gave me an endorsement on my first book."*

*"Do you think he'll do that for me?"* A soprano-voiced male said. *"That would really help me sell my novel."*

Cole switched to Garth's frequency. He was met by total silence. Not even static.

Cole fiddled with the volume control. At maximum the headphones emitted a slight hum.

"When's the last time you monitored Garth, Blackie?"

"A little while ago, boss. I got the same background noise from him I was picking up off the others."

"I'm not getting anything now," Cole said. "Manny, contact Judy. Have her find out where Garth is. Maybe his transmitter's failed."

Judy was on a separate system from the others. They could contact her on a two-way hookup, which she could hear by way of a small receiver, the size of a hearing aid, in her ear, concealed beneath her wig.

Manny picked up the microphone. "Base to High Priestess. Base to High Priestess. Come in."

Blackie and Cole exchanged looks. Manny had given Judy the code name.

Judy was browsing at the book display next to the table where Barbara Zorin was conducting the registrations. She was reading the book jacket of Hutch Holiday's most recent novel. Two clerks from the Scotland Yard bookstore in Winnetka operated the display.

"What is it, Manny?" Judy whispered into her transmitter, which was disguised as an American Flag lapel pin.

One of the clerks looked over at Judy. "I beg your pardon, ma'am?"

Maintaining her character, Judy said, "Have you read this?"

"Oh, yes, I'm a big fan of Mr. Holiday. He was our luncheon guest speaker two years ago. He's an excellent writer. There's never a . . ."

*"Base to High Priestess. Come in. Base to High Priestess."*

"I hear you," Judy said. "I've been reading his books myself for years."

*"High Priestess, are you talking to me?"*

"We have a full line of his books," the clerk said. "Some say the best one was *Nick Castle, Private Eye*. I loved it."

"I read you loud and clear," Judy said with a smile for the clerk. "I'll take it."

The clerk gave her customer a quizzical frown, as she took the Holiday book and Judy's money. When she turned to make out a receipt and get a paper bag, Judy whispered, "What do you want, Manny?"

The clerk turned around with the book and receipt. "Twenty-three dollars and seventy-five cents out of thirty." She began counting out Judy's change.

"Have a nice day," Judy said, walking away with her purchase.

"Yes, ma'am. You do the same," the clerk called after her. "And, by the way, my name's Edwina, not Manny."

"Of course," Judy said. She was glad this wasn't a drug bust or she would have been in real trouble.

Judy walked from the registration area into the Alpine Room. The crowd was left behind. In an isolated corner, she said, "I told you never to call me here!"

*"Sorry," * Manny said. *"Boss's orders. He can't pick up anything on Mr. Garth's frequency. Do you know where he is?"*

"I know right where he is."

*"Where?"*

"Sitting on the other side of this room. He's by himself going over some papers or something."

*"Judy,"* Cole's voice came over her ear piece. *"Go over and see if his transmitter's working."*

"Ten-four. On the way."

Garth was seated on a folding chair going over the notes for his class. He had been alone like this for some minutes. When Judy checked his transmitter it worked perfectly. Cole had been unable to hear anything because there had simply been nothing to hear.

Following registration, things settled down. Barbara Zorin, as chapter president, provided a brief greeting in the Alpine Room. The participants then broke up for the nine-o'clock classes. Three classes would be going simultaneously during each session throughout the day.

Inside the van the cops monitored the classes that members of the brain trust either attended or gave. At ten-thirty the second round of classes began. This was the series in which there was a scheduling conflict between Garth and Zorin. There were no problems.

The interior of the van was becoming stiflingly hot. They did what they could to stay cool, but as midday approached, this proved to be an impossible task.

"You know this mystery writing sounds interesting," Manny said, monitoring a transmission inside the center. "I mean these people are very serious about crime. They really know a lot about disposing of people. And they could probably get away with a crime or two, if you ask me."

Cole and Blackie didn't comment.

As the noon luncheon approached, Margo DeWitt had yet to make an appearance.

Blackie opened a can of Coke. Before taking a swallow, he rubbed the cool metal across his forehead. He sat down beside Cole, who was reading *Bless the Children.*

"What do you think, Larry? She gonna show?"

Cole sighed. "I've been thinking about that. Maybe she won't. Then it's possible, if she's such a great fan of this McGhee's Magda, that she wouldn't miss this for the world. It's too much of a challenge for her to pass up. Then . . ."

"Then what?"

"She might already be in there. Judy's not the only one who can put on a disguise."

Blackie started to say something, thought better of it and instead drained off half his Coke.

Inside Norris Center, the seminar participants broke for lunch. The entire 153-strong group, including Cole's brain trust and Judy, headed for the luncheon.

Debbie caught up with Barbara and Garth as they entered the room, which had been outfitted as a buffet dining area. "I've got a surprise for you."

"What?"

"Guess who's here?"

In the surveillance van, Blackie manned the headphones. "Something's happening!"

This galvanized Cole and Manny. In an instant they were standing beside him.

"What is it?" Cole said tightly.

"Bass said somebody's there with them."

"Did she say who?" Cole pressed.

"No, but it's got to be our girl."

Cole took the headphones, which were slick with Blackie's perspiration. Ignoring this, Cole put them on.

"*Harry McGhee*!" He heard Barbara Zorin say. "*I thought he was still in California*."

"*I called him and invited him to come at my expense*," Debbie said. "*He agreed not only to fly in, but to speak briefly after lunch.*"

"*I guess we have another member of our little brain trust,*" Garth said.

"Dammit!" Cole shouted. "Why in the hell did she do that?"

"Do what, boss?" Blackie asked with confusion.

He explained.

"Do you think she told him what we're doing?" Manny asked.

"How the hell do I know? This thing is getting out of hand. Maybe we should just shut it down."

"I don't think it's going to be that easy," Blackie said. "How're we going to get them out of there?"

"I'll get them out," Cole said. "One way or another."

"What's that?" Manny asked, looking up at the ceiling of the van.

Cole and Blackie heard it too. A helicopter was flying low over the campus and coming closer.

"Now what?" Cole said.

The black and silver Hughes Gulfstream helicopter bearing the DeWitt Corporation logo circled low over the south end of the campus. The few students and idle strollers in the area looked up as the aircraft cast its shadow on the lawns and buildings.

Margo DeWitt was at the controls. She was alone. On the first pass she spied a campus policeman standing at the cordoned off end of the Norris Center parking lot. He was waving his arms at her and the Mars lights of his police car were revolving. She couldn't tell if he was attempting to wave her off or inviting her to land.

"In a moment, my friend," she said, swinging the copter over Norris Center and the surrounding grounds in a slow, gentle circle.

On the lake side of the center she could see people standing at the windows of the Alpine Room. They were staring out at her.

Margo completed her flyby and could detect nothing amiss from the air. She would have to land, get out and go into the conference. Then she would decide which one of them would die first. She began her descent.

# CHAPTER 71

**JUNE 20, 1996**
**12:12 P.M.**

Cole's brain trust watched the silver and black helicopter land in the parking lot. The other participants at the conference strained forward to see what was happening outside.

Comments flew back and forth.

"Must be a promotion for a new book."

"They're probably going to have a stuntman parachute out of that thing when it takes off."

"Why can't a stuntperson do the parachuting? There's a woman flying the helicopter!"

"Who is she? Does anybody know? Is she a famous writer? Maybe she's an actress?"

As they watched, the campus cop lost his hat in the prop wash as he ran to assist the pilot from the helicopter. The saucer cap flew across the lot, skidded and slammed into a window of the Alpine Room with a dull thud. The noise made the brain-trust members jump. For the first time, the very real fact was upon them that this was no fiction plot. The woman who had just landed outside was very dangerous. Margo stepped from the helicopter and stared at the windows from which she was being watched by so many. She wore dark glasses, but it was obvious she was concentrating her gaze at the spot where the brain trust stood.

Heading for the entrance to Norris Center, she walked away from the copter.

"What do we do now?" Marty asked, a noticeable tremble in his voice.

"Just what we planned," Barbara said. "She will sit at our table for lunch. She can attend any afternoon class she wants as our guest. Then at three we conduct the panel discussion on *Bless the Children.*"

"Who's going to greet her?" Debbie asked.

"I'm the chapter president," Barbara responded. "That's my job."

"I'm going with you," Garth volunteered.

"You don't have to."

"Yes, I do."

"Okay." Barbara turned from the windows. "Have everyone else head for the buffet tables while we collect . . . our guest."

"I was going to have Harry sit with us too," Debbie said.

Barbara frowned. "I wish you had told us before you invited him."

"I'm sorry."

Garth stepped forward. "Barb, we don't have much time. She should be on her way up here by now."

"Okay, let's go." As they started across the room, she said to her American Flag lapel pin, "I hope you gentlemen are paying attention out there. Things are heating up very rapidly in here."

Margo saw the two authors at the top of the stairs and recognized them immediately from photographs on their book jackets. Barbara Zorin looked pretty much like her picture, only her hair was shorter. Garth was grayer and heavier in the flesh. She also noticed their tension.

Margo wore a simple black jumpsuit that cost enough with accessories to send a student through a full semester of classes at Northwestern. When she reached the top of the stairs, her high heels brought her up to eye level with Garth. She removed her sunglasses and waited.

"It was very nice of you to come on such short notice, Mrs. DeWitt. I'm Barbara Zorin. This is Jamal Garth."

Margo swung her eyes slowly from one author to the other. They managed to maintain eye contact with her. "I wouldn't have missed the panel discussion on dear Harry's book for the world. I'm one of his biggest fans."

"Then you'll be delighted to know," Jamal said, "that Harry's with us today."

"We were also just about to have lunch," Barbara added. "Won't you join us?"

"I'd be honored," Margo said. They led her into the Alpine Room.

And there he was: Harry McGhee. Margo recalled that a book reviewer had once compared the venerable writer's appearance, temperament and appetites to Babe Ruth's. Yes, now that Harry had gotten on in years, he did look very much like the dead baseball legend. He had to be at least eighty, maybe older, but he struggled to his feet to greet them.

Margo stepped forward and took Harry's wrinkled but still strong hands. He walked with a slight stoop and his hair was snow white, but he was dressed in a dazzling green blazer, white slacks and white shoes, and there was still a hint of the mischievous, hard-drinking rogue he had been in his youth in those sparkling blue eyes.

Margo kissed him on the cheek. "It's been a long time, Harry."

"Margo," he said, surprising her with his memory. "It has been a few years. As I remember it, you married into money."

"You remember me?"

"Of course," McGhee said, grinning. "Nowadays that's all I can do is remember, because nothing else on this old body works."

This brought chuckles from around the table. Exhausted, he slumped back into his chair. "You've got to excuse me. I had to catch the red-eye out of LAX. Didn't get into O'Hare until seven-thirty. By the time I got to the hotel, showered and changed it was almost eleven. I barely made it in time for lunch."

Everyone resumed their seats with Margo between Barbara and Garth. "Couldn't you have flown in yesterday? I would have made arrangements for you to stay at DeWitt Plaza."

"Didn't know about it until this time yesterday myself," Harry wheezed. "That's when this little lady called and invited me." He patted Debbie's hand. "I thought they'd forgotten about me out this way."

"No one who's ever read a Harry McGhee book will ever forget you," Debbie said, before turning to look at Margo. "Especially with all that's been going on in Chicago."

"My dear Ms. Bass," Margo said. "Whatever do you mean?"

"There'll be plenty of time to discuss that later," Garth said. "Why don't we head for the buffet before all the food is gone?"

"Good idea," Marty said, looking relieved to be getting away.

Harry McGhee was full of anecdotes about the trade.

"So I got an advance for *Bless the Children*, if you could call it that. Five hundred bucks from that cheap publisher, and my agent had to fight for that. I moonlighted doing feature articles for local newspapers and magazines to stay alive while I did the writing. Even then I found it hard to make ends meet.

"Book comes out in October of seventy-two. Didn't make a big splash on the market, but I had a bit of a name by then. Agent I had doubled as my publicist. Signed me for a thirty-city book-signing tour. Hell, I was still on the booze then, so letting me loose on America like that almost killed me."

"I bet it did some damage to a few ladies along the way," Margo quipped wickedly.

Only she and Harry laughed.

Harry continued. "By Christmas the book caught on by word of mouth. Sales reached into five figures, but instead of ordering another hardcover printing that cheapskate publisher of mine rushed into paperback. Then *Bless the Children* really took off."

"You were still on the book tour then, Harry," Margo said. "I came to one of your signings in Denver. I owned a paperback copy of *Bless the Children.* I left it in Colorado when I moved to Chicago."

They went back for dessert. Margo brought Harry a huge slice of German chocolate cake. She had a small slice of cheesecake.

"Tell me something, Jamal," Margo said, turning in her seat to face him.

He dabbed at his mouth with a napkin. "Sure. What is it?"

"The lapel pins," Margo said.

"I beg your pardon."

"The lapel pins. Yours and all the others. Even yours." Margo spoke directly to Judy Daniels for the first time.

Judy had maintained an almost invisible presence at the table. So far she thought Margo DeWitt hadn't noticed her.

"I'm sorry," Margo said, "but I don't think I caught your name."

The tension level at the table went up a notch or two.

With her head down, she responded, "Judy Davis."

"Tell me, Miss Davis," Margo asked. "Are you a full-fledged member of MWA?"

"Yes, ma'am."

"What have you published?"

The confusion came across despite the disguise.

"I don't think Judy completely understood you," Barbara said. "She's not a regular member, only an associate one. She hasn't been published yet."

Margo's smile was as cold as a gust of wind blowing through a cemetery vault door. "Well, she should have no problems breaking into print. After all, she keeps such impressive company. And she does have her lapel pin."

"Oh these!" Debbie said. "They're just a fad. I had no idea the others would be wearing them when I put mine on this morning."

"Yes, quite a coincidence," Margo said. "And they're all so different and yet so very similar. All the same size in diameter and all worn on the left side of the collar. I'm surprised there are no stars."

She watched their reactions with interest. The badges of the Chicago Police Department were star-shaped. "I mean like in the star of David. Don't we have any members of the Jewish faith present? Of course, Harry and I have been left out. What do you think we have to do to get our lapel pins, Harry?"

"Beats me," he said with a shrug.

Out in the surveillance van, Cole monitored the luncheon table talk from Judy's transmitter. "She's made them," he said glumly.

"Now what?" Manny said.

"She ain't gonna pull nothing in there, boss," Blackie said. "Right now she's just blowing smoke. Playing with them."

"I didn't expect her to react this way," Cole said, chewing on his thumbnail. "She's got to be either the coolest or the craziest chick in the world."

"I think she's both," Blackie said. "Cool and crazy."

# CHAPTER 72

**JUNE 20, 1996**
**1:27 P.M.**

Harry McGhee gave a short talk after lunch, but tired quickly. When he returned to the table, he said, "So what's next on the program?"

"Are you sure you feel up to it?" Barbara asked, with concern.

"I'll have you know, young woman," he rasped, "that I'll be going strong long after you've cried 'uncle' and scurried home for a well deserved rest."

"We've got three afternoon classes you can attend if you'd like," Garth said.

"What are they?" McGhee sank back into his chair.

Debbie said, " 'Plotting the Modern Mystery,' 'Police Procedures in the Police Procedural,' which will be given by a deputy chief from the Chicago Police Detective Division . . ."

"Oh," Margo said. "What's the policeman's name?"

"Frank Dwyer. Do you know him, Mrs. DeWitt?"

"No, my dear. Should I?"

Debbie shrugged and turned back to McGhee. "The last one you'll get a kick out of, Harry. It's called 'Mystery Poetry.' "

"What in the hell is Mystery Poetry?"

"Beats me," Debbie said. "So I take it you're not interested."

"I think I'll take a look at this Deputy Chief Dwyer. See what's he's got to offer an old broken-down writer. Maybe I'll pick up a tip or two."

As McGhee got slowly to his feet, Margo slipped up beside him and grabbed his arm. "I'm with you, Harry. After we see the cop comes the exciting part."

"What's so exciting about a panel discussion on an old book?"

"They're going to compare crimes in *Bless the Children* with real murders that have been occurring recently in Chicago. Isn't that right?"

"We're going to explore a couple of unique angles," Barbara said. "I think you'll find it very interesting, Harry."

"I bet I will, but right now I'm going to see what this cop's got to say and enjoy the company of this young lady."

The brain trust followed Harry McGhee and Margo DeWitt to Frank Dwyer's class, "Police Procedures in the Police Procedural."

"So what you're saying, Chief," Harry said from the front row of the room, "detectives, that is real detectives, solve the majority of their cases by either a tip or a confession?"

"That's right," Dwyer answered. "That is, in a somewhat oversimplified fashion. It takes hard work, more than a little bit of skill, and a break or two to solve difficult cases. But a confession, if handled right, always makes things a lot easier for detectives."

Debbie and Garth were seated behind Harry and Margo. She turned to them and said, "How do you feel about confessions, kids? Think you'll luck out and get one today?"

Neither of them could find a voice to respond before she turned to face Dwyer again.

Margo was once more draped on Harry's arm as they trudged back to the Alpine Room for the panel discussion.

Harry's exchange with Dwyer perked the aging writer up a bit, but he still appeared exhausted.

"You mind telling me what's going on between you and my colleagues, Margo?"

"Whatever are you talking about, Harry?"

"You keep speaking in riddles and every so often one of

them looks like they're going to jump out of their skins. And those lapel pins look like body mikes. If they are, the question I have to ask is, who's listening in?"

"Very astute," she said. "What else have you noticed?"

"Deduced, my dear girl, deduced. It's quite obvious from all the unfinished phrases and sidelong glances they've been exchanging that they suspect you of using my book for something other than simple entertainment purposes. Possibly even murder."

"What do you think?"

"I remember years ago you asked me a lot of questions about Magda. You seemed very impressed with that little figment of my warped imagination. In fact, you knew things about her that not even I did, and I created her."

"Interesting. Go on."

"So maybe you decided to become Magda."

"And how would I do that?" Her shrill laugh made him stop and stare at her.

"With your money I'm sure you could figure out a way."

They entered the Alpine Room. "Let's sit over by the window." He allowed her to lead him there. "And, Harry, you wouldn't want me to classify you in the same category as the others."

"What category is that?"

"Let's just say that being placed in it can be very hazardous to your health."

# CHAPTER 73

**JUNE 20, 1996**
**3:00 P.M.**

The panelists' table was set up in front of the room. There were four microphones on the table and four folding chairs behind it. The audience, consisting of everyone who had registered that morning, including Margo DeWitt and Harry McGhee, were seated facing the panelists. After a brief meeting in the hall outside the Alpine Room, the brain trust entered and took their seats.

Before beginning Barbara waited a moment to make sure everyone was ready. "We are all interested in crime. For many of us it is a hobby. For some it is bread and butter. One of the slogans of this organization is 'Crime does not pay enough.' "

There was a smattering of laughter.

"Madelyn, Jacqueline, Margaret, Audrey and Marcellina. All the names of young, white female children murdered in the city of Boston circa eighteen ninety-eight. Madelyn and Jacqueline were mysteriously strangled while they were at play. Margaret fell off a bridge near the city's zoo. Her body was discovered in eight feet of water beneath the bridge on the following day. Her neck was broken.

"Audrey climbed a tall tree in a park. She was found by the police with her head wedged between the branches of that tree. Her neck was also broken; however, there were no other injuries sustained as a result of the fall. This made Inspector John Lemieux of the Boston Police Department suspicious. He began an investigation. An investigation which led to one of that city's most prominent and wealthy citizens. Her name was Magda Gibson."

Barbara turned to Jamal Garth. He took up where she left off.

"As many of you know, Magda Gibson was the villainess created by our own mystery and horror novelist Harry McGhee." Garth swung his hand up in Harry's direction. Heads turned to catch a glimpse of the author. There was brief applause. Harry, seated beside Margo DeWitt, had his chin resting on his chest and his eyes closed. He did not acknowledge the salute. Margo never took her eyes off Garth.

"In *Bless the Children*, Inspector Lemieux began his pursuit of Magda believing her to be a normal human being. He was soon to discover that she was not.

"The inspector learned that she was a supernatural creature with many powers, which she used in pursuit of her evil schemes. One such power was the ability to swim great distances underwater without any need of oxygen. Utilizing this power, she trapped eleven-year-old Marcellina, her next victim, who was wading in the shallows off a public beach. Magda pulled the child under the water and drowned her.

"John Lemieux had accumulated enough data on the entity Magda not only to know what she was doing, but to destroy her. This could only be done by fire, but before he could trap her in St. Mary of the Heavens Cathedral in Boston, Magda kidnapped Lemieux's son Jonathan and killed him."

Garth looked across Barbara Zorin at Marty Wiemler. Wiemler didn't look back. They waited. There was only silence.

"Marty?" Barbara leaned toward him.

He jerked, but remained silent.

She placed her hand over her microphone. "It's your turn, Marty. Please continue."

"Of course," he said, looking across the room and making eye contact with Margo. He looked away quickly.

"Inspector Lemieux set fire to the cathedral. . . ."

"Louder!" someone called from the rear of the room.

"We can't hear you back here!"

"Speak up!"

Wiemler's voice rose half an octave. "Inspector Lemieux set fire to the cathedral. Magda was destroyed by it. That was the end of the book." He lowered his eyes so he wouldn't accidentally look in Margo DeWitt's direction again.

When it became evident he was not going to continue, Debbie Bass stood up and defiantly stared at Margo. Their eyes locked.

"They say that life sometimes imitates art. Perhaps we have run across a series of real murders in Chicago that are not only a very close imitation of the ones Harry created in *Bless the Children*, but which actually copy those murders!

"Now, in nineteen ninety-six in Chicago, we have real dead bodies. Their names are Jason, Jeremy, Dion, David and Brian. They are young, black male children, whose ages are nearly identical to each of the fictional children murdered in Harry's book. They also died the same types of horrible, mysterious deaths and in the exact same sequence of those occurring in the book."

Margo raised her hand. This startled Debbie. She looked over at Barbara and Garth.

"We were going to save the questions and comments until the end," Barbara said, covering her microphone with her palm, as Garth did likewise. "What do you think?"

"Let her have her say," Garth replied. "We've gone too far to turn around now."

They nodded to Debbie, who turned and said, "Yes, Margo. Do you have a comment or question?"

"Let's say, to start, I have several questions," she said, standing up. "I might have a comment or two later as well." All eyes in the room swung to her. "Should I address my questions to you or to the entire panel?"

"I think all of us are qualified to help you," Barbara said, "but if there's a panel member you prefer, please feel free."

"Of course," Margo said with a smile. "As I see it you're all in this together, so to speak."

"She's overplaying her hand," Cole said. "I hope they let her talk. The way she's going now she'll put her own neck in the noose."

The wail of a police siren could be heard approaching from the south. As it grew louder, Blackie said to Manny, "Check it out."

Manny went to the rear door of the truck and opened it. The fresh air rushing in was like cold water to a thirsty man. Looking out, he could see the red revolving Mars lights of one of the campus police cars coming up Sheridan Road. It sped past their location, heading for Norris Center. Manny reluctantly closed the door of the van.

# CHAPTER 74

**JUNE 20, 1996**
**3:15 P.M.**

Margo was talking. "Are you saying that an evil supernatural being is responsible for the deaths of the black children you mentioned?"

Debbie answered, "It isn't necessary to have supernatural powers to commit murder."

"But doesn't Magda swim underwater and fly through the air?"

Barbara said, "In eighteen ninety-eight those things would have been considered unusual. Possibly even supernatural. In nineteen ninety-six they're commonplace. You flew through the air to get here, Margo."

Garth added, "And I understand that you own a boat."

Margo's eyes flared. At that moment all the members of the brain trust realized this woman was insane.

A campus cop in uniform marched into the room. Stopping

at the door, he announced, "I'm looking for a Mr. Harry McGhee!"

Barbara got up from the table and walked over to him. "What is it, Officer?"

"Are you Harry McGhee?"

"No, but . . ."

"Then this is none of your concern." He again bellowed to the room. "I'm looking for a Mr. Harry McGhee!"

Barbara managed to control her temper. "If you'll stop that shouting, I'll take you to Harry."

"Lead the way."

Turning, Barbara led him across the room to Harry. He had not moved since the presentation began.

"This is Harry McGhee," Barbara announced.

The policeman stepped forward. "Sir, your doctor called from California. He said you were endangering your health by coming here. He also said . . ."

When Harry did not move, Barbara checked his pulse. "Oh, my God, he's dead."

As this news sank in, the blades of Margo DeWitt's helicopter started to spin. The members of Cole's brain trust stood over Harry McGhee's body as the helicopter lifted into the air.

# CHAPTER 75

**JUNE 20, 1996**
**4:02 P.M.**

Paige finally mustered up the nerve to put on a bathing suit and go out to the pool. As she walked down the stairs at about two-thirty that afternoon, she wished she'd owned something other than skimpy string-tied bikinis.

When she had purchased the plain white number she wore now, she'd been in the business of advertising her body for the purposes of negotiating a sale.

There were few people around the pool when she arrived. All were residents. A few curious looks were cast her way, but no more. She found a deck chair that didn't place her directly in the sun and stretched out. She had brought a book from the apartment. It was a gothic romance novel. She'd had her fill of mysteries for a while.

As the afternoon progressed, the others kept their distance. In fact, once or twice when she looked up, no one was paying her the slightest attention. Mack had been dead, what . . . ? Two weeks? No, it was closer to three. She was old news now.

The heat and fresh air made her drowsy. Twice she dozed off. The first time she awakened and took a dip in the pool. The water was cold, but after splashing around in it awhile, she felt wonderfully alive.

She climbed out with her hair dripping and her bikini clinging to her flesh. She didn't look around to see if anyone was looking at her. Hell, she didn't care. Let them look. She definitely had the body for it.

She dozed again, repeated her dip in the pool, and returned to her book. After only a few minutes she nodded off again. When she awoke Ronnie Skyles was standing over her.

Skyles was a pimp. He dressed like a pimp, in flashy clothes, having a tendency to be a bit gauche. His hair was elaborately styled, and he wore diamond and gold jewelry around his neck, on both wrists and on the fingers of each hand. He was a good-looking white man considered more pretty than handsome. There was a story going around about Ronnie. A rival pimp in the now defunct DeLisa organization once said, "Ronnie Skyles would give his left nut to be a nigger."

The DeLisa pimp was found in the trunk of a car with his throat cut. The organization suspected Ronnie as the slasher, but it was a personal thing about honor between him and the deceased, so they did nothing. For his part, Ronnie let it be known to a select few that he was indeed responsible for dispatching the man who had insulted him. The reason? Ronnie didn't mind being compared to a black man, but he took offense at being called a nigger.

Paige hadn't understood it until she told Mack the story and he explained.

"It's the word 'nigger,' Paige. I don't think there's a worse insult in the English language."

Now Ronnie Skyles was there with her. She didn't think he just happened to be passing by.

"How ya doin', Paige?" He didn't have an accent, but he did talk slow.

Paige sat up and wrapped a towel around her shoulders. "I'm okay."

He sat down in the chair next to hers, then swung his eyes around the courtyard. "Nice, but I seen you living better."

She caught the scent of his cologne. It was expensive, but he smelled as if he'd doused himself with half a bottle of the stuff.

"Is that why you're here? To talk about the way I live?"

Ronnie held up his hands. "Easy, baby. You and me used to be friends before you met big brother the cop. I just wanted to say how sorry I was to hear about him."

Paige felt tears sting her eyes, but she blinked them away. "Why don't you get to the point?"

His smile never wavered. His eyes, a startling pale brown under long lashes, locked with hers. She'd heard a girl in the trade once say that Ronnie Skyles had hypnotic eyes. Paige looked away.

"I didn't come to intrude on your period of mourning, honey, but I thought we could have a little talk."

"About what?"

"You don't want to discuss anything out here. Why don't we go up to your place?"

She started to refuse, but finally relented.

Paige stood up and started for the staircase. She knew Ronnie was behind her. She could feel him.

At the apartment door she fumbled with her keys as she tried to unlock the door. He stepped forward and took them from her. She stepped back. He wasn't tall. In fact, he might have been a shade shorter than her. But he was well built with broad shoulders, muscular arms and a narrow waist. The hair on his chest and arms was thick beneath the short-sleeved, open-necked shirt he wore. And the cologne now seemed to envelop her like a fog.

He opened the door and stepped inside. For a brief instant, she hesitated before following him. Then she walked in.

"Can I offer you something to drink?"

"What you got, baby?" he asked, standing in the center of the living room and looking around.

"Beer," she managed.

"That'd be nice. Long as it's cold."

She opened the refrigerator. The two six-packs, minus one bottle, were still there. She had not touched them since . . .

She snatched a bottle out and slammed the door shut behind her. She turned around. Ronnie was standing at the kitchen entrance.

Paige set the bottle down on the counter and turned to get an opener from the drawer beside the sink.

"I can handle it, sweetheart." He picked up the bottle.

To have something to do, she opened the drawer and removed the . . . ? What had Mack called it? A church key. The thought made memories of him flood back into her mind.

Turning with the opener in hand, she found Ronnie Skyles struggling with both hands to twist off the cap. But it wasn't the twist-off type. Mack could open a bottle like this with one hand. Mack was a man. Ronnie Skyles was a pimp.

"You'll need this," she said, handing him the opener. She stepped back. "What do you want, Ronnie?"

He took his time answering. "Just came by to see how

you was doing. How you were fixed for bread. Maybe find out if you had any plans for the future."

"Plans that might coincide with yours?"

His smiled broadened. He had very white teeth. "You were good at what you did, Paige. Damn good. That is, before the cop came along. Now . . . ?"

"Excuse me a minute," she said.

"Don't be too long, baby," he said.

In the bedroom she unlocked the bottom drawer of the dresser. Larry had made sure Mack's guns were returned to her. She looked through the assortment of firearms. She didn't think she would need anything too large for the likes of Ronnie Skyles. She selected a .38 nickle-plated Colt Detective Special with a white pearl handle. This was the gun she always liked the best, because she thought it was pretty. She also knew how to use it.

Back in the front of the apartment, she confronted the pimp. He had about a swallow of beer left in his bottle. When he spotted the gun he looked about to upchuck the rest.

She didn't point it at him, but instead let it hang down at her side loosely, ready to swing up into a position for doing business just like Mack had taught her.

"As for your concerns, Mr. Skyles," Paige said. "I'm doin' fine. Mack had a nice money-market account he left me that's got over fifty grand in it, so my money's okay. As for my plans, that's none of your business!"

He placed the empty bottle down on the counter and backed toward the front door. He looked scared now, and this made his phony front crumble to show him up for exactly what he was. A pimp. A cheap pimp. There was no other variety.

"Well, it was nice talking to you, uh . . . Paige. I'll tell all the old crowd you said hi." Then he was gone.

Handling the snub carefully, Paige crossed to and double-locked the door. A smile played across her lips. She was proud of herself.

# CHAPTER 76

**JUNE 20, 1996**
**5:55 P.M.**

The brain trust rode back to Chicago Police headquarters in the surveillance van with the cops. A tense silence reigned nearly the entire way. Blackie drove, and Cole sat in the front with him. In the back, Manny studied the writers. The bravado and self-assurance they had exhibited that morning were gone. There was fear here now. A great deal of fear.

Cole's office was dark. The brain trust came to an abrupt halt before entering, until Cole turned on the lights.

They sat at the conference table. Cole made a brief telephone call, which he conducted in whispers. When he finished, he turned to face them.

"The preliminary medical examination indicates that Mr. McGhee died of natural causes," Cole said. "I have a friend in the Cook County Medical Examiner's Office who's going to take a real close look at the body when it's brought in."

"She killed him," Marty Wiemler said in a quiet voice.

They looked at him.

"She killed Harry and now she's going to come after each one of us."

"That's what we planned, wasn't it, Marty?" Barbara Zorin said. "Just like in the book."

Wiemler slammed his fist onto the table surface. "Goddammit, this isn't fiction! This woman is real! She's filthy rich and she's a killer! Our lives aren't worth spit now!"

"Oh, look who's throwing the temper tantrum," Debbie Bass taunted. "Cat had his tongue back at the conference when his words would have meant something. Now he's in a nice safe police station, so he rants and raves. What a bleeding coward you are, Marty!"

"Don't call me that, you . . . !"

"That's enough!" Cole's roar brought silence to the room. "You all seemed pretty eager to get into this thing a short time ago. Now you're in it to stay and I'm in it with you for better or worse."

"What's next?" Garth said.

"I've given that a great deal of thought. Listening to her this afternoon gave me a much clearer picture than I had before. She's powerful, extremely formidable and above all arrogant."

"So was Magda," Barbara said.

"Exactly. Now the question is how far she'll take it."

"You know the answer to that," Marty said. "If she killed all those boys and Harry too she won't hesitate to kill any of us."

Debbie bristled. "He said Harry died of natural causes, Marty. He should never have left California."

"And who invited him?" he shot back.

Cole held up his hands. "This isn't getting us anywhere. I think our concern should be for the living and how we're going to close the show on that monster you encountered this afternoon. She never admitted openly to killing the children, but you could tell by the way she talked that she is responsible. And that goes for not only those little boys, but also for her husband, a cabdriver and a college exchange student."

"A genuine homicidal maniac," Garth said.

"A human menace," Barbara echoed.

"And somebody I'm going to nail, with your help. That is, if you do exactly what I say," Cole concluded.

# CHAPTER 77

**JUNE 20, 1996**
**6:10 P.M.**

Margo DeWitt was dressing for dinner. She took more time with her hair and makeup than usual. She wanted to make a good impression on her dinner guests. The private dining room of Medici's Restaurant on the twentieth level of DeWitt Plaza would also impress them.

She studied her reflection in the mirror. There was a self-satisfied smirk on her face. "You look rather pleased with yourself," she said to the image. "But it really was too bad about Harry. Must have been his heart, poor thing."

Finished with her primping, Margo left her bedroom. She climbed to the third level just below the roof observation deck. At the top of the stairs, she came to a metal sliding door with no knob. A signature palm-sensor panel was located in the brick wall at waist level beside the door. Placing her right hand flush on the panel caused it to illuminate and emit a dull hum. The door slid open and closed automatically once she was through it. The room she entered had been designed by the same German firm that had constructed the underground bunkers for Iraqi strongman Saddam Hussein. An artillery shell could not penetrate the metal outside door, and if the secured top level of DeWitt Plaza had been constructed belowground it could have taken a direct hit from a long-range missile and suffered minimal damage. The interior of the room was divided into four large cubicles. Each contained one of Margo's projects.

It had been a long day for Margo, but she seldom needed sleep. Since before daybreak, she had been traveling the city and suburbs conducting her own surveillance operation, which had succeeded in planting radio-transmitting eavesdropping devices on each member of the brain trust. She also had listening devices in Larry Cole's home and Judy Daniels's apartment.

Each device was nearly as small as the collar pins the writers had been wearing at the conference. Each was also artistically disguised. It was ironic that while they were planning to listen in on her, she had been in the process of bugging them.

Each transmitter was connected to a voice-activated tape recorder back in Margo's penthouse electronics cubicle. She studied each recorder. Only Cole's was running. She flipped the audio switch.

"*We will destroy the* Enterprise *if you don't comply with our wishes immediately, Captain Picard!*"

"*Your wishes amount to no more than blackmail and you will find that destroying . . .*"

"*Butch!*" A woman's voice called faintly in the background.

"*Yes, Mom.*" Margo stepped closer to the recorder. Her breathing quickened. It was almost as if she could reach out and touch him. To run her hands through his curly hair. To feel her fingers tightening around his throat.

"*Dinner's ready,*" the woman said.

"*Can I wait until 'Star Trek' goes off?*"

"*Okay, but as soon as it ends I want you to wash your hands and get in here.*"

"*Yes, ma'am.*" But then the little boy mumbled something under his breath.

Margo waited for the mindless chatter of the TV to resume before pressing the Automatic Function override button to halt the tape. She ran it back. She enhanced the audio and played with the voice filters to mask out the television noise. Then she played the end of the conversation again.

"*Yes, ma'am,*" came across at high volume. Then, almost in a whisper, "*I wish I could wait for my dad.*"

"Of course you do, little man," Margo said to the unhearing tape. "He doesn't spend enough time with you, does he? Too busy playing policeman and sticking his nose into things where it doesn't belong. Well, don't worry. Margo's going to relieve you of your problem with Daddy very soon."

# CHAPTER 78

**JUNE 20, 1996**
**7:00 P.M.**

As darkness fell, Manny drove Cole north on Michigan Avenue toward DeWitt Plaza. Blackie had been left in charge of the brain trust and the teams of detectives and tactical officers who would be assigned to guard them.

Cole had showered and changed from his surveillance clothes into a blue blazer, tan slacks, a blue pinstripe shirt and a blue-and-gold-patterned tie. While Manny was waiting, Blackie told him that Cole was going to pay a social call on Margo DeWitt.

Cole had been Manny's first commander in the Detective Division five years before. The young sergeant had developed a tremendous respect for his boss, a respect that had turned to deep admiration, possibly even affection. He also knew that Cole possessed one of the most astute police minds in the department. Manny had no doubt that somehow, some way, Cole was going to nail rich bitch Margo DeWitt.

After getting in the car at headquarters, Cole did not say a word until they were passing Roosevelt University at Congress and Michigan. "Most crimes have a discernible motive. Greed, hatred, revenge, something you can put your finger on and say, Now, that's why this happened.

That's why I've got this dead body or this machine-gunned storefront or this ransacked apartment."

"Yes, sir," Manny agreed. "That's true in most crimes."

Another short silence followed. "Probably the worst criminal to pursue is a psychopath. They never play by the rules—that is, if there really are any. They can kill because it is sexually gratifying to them, or they can kill because by the act of murder they can demonstrate their superiority and control of the victim.

"They always think of themselves as superior to us poor, lowly mortals. They feel they can do what they please to whomever they please, and then thumb their noses at the cops because we're just too stupid to catch them."

"Margo DeWitt didn't strike me as being that intelligent, sir."

"Oh, she is, Manny. When Garth was out in Colorado he found out that she was the smartest in every class and maintained the highest averages in each of the schools she's ever attended. She has an advanced degree in chemistry and completed enough required courses at the University of Colorado at Boulder to qualify for a bachelor's degree in electronics. Then she went to Colorado State University and got a degree in pharmacology. Hell, she could qualify as a licensed pharmacist in Illinois with her background."

"Could that account for the poisons?"

"Probably, but I'll need a lot more to bring her down and I think she's given me a way to do it."

They pulled up in front of DeWitt Plaza.

"I won't be long," Cole said, getting out of the car.

"Deputy?"

Cole stopped and looked back in the car.

"I know you'll get her," Manny said, giving him a thumbs-up.

Cole smiled. "Thanks."

Manny watched his boss stride into the building.

# CHAPTER 79

**JUNE 20, 1996**
**7:05 P.M.**

When Cole told the security officer in the lobby that he was there to see Margo DeWitt, he was directed to Medici's Restaurant on the twentieth floor. The maïtre d' graced him with a tolerant smile that stretched into open-mouthed alarm when Cole flashed his police ID.

"Is there some problem, Officer?"

"I don't think so. I'd like to talk to someone who is having dinner here."

"Whom do you wish to see?"

"Margo DeWitt."

When Cole said the name, the maïtre d' froze in place. For a brief moment, Cole thought he was having a stroke.

"I'm, I'm, I'm . . ." he stammered.

"Take it easy," Cole said. "You can just point me in her direction."

"No, I've got to tell her first. She has guests. Excuse me."

Cole watched him run across the restaurant. He was gone less than a minute. When he returned, he said a stiff "Mrs. DeWitt has asked that you join her and her guests in their dining room. Right this way."

The maïtre d' led Cole through the main dining room, where a violin quartet serenaded the diners, into a corridor running at right angles from the restaurant proper. The maïtre d' stopped at a set of sliding doors and opened them.

Cole looked inside. What he saw there stopped him.

There was a single table set for ten. Margo DeWitt sat at one end. To her left was Wayne Tolley. Cole also knew most of the others. There were a couple of U.S. congressmen, a well-known local television personality, and the manager of the Chicago White Sox. Seated beside Tolley were the mayor and the police superintendent.

"Deputy Chief Cole," Margo said, rising and coming to greet him. "Isn't this a pleasant coincidence. We were just talking about you." She took Cole's arm. "And we have an empty place because Phil Jackson can't make it. You will stay, won't you?"

"I'd be delighted, Mrs. DeWitt. That is, if I'm not intruding."

"Nonsense! You're almost like a member of the family, but you must promise to call me Margo from now on."

"Okay, Margo," he said. "And you must call me Larry."

"Goodie," she said, leading him to a space at the opposite end of the table from hers.

Margo instructed a waiter to take the new arrival's drink order.

"Just orange juice," he said.

Margo's eyes widened. "Are you on duty, Larry?"

"Yes, I am," Cole said easily.

The superintendent and a bewildered mayor looked down the table at him.

"Actually," Cole continued. "I'm doing a favor for Chief Cooper of the Evanston PD. His people are conducting a death investigation, and since I was going to be in the vicinity, they asked me to come by and interview one of the witnesses."

"The witness to a murder?" the superintendent asked.

"No, ma'am. It was apparently due to natural causes, but there were some unusual surrounding circumstances."

"Such as?" the superintendent queried.

The waiter placed a glass of orange juice down in front of Cole. He took a sip before looking at Margo. "Although the deceased gentleman was very elderly and under a California doctor's care for severe coronary problems, some of his colleagues are making accusations of foul play."

"His colleagues?" the superintendent said.

Margo interrupted. "Perhaps I can explain the situation for the superintendent, Larry. Do you mind?"

"Not at all, Margo."

"I attended a conference given by the local chapter of Mystery Writers of America earlier today, Superintendent. One of the truly great suspense authors of our time, Harry McGhee, flew in from California to attend. He was quite advanced in years and, as Larry has already told you, succumbed to a heart attack during the conference."

A few present remembered Harry McGhee's work, but none of them had ever met him.

"But why would anyone suspect foul play?" The superintendent demanded from Cole.

"With all due respect to the writers and their organization, boss, I would say they're the victims of overactive imaginations."

Margo displayed open surprise at his statement. Cole pressed on.

"It's my understanding from Chief Cooper that a portion of the mystery-writing conference was devoted to comparing fictional crimes created by this McGhee with the rash of child deaths which have occurred recently in Chicago."

The mayor spoke up. "How could fictional crimes relate to real ones?"

"That's the same question I asked, Your Honor," Cole said. "I mean, as a fiction exercise, it might have some merit, but in real police work it's a total waste of time. Wouldn't you agree, Margo?"

The question startled her. "I don't know if it was a complete waste of time. I mean, they were drawing some startling parallels."

"What kind of parallels?" the superintendent asked.

Margo squinted as if she had just come down with a severe headache. "Oh, I can't really recall. Something about swimming under water and flying through the air."

"Chief Cooper filled me in a bit, Superintendent," Cole said. "Seems that the guy . . ."

"It was a woman!" Margo's outburst startled the diners.

"Oh, no, Margo. I can assure you Harry McGhee was a man. My wife's read his book."

Margo was as tense as a taut violin string. "I wasn't talking about Harry. I meant Magda."

"Who's Magda?" Cole asked.

"The villainess in *Bless the Children*! Don't you people ever read books?!"

Cole let the insult pass, but the superintendent gave their hostess a disapproving look.

"Well, anyway," Cole said with a shrug, "there's no way that this Margo swam under water or flew through the air to kill anyone. It's great fiction, but . . ."

"Excuse me, Larry," the superintendent said. "But you said Margo instead of Magda."

"Did I? Must be all those 'M' names. Can't keep up with them. I really should read more."

Margo's eyes locked on Cole. "So you really meant Magda then?"

"Definitely," Cole said. "After all, you can't swim under water without oxygen or fly through the air, can you?"

"Perhaps not like Magda," she said, "but my boat is equipped with the latest scuba-diving equipment and I do own a helicopter. In fact, it is temporarily parked on the roof of this building."

Cole looked thoughtful for a moment. "You know, I never thought of that, Margo. Do you think that's what those mystery writers were talking about? I mean your swimming under water and flying through the air?"

"I don't remember them accusing me of committing murder, Larry."

The superintendent looked from the hostess to her deputy chief.

Using his thumb, Cole wiped the condensation off his glass and said, "Oh, I didn't mean to imply that you actually killed anyone. Perhaps it was my poor choice of words. But I guess whatever they were talking about is irrelevant anyway. This guy McGhee is dead from a worn-out ticker. All Chief Cooper wanted to know, Margo, was your impression of what happened this afternoon."

"My impression?"

"Yes. Do you think Harry McGhee was murdered?"

"Of course not. Like you said, he had a bad heart. People a lot younger than him die from heart attacks every day."

"Chief Cooper wanted me to ask you one more question."

She waited.

"Why did you leave the conference so suddenly?"

She smiled. "As you can see, I was having guests for dinner and there was really nothing anybody could do for poor Harry."

"I guess you've got a point there," Cole said. "Old guy probably didn't know it, but he was a dead man the moment he set foot on that plane."

"Could we talk about something more cheerful than murder and death?" the mayor said.

"Of course, Your Honor," Margo gushed. "What would you prefer? Politics?"

The mayor laughed his characteristic guffaw. "I said something 'cheerful.' "

As they all chuckled, Margo looked down the table at Larry Cole. He smiled back at her.

# CHAPTER 80

**JUNE 20, 1996**
**9:12 P.M.**

Tolley rode to the penthouse in the elevator with Margo. He was drunk.

"You know that Cole strikes me as a pretty smart cop," Tolley slurred. "Seems to really know his business."

He didn't notice the look Margo gave him.

"I had my doubts that a woman could run a police department the size of Chicago's, but it looks like that superintendent has really got her act together. As for the mayor . . ."

"Shut up, Wayne!" she snapped.

"Now, you just hold on a minute, Margo! You have no right to talk to me in that fashion. I'm . . ."

The elevator halted and the doors opened. Margo spun toward him. "No, you listen! You're nothing but a two-bit, chiseling lush who's lucky he's not rotting in some jail cell taking it in the rear end from a three-hundred-pound queer. You should count yourself damn lucky I even put up with you."

"I don't have to tolerate this," he said, stifling a belch. "You're not pure as the driven snow yourself, honey."

She reacted before she was completely aware of what she was doing. Her hand came up to slam knuckle first across Tolley's face. The blow knocked him against the wall of the elevator. Landing with a thud, he slid down into a sitting position on the floor. Blood began flowing from his face down his shirtfront.

"Oh, for crying out loud!" she said.

Stomping off the elevator, she headed for the library, without looking back at Tolley.

She picked up the house phone. A security officer answered.

"Governor Tolley fell in the elevator. He's intoxicated and looks to be bleeding from the mouth. Have first aid provided for him and then drive him home. And let's be discreet."

She slammed the phone back on its cradle. Then she caught herself.

"You are out of control now, aren't you, Margo?"

She held up her right hand with the fingers extended. She was trembling. Crossing to one of the bookcases, she pressed a button concealed beneath the shelf. A false front swung away to reveal a bar. She selected a decanter of blended whiskey and poured a neat shot into a cocktail glass. Downing the liquor, she inhaled a deep breath and exhaled slowly.

Margo knew what was wrong. It was Cole. He had done this to her with his inane, stupid dinner-table talk. She was surprised she had let him get to her. But she had been unable to help herself. All that talk about Magda or Margo or vice versa.

She was pacing the floor of the library. Back and forth like a caged animal. Now she stopped. A game? Could he have been playing a game with her?

Cole had gotten the superintendent and even the mayor interested in what had occurred at the mystery writers' conference. But then, he could have been simply baiting her. And it had worked.

Margo stood in the center of the library clenching and unclenching the fist she had struck Tolley with. She hadn't the slightest bit of remorse for what she had done to her attorney. Hell, he shouldn't have drunk so much. Cole was her problem now. Cole and his friends the writers.

She left the library and climbed rapidly to the third level. In the electronics cubicle she studied the recorders connected to her listening devices. Debbie Bass was Margo's first choice. Reaching out, she switched on Debbie's audio.

# CHAPTER 81

**JUNE 20, 1996**
**10:02 P.M.**

Debbie Bass lived in Olympia Fields, south of the city. Tactical Officers Jane Malecki and Tom Benteen of the Third District were assigned as her bodyguards. They would work a twelve-hour shift, which commenced at 8:00 P.M. and would end at 8:00 A.M. on Sunday morning, when they would be relieved by another crew.

All of the officers assigned to guard the brain trust were briefed by Blackie in the O. W. Wilson Crime Lab auditorium at police headquarters. There were eight officers present: four detectives and four tactical officers.

"You've all had some type of bodyguard detail before," Silvestri said from the podium. "Usually it's been some politician with an overinflated opinion of their own importance."

There was a smattering of laughter.

"This assignment is different. These people could possibly be the targets of a psychopath. And they're not politicians, they're writers. They'll do whatever you tell them. If there's a problem, you are to immediately contact me or Deputy Chief Cole. Write these numbers down."

Malecki and Benteen were two of the most highly decorated officers on the Chicago Police Department. That past April, after responding to a silent bank alarm, they had come upon an armed robbery in progress. Four masked and heavily armed men had entered the bank and forced all the tellers and patrons to lie on the floor. They were looting the cash drawer and vault as the tactical officers carefully observed them through the windows.

Malecki and Benteen patiently waited until the stickup men made their exit before confronting them. A gun battle ensued with the two cops against four robbers. When the smoke cleared the score was cops, four—stickup men, zero.

Janie Malecki was short and stocky, but rumored to be the "fastest two-hundred-pound, five-foot-three-inch person on Earth." She was also known as the "She-Devil," because of her pronounced resemblance to Roseanne Barr, who had played the lead in the movie *She-Devil.*

Benteen's unofficial nickname was "Pee Wee" after Pee Wee Herman. No one ever called him that to his face, because doing so would be extremely hazardous to the nickname caller's health. In fact, Tommy Benteen was the spitting image of Pee Wee Herman, but the resemblance ended with the physical. When he talked, Benteen sounded a lot like Hulk Hogan, and beneath that mild-mannered, wimpish exterior lurked the body of a 160-pound man who could bench-press 250 pounds and tear suburban telephone books in half with his bare hands.

They picked Debbie up at Cole's office. When she saw them, she was seriously not impressed.

"Don't worry, ma'am," Janie said. "Nothing's going to happen while you're with us."

"Yeah," Tommy rasped in that deep, Hulk Hoganish voice, "we got ya covered."

Debbie was starting to think like Marty Wiemler. Maybe the four of them were in over their heads.

When they reached the police parking lot, where the battered, unmarked tactical car was parked, Janie and Tommy removed the jackets they'd been forced to wear inside headquarters. Debbie was definitely impressed by their weaponry. Both carried combinations of extended-clip automatics and large-bore revolvers. They also carried smaller-caliber guns in ankle holsters and various-sized knives secreted at clever locations on their bodies. It took Debbie's writer's eye to locate the cutlery. The weapons, combined with the lightweight body armor, convinced her that they were indeed bona fide street warriors.

By the time they reached her suburban home, the three of them were fast friends.

"So this guy climbs out on the window ledge," Tommy said, "and threatenes to jump. I'm standing there not knowing whether to crap in my pants or go blind when Janie walks right past me and says to this punk, 'Look, asshole, I ain't had lunch yet and we got less than an hour left on the tour, so if you're gonna jump, then jump!' "

They parked the police car in Debbie's driveway and walked up to the front door. Debbie was laughing so hard her eyes teared. "Well, did he?"

"Did he what?" Tommy said deadpan.

"Did he jump, Officer Thomas Benteen?" The writer stopped, faced him and placed her hands on her hips.

"Yeah. But at least we had lunch on time."

Janie punched him in the arm hard enough to make him wince. "He didn't jump," she said. "He climbed back in that window and apologized for all the trouble he caused us."

"I thought so." Debbie opened the front door.

They followed her inside.

"Wow, what a layout!" Janie said of the ranch-style, three-bedroom house. "And you ain't got no brats nor an old man. Kid, you got it made."

Debbie kicked off her shoes and picked up the mail. Sifting through it, she said, "Sometimes I wish I'd never bought this place. It's so out of the way."

"You don't know how good you got it," Tommy said.

There was a package with the mail. Opening it, Debbie found a book from something called The Mystery Book Guild. The novel inside was *Nick Castle, Private Eye* by Hutch Holiday.

"I didn't order this."

"Let me see it," Janie said. "Says here it's a free sample. Being a writer you must get a lot of stuff like this."

"No. I've never gotten a free book before. But this is an excellent novel and the binding looks expensive."

Debbie changed clothes and had just offered to make them one of her special vegetable omelets when the telephone rang. She picked up the kitchen extension.

"Hello."

*"Miss Bass, this is Deputy Chief Cole. Could I speak to one of your bodyguards?"*

"Sure, Larry. Is everything okay?" He sounded strange.

*"Everything is fine."*

She motioned to Janie. "Deputy Chief Cole wants to talk to you."

The tactical officer took the phone. "Yes, sir." She listened for a moment before taking a worn notebook from the back pocket of her jeans. "I'm ready. Go ahead."

After scribbling instructions, she concluded the conversation with, "Yes, sir. We're on the way."

She turned to Debbie and Benteen. "We've got to vacate this place right now!"

All the color drained from Debbie's face. "What's wrong? Has something happened to one of the others?"

"The deputy didn't have time to go into all that. He wants us back downtown, but we have to take a different route than the one we came in on. Tommy, check the front. I'll bring her out when you give me an all-clear."

Benteen headed for the door, pulling a .45 Smith and Wesson automatic from his shoulder holster and checking the thirty-round clip. He shut off the lights, plunging the house into darkness. Edging open the door, he peered cautiously at the street. It was deserted. He slipped outside.

Malecki grabbed Debbie's arm and escorted her to the spot Benteen had vacated.

"Listen, honey," Janie said. "I want you to do exactly like I say. When Tommy gives us the signal we're going out of here like we were shot out of a cannon. We're going to run, and I do mean run, to the car. Me and you will get in the backseat, Tommy'll drive. Once inside I want you as far down in the seat as you can. If anything happens, I want you on the floor. Got me?"

Debbie's head bobbed up and down.

Janie turned to look out the door. She pulled a six-inch-barrel, stainless-steel .357 magnum revolver and held it down at her side. When her partner waved, she turned to Debbie.

"Ready?"

"Ready," Debbie said.

"Hit it."

The two women left the house at a dead run with Janie slamming the door behind them. It took less than four seconds to reach the car. Janie snatched the door open and shoved Debbie inside. She dived in behind her.

Tommy yanked the car into gear and peeled rubber backing it out of the driveway. Out on the street he twisted the wheel and floored the accelerator.

"Which way, Janie?" he said, as they raced away from the house.

"Head for Forest View Lane, four blocks straight down this street. Then make a left."

"I don't understand," Debbie said. "Going west on Forest View Lane will take us away from Chicago."

"Cole wants us to take a shortcut back to the expressway about two miles east on the lane."

"But that's an isolated area. There aren't any houses or anything else out there."

"Don't worry, honey," Janie said, as Benteen negotiated a screeching turn onto Forest View Lane, "Cole's got his reasons for sending us this way. Probably your psycho friend is waiting for us the other way."

"But . . ." Something was bothering Debbie; however, she couldn't pinpoint what it was. ". . . wouldn't it be better for us to stay in the house and have him send some backup units?"

"We'd have been sitting ducks that way, Deb," Tommy said, flicking on the bright lights to negotiate the pitch black strip. The two-lane highway cut through an area of fields dotted with trees and devoid of any sign of life. "I'd rather be out in the open and movin'."

Debbie couldn't find the voice to argue with his logic, even though she didn't agree with him. She played back in her mind everything that had happened since she picked up the phone. She had to do it twice before the thing that was bothering her came to light.

"How do you know that was Larry Cole on the telephone?"

Janie looked at the reflection of Tommy's eyes in the rearview mirror. He squinted skeptically.

"I've heard him talk a couple of times on television," Janie said. "It was him all right."

"But I've talked to him personally maybe five or six times in the last two weeks and that voice on the phone didn't sound like him."

"Maybe he has a cold," Tommy offered.

The faint thumping of helicopter blades high above them became audible.

"But he called me 'Miss Bass'! He's never done that before. It's always been just Debbie. And he referred to himself as 'Deputy Chief Cole.' I've heard other people call him that, but he's never said it himself."

Janie laughed. "Honey, when the guys and gals who wear the brass downtown get their habits on they can be real formal. You can bet that . . ."

The sound of the helicopter engulfed the car at the instant a blinding light pierced the windshield. The aircraft was directly ahead of them. Tommy threw his arm up to deflect the glare, but he couldn't see anything beyond the light. He hit the brakes, but he was unable to see, and they ran off the road.

The car bounded over the shoulder and became airborne as it plunged fifteen feet into a barren field. They crashed at an angle and rolled over once. Debbie and Janie were thrown around the interior of the car. Flying glass flew through the passenger compartment, slashing them.

Both cops were knocked unconscious by the impact. Bleeding from head and facial wounds, Debbie was still conscious, but groggy. She looked out through the spider-webbed windshield to find that they were still held in the beam of the brilliant light. The helicopter blades sent a continuous, throbbing pulse through the car.

"No," she moaned, as she struggled from under Malecki. "No, this can't be happening."

The back door stuck and she kicked it twice before it would come away from the frame enough for her to squeeze through.

She fell to the ground in the field. The prop wash from the hovering helicopter blew dust and debris into the air. The light was still trained on the smashed car.

Debbie tried to get to her feet, but her legs wouldn't support her. As tears streamed from her eyes, to mix with the blood on her face, she began crawling away.

A hundred feet above her Margo DeWitt hung in the air and looked down at the writer's pitiful escape attempt.

"No, no, no, my dear Debbie. You of the acid tongue and fiery gaze. There's really no place to go."

A gallon container filled with an explosive liquid hugged the bottom of the helicopter. A release lever was located near Margo's hand on the control panel. Flipping the lever up released the container and caused a five-second-delayed detonator to become activated. Casually, Margo flipped the switch. The container dropped into the field below, landed on top of the police car and exploded, spewing jets of flaming liquid. The liquid splashed on the still crawling writer, and in an instant she caught fire with a scream that easily carried to the woman in the helicopter.

With a satisfied grin, Margo banked the helicopter and headed back for Chicago.

# CHAPTER 82

**JUNE 20, 1996**
**10:22 P.M.**

Detectives Jeff Reed and Patrick Hughes of Area One Detectives were assigned to guard Martin Wiemler. Blackie had selected them because the overweight writer was developing a very serious case of nerves.

Reed and Hughes were the two biggest cops assigned to the brain-trust detail. Both stood over six feet four inches tall and weighed in excess of 250 pounds. Reed was a former professional wrestler who had gone by the name "The Masked Assassin." Wearing a stocking mask and acting the role of a street mugger in the ring, he'd had a fairly successful career against good guys such as "Adonis," "The Gladiator," "Captain U.S.A." and "Pretty Boy Roy." After 132 matches, Reed retired from wrestling to become a cop.

Pat Hughes had been the perennial starting center for the Gary, Indiana Rough Riders of the North American Football League semi-pro team. After graduating from Lane Tech High School in Chicago as an All-City lineman, Pat hadn't been good enough to go to a major football power and instead ended up at a junior college. From there he had gone on to the Rough Riders, where he was paid a hundred dollars a game on a good Sunday. He had worked in the steel mills of South Chicago and Northern Indiana to stay in shape; that is, until the mills began closing and the emergence of the World Football League dried up the pool of amateur talent the Rough Riders depended on to stay in business. So Pat began looking for a steady line of work and, like Jeff, ended up on the CPD.

Jeff and Pat had been in the same recruit class hired in May 1986. They had also been in the same Detective School class of December 1990. Along with Sergeant Sherlock, they were assigned to Area One Detectives under the command of then Commander Larry Cole. Jeff Reed and Pat Hughes had the same admiration for Cole that Manny Sherlock did.

They had been the only pair of bodyguards that Blackie called to the side away from the others.

"The guy you're getting's real shaky. Looks about to crack, so the least little thing'll set him off. Watch him and if anything does happen, be ready for him to do the unpredictable on you."

When the three of them left headquarters, Marty Wiemler looked a lot like Jackie Gleason's "Poor Soul," as he walked between the behemoth-sized, former professional athletes. During the ride to his Wrigleyville apartment, the writer sat in the backseat alone, his eyes darting nervously at everything and everyone they passed.

When they got to his place and doffed their jackets, Marty noticed with dismay that they were only carrying snub-nosed revolvers on belt holsters. The guns looked even smaller in relation to their immense bodies.

"Nice place you got here, Marty," Jeff said, looking around the bachelor apartment two blocks north of Wrigley Field. "Lived here long?"

"Seven years. Look, guys, do you think it's such a good idea coming back here? Don't you think this would be the first place she'd come looking for me?"

"That's what Deputy Cole's hopin', Marty," Pat said. "She'll make her play and then we'll make ours."

This didn't leave him very happy. In fact, he looked as if he was going to be seriously ill.

They settled in for the evening.

Marty couldn't sit still. He paced the floor, sat down, stood up and finally headed for the windows.

Jeff and Pat were watching a Dirty Harry movie rerun on the writer's living-room television. Jeff glanced up at Marty.

"I wouldn't go near those windows, Marty. You're a big guy like us. Make one helluva target."

Marty darted across the room and sat down in the easy chair next to the couch the two big cops were sitting on. He fidgeted nervously as he watched Clint Eastwood dispatching bad guys on the screen.

"You think we could watch something else?" Marty asked.

"Be off soon," Pat said, without turning to look at him.

Marty started to get up, but now he was aware of the windows. Feeling like a prisoner, he remained glued to his seat.

When the movie went off, Jeff asked, "You play cards, Marty?"

"What?"

"Man asked if you played cards," Pat said, in a less than cordial tone. "You know, like pinochle, poker, gin rummy, whist?"

"Sure."

"You got cards?" Jeff asked.

Marty produced a worn, dog-eared pack with the deuce of spades missing. Pat made the Big Joker the deuce, while Jeff produced four boxes of wooden matches from the pockets of his size-fifty-two-long sports jacket. After distributing the matches into three even piles on the cocktail table, Jeff and Pat cut for the deal.

They played seven-card stud. At first Marty handled the cards listlessly; then, when he began winning, he shuffled and riffled the cards with more enthusiasm. Finally, after winning three hands in a row, he was so involved he almost forgot his life was supposed to be in danger. By this time he'd also won all the matches.

"Let's play for money!" Marty said.

"Can't," Jeff said.

"We're on duty," Pat added.

"Suppose it was my money and I gave it out like you guys did the matches?"

Jeff and Pat exchanged looks before finally shrugging.

"Don't see a problem," Jeff said. "As long as we give back everything when it's over."

"Great!" Marty said, dashing to the rear of the apartment. He returned with a gallon pickle jar so full of quarters he had trouble carrying it.

"Where'd you get all those?" Pat asked.

"Habit I picked up when I was on the road as a salesman," Marty said, opening the jar and dumping piles of quarters in front of the two detectives. "I'd empty my pockets of change every night and separate the coins. I'd load them into these jars when I got home. You can see what this one holds."

"You saved a lot of quarters here, Marty," Jeff said. "You ever counted them up?"

"No," Marty said, just as all the lights went out. His gasp of horror split the darkness.

"Just sit tight," Jeff said calmly. "We have blackouts like this every summer."

"Yeah," Pat added. "Too many people running too many air-conditioners."

"I can't stand this!" Marty screamed. "I got to get out of here!"

"Hold it, Marty!" Jeff said, lunging for the last place he had seen the writer before it went dark. "Shit!"

"What's wrong, Jeff?"

"I hit my knee on the damn cocktail table."

"Where's Marty?"

Pat's question was answered by the apartment's front door being flung open to crash into the living room wall.

"Marty! Hey, Marty!" Jeff shouted. There was no answer.

"Come on!" Jeff said into the pitch blackness surrounding them.

"How can we go anywhere, man! I can't even see my hand in front of my face!"

Martin Wiemler's scream could be heard from somewhere below. It was a scream of terror. It became a scream of pain.

"Jeff?"

"I'm over by the wall! I'm going to follow it around. . . ."

The lights came back on suddenly. Pat hadn't moved from his position on the couch. Jeff was standing over by a wall that would have led him into the kitchen.

"Let's go," Jeff said.

The two big men lumbered from the apartment like a pair of rampaging mastodons. They hit the stairs and started down. They found Marty on the first-floor stairs. He had been disemboweled by someone using a very large, very sharp knife. His internal organs protruded through the gaping hole in his abdomen, and there was so much blood the landing looked like the floor of a slaughterhouse. The writer's eyes were closed and his face had gone an ashen shade. He wasn't breathing.

Without hesitating, Jeff stepped over the body and, being careful not to slip in the gore, headed for the street. After stopping to stare at the dead man, Pat followed.

The street in front of Wiemler's apartment building was deserted, except for a tall, thin woman in black walking rapidly toward the corner.

"Hey!" Reed shouted. "Hey, you! Stop!"

Casually, she turned and looked directly at them. Even though they were a hundred feet away, both detectives would later positively identify this woman as Margo DeWitt.

She gave them a chilly smile as she waved and disappeared from view around the corner.

Reed and Hughes ran as fast as they could to the corner. But by the time they got there she had vanished.

# CHAPTER 83

**JUNE 21, 1996**
**6:15 A.M.**

Larry Cole's eyes burned with fatigue as he turned his car onto the street where he lived. He pulled into the curb and shifted into Park. Emitting a deep sigh, he shut his eyes and leaned his head back against the headrest. The police radio was silent. The commercial AM/FM radio was turned to an oldies station that Cole didn't remember dialing. The only other person who had driven his car lately was Manny. Cole figured the sergeant was into nostalgia.

Cole's plan had worked. At least almost. He had Margo DeWitt behind the eight ball. The evil-tempered Anne Johnson had approved four felony murder warrants against DeWitt. All they had to do now was catch her. And they would. But the price had been high.

Last night he had been in the superintendent's office briefing her when his beeper went off. It was Blackie.

*"Our girl Margo got Marty Wiemler."*

"What? Where in the hell were Reed and Hughes?"

*"Take it easy, boss. We've got her dead to rights. She managed to disable the Edison transformer providing power to Wiemler's block. In the dark the writer panicked. He got out of the apartment before the dicks could do anything to stop him. DeWitt caught him on the stairs and ripped his gut open with an antique knife."*

"You've got the blade?"

*"Reed found it out on the sidewalk. It's on the way to the Crime Lab. I'll bet our girl's prints are all over it."*

"Don't be too sure of that," Cole said. "She's not that careless."

*"Well, there're a couple more things indicating that she really slipped up on this one."*

"Such as?"

*"Reed and Hughes both eyeballed her outside the apartment building. They yelled for her to stop, but she just waved at them and kept going."*

"They're certain it was her?" Cole said tightly.

*"I showed them her photograph personally, boss, and there's more."*

Cole waited.

*"Groundskeeper at Wrigley Field's throwing a conniption with the Twenty-third District watch commander. Somebody parked a black and silver Hughes Gulfstream helicopter right down on the playing field behind second base. Aircraft belongs to the DeWitt Corporation. Wiemler lives, or shall I say lived, two blocks away."*

"What about the others?"

*"I'm having them brought back to headquarters. Zorin and Garth are on the way. I got no response from Bass. She's got two pretty good tactical cops from Three with her. But there's no answer at her place. I sent an Olympia Fields patrol car to check her house in case there's something wrong with her phone."*

"What about their radios?"

*"No response."*

Cole was still briefing the superintendent when Blackie beeped him again.

*"She got Bass and the two tact people,"* Blackie said quietly. *"Squad car was found in a field a mile or so from Bass's place. Thing was totally incinerated. Sergeant I talked to from out there says it's been burning like an oil-well blaze for the last hour. He also said there were reports in the area earlier of a low-flying helicopter. That's another nail in this broad's coffin."*

"Okay," Cole said, now numbed by the bad news, "call

the FAA and see what we can get on her flight plan. I'll see you later."

He had hung up and turned to give the superintendent more bad news.

Margo DeWitt had contacted Midway Control via radio at 9:45 P.M. on June 20, 1996, requesting clearance for a flight to Aurora Airport, southwest of Chicago. Clearance was given for her to lift off from the DeWitt Plaza sky pad and fly on a southwest vector across the city, maintaining an altitude of two thousand feet. At 9:59 P.M., Midway Center handed the helicopter over to Aurora Center. Aurora Center had no record of her flight.

At 10:04 P.M., Midway Center received a transmission from the DeWitt flight that she was returning to Midway space. Her destination was DeWitt Plaza. At 10:09 P.M., Midway Center lost contact with her and the transponder aboard the aircraft had stopped transmitting.

A report of a possible aircraft down in the city was called in to Chicago Police communications. Patrol units along the helicopter's last known route were alerted, including Lake Michigan marine units.

At 10:37 P.M., a call was received from the groundskeeper at Wrigley Field. The DeWitt helicopter had been found.

Cole had led a raid on DeWitt Plaza, as additional units cordoned off the multistory building. Three special-weapons-team cops took up positions in skyscrapers surrounding the Plaza. The snipers selected perches providing them with clear lines of fire at the penthouse.

Search and arrest warrants were presented to the head of security and a quite-taken-aback female business manager. The assistant security director blocked access to the penthouse elevator with his body.

"This is a search warrant," Cole said. "I suggest you get out of the way."

"I'm not letting anyone up there until I talk to either Mrs. DeWitt, Governor Tolley or Mr. Winbush."

Detectives Reed and Hughes had accompanied the raiding party. Cole glanced in their direction. The assistant security director was snatched from the doorway and handcuffed. As he was whisked away, he was bellowing about police brutality and violations of his civil rights.

Twelve cops, including Cole and Silvestri, had entered the penthouse with guns drawn. They searched every room on the first two levels looking for Margo DeWitt. Locked doors were smashed open, closets searched, and the books written by the members of Cole's brain trust and the specially bound edition of *Bless the Children* by Harry McGhee catalogued and inventoried.

The entrance to the third level had halted them.

Cole and Blackie studied the palm sensor, the metal sliding door and the reinforced concrete walls.

"We'll need some heavy-duty explosives to get in there, boss," Blackie had said.

"See if we have someone who might know a way to get in."

Sergeant Bennie Cappetto of the special weapons team was the closest thing they had to a demolitions expert on the scene. He studied the sky bunker's exterior and shook his head. "This place is damn near impregnable from anything we got, Deputy. We'll have to call in the army."

"Then call them," Cole had ordered.

Cappetto hurried off to contact the Fifth Army duty officer stationed in the downtown Federal Building,

"She could be in there, boss," Blackie had said.

Cole studied the steel door. "An hour ago I would have said you were wrong, but now I don't know. She's making mistakes tonight. Holing up inside this place could be another."

"You think her being eyeballed at the Wiemler hit was a mistake?"

Cole looked at Silvestri. He respected Blackie's hunches. "You don't think it was?"

Blackie shook his head. "She waved at them. Parked her helicopter in a place where it was sure to be found even if the Cubs are playing on the West Coast. She's not running. She's playing this thing methodically step by step. I'd say she had a plan. A plan that wouldn't allow her to be cornered in there." He nodded at the sky bunker.

Cole had thought for a moment. "I think there's someone we can ask about that."

Wayne Tolley had been sleeping the sleep of the inebriated when the flashlight beam shone full in his face.

"What the . . . ?" The ex-governor came awake with a start.

"Let's go, Governor," Sergeant Manny Sherlock said from behind the flashlight beam.

"I'm not going anywhere until you explain the full meaning of this intrusion!" His words were badly slurred, but he was sitting up straight in the bed glaring at the blackness behind Manny's flashlight beam.

"Very well, sir," Manny said. "I have a warrant for your arrest charging you as an accessory in four murders. 'You have the right to remain silent. If you give up . . .' "

They had interrogated Tolley at Area Three Police Center at Belmont and Western.

When Cole, Blackie and Anne Johnson entered the interrogation room, Tolley glared at them. Cole noticed the contempt on his face.

Cole walked to the wall directly across from Tolley's chair. He studied the prisoner's swollen lips and puffy nose. "What happened to your face, Governor?"

Tolley refused to look at Cole. Instead he stared at Anne Johnson. She refused to return his gaze.

"I asked you what happened to your face?" Cole repeated.

"One of your cops hit me when they broke into my apartment."

"Bullshit!" Blackie exploded.

Cole silenced the lieutenant with a look. "Why don't you get real, Tolley? None of my men laid a hand on you and you know it!"

"You refusing to take my brutality complaint? I thought you people didn't have a choice in these things. You already have a state's attorney here. Now all you need is an OPS investigator."

"Okay, which one?"

"Which one what?"

"Which one of my people hit you?"

Tolley had thought for a moment. Then, "Sherlock. Sergeant Manfred Wolfgang Sherlock."

# CHAPTER 84

**JUNE 21, 1996**
**6:20 A.M.**

The police radio emitted three warning signals prior to the broadcast of an "All Call." The warning succeeded in snapping Cole out of his semi-doze. It took him a moment to recognize his street. He was so tired he could barely remember driving home.

The radio message began: *"All Call Message Number 96–374. Wanted for murder. Margo Monica DeWitt. Female, white, thirty-seven years of age. Approximately five feet seven to five feet nine inches tall; weight one hundred and fifteen to one hundred and twenty-five pounds; slender build, black hair worn short, light complexion, brown eyes. Has no distinguishing marks or scars.*

*"Offender should be considered armed and dangerous. . . ."*

Cole listened to the conclusion of the transmission. It had been sent on his authority. At the time there had been nothing more they could do. Margo DeWitt had vanished.

With the help of a Fifth Army demolitions squad, they had forced their way into the third level of her penthouse. It had been empty and there had been nothing there to give them any clue to where she had gone. But there had been a laboratory that the day-watch crime lab would be going over with a fine-tooth comb in an attempt to link Margo with the deaths of Shafiq, Vukhovich and her husband. Even Soupy McGuire was going to look in at DeWitt Plaza later today.

But they still had no idea where she had gone and Cole was certain that somehow she had not given up on killing Zorin and Garth.

Cole felt himself nodding off again. Forcing his eyes open, he got out of the car and made his way into the house.

He could hear the television set before he unlocked the door. When he stepped into the house, he found Butch in pajamas sitting on the floor. A very old, black-and-white episode of "The Adventures of Superman" was running on the tube.

"Hi, Dad!"

"Hi, Butch. How long have you been up?"

"Just a few minutes. I'm goin' to church with Paige at nine o'clock."

"Where's your mother?"

"I think she's in the laundry room. She's ironing my church clothes. She said I could watch TV before I took my bath."

There was a flat brown cardboard box on top of the television set. Cole picked it up. It was addressed to: "Mr. and Mrs. Larry Cole, Sr." It was from The Mystery Book Guild.

Cole started to open it.

"Well hello, stranger," Lisa said, walking into the room

carrying little-boy-sized blue-and-white plaid slacks, a white short-sleeved shirt and a blue blazer. She took one look at her husband's face and stopped. "You'd better run your bathwater, Butch."

"Could I wait . . ."

"Do it now!"

The child shut off the television and headed for the stairs. His disappearance at the top of the stairs was followed by the bathroom door closing quietly.

"I shouldn't have yelled at him," she said, hanging his clothing on a hook inside the downstairs closet door. "He doesn't understand what's going on."

Cole placed the cardboard carton back on top of the television console. Slowly, he walked across the living room. "Sometimes I don't understand what's going on myself."

He entered the kitchen and emerged with a sixteen-ounce can of beer.

"Isn't it kind of early for that?" Lisa said.

"It's late," Cole said, sinking wearily onto the couch. Before opening the beer he ran its cold sides across his forehead. "Very late."

She came over and sat down on the arm of the couch. "What happened?"

He told her.

When he was finished, she was numb. "Do you think you'll catch her today?"

"She's probably long gone by now. Europe, maybe South America. The Financial Crimes Section was able to find out that the DeWitt Corporation is not only multinational, but has a labyrinthine system of holdings worldwide. And our Margo's the girl. She owns it all. We're going to request the U.S. Attorney's Office to file suit in federal court freezing all her assets until she's apprehended. But that can't be done until Monday. There's a possibility the judge won't buy our argument. With her kind of dough, she could run forever, and in style."

"Do you think I should let Paige take Butch to church?"

"She taking him alone?" Cole attempted to stifle a jaw-popping yawn.

"No. Judy's going with them. She's cooking up a special disguise for Butch. One she claims is foolproof."

"Lucky girl."

"Who, Paige?"

"No," Cole said. "Judy. She was supposed to relieve the team assigned to Debbie Bass at eight o'clock this morning. She was going to be with a detective named Davis from Area Three. I had Blackie call and cancel the detail earlier this morning. So I guess she's going to church with Paige and Butch."

"Larry, I wouldn't let him go unless she was going with them."

But he hadn't heard her. Still holding his barely touched beer, Cole had fallen sound asleep.

Across the room, the unopened book carton remained on top of the television set. Inside the wrapping was an expensively bound hardcover book. Its title: *Nick Castle, Private Eye* by Hutch Holiday. Exact copies of this same book had been delivered to all the writers in Cole's brain trust and Detective Judy Daniels. Debbie Bass had opened hers. Martin Wiemler's had rested on the cocktail table he, Reed and Hughes had played cards on. Jamal Garth's had gotten lost in the mail room of the Presidential Towers condominiums, where he lived. Barbara Zorin's was buried under a pile of unopened mail in her study.

Judy Daniels had removed hers from its carton and read the first thirty pages before dozing off the night before. It now rested on her nightstand.

Each book contained a transmitter. A transmitter broadcasting back to Margo DeWitt every word spoken within a fifty-foot radius of the book. As Cole fell asleep, she had been listening. She had not left the city.

# CHAPTER 85

**JUNE 21, 1996**
**7:00 A.M.**

The alarm clock went off in Judy Daniels's apartment. She stared up at the ceiling for a moment. A smile played across her face. She didn't have to work today. Blackie had called to tell her last night.

She swung her feet to the floor. Something had gone wrong with the deputy's plan. Two of the writers were dead. Two cops, too. She shivered. This Margo DeWitt was really turning out to be something else. Judy remembered hearing somewhere that the rich are different. Being rich couldn't explain the DeWitt woman. Nothing could, except maybe "homicidal maniac."

A thought struck Judy. It made her smile twist into the evil leer of the Wicked Witch of the West from *The Wizard of Oz*. "Yes, my little Butchie," she cackled. "Today is the day. Your string of victories is over."

Contorting herself into an Igor-the-hunchback shape, she shuffled to the closet and, swinging it open, revealed Sister Mary Louise Stallings's habit hanging behind the door. Again she cackled, "In this no one will recognize me. Not even my own moth—"

The heavy-handed knocking on her front door stopped her. Igor vanished. The knocking was repeated. "Who in the hell is that?" Her voice was back to normal. She snatched on jeans and a sweatshirt before picking up her Beretta from the nightstand. In her narcotics days she had made a great many enemies.

A few feet from the front door she stopped. The banging

outside was so insistent that the frame shook violently. This frightened her. She lifted the automatic and leveled it at the door.

"Who's out there?!"

"F.B.I.! Open up!"

"What do you want?"

"Are you Judy Daniels, owner of a nineteen ninety-five Toyota Tercel, license number XCB-four-six?"

"Yes." Her brow wrinkled in confusion.

"We have a warrant for your arrest."

Judy felt her knees go weak. "How do I know you're an F.B.I. agent?"

"I'm slipping a copy of the warrant under the door. You can check my ID through the peephole."

She watched the folded sheet of paper slide onto the living room rug. Without putting herself directly in front of the door, she picked up the paper.

She had seen federal warrants before. She had even done some with the DEA. This warrant was authentic right down to the United States Seal, but it stated that she had violated some kind of FCC regulation. That didn't make sense.

"What's your name?" Judy called.

"Look, ma'am." The FBI agent was losing his patience. "You've seen the warrant. Now, if you don't open up, we're going to force this door."

"Hold it! I'm a Chicago Police officer and I've got a gun in here."

"There's no need to turn this into a problem, Miss Daniels. This is a minor Federal Communications Commission beef. Resisting federal officers is a great deal more serious."

"Just a minute." She crossed to the telephone and dialed Blackie's number. The line was busy. She started to call the deputy. The living-room telephone was on a table overlooking the street below. She could see a Dodge sedan parked in front of her building. It was definitely a federal car. In fact, she recognized the guy leaning casually against it. He wore sunglasses and an off-the-rack suit. His name was Ted

Raines and he was an F.B.I. agent. She's met him on a DEA job.

With a sinking feeling in the pit of her stomach, she removed the magazine from the Beretta and ejected the chambered round. She laid the weapon and ammo on her cocktail table. Then she went to open the door.

Back in the bedroom of her small apartment, the novel *Nick Castle, Private Eye* rested on her nightstand.

# CHAPTER 86

**JUNE 21, 1996**
**8:45 A.M.**

Paige and Butch went to the church they'd buried Mack from. She parked her Mustang in the lot of the funeral home across the street and, taking Butch by the hand, crossed to the entrance to the cathedral-like building. She held the little boy's hand as much for her own moral support as to guide him across the street. She was apprehensive, maybe even a little afraid. She'd dreamed last night that the people in the church recognized her as an ex-prostitute and had begun picking up rocks to stone her. It took her most of the night to rid herself of the images churned out by her imagination. Now, as they walked toward the church, the frightening nightmare returned.

As if sensing her fear, Butch gave her hand a gentle squeeze. She looked down at him walking beside her and smiled. It would be just fine, she kept telling herself.

They entered the cool vestibule and paused for a moment to permit their eyes to adjust to the dimness. Beyond the vestibule was the main section of the church. Paige hadn't remembered it being this big the day they'd buried Mack.

An elderly man wearing a neatly pressed suit that had been in style about half a century ago was handing out hymnbooks and missalettes at the rear of the church. He smiled at Butch and said, "And how are you today, little man?"

Solemnly, Butch said, "I'm fine, sir. How are you?"

The usher was surprised. "My, you're polite. Your momma must be very proud of you." He looked up at Paige. "Good morning to you, ma'am."

"Good morning," Paige said.

They walked down the center aisle past a cross aisle bisecting the pews in the middle of the church. Paige selected a pew a couple of rows up from the cross aisle. Once they were inside Butch knelt down and crossed himself. Taking his lead, she did likewise.

Lisa and Larry were Catholics and were raising their son in the faith, but at times Cole's working hours made regular church attendance impossible. Lisa would have come with them, but she'd stayed home to take care of her exhausted husband.

Butch finished praying and sat down on the wooden bench. Again Paige did what he did.

They sat in silence for a time. There had been a few people in the church when they came in, and a few more drifted in after them. Paige checked her watch. It was a couple of minutes to nine.

Two servers, a boy and a girl of about Butch's age, came from somewhere up in front. They were followed by a robed priest. Paige watched them walk to the rear of the church.

"That's where they start from," Butch whispered.

"Oh," Paige said, nodding. This was all very new to her. She'd have to take it one step at a time. Whose idea was this anyway? Judy's! She wondered where Judy was. Besides going to church being a good thing to do, Judy was also trying to see if she could fool Butch with one of her disguises.

The priest gave the signal to the choir director to start the opening song. To the music of "We've come this far by faith," the procession of priest and servers started toward the altar from the back of the church. The elderly usher watched them go. He turned back to straighten the remaining hymnbooks and missalettes when the vestibule door opened. A nun stepped from the bright June sunlight into the vestibule shadows. The usher frowned. This parish had no nuns assigned to it.

He watched her cross to the holy-water fountain with pronounced decrepitude. The usher was seventy-two, but when he first saw the nun's face he figured she had him by at least twenty years. Every inch of visible flesh on the woman was crosshatched with wrinkles. He couldn't see her eyes, because of a pair of glasses with black oval lenses. Probably, he figured, she was almost blind. How she had gotten here by herself was a mystery. He rushed forward to help her.

He attempted to take her arm, but she snatched it away from him with a gesture so quick and agile that it contradicted her other movements. She hissed, "Don't touch me, you damned old fool."

Shocked, the usher stepped away from her.

She stood at the back of the church scanning those assembled for the nine-o'clock mass. She stood this way for a long time. Finally, she began moving slowly forward. She was headed for the young woman with the polite little boy who had come in before Mass started.

The usher watched her for a time before kneeling and saying a prayer. He prayed for God to forgive the old nun for swearing in His house.

# CHAPTER 87

**JUNE 21, 1996**
**9:15 A.M.**

Margo DeWitt flew through the air. Cole ran on the ground beneath her. She swooped out of a dark, cloudy sky toward him. He leaped to grab her and missed. She dived toward him again. Again he jumped and missed.

She flew away toward a lake. He ran as fast as he could. She dived into the black water. He jumped in after her. Suddenly, he was drowning.

He fought the undertow. Wayne Tolley was underwater with him. The ex-governor was laughing and shouting over and over, "Sergeant Manfred Wolfgang Sherlock hit me, Cole. Sergeant Manfred Wolfgang Sherlock hit me."

Cole reached for Tolley, but like Margo DeWitt, Tolley remained out of reach, shouting something else at Cole.

"Mr. and Mrs. Larry Cole, Sr."

Cole opened his mouth to ask Tolley what he meant, but no sound came out. Then he woke up.

He was lying on the living-room couch. His shoes and socks, along with his gun, had been removed. A lightweight blanket covered him. He checked his watch. It was mid-morning.

Cole sat up. He felt like hell. He could use eight hours of uninterrupted sleep, but experience had taught him it would be best to fight it until tonight. If he slept all day he'd be awake all night and his system would be screwed up for days.

The house was quiet. Usually he could detect Butch's presence somewhere inside. The little boy seemed to come with his own noise zone. Then Cole remembered that his son had gone to church with Paige and Judy.

Cole forced himself off the couch and crossed to the front window. He peeked through the blinds at the sun-drenched lawn. It was a beautiful day. Lisa's car wasn't in the driveway.

He was turning from the window when he again noticed the book carton on top the television set. It was addressed to Mr. and Mrs. Larry Cole, Sr. The dream came back to him. In the dream, Tolley screamed the same thing at him. But he and Lisa never called themselves Mr. and Mrs. Larry Cole, Sr. Maybe someday, when Butch was older, they'd have to.

Cole carried the book with him into the kitchen. There was a note from his wife held on the refrigerator by a sunflower-shaped magnet.

"Went to the store. Be back soon. Tuna salad in the fridge if you're hungry. Lisa."

He was toasting a couple of slices of bread to make a sandwich when he noticed the book carton again. He opened it. *Nick Castle, Private Eye* by Hutch Holiday. He wondered if Lisa had ordered this? Hell, they belonged to enough book, record and videocassette clubs as it was.

Cole's toast popped up.

A moment later he sat down at the kitchen table with the sandwich and a glass of iced tea. He examined the book. The binding was expensive and the pages gold-edged. On top of that the burgundy binding looked familiar.

The kitchen telephone rang. Leaning back in his chair, Cole was able to stretch far enough to reach the wall extension.

"Hello?"

*"May I speak to Deputy Chief Cole please?"*

Cole recognized the voice of Sergeant Carlo Amato from headquarters.

"This is Cole. What's up, Carlo?"

*"I got a funny call a little while ago, Boss. Agent-in-charge of the Chicago office of the F.B.I."*

"Dave Franklin?"

*"That's him. Well, he first asked to speak to the chief. When I told the fed he wasn't here, he asked for you. I mean, it is Sunday. I don't know why he'd expect either of you to be here."*

"Did he say what he wanted?"

*"No, sir. Said if I heard from you today to have you or Chief Govich give him a call. He left his office number."*

"I've got it. I'll call him back in a bit. Anything else on the DeWitt case?"

*"Nothing since you left. Guy from the M.E.'s office is down at DeWitt Plaza looking through some laboratory in the penthouse."*

"If anything comes up, Sarge, you let me know. Tell your afternoon relief the same thing."

*"Yes, sir."*

When Cole hung up, his mind dwelled on the serial-killing fugitive. Where could she be? He chuckled softly to himself. With her money, anywhere. Then another thought hit him. What did Dave Franklin of the F.B.I. want with him or Govich on a Sunday morning?

Cole picked up the telephone and dialed from memory the number of the Chicago office of the F.B.I.

# CHAPTER 88

**JUNE 21, 1996**
**9:22 A.M.**

When Jesus talked about the Prodigal Son, He didn't only use this parable of the man who leaves his father's house to squander his fortune on the wicked to stand for those who leave the faith, but He also meant the symbol of the Prodigal Son to stand for all those who possibly have never felt a strong enough call to the faith."

Paige was listening to the priest's sermon intensely. Butch had lost interest quickly and was looking around at the statues, murals and stained-glass windows. Neither of them noticed the ancient nun seated four rows directly behind them.

"Jesus allowed everyone to come to Him without reservation," the priest continued. "Little children, tax collectors, prostitutes, beggars and anyone else who wanted to talk to Him could come and receive His grace, love and understanding. Even after His death and resurrection . . ."

The priest's words echoed through Paige's mind. She had never heard anything like this. She was certain that her sins of the past would go with her to the grave. Now this priest was saying that perhaps she could be forgiven.

The mass continued.

The priest extended his arms to the congregation. "Let us offer each other the Sign of Peace."

Paige didn't know what to do. Butch turned to her and extended his hand. "We're supposed to shake."

She took the hand and looked around the church. Some of the others were also shaking; a few embraced and even kissed. She bent down and kissed Butch on the cheek. It shocked him.

"Why'd you do that?" he said.

"Because I love you."

He looked around to see if anyone had heard her. He was embarrassed. Paige almost laughed out loud at the little boy's predicament.

A hand touched her shoulder. Paige turned around.

Initially, she was startled by the nun's ugliness. But when the woman extended her hand, Paige took it. She was amazed at the old woman's strength.

"Bless you, daughter," the nun said.

"Bless you too, ma'am," Paige responded awkwardly.

The nun looked past her at the little boy. She held out her hand to him.

Paige noticed Butch's apprehension. He kept his hands rigidly at his sides.

"Shake with her, Butch," Paige said.

Without looking up at the wrinkled face behind the black oval lenses, Butch held out his hand. The nun took it and said, "Bless you, little one."

Butch snatched his hand away. Paige frowned. She started to apologize to the nun, but the old woman whispered something to her. At first Paige didn't hear it. The nun said it again. "Don't recognize me, do you, Paige?"

She was so shocked she almost blurted out, "Judy!" But she held her tongue.

The nun turned and shuffled back to her pew. Paige fought the urge to turn around and look at her.

Butch sniffled. Paige looked down at him. He was rubbing his hand.

"What's the matter?" she asked.

He was close to tears, but he fought them back. "She hurt me."

Paige felt a sudden unease. Judy would never hurt him. "I'm sure she didn't mean it."

He looked up at her. His eyes were moist, but he was under control. "Yes, she did. She did mean it."

# CHAPTER 89

**June 21, 1996**
**9:30 a.m.**

Lisa was shopping for a few odds and ends at the local supermarket. So far she had placed a gallon of milk, a box of detergent and two rolls of paper towels in her cart. She remembered that she was making spaghetti for Monday night's dinner. She was crossing to the bakery section to pick up a loaf of Italian bread when she saw her husband. He was running down the aisle toward her.

Before she could say anything he shouted, "What church did Paige take Butch to?"

"What's wrong?" She was near panic.

He gripped her shoulders hard enough to make it hurt.

"Judy's not with them. The F.B.I.'s got her on some bullshit charge. Might be a frame. Paige and Butch are alone. Margo DeWitt could have set this entire thing up!"

"Oh, God, no!"

"What church, Lisa?"

"The one they buried Mack from," she said.

"St. Columbanus?"

All she could do was bob her head up and down. Terror had taken control of her voice.

"C'mon!" He grabbed her hand. Together they ran from the store.

# CHAPTER 90

**JUNE 21, 1996**
**9:45 A.M.**

The Mass concluded and they followed the priest and servers to the rear of the church. The priest stood outside saying goodbye to the Mass participants. With an unusually quiet Butch in tow, Paige walked over to tell him how much she had enjoyed his sermon.

"Thank you," he said with a smile. "You're not from here, are you?"

"No, I'm not."

"I could tell by your accent. The Southwest?"

"Texas by way of Oklahoma."

"Never been down there myself. I heard . . ."

"Excuse me, Father."

They turned to find the old nun standing a few feet away. Butch slipped behind Paige.

"I think these people are waiting for me," the nun said in a cracking, raspy voice. "If you don't mind, I'm very tired and would like to be going."

Paige was aware of Butch clutching at her dress. She had never seen him frightened of anything before. She didn't know what Judy had done, but whatever it was had definitely worked, maybe too well.

"I saw you in church, Sister," the priest said congenially. "Is your Mother House near here?"

"I just told you that I'm tired, but you still want to keep me here answering your stupid questions!" the nun said testily.

"I'm sorry, Sister," the priest said with a forced smile. "I wouldn't want to detain you. Please feel free to come back to our parish again."

The nun was already moving slowly down the church steps. She didn't look back.

"And God bless you, Sister," the priest called after her.

She kept going.

"I guess we'd better be going too, Father," Paige said. "You have a nice day."

"The invitation is open to you and the little boy to come back too," he said. "And do remind Sister . . . ?"

Paige thought quickly. "I think she just likes to be called Judy."

"I beg your pardon?" he said, with a confused frown.

"We really have to go," Paige said, grabbing Butch's hand.

They left the priest standing in front of the church.

They were forced to wait for traffic to clear on Seventy-first Street before they could cross.

"Paige," Butch said in a near panic, "she's not going with us, is she?" He pointed at the old nun, who had just begun creeping across the funeral-home parking lot toward a black van parked beside Paige's Mustang.

As they crossed the street, Paige said, "Of course she is. Don't you know who that is?"

He shook his head violently in the negative. "That's not Judy!"

"Ha!" Paige said. "So she finally fooled you!"

"No, Paige, please!" He tried to stop her by pulling back with all his might. They were in the parking-lot driveway.

Paige stopped and looked at him. "What's the matter with you, Butch? Of course that's Judy."

"No, it's not!"

"Butch, stop it!"

Suddenly, the nun was there with them. When Paige turned, she was standing so close Paige could see her reflection in the black lenses.

"He's such a smart little boy." The nun's voice had changed; it was now younger and more cultured. However, the stooped, decrepit posture had not altered. "He's also right, Paige. Now, if you don't want me to kill the both of you right where you stand, pick him up and carry him over to that van."

For just the briefest second Paige thought this was a joke—a very bad joke, but a joke nonetheless. Then she saw the ugly black automatic. Mack had shown her a picture of one once. It was called a Glock. Paige was also aware that at such close range neither she nor the child could escape.

"Do it now, bitch!"

Butch had stopped struggling when he saw the gun. He was frightened rigid.

"I think he can walk," Paige managed. "But why are you doing this? We don't have anything you want."

The woman's in the nun's **habit** laughed. "Oh, but you

do, Paige, you do. You *and* him. Now, walk over to that van!"

Slowly, Butch and Paige walked to the van. Still standing in front of the church across the street, the priest watched.

# CHAPTER 91

**JUNE 21, 1996**
**9:54 P.M.**

Barbara Zorin and Jamal Garth were returned to police headquarters from their homes after Martin Wiemler was killed. Using the Superintendent's Contingency Fund for expenses, Cole put the writers up in a suite at the Essex Inn on Michigan Avenue a few blocks from headquarters. Heavily armed officers from the Special Weapons Unit were placed on the roof, and additional officers were detailed to the outdoor pool, to the corridors outside their top-floor suite and also within the suite itself and in the lobby. Despite the precautions, the occupants of the Essex Inn Sky Suite spent a sleepless night huddled together in the living room.

When she reported for work in the 24th District that morning, Officer Liz Fletcher, the heroine of the shootout with Neil DeWitt, found herself relegated to another detail by her sour-faced lieutenant. As the second watch progressed on this sunny Sunday, she'd gotten over her initial disappointment at being yanked from a field assignment for more bodyguard duty. She'd even become friendly with Barbara Zorin and Angela DuBois. Zorin's sons—Brian, twenty-four, and Paul, seventeen—had finally succumbed to the need for sleep and crashed in one of the bedrooms. Jamal Garth was at the lone living-room desk studying a thick file. He had been at it since Liz arrived at eight.

The policewoman's radio was turned to a special citywide frequency designated for units engaged in the hunt for murderess Margo DeWitt. As the day progressed there was a minimal amount of traffic on the frequency.

"You know," Liz said, "after I get a couple of years on the force I could probably write a pretty interesting book."

"I'd say you would have a lot to write about in that time," Barbara said. "You've already had some very interesting experiences."

Angela DuBois had been somewhat reserved earlier, but she found the young police officer to be completely different from her idea of cops, at least from her idea of male cops. "How does a woman do such a difficult job as this," Angela pointed to Liz's uniform, "in a place as dangerous as Chicago?"

"Very carefully," Liz said.

They laughed.

Traffic on her radio went from silence to bedlam in a matter of seconds. Even the absorbed Garth looked up from his papers.

"What's happening?" Barbara asked, attempting to focus in on the garbled transmissions.

"Nothing here at the hotel," Fletcher said. "But they've got some kind of flap on about Deputy Chief Cole's son."

Garth walked over and listened. He understood instantly what was happening. "Just like Magda in the book, she's kidnapped the son of the policeman hunting her. She's bypassed us to do it."

"Oh, poor Lisa," Barbara said. "She must be hysterical."

"There's no time to worry about her," Garth said. "There is time to save the boy! She won't kill him right away."

He turned to Fletcher. "I need to speak to Cole or someone in charge in his office at once!"

"I don't know . . ." she began.

"Do it, woman! Every second we waste brings that little boy closer to an appointment with dismemberment."

She unsnapped the microphone of her walkie-talkie.

# CHAPTER 92

**JUNE 21, 1996**
**10:05 A.M.**

Paige was forced to drive the black van at gunpoint. The woman in the nun's habit held the automatic in her lap and sat next to the passenger-side door. A very frightened Butch Cole was between them.

They traveled north on the Dan Ryan Expressway from Seventy-first Street.

"Stay in the local lanes," the woman ordered.

Paige obeyed. "Look, this is only going to cause you a bunch of problems. Kidnapping is a federal offense."

The wrinkled face behind the black glasses twisted into a grin. "Cause me a bunch of problems," she said, ridiculing Paige's accent. "Kidnappin' is a fedral of-fense. How very quaint. Tell me, did you ever slop the pigs and call the hogs where you came from?"

Paige's cheeks reddened, but she controlled her temper. She had to consider Butch's safety before her own.

"Get off here!" the woman snapped.

Paige pulled the van onto the exit ramp. As she started up the ramp, she realized that if she hit the brakes a little harder she might be rear-ended by the car coming up behind them. But then, what good would that do? The woman with the gun would still be in here with them.

"At the next intersection you're going to make a left." As if sensing the plan forming in Paige's mind, she added, "So far your driving's been very good. Let's keep it that way."

They entered one of Chicago's more depressed neighborhoods. The area was dotted by rotting tenements, abandoned buildings and vacant lots. The few people they passed on the street seemed to be shuffling along aimlessly, neither looking to the left or right, as they made their way to unknown destinations. No aid would come from them.

Paige's eyes scanned the desolation for a police car. Mack always said there were more cops in ghetto areas than anywhere else in the city. According to him, it was among the poor and the disenfranchised that the police were needed most. Yet there was no sign of one of the distinctive red, white and blue cars.

"At the next corner make a right."

They were going someplace specific. That meant that this crazy woman in the phony religious habit had a plan. She'd told them back at the church that they had something she wanted. Paige shuddered as she considered the possibilities of what that *something* might be.

She made the turn. They were traveling down a totally deserted, dead-end street. A couple of abandoned buildings, their vacant windows gaping, looked ready to collapse on one side. On the other was a church/school complex surrounded by a six-foot cyclone fence topped with barbed wire. The complex took up half the short, garbage-strewn block.

"Slow down."

Paige did so.

"Pull up to the gate."

The gate was at the far end of the fence. Beyond it was a driveway leading behind the church. Paige was able to see the name engraved in stone above the church's front entrance: ST. MONICA'S.

Paige experienced one brief ray of hope. The gate was locked. Someone would have to get out and open it. If the nun let her do it, this would be the only chance she was likely to get. She wouldn't like leaving Butch, but then there was little help she could provide him if they both stayed under the control of this crazy woman.

Her hopes were dashed when the woman removed a remote-control device from the folds of her black robes and pointed it at the gate. It swung open with a soft hum.

"Drive inside."

Paige looked at the driveway beyond the gate. High, dense trees shrouded it in shadow, and little care had been taken of this place in quite some time. There was no sign of life anywhere. The church was abandoned.

Paige looked down at the gun in the woman's lap.

"It won't work, Paige. You'd be dead before you opened the door. And this is a particularly nasty weapon. I've used it before. Leaves nice, big, messy holes."

Paige looked up at the woman's horrid face. "Why are you doing this?"

"You do deserve an explanation and I definitely plan to give you one. But first we must go to church. My church. After all, we've already been to yours."

Paige looked down at Butch. He looked back at her. There was fear in his gaze. Fear and something else. Under other circumstances she would have thought it was anger.

She eased her foot off the brake, and the van rolled through the gate. Once they were on the other side, the woman activated the remote control. Paige watched in the side-view mirror as the gate swung shut behind them with a finality that nearly made her cry out.

The shadowed driveway led around to a courtyard. A moving van and a late-model Jaguar were parked there.

"Pull over to the church doors."

When Paige had complied, the woman reached over and turned off the ignition. Snatching the keys, she said, "Both of you, out!"

Slowly, Paige obeyed and Butch followed her. The woman came out behind them. Her stooped posture and decrepit movements were gone. Standing up straight, she was as tall as Paige. This addition to her appearance made her even more terrifying.

They entered the side door of the church. Paige, with her

arms around Butch, walked in front. The woman followed, gun in hand, keeping a distance of six feet.

The inside of St. Monica's Church had been gutted down to the bare brick of the walls. All the religious trappings—altars, statues and most of the pews—had been removed. Scaffolding rose from the floor to the choir loft at the rear of the church proper, and ropes hanging from pulleys were still in place at the location where the organ had been lowered to the main floor for removal. The electricity had long since been disconnected, but four rusted racks of candles remained. They had been shoved to the center of the church to surround a heavy wooden table resting at the approximate location where the altar had once been. Each rack held about fifty small candles. All of them were burning, adding illumination as well as unwanted heat to the stuffy interior.

As they proceeded through the hazy gloom, Paige noticed six large, battery-operated tape recorders, a small table containing vials of multicolored liquids and a small propane gas tank connected to a rubber hose arranged against the far wall.

"Go over to the bench," the woman ordered.

Paige, still holding Butch, crossed the floor to the bench. The immense emptiness of the building dwarfed them. Unlike the church they had just left, this vastness frightened rather than comforted.

"Sit."

The bench was covered with dust. Paige reached into her purse for a handkerchief. Their backs were to their captor.

"Stop!"

The woman's voice made Butch jump.

"What are you doing?"

In a tremendously tired voice, Paige responded, "I wanted to wipe the bench off. It's filthy."

A silence ensued in which there was no sound and nothing moved.

Something landed at Paige's feet. Looking down, she found the nun's veil.

"Use that."

Releasing Butch for an instant, Paige bent down and picked up the veil, folded it twice, then wiped a place clean on the bench and dropped it back to the floor.

They sat down together on the bench and turned to face the woman. At the sight of her, Paige stiffened and Butch gasped. Without the veil covering her wrinkled face, she looked even more horrible. Even monstrous.

A chuckle escaped the black-robed apparition. "My face isn't very pleasant, is it, children? But the disguise was effective. Now the time for unmasking has arrived."

Reaching up, she peeled the latex mask off. It came away in one piece. Shaking her short hair, Margo DeWitt smiled coldly at them.

"I know you," Paige whispered.

"She's the lady at the Historical Society that day," Butch said. "The one who asked me my name at the carriage."

"What are you after, Mrs. DeWitt?" Paige said.

Margo's eyes took on an unnatural glint of unbridled insanity so intense that Paige and Butch shrunk back on the bench away from her.

"But you see," Margo said in a whisper. "That is the rub, isn't it. I'm no longer Mrs. DeWitt, as you called me. Margo DeWitt passed from this life sometime last night as I flew through the air over the city. Flew through the air to kill two bungling, interfering writers."

She advanced on them. As she did so, the gun dropped slowly to her side.

"Now I have returned. Returned to feed on the less fortunate, the young, the vulnerable."

She was close enough to reach out her hand toward Butch's head. He buried his face in Paige's shoulder. "No, no, no, little one. Magda knows what is best for you. Magda . . ."

Paige grabbed Butch by his shoulders and shoved, propelling the little boy away from her. He slid across the bench onto the floor five feet away. In one motion Paige reached out and grabbed the woman's gun hand.

"Run, Butch! Get out of here!"

Paige kept a firm hold on the woman's wrist. The hand holding the gun never moved. Paige reached for the barrel. The woman swung her free hand up and struck Paige across the side of the face with a clenched fist. The blow knocked Paige off balance and she fell back onto the bench, seeing stars as the gloomy interior of the gutted church dimmed slightly before brightening once more.

The woman stood over her still holding the gun. The attack hadn't fazed her at all.

"That was very stupid, Paige. You really have no idea who I am. I think it's time you learned."

She removed the clip from the automatic's housing. After she ejected the chambered round onto the floor, both gun and clip vanished beneath her robes. She held up her empty hands for Paige to see.

Paige looked at Butch, who had scrambled to his feet but had made no move to flee. He stood there looking from Paige to the woman in black.

"Lady," Paige said, standing up and slipping out of her heels, "you just made a big mistake."

The woman didn't move. Her hands remained placidly at her sides.

Paige hiked up her skirt to free her knees and thighs as she went into a fighting crouch. Her hands formed into claws tipped with long painted nails. She circled the woman, moving to the right away from Butch; then, with a snarl of fury, she charged.

The woman waited until Paige was within arm's length before pivoting to the side and tossing the charging woman over her hip. Paige did a complete somersault before landing on her back. She tried to get to her feet, but the woman was too fast for her. Grabbing Paige from behind in a choke hold, she lifted her from the floor.

"Now do you understand that Magda is so much more

formidable than you?" the woman whispered in Paige's ear. "I want my voice to be the last thing you hear, my little whore. The last thing before you die."

The arm tightened unmercifully around Paige's throat, as she fought for oxygen and the darkness of eternity closed in around her. She could hear Butch shouting as if from a great distance, but she couldn't understand what he was saying. Then, suddenly, she was released.

It took a moment for her oxygen-starved senses to respond. Finally, she was able to look around. Her attacker had staggered back to the bench where only seconds before they'd been held captive. The woman was rubbing her leg. Butch was gone.

"The little bastard kicked me!" the beast called Magda screamed.

"Good . . . for . . . him," Paige rasped through her bruised throat. "Hope he . . . gets away and . . . they . . . hang your . . . ass!"

Paige managed to get up on all fours, but could go no farther. Magda crossed to stand over her.

"He really has no place to go, Paige. I'll catch him and then I'll be back for you!"

Paige didn't hear the last words, because her head exploded in a searing flash of pain as Magda slammed the butt of the automatic across her skull.

# CHAPTER 93

**JUNE 21, 1996**
**11:03 A.M.**

They were seated at the superintendent's conference table. The superintendent herself was at the head of the table. First Deputy Superintendent Terry Kennedy, Chief of Detectives Jack Govich and a host of other Chicago Police brass were arranged in descending rank in the other chairs. Larry Cole, with his wife, Lisa, had remained in his fifth-floor office. The superintendent had decided it would be best if he were excluded from this meeting.

An unnatural silence had reigned for some time, intensifying the already unbearable tension. Each of them had some form of family, whether it was a wife and a houseful of kids, or an aging parent, or simply a significant other. At most times these loved ones were bit players or no more than extras in their lives. But when something like this happened, the importance of having someone came back to them with stunning urgency. What had happened to Cole's child could happen to any one of their loved ones.

The superintendent was waiting for one of them to tell her something positive. Since Cole's beeper had gone off last night in this office everything had been negative. At least they had the suspect identified, but even then Margo DeWitt, after killing two people under police guard and while wanted nationwide, had kidnapped the son of one of Chicago's highest-ranking officers. This was intolerable and she damn sure wasn't going to stand for it any longer!

Kennedy had been the last one to speak. He had laboriously catalogued everything they'd done in search of the bogus nun who had been seen driving away from St. Columbanus Church with Paige Albritton and Cole's son. Flash messages, strategic roadblocks, numerous street stops of any vehicle spotted in the city containing a nun, shaking up informants and even stepped-up surveillances of radical groups with any kind of grievance against the Catholic Church had been implemented. The results? Negative.

"So what you're telling me is that we've failed," she said quietly.

Blackie Silvestri was representing Cole's office. He was at the far end of the table, down on the left. From where the superintendent sat, he was almost invisible in the sea of command officers. Blackie leaned forward and looked down the table at her. She was in full uniform with the four stars of her rank gleaming in the overhead lights. And she looked as tough as she was rumored to be. She had been known to slay the messenger for bringing bad news, or at least to make the messenger wish he were dead.

Nevertheless, Blackie raised his hand. Butch was like his own child and he was in as much agony over his kidnapping as Larry and Lisa were.

The superintendent's gaze locked on Silvestri. Now he understood what was meant when someone said they felt like a fly trapped on the head of a pin. He could even feel a couple of the people sitting around him shifting almost imperceptibly to put as much distance between him and them as possible.

Well, what the hell, he was in too far to back out now.

"Margo DeWitt's been living out some kind of fantasy with this book, Superintendent."

Her gaze never altered. "Are you talking about *Bless the Children* by Harry McGhee?"

"Yes, ma'am," Blackie said. "She thinks that she's . . ."

The superintendent raised her hand, silencing Blackie in midsentence. "I know all about that, Lieutenant, but I hardly see how it's going to help us now."

Blackie was about to add more, but then the eyes of the others made him hesitate. A couple looked as if they were pleading with him to simply shut up and not make things worse than they already were. A few refused to even look in his direction, as if not seeing him could somehow relieve them of any responsibility for his actions. He'd been around long enough to know how to play it. On top of that, he doubted that anything that occurred in this room would help Butch and Paige. Hell, they should be out in the streets, not sitting here playing twenty fucking questions with the Iron Maiden.

There was a soft knock at the door leading to the outer office. The superintendent glanced at an aide, indicating that he should answer it. The door was opened and a brief conversation took place between someone out of sight and the aide. The door closed and the aide crossed the office to Deputy Chief Frank Dwyer. Brief whispers were exchanged before the deputy excused himself and left the conference room.

# CHAPTER 94

**JUNE 21, 1996**
**11:10 A.M.**

Probationary Officer Fletcher was waiting for Dwyer in the outer office. She was so nervous she could feel her knees shaking, and when she saw Dwyer's grim face, she was certain that she was doomed.

"Yes?" he said in a less than cordial voice.

"Someone would like to speak to you, sir." She was surprised her words came out so steady.

"What?" He looked like he was getting really pissed.

"They're right out in the hall."

Dwyer looked across the reception area at the glass doors. Jamal Garth and Barbara Zorin were out there waiting.

"What are you doing here?" Dwyer demanded. "You're supposed to be under heavy guard over at the hotel!"

"We haven't got time for that now, Frank," Barbara said. "Margo DeWitt is no longer interested in us. She's got Cole's son."

"It's the last act in her parody of McGhee's book," Garth added. "It's the same as Lemieux's son. She's taken him to a church to dismember him. Then she's going to send the pieces back to Cole. That's what Magda did in the book."

"We've got to find that church, Frank!" Barbara said.

Dwyer grabbed them each by the upper arms and led them away from the entrance to the superintendent's office. "Look, I know you mean well, but nobody in there's going to buy this fantasy thing about McGhee's book."

"How do you know?" Garth challenged.

"Silvestri already tried it. The boss shot him down."

"What about you, Frank?" Barbara questioned. "What do you think?"

"I think . . ." Dwyer began before stopping and exhaling a deep sigh. "I think the kid and the Albritton woman are already dead. It's just a matter of time before we find the bodies."

"I disagree," Garth said.

"Well, it doesn't really matter whether you agree or not, does it, Jamal? You've got no business being involved in this anyway!"

"The hell I don't! Cole asked me in now I'm in to stay."

"Relax, fellas," Barbara said, stepping between them. "This isn't getting us anywhere."

Dwyer spun on Officer Fletcher. "I'm giving you a direct order to escort them back to the hotel. And, Fletcher, I'm going to make a full report of this to your commanding officer."

As Dwyer stormed back into the superintendent's office, all the blood had drained from Fletcher's face.

"What now?" Barbara Zorin said.

"I don't know," Garth sighed. "Maybe he won't listen because of what I did."

"That's nonsense."

"I'm listening," a voice said from down the hall.

They turned to see Larry and Lisa Cole standing just inside the stairwell door. They looked like hell, but they were both listening.

# CHAPTER 95

**JUNE 21, 1996**
**11:15 A.M.**

Butch was confused when Paige pushed him off the bench onto the floor. Paige and the lady who called herself Magda had fought, and the lady had tried to hurt Paige by choking her. That's when Butch ran up to Magda and kicked her as hard as he could. He knew it hurt, because he felt the solid tip of the sturdy dress shoes Mom had bought him for Easter make solid contact with a bone in Magda's leg. She immediately let Paige go. Then she came after him.

He ran first for the door they had entered through, but Magda had locked it. He looked back and found her coming after him, but she was moving slowly. His kick had hurt her! Good! He looked around for a place to run to. Although the main church had been gutted, the walls of the sacristy in the front and the vestibule in the back were still standing. The vestibule was closest. He darted toward it. She followed silently, but with a menace he could feel. She said nothing, she just came on, favoring her injured leg.

There was no light in the vestibule and fright stopped Butch dead in his tracks. He could hear the heavy rasp of his breathing from the fear and exertion roaring through his head, and his heart pounded furiously.

He scrambled forward. His hands touched the banister of a stairwell leading up. He could hear Magda coming toward his hiding place. He crouched down, felt for an opening under the staircase, found it, reached into the dark and touched something soft that moved. He froze, barely managing to stifle a scream. Then Magda was there with him.

# CHAPTER 96

**JUNE 21, 1996**
**11:20 A.M.**

Father Michael Ivers's beeper went off just as he was finishing the sermon for the eleven-o'clock Mass at St. Agatha's Catholic Church. He silenced the instrument and returned to his seat behind the altar. As the congregation pondered his words, he leaned over to whisper to the deacon assisting him. "Take over for a few minutes, George. I've got to make a call."

The deacon nodded.

In the sacristy Father Mike opened the case containing the portable telephone the Department had issued him when he was appointed police chaplain. He dialed the department number on his beeper display.

*"Deputy Chief Cole's office, Sergeant Sherlock speaking."*

"Sarge, this is Father Mike Ivers from the chaplain's unit."

*"Hold on, Father."*

Cole's voice came over the line. *"Father, I need your help and it's very urgent."*

"Whatever you need, Deputy."

*"Do you know of any church in the Archdiocese called Our Lady of the Heavens?"*

Father Mike thought for a moment. "No. I'm almost sure we have no Our Lady of the Heavens in the Chicago archdiocese."

Father Mike heard someone say in the background, *"Ask*

*him if there's a Mary Magdalene, or a church with the name Magda or Margo in it?"*

Cole asked.

Father Mike, again after brief contemplation, replied in the negative.

Dejectedly, Cole said, *"I want to thank you for taking the time, Father. I guess we'll have to think of something else."*

Father Mike was just about to hang up when the voice in the background said, *"Her middle name is Monica! Ask him if there's a St. Monica's in the area!"*

*"Are you still there, Father?"* Cole said.

"I'm here."

*"Is there a St. Monica's in Chicago?"*

"Yes and no. The old St. Monica's on the South Side is closed. The building's still standing but it's slated for demolition. A private firm purchased the land. I think it's now owned by the DeWitt Corporation."

# CHAPTER 97

**JUNE 21, 1996**
**11:23 A.M.**

Magda's leg was bleeding. Butch Cole's kick had broken the skin. It had been a long time since she had been injured. The last time had been when she was trapped in Boston by Jonathan Lemieux of the Boston Police. The year was 1899.

But how had the child been able to do this to her? Sorcery? Of course. The only way Magda could be hurt was by some form of sorcery or . . . She hesitated before allowing the image of flames and shimmering heat waves to invade her delusions. Fire was not her problem now; the child was. If he was indeed a sorcerer, he was a fledgling, due to his age. By slaying him she would absorb his power.

She watched him dash into the darkness behind the vestibule wall. She followed. Taking a step into the shadows, she gathered all her senses, expanding her being to fill every nook and cranny of the pitch black area.

Something moved. There. A noise ascending. She followed it, discovered the staircase and . . . there was another noise below her, a sigh or expulsion of breath. She stopped. Her hands began probing the dark at waist level. No. The noise had been lower. Nearer the floor.

The light thumping of something running in the choir loft above her head distracted her. For a moment she was confused. In one quick lunge she thrust her hands down until she touched the dust-covered floor. She felt around. There was nothing there. The sounds above her were repeated. They were now more distinct. She found the staircase again and started up.

Last night she had used infrared, night-tracking glasses when she'd gone after Wiemler. Of course, Magda did not need such things, but some of the weaknesses of Margo's mortal body remained. The night glasses were in the trunk of her Jaguar. She wasn't going out now to get them. She would find the boy using Magda's powers.

She climbed the stairs in the dark, feeling the ancient wood squeak and groan under her weight. The loft was dimly illuminated from the church interior. As she crossed it toward the scaffolding built from the floor of the church, she saw movement at the far end. She smiled. Her prey was cornered. She moved toward him.

She detected movement out of the corner of her right eye. Turning, she looked down at the floor thirty feet below. Her eyes widened when she saw the little boy running back toward the prone form of Paige Albritton. Magda spun back to the place where she had seen the movement in the choir loft. The yellow eyes of a large black cat flashed at her.

With a snarl of anger she turned toward the stairs. As she did, the rotten wooden planks gave way beneath her.

# CHAPTER 98

**JUNE 21, 1996**
**11:24 A.M.**

They were traveling south on the Dan Ryan Expressway with lights and siren going. Cole was driving with Lisa beside him. Jamal Garth and the recently released Judy Daniels were in the backseat. In the car driven by Manny Sherlock, hanging close on Cole's bumper, were Blackie Silvestri and Barbara Zorin. Cole had permitted the writers to come because he owed them. Whatever the outcome of this thing with Margo DeWitt and his son, they would never have gotten this far without the brain trust. Now he could only hope that they weren't too late.

They swung off the Dan Ryan at Garfield Boulevard. The two unmarked police cars were joined by two marked cars from the 7th District. Local units in the area of the deserted St. Monica's had been alerted. Now ten police cars were converging on the old church.

# CHAPTER 99

**JUNE 21, 1996**
**11:27 A.M.**

Paige was enveloped in a fog of pain. Her head, face and back ached. When she attempted to open her eyes, the ceiling above her began to spin, making her nauseous. She tried to turn over on her side, but her body simply wouldn't respond.

"Paige! Wake up, Paige!"

Again she attempted to open her eyes. She caught a glimpse of Butch before waves of dizziness washed over her. Then she felt his cool hand massaging her forehead. His touch was comforting in the airless, musty heat of the old church.

"Butch," her voice was weak, "where is she?"

"Up in the loft. I heard her fall. We've got to get out of here!"

Urgency fed adrenaline into Paige's system. With help she managed to struggle into a sitting position. Her head felt as if it had doubled in size.

"Can you get up?"

She turned to look at Butch. His face was soot-stained and his eyes bright with fear, but he seemed very much in control. His strength helped her find her own. She struggled to her feet and would have fallen had he not been there to hold her up.

"Okay, Butchie, let's get the hell out of here."

"The doors are locked!"

"Then we'll find a way to break them open."

Paige looked around the church and then up at the choir loft. What she saw there froze her in place.

The woman in black robes, who called herself Magda, was standing with the arms of her gown extended like wings. In one hand she held a rope attached to the top of the scaffold. As Paige continued to stare, she grasped the rope with her other hand and leaped into space.

Like a huge bat she swooped toward them.

"Run, Butch!" Paige shouted, attempting to push him away from her.

"No! You're coming with me!" He held tightly to her, pulling her with him. Too weak to resist, she came along at a snail's pace. Magda was coming down right on top of them.

Paige made herself move faster, feeling the pain in her head intensify as quickly as her legs weakened. She and Butch made it as far as one of the candle racks before Magda reached the bottom of her arc and dropped to the floor a scant yard and a half away.

Paige and Butch slipped behind the candle rack.

Bleeding and tattered, Magda stood before them, her face bruised from the plunge through the floor of the choir loft, blood flowing freely from her cheek and forehead.

"Did you really think you could escape, little one?" she said to Butch as she removed the automatic from her robe pocket. "I have plans for you after I get rid of your friend."

She began reaching into the other pocket for the magazine when the sounds of loud banging from outside echoed through the church.

Magda spun toward the boarded-up doors below the choir loft.

Paige looked down at the candle rack and then at their diverted captor. Placing her hands against the back of the rack, Paige attempted to push it over, but she was too weak. Initially puzzled, Butch watched her. Then he caught on and helped.

The rack tilted slightly and then rolled completely over

to smash onto the stone floor. Magda spun back toward them just as a score of lighted candles rolled around her feet. Her gown ignited.

Paige and Butch were already hurrying as fast as they could toward the rear of the church. A hideous scream came from behind them. Looking over their shoulders they saw Magda, her gown in flames, rushing toward them. She was gaining rapidly.

"No!" Paige screamed.

Sunlight pierced the dark interior as Cole, Blackie and Manny Sherlock, followed by four uniformed cops, stormed into the church.

The figure of Magda, now totally immersed in flame, reached for Paige and the boy just as a volley of gunshots reverberated off the barren brick walls of the abandoned House of God.

# EPILOGUE

**September 10, 1996**
**7:26 p.m.**

On the television set in the Coles' living room, a group of actors with drawn guns advanced toward a burning figure lying on the floor of an abandoned church. The scene switched to take in a woman clutching a little boy. They stood with flames from the burning body reflecting off their tearstained, dirt-smeared faces. The scene switched again. The next shot showed Larry Cole, dressed in a neat blue suit, a white shirt and a dark maroon tie, standing in the lobby of DeWitt Plaza.

A cheer went up from the audience assembled in the living

room. Seated beside his wife on the couch, Cole looked sheepishly over at Blackie.

"You look good, boss," Blackie said. "You could probably host one of those cop shows yourself."

"Ssssh," Lauren Sherlock admonished.

On the TV Cole was talking.

*"The investigation which followed the death of Margo DeWitt revealed an odyssey of death that began in Colorado. There Margo Rapier killed twenty-two-year-old Jennifer Raymond of Boulder over the Christmas holidays in nineteen eighty-six. Neil DeWitt was the last person to see Miss Raymond alive, but was cleared following an investigation by the Colorado State Police. Modern crime-detecting technology not available in nineteen eighty-six revealed that both Margo Rapier and Neil DeWitt were at the location where Jennifer's body was found."*

"I thought Margo's thing was boys?" Manny said.

On the screen Cole answered, *"Although her victims were generally young black male children between the ages of seven and thirteen, Margo DeWitt's sociopathic personality enabled her to kill anyone at any time without compunction or regret.*

*"The DeWitts' reign of terror in the summer of nineteen ninety-six came particularly close to me because she kidnapped my son, planning to dismember him in an abandoned church. Now, every night in our home, we thank God that our little boy was saved by a combination of his own personal heroism and the valiant efforts of Ms. Paige Albritton."*

There was applause from the living-room audience once more. This time Paige acknowledged with a wave the accolades meant for her.

The scene switched. Cole was now outside police headquarters.

Cole in the flesh said a frowning "They cut it!"

"How do you know?" Lisa asked.

"This next part was supposed to mention Barbara and

Jamal's book. I put in the plug while we were filming at the Plaza. The part at headquarters was simply a wrap-up."

"Well, Jamal," Barbara Zorin said, "I guess we ended up on the cutting-room floor."

"Those bastards," Blackie swore quietly around his cigar.

*". . . no matter who they are, or what they have, the police will hunt killers down and bring them to justice in the hopes of making the cities and towns of this country safe for everyone,"* Cole concluded on the screen.

An announcer's voice offscreen said, " *'Police Case Book' will continue after a message from our sponsors."*

"Well, so much for free publicity," Jamal Garth said.

Cole was still agitated. "But that wimpy producer promised me it would be in! That's the only way I'd give that syrupy, flag-waving, closing speech!"

"I wouldn't worry about it, Larry," Barbara said. "The book won't be out until Christmas anyway."

"On top of that," Garth added, "with the advance we got, I'm sure the publisher's advertising budget for *The Strange Case of Margo and Neil DeWitt* will be substantial."

"I take it you've had no more problems with Tolley trying to block publication?" Paige said.

"We have Larry and Blackie to thank for that," Barbara said.

"What did you do?" Lisa asked her husband.

"Tolley tampered with our investigation by obtaining unauthorized information from City Personnel on me, Blackie, Judy and Manny. He used Anne Johnson and Dick Shelby to do it. We could have gone after him both criminally and civilly after what happened, so he managed to convince the chairman of the board of the DeWitt Corporation not to interfere with the publication of the book."

"That Johnson and Shelby sure landed on their feet after what they did," Paige said, with an angry edge in her voice.

The acid-tempered state's attorney had resigned when an investigation into her conduct during the DeWitt investigation was launched by her superiors. Almost simultaneously,

Dick Shelby had taken an early pension from the Department. Johnson went to work as an associate in Tolley's law office. Shelby got a job as chief investigator in the same office. With what each had on Tolley, it was an unholy alliance of convenience.

As the closing credits of "Police Case Book" began to roll, Butch said from his usual spot on the floor in front of the set, "Can I see it again?" The program had been videotaped.

"Later, Butch," his father said. "We'll all take a look again after dinner."

They did watch it again; however, the second time around it had lost some of its initial impact.

The sound of an ice-cream truck outside the house absorbed Butch's attention. He looked at his mother and father.

Larry looked at Lisa. "Did he eat all of his dinner?"

"Just about. He did leave a carrot or two."

Butch's face fell.

Lisa quickly added, "But I gave him more than usual, so I guess he can have some ice cream."

The little boy jumped to his feet. "You gonna come with me, Paige?"

"I sure am, Butchie, and I'm gonna buy too. Two scoops or three?"

Butch started to say "three," but his dad held up two fingers.

The Tastee Freez truck had its chimes playing softly as the female attendant with blond hair and a mass of freckles dispensed ice cream to the children lined up at the window. Butch, with Paige holding his hand, got in line.

At the window, they ordered double scoops of black walnut in sugar cones. Paige paid, but as they turned from the window Butch stopped. He went back to the attendant.

"Hi, Judy. You coming over later?"

"I beg your pardon?" she said with a frown. "My name's

Mary Anne. I think you've got me confused with someone else."

"No, I don't, but I won't tell anyone. Your secret's always been safe with me."

He turned back to Paige as the truck pulled away.

"Are you sure that was Judy?"

"Certain," he said, licking his cone.

They walked slowly up the driveway. "But how can you be so sure?"

"I know her," he said. "Like I know you, Mom and Dad. If you put on a disguise I'd know it was you too."

"That's how you knew the nun was Margo DeWitt?"

He got very quiet. "I didn't know it was her. I just knew it wasn't Judy."

They entered the house. The tape of "Police Case Book" was almost over. Everybody was in the living room just like before. With one addition.

"Hey, Butchie," Judy said from where she was seated in his usual spot on the floor. "Let me have a taste of your ice cream."

In wide-eyed amazement Butch and Paige stared at the Mistress of Disguise/High Priestess of Mayhem. She was dressed completely differently than the woman on the Tastee-Freez truck had been, and there simply wouldn't have been time for her to have gotten inside that fast. They could still hear the chimes of the ice-cream truck receding in the distance.

Butch gave Judy a bite of his cone. Then he went to sit between his mother and father. He stared at Judy.

Paige crossed and sat down on the floor beside her. "You want some of mine?"

"Sure," Judy said, taking the cone. "And by the way," she whispered, " 'my name's Mary Anne.' "